THE LIVING INFINITE

Chantel Acevedo

THE LIVING INFINITE

A NOVEL

Europa
editions

Europa Editions
214 West 29th Street
New York, N.Y. 10001
www.europaeditions.com
info@europaeditions.com

Library of Congress Cataloging in Publication Data is available
ISBN 978-1-60945-430-2

Acevedo, Chantel
The Living Infinite

Book design by Emanuele Ragnisco
www.mekkanografici.com

Cover image: Princess Eulalia, Infanta of Spain

Prepress by Grafica Punto Print – Rome

Printed in the USA

CONTENTS

For Orlando, Penelope, and Mary-Blair

"If his destiny be strange, it is also sublime."
—JULES VERNE, *Twenty Thousand Leagues Under the Sea*

"It is my final realization of freedom
that I celebrate now in these pages.
I have escaped, mind and body, from my gilded cage."
—THE INFANTA EULALIA OF SPAIN, *Court Life from Within*

February 25, 1893

To HRH, Eulalia, Infanta of Spain:

It has been my honor and duty to give prolonged attention to your reflections. I attach great weight to the work therein, and will always treasure as a compliment that you entrusted your writings to me.

For an editor, the question first and foremost in regards to a manuscript should be: Do you think well of the project?

I lament that I do not.

I say: women cannot demand perforce their share in the freedoms afforded to men. This applies, I daresay, even to an Infanta of Spain.

I say: silence, too, is an act of moral courage.

The celebrity of your person will, undoubtedly, sell many copies. However, public opinion, which in Spain and all of Europe trammels over logic, will be against you, and in its wake profitability will soon turn to unhappiness for me, my fellow editors, the bookshop owners, and all who care to sell your little joys and little sorrows to the people.

I have no doubt that there is a great deal of truth in what you say, that you have been ringed about by so many limitations, which you consider without meaning, and that your democratic inclinations have been achieved without malice.

However, if I may be so bold as to offer you advice, I would urge you to be content with hope for the future, and the belief that the traditions we hold dear in civilized Europe, when in dispute with the modern sensibilities of the New

World, will win out in the end. Those traditions, which you seem determined to cast aside, are the sole certainties one can rely upon.

I have tried not to abuse the privilege that you have offered me in allowing me to read your story, and I will speak of it to no one. This, I promise. But for the advantage and protection not only of my company but of certain values/principles that I hold to be true, I regret that we will not, today nor ever, publish this book.

Very sincerely yours,

Pedro Medina
Editor in Chief, Ediciones Medina

SPAIN

Su Alteza Isabel II, Reina de España, carried ten relics on her person during her last few weeks of pregnancy. These included the desiccated right arm of John the Baptist, which, wasted and ancient, resembled a piece of driftwood, and a rosary belonging to Saint Francis of Assisi that smelled of flowers at all times. No one could blame her for taking every possible precaution. Out of twelve deliveries, each ferocious and hard-fought, only five of Isabel's children survived.

And the queen was determined that this child would live.

In February of 1864, two days before Saint Valentine's feast day, Isabel delivered a blue, half-asphyxiated child. The jawless skull of that love-feasted saint, bedecked in preserved flowers, stared out at her from its small crystal coffin—a relic sent to the queen from Rome. Upon seeing the infant's skin going from pink to pale lavender, to indigo, Isabel cursed the date, and thought, desperately, that had she held the child in for two more days, just two more, then Saint Valentine might have intervened.

Whisked away by her formidable doctors, the baby was doused with holy water, el agua del socorro, so that her soul might not be trapped in purgatory forever. But events unfolded in unexpected ways. The child recovered her breath, and, soon enough, rested comfortably in her mother's arms.

Outside of the Palacio Real de Madrid, a white flag was hoisted, and fifteen salvos rang out, indicating a girl, an infanta, had been born. The noise infiltrated the room of Isabel's labor.

It disrupted the first song Isabel sang to her daughter, a tune that no one recalls, and, thankfully, interrupted, too, her memories of the other babies who had lived only an hour or so after birth, who had turned blue, who had gone still and cold in her arms.

Isabel let out a bark of laughter when the little infanta sneezed, but the sounds converged with shouts of anger and cries of anguish coming from the streets of Madrid—anger because the flag and the salvos had announced a girl, and anguish because there would be no spare son, so ardently hoped for in those dark, frightening days. She was named Eulalia, which meant "well-spoken." No other Spanish royal had shared the appellation, and so it was a name for the present and the future, a name without a past.

The baby was placed on a silk cushion of royal blue, and the cushion was laid on a silver platter. Baby, cushion, platter were paraded before the ambassadors and palace folk waiting in the main hall. Wearing their silks and furs against the chilly air, the men and women of the hall clapped and peeked at the small rosebud that was the baby's genitals and sighed. The baby made no sound, but peered at them all with damp, lively eyes. A man commented how she appeared to be thinking hard about something. Another said she resembled no Bourbon he had ever seen. Another lamented that she was not the son they had hoped for. But the important thing was that she would live. That was certain, and there was relief and happiness at that.

2

The milk brother, too, was born in this time of peace, three months before Eulalia. The Carlists, those pretenders to the throne, had gone quiet in the years before he was born, meeting in secret, biding their time. Amalia, his mother, remembered that on the day that peace was declared, the children in her village were given pots and pans and bells to ring, and that they trooped through Burgos in celebration. The priests had been angered by the display, for many of them had supported Don Carlos, since he had promised the church land and wealth. Though peace was declared, the fighting went on for a few years, and Amalia, who was only nine years old at the time, would lie awake, listening to gunfire in the distance at night, like the cracking of giant bones in the hills.

The milk brother, whose name was Tomás, was born in a small, dusty room in a house in Burgos, attended by the same midwife who had been at all of his mother's deliveries—a woman named Gisela Castillo. She had delivered half of Burgos's women of their babies, mainly because she was talented, but also because everyone thought she was good luck embodied. Her curious eyes, one blue and one brown, were what started the rumor, and Spaniards being the superstitious people they were, Gisela Castillo became a very busy woman. But her luck had not held when it came to Amalia. She'd come to Tomás's birth dressed all in black, ready to grieve another dead Aragón baby.

At once, Amalia shouted at her to leave. "You're bringing bad luck in here, dressed in mourning!" she said before a wave of pain silenced her momentarily. When it passed, she threw her discarded Sunday dress at the midwife—light blue and dotted with white daisies—one she had embroidered herself. A heavy sleeve slapped the midwife across the face. "Put it on," Amalia told her.

"But it will get ruined, Amalia. Be reasonable."

She gritted her teeth. "Put it on."

In the end, the midwife did as she was told, changing into the dress immediately. It draped over her body like a formless sack. Gisela was quite small. She was slim and brown, her skin retaining some of that sun from the island where she'd been born and raised. They were the same age, Gisela and Amalia, and the latter noticed, as the former dressed herself, the way Gisela's tiny belly button resembled a knot in a tree. Amalia hadn't seen her own belly button in months, she thought between spasms of pain. Gisela rolled up the sleeves and got to work, her mouth set in a pucker. Later, Amalia would apologize, and thank Gisela for changing out of her black dress, but in that moment, they could do nothing but glare at one another. Into this volatile air came Tomás, screaming.

"He sounds like a peacock," Gisela said, bundling the baby and giving him to Amalia. "Have you ever heard one? They cry like infants, but twenty times louder. They stroll around certain parts of Havana, like princes."

"You are ridiculous, Gisela," Amalia told her, teasing, the air simmering between them cooled now that the baby had arrived, pink and vociferous and large. Amalia had never seen such a large baby, in fact, nor had Gisela. Even so, they watched over him like a pair of lionesses through the night.

Rubén, the milk brother's father, who never got the chance to hold any of his previous babies while they still lived, cried fat tears when Tomás was first put in his arms. "Ay, mi vida," he crooned at the baby, and kissed the top of his still sticky head again and again. Both Amalia and Rubén had buried, deep in their hearts, their blighted hopes for the children they had lost. Now, they placed them all on Tomás, young as he was, and imagined the paths he would follow, the man he would become.

Outside, no one waited to hear the sex of this child. There were no cannon shots. Rather, the road outside was quiet, because it was a Sunday, and because the Aragón neighbors had come to expect only sadness from this particular family.

Two weeks after Tomás was born, Gisela came over, a new

dress draped over her arm. She'd made it herself, and she'd embroidered the deep blue eyes of peacock feathers along the hem.

"Ay, Gisela, you didn't have to," Amalia said.

"Your old dress was ruined. And besides, this particular birth is one to celebrate. Look, look at the peacocks. Fit for a queen."

Amalia examined the exquisite sleeves, ran her finger against the silky threads of the embroidery, tested the whalebone in the bodice against her thumb and forefinger. She was all business, all poise until she felt her eyes sting.

"Don't cry," Gisela said. "If you don't like it—"

"I adore it," Amalia said. "Gracias." Then she sobbed and sobbed until Gisela had to take the baby from her. "It's normal, this crying," Gisela said, but Amalia felt as if she'd been suddenly dropped into very deep water and could only beat her legs for so long.

Tomás was Amalia's fifth baby. Gisela had been there through all of them—Emilia, Francisca, Rubén, who looked as if he might survive, then decided that he'd prefer to follow his sisters to the grave, and finally, Alicia. Each time, Gisela had tucked herself behind Amalia like a pillow, cradling her while she cradled her darlings. She'd whispered "Ya, ya, basta," into Amalia's ear when her sobs had left her breathless. Sometimes, Gisela would sing Cuban songs, and the rhythms of her voice seemed to mimic the coming and going of the sea. It was Gisela who would take the babies away at last, her spine curved, her body a hollow of shared grief.

For Amalia, holding Tomás in those early days felt like trying to cradle a porcelain tea set. His tiny ears were teacups of bone china, and his long calves were like delicate handles. His nose was a spout, his cheeks were creamers of the thinnest ceramic. At any moment, Amalia feared she would drop him and he would shatter, as all the others had done.

But Gisela had come by every day, repositioning Amalia's arms, helping her when Tomás kicked so hard that he was impossible to diaper, feeding Amalia malted drinks and cooking up bacalao for dinner, and holding Tomás when Amalia could no longer bear his weight.

"Big boy, the biggest," Gisela would say to him, nose to nose. He would try to focus on her strange eyes, then he would turn his head and squall.

Amalia knew that Tomás's birth and survival would keep Rubén close by forever. She would observe him with their son, how her husband would lower his face toward the baby and touch noses with him, and she would think, "I have won him now." She had felt him growing distant with each birth, each death. He would take on more work, and that work made him more tired at night, so that he would skip the dinners she made and eat only bread, too exhausted even for conversation. In bed, he would roll over onto his side, away from her. Amalia would rub his arm, slide her hand down to his stomach, lower still, and he would not stir. "Buenas noches," he would whisper and become very still until she removed her hand. That Tomás was even conceived was a wonder to her, and Amalia could not remember what the night had been like, whether she had wept afterwards, as she sometimes did, or if he kissed her mouth.

Now, his son alive and thriving, life thrummed in Rubén again. He smiled often, and snuck up behind Amalia to kiss her ear loudly, and she would smack him playfully complain about her ringing ear. Amalia prayed that Rubén would not change again, that God would allow him to remember the happiness of their life in that moment when the winds changed, as they would, inevitably.

3

It was Gisela who first told Amalia about the doctors from the palace, the ones who had selected Burgos as the place to search for the new nodriza. "You should apply," Gisela suggested. "It's only for two years, and Tomás here will be like a little prince."

Even then, in the flush of the idea, Amalia had misgivings. "A milk brother is far from a prince."

"I'd rather live in a palace if I had a choice," Gisela answered.

"Away from my husband?" Amalia asked, and Gisela stared at her feet. "Rubén will not be easily convinced, and he won't want me to—"

"It says here," Gisela said, reading from the newspaper, "that there is a stipend of 24,000 escudos for the selected woman."

Rubén came in at the moment, his hands blackened with soot. He'd been on the roof, fixing the top of the chimney, which had blown over in a storm. "Twenty-four thousand escudos? Who has that kind of money?"

Gisela read the announcement again, while Amalia bounced Tomás.

"Tomás would be a little prince," Gisela repeated, then turned to Amalia and said, "The odds are you won't be selected."

Amalia and Rubén debated the merits of the position for days, trading opinions back and forth, as if they were playing a card game. One moment it made perfect sense, a provident choice. The next, it didn't.

"My mother was a wet nurse," Rubén said one night. Amalia had not known this. "When my brother was born," he said, and they both crossed themselves, for Rubén's older brother had died young of scarlet fever. "Not for the queen, of course. For a well-to-do Italian family that lived in Burgos for some time. She loved that baby of theirs, a girl."

"Your brother's milk sister," Amalia said.

"I suppose so. The money was good, my mother always said. It paid off the house I grew up in." Rubén looked at his hands, turning them over this way and that. Silently, he pointed at his calluses, one at a time, and Amalia reached over to make him stop. Her own hands weren't soft, and already, a single, pale sunspot had emerged beneath a knuckle on her left hand. She'd forgotten what they'd looked like when she was very young. Near them, Tomás snored in his sleep.

So they decided it, in silence and together, that being a milk brother to a princess of Spain was no bad thing.

The queen's doctor, Bruno Aguilera, and a palace administrator, Manuel Izquierda, came to the countryside to interview and examine sixty-four women for the job. The examinations lasted only two days, and the same procedure was followed for each applicant. The doctor and the palace manager palpated one hundred and twenty eight breasts with their small, cold hands. They peered into the women's mouths and compared the redness within to a little piece of crimson fabric. They weighed the women, measured their height with golden measuring tapes. The men took turns sniffing their ears—too much wax inside meant the woman was lazy about hygiene. If the woman made the cut, they would ask to see the child the woman was nursing, the future milk sister or milk brother to the royal baby.

While the doctors examined Amalia, Rubén and Gisela waited outside, at the doctors' request. Before going out, Rubén had whispered in his wife's ear, "Don't tell them about the others," and she knew he meant the babies who had died. Later, she would learn that Rubén had gone to the church and removed the babies' death certificates when the office was empty, just in case the palace doctors went looking for them.

Amalia unbuttoned her shirt, and cold, manicured hands

felt her breasts, squeezing her until she cried out, and a thick drop of milk trickled down her stomach. Her own mother came to mind as it was happening. It was a nun who had first revealed to Amalia that her mother had been a prostitute. "Nearly all the children had whores for mothers," she'd said with a pitying look, and Amalia had replied that nearly all nuns were kicked out by their villages for their ugliness. She had been made to wash all of the habits in scalding water that afternoon. But the punishment had not made the memory of the nun's accusation, that her mother had been a prostitute, fade. Amalia thought of her as she was touched and prodded by the men from the palace, and wondered if the deep shame she was feeling, so deep that she forgot where she was for a moment, had been her mother's constant companion.

Before Amalia was allowed to dress herself again, one of the doctors asked, "Tell us about your parents during the war. They were not Carlists, of course." He smiled strangely, stiffly.

Amalia swallowed hard, told them what the nuns had told her, that her mother had run from the Carlists on the Basque border, and had left Amalia at the orphanage for safekeeping. For good measure, she added, "My father was killed by the Carlists for joining the Liberales." Amalia made that part up for good measure.

"So much bravery from our men," the questioning doctor said sadly. Gooseflesh prickled Amalia's arms. "We are finished, señora," the other doctor said. They would not look Amalia in the eye, though she bore her own gaze into their faces.

When she brought her son out to meet the men, blinking at them with still sticky eyes, they commented on his size—"He's a large one, no? Well done, señora," and on the size of his penis—"Excellently formed," they said—and decided that Amalia's milk was fortified with nutrients good for growing. The baby cried, and clawed at the air in their arms as if he mistrusted the doctors' ability to keep from dropping him, and this was the first time Amalia realized that her son had a brain in his head.

Holding Tomás, feeding Tomás, watching as his small stomach grew and his sighs became contented and happy, was the single most wonderful thing Amalia did each day. She thought often of Queen Isabel, who would never know the sweet feeling of a suckling child, how it felt as if her entire self was being funneled into that little body. Amalia thought that, perhaps, having never known it, Isabel imagined that the child would be like one of those doctors, exposing her, shaming her. Perhaps royal people could not bear to have themselves diminished in any way, dispossessed of any thing, including milk.

"I don't think I want the job," Amalia said to Rubén one night. She had seen a picture of Isabel in the newspaper, and she seemed grim and awful. The artist had drawn her in profile, and had done her the disservice of drawing an accurate portrait.

"Think of Tomás," Rubén said. "We'll save the money for him. Twenty-four thousand escudos, Amalia!"

"But—"

"He may not be a real prince, but he'll have land and money."

"What if he doesn't want to be a landowner?" she asked. Tomás had his hand wrapped around her finger. It looked like a farmer's hand. It was fat and strong, and the knuckles twitched as he gripped his mother.

Rubén laughed. "Look at him. He was built for that life."

"He likes it when I read to him," Amalia said quietly. Earlier that day, Gisela had brought a book of child's verses as a gift, and Tomás had seemed to enjoy them. Rubén, who could only read and write a little, fidgeted through the reading, making noises in the kitchen and stomping about in his heavy boots.

When the baby woke for a feeding, Amalia made the sign of the cross on his forehead. Tomás drank and slurped and grunted against her skin, like a small pig.

A few weeks later, a letter arrived with the news. Amalia was to become the new palace nodriza, which made her son, Tomás Aragón, the milk brother to the prince, or, heaven forbid, princess, destined to drink only after the royal child was satisfied. But first Rubén had to sign a letter granting Amalia permission to enter into the service of the palace. He scribbled out a few phrases, "I give permission," and "My wife is respectable," and "I expect payment."

4

They waited up in bed for the new year, Rubén and Amalia, with Tomás between them, like petals guarding a precious center. Faint whoops and cheers could be heard after the cathedral bell clanged twelve times, once for each month of the year. The following day, Amalia would leave for the Palacio Real in Madrid. She had a small bag packed with clothes and diapers for Tomás, and two plain traveling dresses for herself. She would be given a uniform, including shoes, and was instructed to leave the rest of her things behind.

Lying there, they parsed through their worries the way one picks through seeds, finding and discarding the bad ones quickly, without a second thought. Out loud, they talked about bills, about Tomás learning to walk and talk away from his father. In silence, Amalia brooded on her worries about living in a palace, her fears about Rubén left alone in the house. These were the bad seeds she tossed away. There was no point in bringing those worries to light again.

"Don't forget me," he said.

"I'll get a day off once a month and you'll come to Madrid then."

"Of course," he promised, but Amalia knew it would not be so easy for him to travel to Madrid. "Tell Tomás about me, even if you think he is too little to understand. Tell him he has a father."

Amalia nodded. "Eat well, promise? And keep an eye on the well."

Rubén nodded. "Remember me in your prayers, yes?"

Amalia was quiet then, this litany of promises threatening to make her cry. There was one thing she wanted to ask, one thing above all, but all she could muster was "Be true." Then she burst into tears.

Amalia settled Tomás in his cradle, and reached out for Rubén in the darkness. They found each other hungry, and filled with both sadness and desire. The taste of his mouth reminded her of the grass after the rain, and his skin was salty. His hands were rough and bumpy, like cobblestones, and the skin on his back was bristly with wiry hair. Sensing Rubén this way, with her eyes closed, with only her mouth and hands guiding her, was to understand the infinite characteristics of Burgos. He was Burgos, and she was leaving him for the capital, which was, in her mind, all marble and stone.

"Don't forget me," Amalia said in his ear. "Not even little by little, the way a person forgets the winter when it turns to spring."

He responded with a grunt and a sigh, and sweet kisses behind her ears. Later, they took turns kissing their boy, who had become a vessel of their competing hopes. Amalia thought of Isabel, possessed of everything, including her own future, and how she and Rubén, parents now, had no sense of a future of their own. It was all about Tomás's tomorrows. Finally, Rubén fell asleep, and all was quiet in their house in Las Trinas, which sat behind a crumbling convent, where they breathed in the dust of ages and dreamed of what was yet to come.

The carriage arrived in the morning. Amalia peered at it through the kitchen window. It was black and shiny, and the horses that pulled it were equally black. They snorted together, and their breaths formed clouds before them.

They stepped outside, Rubén and Amalia, walking slowly. Gisela, who had come to see them off, followed closely behind.

"Look," Gisela said, and gestured toward the carriage driver, who came off of his perch and shook hands with Rubén. They exchanged a few words while Amalia peered into the carriage. Expecting an empty seat, what she saw made her yell out in surprise. She met the eyes of a woman, slender and all in black, who was staring at Amalia with a grim press of her lips. In her arms was a baby, swaddled in a tattered linen blanket.

"Forgive me," Amalia said. "I was startled."

The woman betrayed the slightest smile, but said nothing. The baby in her arms gave a sudden wail, but the woman did not seem to acknowledge the sound. Amalia glanced away a little, settling her gaze on the woman's shoulder. "Leonela Garcia," the woman said at last, over her baby's cry. "Nodriza, like you."

So one of us is the spare, Amalia thought to herself.

"Be quiet," Leonela said to the baby, and Amalia watched as she pinched the fabric over the baby's thigh, a morsel of flesh certainly being squeezed. The baby stopped crying at once. Leonela then slid back into the depths of the carriage without a word.

Amalia turned away from her uneasily, facing her husband. She and Rubén had said their goodbyes last night. Now, at the last moment, he took Tomás in his arms and put his forehead against the baby's. Rubén's face grew ugly trying not to cry, not now, not in front of the carriage driver with his thick, caterpillar eyebrows and royal red uniform.

Gisela drew Amalia aside. Amalia thought she meant to give Rubén privacy with his son, but what she said was this: "Remember that your devotion should be to the royal baby. Outwardly, it should be so. But in your heart, never forget who your child is. That one, that big boy in his father's arms, loved you before you even knew he'd been formed."

Amalia shook her head. "Gisela, por favor. Why would it ever be otherwise?"

"You will be dazzled by it all, and by that baby, perfumed and well-dressed at all times, and who might one day sit on the throne. You will look at that baby and, if he is a boy, call him 'mi rey,' and he will drink your milk before Tomás."

Amalia shook her head again. Here was another worry, another bad seed she tried dropping away.

"Don't forget which one is your true son," Gisela said. She'd gripped Amalia's shoulders, a biting fire in her strangely colored eyes, from which Amalia recoiled.

The carriage driver cleared his throat. Amalia took Tomás from Rubén's arms.

"I'll see you in a month," he said. "And you," he added, kissing Tomás once more.

"Not even little by little?" Amalia whispered, wondering if he remembered what she had asked him the night before.

"Not even an inch," Rubén said. He helped his wife and son into the carriage, then settled Amalia's bag at her feet. The door closed and they were gone with a jolt that knocked Amalia back into her seat. Tomás let out a squeal.

"It's fine, mi hijo, we're fine," she told him, though her hands were shaking.

"I'm glad you think so," Leonela said, and her voice cracked. She lifted a bit of her baby's blanket to cover her face, and she turned her head toward the window, her neck long and luminous like a crane's.

They arrived in Madrid on the fourth of January, in a drizzling snow. Leonela hardly spoke a word over the course of the two-day trip. Amalia learned that she was from northern Burgos, that her husband was an iron-worker, that her baby was a three-month-old girl named Luz María. And that was all. Leonela had a habit of taking the baby's linen blanket into her mouth, as if she were sucking something out of it. But her breasts were ample, bigger than Amalia's, and her baby was also quite large. Together, their children were probably some of the heaviest and sturdiest babies in Burgos, and both women knew at once why they were selected. Neither one had brought up the question of which one of them was the secondary nodriza, but the matter hung over them, thicker than the velvet lining of the carriage's ceiling.

At the palace they were met by Celia Garcia, nanny to the two-year-old Infanta Paz, and the Infanta Pilár, who was four. Paz's nodriza had been recently dismissed, Celia told them. "She wrote the most pathetic letter to Her Majesty, asking to be reinstated. But we all know the milk goes bad after two years, don't we? I'm telling you now, to save you the embarrassment. When the baby turns two, out you both go. If not earlier. Understood?"

This was her greeting to them, and both said, "Sí, señora," without pause. Celia was a commanding woman, shorter than both Amalia and Leonela, but so settled in her grandmotherly ways that she acquired a royal bearing herself. Amalia very nearly wanted to curtsy before her, but she stood straight, shoulders back. Leonela straightened up, as well, her shoulders too far back, as if she were showing off her bosom. Celia raised an eyebrow at Leonela, who slumped over at once.

Celia peered at the babies that the women were carrying. When she tugged at the corner of the blanket hiding Tomás's face, she gasped. "He is a beautiful child," she said, and she smiled at the baby. Amalia felt herself puff up with pride.

They followed Celia into the palace, leaving behind tinkling fountains and serious guards. Inside, the palace opened up like a cathedral, with ceilings so high that Amalia had to squint to see the paintings on them. Marble veining shot out under their feet in rosy pinks and oranges, and massive archways led to halls in every direction. It was like being inside the rib cage of a tremendous, beautiful beast—there were angles, curves, organic colors everywhere. It was an architecture that seemed to be alive.

"This way," Celia said, and they went up a wide staircase, large enough that a carriage and horse could thunder their way to the top. They passed statues in alcoves of short men in knights' armor, and portrait after portrait of serious, gold-flecked people. They drew close to another door, left ajar. From within, they heard the small voice of a child, counting to six again and again.

"Muy bien, tesorito," Celia boomed, and pushed through the door. There was a little girl in a red and white striped dress. She wore the whitest shoes Amalia had ever seen, and a red bow in her short, curly hair. Her cheeks were pudgy, and she held her hands against them, feeling her face change as she counted at the top of her voice.

"Nana," she cried when she saw Celia, and plunged into the woman's skirts.

Celia picked her up and nuzzled her nose, then put her down again.

Celia turned to the nodrizas sharply. "You may call her Paz while in the nursery. Outside of this place, she is 'your highness.' Same goes for Pilár, who is taking a music lesson at the moment. Questions?"

Paz danced around Celia, calling, "Nana, Nana, I love you, Nana." A corner of Celia's mouth twitched into a smile at the song. The little princess was sweet, and if not beautiful, certainly pretty, having inherited the blond hair and blue eyes of the Bourbon family. Her manners were gentle, and she squinted her eyes at all times, as if she were about to laugh at the slightest joke.

Celia lifted Paz onto her hip and led them through another long hallway. "My room," she said, pointing to a small, tidy bedroom nearest the nursery. They walked on, and as they did, a strange sound grew. At first, Amalia thought the Infanta Pilár was taking lessons with other children, and that what they were hearing were the discordant sounds of several young violinists. But, as they approached the end of the hallway, then took a left turn, the space opened up in a bright shaft of light, and in the distance, Amalia could see a sliver of blue sky overhead. The hall ended in an iron gate, with a long, beveled glass set between the bars, and a greenhouse lay beyond. Lush flowers were blooming, even though it was winter, and a fountain squirted prettily within. The sound was the squawk of birds, chittering away in the sunlight.

"What is this?" Leonela asked. Luz María, in her arms, had begun to whimper, and she was bouncing the baby to keep her quiet. Amalia watched Leonela warily. She was jostling the child vigorously now. Tomás slept heavily, his mouth open.

"We call it the Birdcage. Her Majesty's birds live here," Celia said. Amalia spotted a white peacock fanning his tail at a dusky female bird that scampered away from him. "And in this room, adjacent to the Birdcage, is where you will both stay." A door that had gone unnoticed was opened to reveal two short beds, pushed against the walls. Cradles were set at the ends of the beds. These were simple, made of wood, with thick white blankets inside.

"Those cradles are for your babies. Never for the royal children, who sleep in the nursery."

Amalia worried out loud about the distance from their room to the nursery. She had always kept Tomás so close by, close enough to hear him breathing.

"I will alert you when the baby needs his milk. My hearing is exceptional," Celia said.

"You'll alert me, too?" Leonela asked loudly, her attempts to calm Luz María having failed. The child was screaming in concert with the white peacock, which voiced its discontent at being rejected.

"There will be no need. You will nurse the baby only once a day, in order to give Amalia a chance to recover her strength. Your other duties will be to assist in the nursery, changing diapers, dressing the children. I suspect we won't have you rocking the children to sleep. You seem out of practice," Celia said, and Leonela clutched Luz María as if Celia had just threatened to throw the child out of a window. Celia dismissed them, but Leonela followed her out. "This is not my first baby, I'll have you know. Luz María is my third. Third. My others are safe and well at home. Strong, too. In fact they—" Leonela paused and said nothing. Celia stopped too. The women stared at each other. "Ask Amalia. Is that boy her first child?" Leonela asked.

Amalia held her breath. She remembered them all at once, the babies she'd lost, felt the old grief bubbling in her heart like a potion.

Celia folded her hands at her waist. "I should have been clearer at the start, I see. Leonela, you are the auxiliary nodriza, Amalia is the primary nodriza, and I am in charge of this nursery and everyone in it." Then, she left them to settle in. Amalia dared not look at Leonela, though she imagined those dark eyes were upon her, marking her every move.

The next morning, Amalia was surprised to find that a very different Leonela greeted her. She chattered all day, complimented Tomás, was tender with Luz María, who Amalia thought was going to grow up to be a dark, heavy-lidded beauty. "Those birds are so loud," or "I feel a long winter coming," Leonela would say, making small talk. But sometimes, Leonela would disrupt a moment of quiet to say something like, "Don't get too comfortable here, Amalia. The queen's babies die more often than not," and a chill would descend upon Amalia at the thought.

"The future cannot be predicted," Amalia said in response.

"You're right. But nothing is promised in this life, is it?" Leonela answered, sighing like a person at a funeral. Amalia felt that Leonela was like a spider trying to get into a house, to find for herself a warm, dusty corner for her web. Amalia observed Leonela's thin arms, covered in dark hairs, and remembered the time Rubén smashed a spider, the million babies that erupted from inside it, and how they had both screamed like children. She stifled a laugh.

"What's so funny?" Leonela asked.

"Just a memory of my husband, that's all."

"Tell me about him," Leonela asked. Amalia almost replied. Honest answers came to her naturally, and so it felt rather foreign to her to say, "He's a good man," and leave it at that.

On the night the child was born, Amalia listened to the queen's agonies through a vent in the ceiling. The vent had been cut in order to install a gas line a few years earlier, and the pipe that jutted out of the hole hissed and sputtered and smelled funny. But other sounds were carried along the pipe, and Amalia, passing by on the way from the kitchen to the nursery, heard the distinct shout of a woman. She returned to the vent an hour later, after Celia had confirmed that yes, the queen was delivering her child. From there, Amalia listened to it all—the doctors' urging, Isabel's grunts and whimpers, muttering she couldn't make out. *Amalia, go*, she told herself, knowing that her eavesdropping was wrong, that she would have nightmares all night, and that her dead babies would come to her in dreams and intrusive thoughts for days afterwards.

But Amalia could not move. Her feet had sprouted roots. When she first heard the new infanta's cries, she cried out too, and her own body betrayed her, gushing milk for a child she had not yet seen.

"You are the new ama?" Amalia heard a man say, and she looked up, startled. He had a thick beard, and his hair was parted severely to the side. He was a little older than she, but not by too much.

"Señor," Amalia said, and curtsied. "I was just—"

"Spying," he said.

"No, no, of course not!" She crossed her arms tight against her chest to cover up the two blooming wet spots on her shirt.

The man put his hands inside his coat pocket, for he was wearing a long jacket indoors. He drew out a pocket watch and glanced at it before putting it back. Above them, the child began to cry again.

The man blew out a puff of breath at the sound, and when he looked at Amalia again, his eyes were bright. "You were only worried about the baby and su alteza, Ama. We have all been worried."

The way he said it slowed the currents of unease within her. "Deliveries are tricky things, señor," she said.

"I know it," he answered, and pronounced the words so clearly and slowly, that it seemed he had revealed something about himself, some inner working of his heart.

"Amalia," she said, curtseying again.

"What? Oh. Miguel Tenorio de Castilla, a su servicio," he said. He nodded, then spun around, headed to the banquet hall where the other nobles were gathered to await the news of Isabel's delivery.

Amalia watched him go in mild astonishment. This man was of the noble class; that was certain. It was in the fine cut of his suit and the trimmed curls on his head, in his fine, white fingers, and in his gleaming pocket watch. Spain was relent-lessly hierarchical—men commanded women, women commanded children, the aging commanded the young. And yet, this Miguel Tenorio had treated her not as a servant but as a fellow witness to a royal birth, both of them anxious and relieved at the sound of the infant's cries. She was not yet well versed in the ways of the court, and the encounter, as short as it was, made her feel welcome for the first time since she had arrived.

At dawn, Eulalia was brought to Amalia, swaddled in a soft, cotton blanket dyed sunflower yellow, the color of the Virgin. Celia settled the girl in the nodriza's arms. "Another girl," she sighed, and Amalia laughed in relief. There would be no little king to replace the boy she loved. And this one was so far down the line, she would never be a queen of Spain. "Mi princesa," Amalia said to her, and put her to the breast.

At that moment, the white peacock squalled, his call so humanlike. Amalia knew it was him, for he was the loudest bird in the Birdcage. "Hush," she whispered to him, but he called out again. She thought of Gisela, and her petition against affections extending toward the royal children. "What's the harm in it?" she whispered, and touched the blond wisps on Eulalia's head.

Just like that, she was in love with the girl. She had forgotten that she shared the room with Leonela, who stared at Amalia from the bed, ignoring Luz María, who was clawing at her breast, her mouth opening and closing. Tomás, for his part, slept on, snoring away. Amalia longed to put Tomás and Eulalia side by side, compare them, introduce them to one another. Celia would frown at that. The new baby took deep breaths, coughed a bit, then latched on again. Her eyes opened for a moment, revealing their blueness, then finding Amalia's. It was her turn to lose her breath.

"Your highness," Amalia mumbled at her, besotted. "Aren't you a hungry one?"

Querida Gisela,

I met the Infanta Eulalia last week, just an hour after she was born, and I thought of you, and your concern for my mother's heart. The child is divine, she is. But she cannot take the place of my son.

In spite of the generally fickle nature of newborns, we have a routine, the infanta and I. Each morning, the nurse brings the baby to me. Tomás, who has begun to pull himself up already, eyes me curiously. Sometimes, his bottom lip quivers and his eyes start to redden, and if I do not say, "Shh, shh, mi hijito," he will start crying. But it is as if he knows I have a duty, and that he, little as he is, has one, too. So he plops his fat little thumb in his mouth and waits.

I wasn't invited to the baptism, which did not surprise me. The other nodriza, Leonela, was offended, as if she were a duquesa who'd been slighted. She is, God forgive, an overwrought and ridiculous woman. Nevertheless, we were both made to go to confession in preparation for the baptismal mass we were not allowed to attend. Leonela quipped that su alteza's confesor, Padre Campion, was probably exhausted after listening to the Queen's sins, and that he would go easy on us.

You should know that the palace is all gossip, much like Las Trinas can sometimes be.

Leonela likes to point out the many ways su alteza's children do not resemble one another, and how none of them resemble the Queen's consort, Francisco de Asis.

I suppose we've all heard those rumors, the newspapers have never shied away from it. When I asked Leonela what she thought of Francisco de Asis, she said, "Several strapping men have come to his rescue, don't doubt it for a second."

Can you imagine, Gisela? The things that come out of Leonela's mouth leave me cold sometimes.

Ay, mi amiga. I am such a long way from Burgos, and I feel the distance physically on some days, as if I have been holding taut a long ribbon between my home and the palace, and suddenly lose my grip on it.

Tu querida amiga,

Amalia

5

The confessional was in the chapel where the baptism would be held. Amalia peeked at the altar, and saw that the preparations had been made—the altar was covered in a cloth embroidered in gold thread. To either side of the altar, a massive bouquet of red and yellow flowers sat in gold vases.

She knelt at a pew and waited. It was courteous not to raise one's head at the sound of the confessional door swinging open. Besides, she did not want anyone to look at her when it was her turn to leave and do her penance. Yet something tugged at Amalia when the door creaked, and she looked up to see Miguel Tenorio, stepping out. He looked much changed—his face was ashen, and he held his hands tightly together, massaging his knuckles as he walked away. Amalia buried her face in her hands, and hoped he hadn't caught her looking.

A rustling sound startled Amalia. A nun had settled herself in the pew. Her eyes were on Amalia, narrowed, her lips moving a little without making a sound. Before Amalia could utter a good morning, the nun said, "I am Sor Patrocinio. Perhaps you have heard of me."

Amalia could not say that she had, and she wouldn't lie, not now, so close to confession. She shook her head, then her eyes fell on Sor Patrocinio's hands, which lay very still on her lap, wrapped in white muslin, so that she could only wiggle her fingers a little.

"Oh, have you had an accident?" was all Amalia could think to say.

Sor Patrocinio only turned her palms up, slowly, as if revealing a gift to a child. There, Amalia could see red stains blooming, seeping into the cloth. "Pray, child. You are in the presence of a miracle," the nun said, and Amalia closed her eyes and did as she said, all of her body itching to get away, as if she were in the company of a terrifying insect one encounters in the middle of the night.

But when she opened her eyes again, Sor Patrocinio was still there, and the nun began to speak with a whispered urgency. "I feel as if there are many miles between you and the one you love. The palace is bereft of love, you can feel that, I'm sure. But I am pure love. This is pure love," she said, gesturing to her hands. "Su alteza seeks me out because of this. As you nourish the child, so do I nourish la Reina." She spoke the way one recites prayers—hurriedly and seeminging without thinking. Amalia thought this might go on forever, for Sor Patrocinio spoke without pauses, her breath hot and garlicky on Amalia's face.

Then, relief. Amalia felt a light touch on her shoulder a few moments later, and looked up to see Padre Campion before her. He nodded towards the confessional, and she stood, leaving Sor Patrocinio behind.

Inside the booth, Amalia knelt. "Forgive me, Father, for I have sinned," she began. Amalia was quiet for a bit, unsure of what to say. That she worried about what Rubén was doing? Or that she would somehow be less of a mother to Tomás now that Eulalia took up so much of her time? These didn't seem like sins, but rather, afflictions of the soul, drawing her away from the present with worries about the future.

"Sometimes I daydream during mass on Sunday," Amalia said at last. This was true, at least. A small sparkling thing caught her eye on the floor, twinkling as if by its own light in the dim space. Amalia thought of Leonela and her claims regarding Isabel. If they were true, she thought, then this Padre Campion had heard far worse. He held his eyes closed, as if listening to the voice of God. He parted his lips to speak, and Amalia expected a soft reprimand, perhaps a recitation of Hail Mary or two.

"You are to recite two rosaries on your knees, and remember that you serve in the household of Spain's regent. Your attention should be sharp and unwavering at all moments." Then he closed his eyes again.

"Amen," Amalia said, her voice limp. She made the sign of the cross, then swept her hand across the floor to pick up the glimmering object. It was small and hard, and she tucked it into her pocket. Leaving the confessional, Amalia decided then and there that she would forego communion if it meant sitting in that dark, wooden box with a man who thought two rosaries on her knees was just penance for day-dreaming.

Amalia tried very hard not to look at Sor Patrocinio as she rose for her turn at confession, but she could see her dark shape from the corner of her eye, and in the center of it was a bright red spot. It was the same effect one feels after staring at the sun.

Later, she heard one of the guards say that the infanta was given ninety-three names. And just as many godparents, if not more.

That night, while Eulalia slept in Amalia's arms, Leonela said, "The queen herself did not attend the baptism. Odd, don't you think? It's been four days since the delivery. Surely, she can get out of bed by now."

"If she wasn't there, who was?" Amalia whispered over the baby's head.

"Half of Spain, I heard. At least, anyone worth anything. Meanwhile, Her Majesty sits around fanning herself. Entertaining her lovers, maybe."

"That's ridiculous," Amalia told her. "No one takes a lover days after birth. You're being vulgar on purpose," she reprimanded.

Leonela dismissed Amalia with a wave of her thin hand and said, "You're pretending to be naive, Amalia. Burgos may be in the country, but it isn't a backwater. You know as well as I do what people are capable of."

"That's what I mean. They are just people! Picture her, the queen, pale and sleepy in her bed, still bleeding, poked, prodded, examined by a host of doctors. Her oldest, María Isabel, is as haughty as any schoolgirl, but she's thick around the waist, like her mother, and her complexion is bad. I saw her this morning. Pilár likes to pick her nose while she plays, I've seen her do it, and Paz is sweet, but she only ever says 'Nana' and 'Ama' like a broken toy. Eulalia cries like any infant, mewling like a kitten when she is hungry, and she scratches her cheeks with her too-long nails, so that I put a pair of Paz's socks over her hands while she sleeps. As for the heir, I haven't seen Alfonso, but I've heard he's overly thin and always getting in trouble for playing pranks. People, just people, Leonela."

"How stupid of me to think otherwise," Leonela said, turning her back on Amalia. Then, in a low voice, she said, "People are capable of terrible things. Even the ones we love. They forget about you, they betray you. I haven't received so much as a single letter from my husband yet. God knows what he's up to. What about you?" The question was not meant to be answered, because Leonela, who eyed all the mail when it came, knew what Amalia's response would be. She flopped down on her bed and feigned an instant sleep.

In the middle of the night, Amalia woke with a start. She listened for the keening sound of a baby's cry, but heard nothing. Even the birds were quiet. Then she recalled the stone she had picked up in the confessional. She got up quietly, peeling back the covers slowly, and tiptoed over to her uniform. She felt for the pocket, and the stone within, which she drew out carefully. Then she left the room and took the stone with her to the Birdcage. Amalia opened the gate, again softly, quietly, and stepped into the lush aviary. There was a full moon, and it blazed through the glass ceiling overhead, catching in the many bevels in the windows, splintering the light. She opened her hand and saw a rectangular stone the color of the sky at dusk. It was the size of large blueberry and looked good enough to eat. It had obviously come loose from some setting—a ring most likely. Amalia turned the stone over in her hand, catching the moonlight. It was a sapphire, or maybe an aquamarine. A blue diamond? Did such a thing exist? She didn't know, but she began to shake with the thing in her hand. If she were to return it in the morning, they would ask why she hadn't done so right away.

The white peacock nudged her with his head, opening his mouth.

"No, no, no," Amalia whispered, but he squawked anyway, a loud, angry noise. She backed away from him, but he followed, fanning his tail and calling out. The brown, female peacock looked down from her nest overhead, as if saying, "Now you know what it feels like to be chased by that one."

Suddenly, Amalia heard footsteps. "What are you doing in there?" Celia said from behind the gate. She was wearing her nightcap and was blinking like an owl.

Amalia gripped the stone. "These birds," she said. "They are so noisy. I was trying to shush this white one."

"I didn't hear the birds."

"They're driving me crazy. The peacocks cry like babies. I shudder to think of the sound if the hen lays eggs. Then it will sound like two nurseries full of infants."

Celia opened the gate, then reached out her hand, palm up, twitching her fingers. Amalia felt as if her heart had stopped. She stood still as a lamppost.

"Your hand, Amalia. Come, child. You need your rest."

Amalia slipped her free hand into Celia's and, when the old woman wasn't looking, pocketed the jewel.

"Let's go down to the kitchens. There's some ham left over from the celebrations this afternoon. We will have a little feast, and then off to bed. How does that sound? Oh, oh," Celia said, halting in her tracks. She drew Amalia in a tight embrace. "No tears, no tears." She pounded her back, like men do to one another.

Amalia couldn't help herself. The stone, the worries about the babies, her husband, the confession, the rumors about the queen, the damned peacocks, Leonela's icy glares. It was all too much.

"I'm sorry, Celia. I miss my home."

Celia looked at Amalia gently, and tugged at a stray hair that had gotten caught in the nodriza's mouth. "You're from Burgos, no? So was I. The Queen and her children, they were all nursed by women from Burgos. It could be said that Burgos is in their blood, quite literally. I'm proud of that."

As promised, Celia led Amalia down to the kitchens and together they ate. They chewed silently, each woman staring off into some inscrutable past or future. The stone sat in Amalia's pocket like a great weight, and the thought of it there troubled her stomach. She told herself that she would say the rosaries Padre Campion had assigned, and add another for the gemstone, though she didn't expect the prayers to do anything to relieve her nerves, or her homesickness. Earlier that day, Leonela had said that the Royal Palace was thick with sin, thicker than any other place in Spain, and Amalia began to think she was right. Beyond the call of the birds, and the wailing of babies, there was a susurration in the air of secret stories. It felt as if Amalia could reach up and cup them to her ear, the way she had reached down and taken something priceless in her hand.

6

It was after lunch one day, when Eulalia was four months old, that Amalia returned to the nursery to find the birds loose. There were doves nestled in the bookcases, songbirds crashing into the frescoes on the ceiling, as if the false blue sky had driven them mad or suicidal. Feathers littered the floor, and the peacock pair was nestled inside one of the cribs. Both Leonela and Celia were dashing about kicking at the birds while carrying children—Paz and Eulalia on Celia's hips, Tomás and Luz María on Leonela's. Pilár jumped up and down in a corner, sucking on the hem of her dress, and crying in jags.

"Help us!" they shouted, and Amalia tried to use her apron as a net. She managed to catch two of the doves that way, but the others eluded her. When she tried to pick up the female peacock, the male bit her, honking, the feathers on his head raised like spikes. "I hate you," Amalia hissed at the bird, and went in search of help. The cook and her four scullery maids followed thereafter, their hands raw and red, shouting about roasted peacock for dinner. Amalia watched as an ibis swallowed a wooden block, the cube rotating down its skinny throat, bulging and spinning until it disappeared in its stomach. "This is madness!" Leonela shouted, and kicked savagely at one of the scullery maids, a girl of no more than fourteen, who had stopped to pluck a feather from the peacock. One at a time, their arms covered in scratches and bites, the women managed to put the birds back in the aviary.

Leonela was slumped on the floor, feathers sprouting from her curls. She looked like a bedraggled bird herself. "Who did it? Who let them loose?" she asked.

"Alfonso. I'm sure of it. That boy has a head for pranks," Celia said, patting at a long scratch on her finger.

Alfonso, Amalia thought. *The future king.* His name was said in low tones, though he was only a child of seven. A small photo of him, a school picture, was set in a golden frame in the nursery. The boy had large, brown eyes, a long nose, his left eyebrow cocked up into his forehead, as if he were questioning the photographer, and thin, crooked lips. His forehead was expansive, his ears positioned low on his head. He was handsome in a very Spanish way. He reminded Amalia of the little boys who played with sticks on the streets of Burgos.

"Her Majesty will be very angry when she hears about the birds," Celia said, clucking as she changed Eulalia's diaper.

"Oh, don't tell her," Amalia blurted, her gaze on Alfonso's picture still. She recalled the punishments at the convent where she grew up. The hours copying Genesis. The silent dinners. The lashes with a man's belt, which the nuns kept only for the purpose of striking the children. Even as a little girl, she had promised herself that she would never hit another child. Rubén once said that Tomás would be spoiled, and Amalia had replied, "Spoiled, but unhurt. I can live with that."

Celia pinned Eulalia's diaper and turned around. "We do not keep secrets from Her Majesty."

Amalia's conscience flew at once to the blue stone at the bottom of her dresser drawer.

"Of course not," she said.

It was because of the prank with the birds that Amalia came to meet Isabel II at last. She appeared in the nursery in the afternoon, her children following her like baby chicks, Eulalia in her arms. Behind her, walking like a shadow, was Sor Patrocinio, her hands in the folds of her habit. The children had spent the obligatory daily hour with their mother, and the little princesses were smiling, cheery. Alfonso, however, walked with his gaze on the ground, as if coming to the executioner. The eldest, María Isabel, studied abroad, and came home only for special occasions.

The queen was so large that she had to squeeze into the door sideways to get through. Her hair, done in dark ringlets like a girl, sat on her shoulders, which sloped downwards. Her eyes were blue and crystalline, and she wore an off-the-shoulder gown edged with lace.

"Your Majesty," Celia curtsied at once, and Leonela and Amalia followed. Tomás and Luz María were sitting on the carpet, handing a rattle back and forth.

"My son has a matter to settle with you. Alfonso," she said, and he stepped forward, brushing against his mother's skirt.

"I deeply apologize," he said in a small voice, "for disrupting your work and the peace of the nursery by letting loose the birds. It will not happen again."

"Of course not, your highness," Celia said.

"Of course not," Leonela and Amalia echoed.

Isabel seemed displeased, though. "Punishments bounce off the child like water off a duck's back."

"Mamá, that isn't true," Alfonso said, thrusting his fists against his thighs.

Isabel whipped around to face him, her heavy skirts knocking down Paz, who began to whimper. Alfonso stared hard at his glossy shoes. "You will write to your father this afternoon and tell him what you've done," she said at last, but when she faced the women again, Amalia caught Alfonso shrugging his shoulders, as if the thought of his father learning of the prank was of no consequence.

Isabel must have seen it in him, too, that sense that her words had not struck his small heart the way she'd intended. She turned to face Sor Patrocinio, who took her cue without words, released her hands from within her habit to reveal them, all white-wrapped and blood-soaked, and said, "Alfonso, you and I will pray a little together today, and ask Papa Dios for forgiveness." The manner in which the nun spoke was different from what Amalia had heard outside the confessional that day—she tuned her voice to a higher key, smiled as she spoke. It was the voice teachers of young children the world over used, and Amalia wondered if that was the voice she used with Isabel, too, who seemed very much like a child all of a sudden, her eyes wide and pleading as she gazed at Sor Patrocinio.

Turning again, the queen seemed to force a smile onto her face. "Your children are quite large, aren't they? Both the boy and girl. Sturdy ones, there," she said, by way of complimenting the nodrizas.

"I give Tomás an extra bottle of goat milk with some ground rice in it for strength, Your Majesty," Amalia said. "Shall I add a supplement to her highness's diet?" she suggested, indicating Eulalia. At that, Isabel paled. She gathered her skirt and whispered something to Celia, who nodded.

"Good evening," the queen then said. She patted each of the children on the head once, and Alfonso twice. Then she left, the future king dragging his feet behind her.

Querida Gisela,

Even as I write this, I do not know how much longer I can withstand the palace. Perhaps Rubén has told you about my last letter to him, when I described the birds in the nursery, and what a mess it was, how I met the queen because of it, what she was like. I mentioned to her that perhaps we might give the infanta a bottle of goat milk a day, to strengthen her, now that she is four months old. Isn't that what we've always done, Gisela? Isn't that what makes them strong? I swear it is what I was taught, what I know in my mother's heart to be right.

Tonight, Miguel Tenorio appeared in the nursery. He is the secretary to the queen, and a man who has been kind to me in the past. The children were all asleep when he came, and the quiet in the room was punctuated by their light snoring. Tenorio held a small brown book in his hand, and a pencil, worn down so small he seemed to struggle to hold it. "I've come on Her Majesty's orders," he said. Then he spoke of the suggestion of the goat's milk, and read a statement from the queen announcing that the palace doctor would be coming in twice a day to weigh Eulalia from now on, and that I should save her soiled diapers so that those, too, can be weighed and measured. Then he warned that I should not introduce my "country ways" into the nursery.

Gisela, I tell you, the solid world under my feet felt like it was shifting, and I might have fallen over at any moment. I am angry and ashamed all at once. But I remember your warnings, my friend, and I will make sure Tomás gets the nourishment he needs, even if I have to milk a goat in the nursery myself!

There. Writing you has already made me feel better, and I imagine you here, at the foot of my bed, laughing at me.

There is one more thing to tell. Tenorio did not leave the nursery right away. Instead, he asked to see the infanta, and the nurse led Tenorio over to the bassinet where Eulalia slept.

I followed quietly and watched as Tenorio stood by the bassinet, his fingers woven together tightly behind his back. It was intensely quiet. Even the birds had fallen silent. A mantel clock tick-tocked the minutes nearby, and Tenorio held his breath.

"Would you like to hold her, señor?" he was asked. "Like you held Paz that time, and Pilár before her?" Then, Tenorio nodded, and Eulalia was lifted in his arms.

"Ay," he said, a soft breath. "Look at that nose, look at those pretty eyes," he whispered. "You are doing everything right, mi niña," he said. Then it was over, and he put the baby back down.

Truly, I felt as if I had caught the man in too private a moment, and so I forgot my embarassment at being chastised. Gisela, I have seen that look before, when Rubén first laid eyes on Tomás. It is a look that a man cannot replicate on his own, no matter how hard he tries. I'm glad Leonela did not follow Tenorio that night, and did not see that moment. If she had, she'd speak of nothing else, gloating in the evidence of gossip, ruining what I think was a beautiful sight to behold.

Tu querida amiga, siempre,

Amalia

7

"Yes, she's asleep. She sleeps so much. Like a baby herself. You are so busy with the children you don't notice." Leonela's voice slipped into the room like a snake. She was outside with Celia. Amalia sat very still, but couldn't make out Celia's response. Then, Leonela again: "I caught her the other day putting her boy in the same crib as Eulalia. Yes, yes, it's true, don't doubt it. He's such a brute of a child, too. Pulled the infanta's delicate little thumb until she cried." Then, more silence. By now, Amalia was tense with fear and anger. She couldn't catch her breath. It's true, she had put the children together for a moment while she helped Paz, who had fallen down and bumped her knee. Amalia had laid Tomás down beside Eulalia, and they cooed and bumped one another with their chubby legs. But it was Eulalia who gripped Tomás's little thumb and wouldn't let go, even though he fussed about it. Leonela and Celia talked in whispers for a while. Then, Leonela came into the nursery and said nothing.

Amalia feigned sleep. But she had murderous thoughts all night, and was caught unawares by the dawn, which seemed to come with the rapidity of a train. In his crib, Tomás was whimpering, making a mewling sound his mother had never heard. She rose at once, thinking that Leonela had done something to him, and was stunned to see her son covered in pink splotches. He was dragging his nails across his cheeks in search of relief, and moaning as he did so. His stomach rose and fell with effort, and when she lifted him, his skin was hot, like the top of one's head outside in the summer. *Sarampión*, Amalia thought with dread, wrapped Tomás in his blanket, and ran out of the room.

"He's sick. My baby is sick," Amalia called out to Celia. Her shouts awakened Eulalia, who began to squeal. Amalia could feel her breasts grow hard, ready with milk for the princess. "Shh, shh," she whispered to Tomás, who had started crying, too. The peacocks began their ghastly calling, and soon, the nursery and the Birdcage were vibrant with sound, every creature shrieking desperately. "Celia!" Amalia shouted, and the nursemaid emerged from her room finally, her hair a nest of curls. "My son," Amalia said, weeping now.

Celia came quickly, and pulled back the corner of the blanket. She sucked in her breath. "Out," she whispered. Then yelled, "OUT! Before the Infantas catch it. Sarampión, here in the palace! Ay!" She milled about, pushing Paz into her bedroom, then returning for Eulalia. "OUT!" she shouted a few more times.

Amalia stuttered at her, didn't know what to do, though she was being instructed plainly. It was as if she had grown dumb suddenly.

"Is it true? Is it true that you put him in the same crib as Eulalia?"

Amalia nodded, Celia a blur through her tears.

"The stupidity!" Celia roared, and peered into Eulalia's crib, turning the baby over and checking her skin for the tell-tale rash. She put her cheek against Eulalia's stomach. "She's not warm, that's good," she said to herself, then whirled to face Amalia. "I said OUT!"

Amalia walked backwards, as if Celia's voice was a force pushing her against her will. "Where do I go? Please call the doctor, Celia," she cried, but all she heard was another angry, "OUT!"

By now, Tomás was wailing, and Amalia was standing in the hall with him. "Shh, shh," she whispered again, and slid down to the floor. Gisela seemed to rise before her like an apparition. *Remember who your real son is*, she had said. Amalia undid the buttons on her blouse, nestled her son against her, and he drank, despite the rash and his hands, which flew to his face, his fingers bent like claws. Amalia held them down and rocked Tomás a little. Then, Tomás opened a perfect brown eye and watched his mother as he drank, as if he understood everything.

Amalia could hear Celia inside the nursery, giving Leonela orders, and she listened as Eulalia stopped crying finally, in Leonela's arms by then. Several minutes passed before Celia appeared in the hallway. She was no longer red-faced, or agitated. But she wrung her hands before her, the soft skin over her knuckles loose like a rumpled bedsheet.

"Why didn't you tell me Tomás was ill? Why did you let it get this far?"

"I didn't know. I didn't," Amalia said. "He just . . . woke up like this!"

Celia shook her head. She lifted Tomás's shirt to reveal another set of angry, red welts. "If that's what you think then you haven't been paying attention. The doctor is on his way. Once he makes the diagnosis, you'll be on your way, back to Burgos for two weeks, at least. Likely more." Then Celia left.

Amalia cradled Tomás, making clucking noises at him. "I'm so sorry," she told him. She hadn't noticed the welts. The fever. The runny nose. *Because I spend so much time with Eulalia*, she realized, thinking how it was that she knew the heat in the infanta's skin, knew when it was right and when it was off, but did not have the same intimate knowledge of her son's flesh. Miserable, Amalia cried in torrents all morning, stopping only to shush Tomás, or feed him, or blow air onto his flaming cheeks.

The doctor arrived at lunch. Amalia and Tomás sat in the hall the entire time, exiled from the nursery. He examined the baby there on the marble floor, as if he were administering to a dog that had been run over by a carriage. "It's sarampión, of course. Keep the fever down with cool cloths."

Celia appeared with Amalia's bag under her arm. "The carriage is waiting outside, Amalia. Here, I'll carry your bag for you," she said gently. "The cook packed you lunch for today and tomorrow," she said. "You'll find that in the carriage, too."

Celia escorted them outside, and helped settle Tomás in beside Amalia, who could not speak for the tears. Celia patted her knee. "He'll be fine. Most babies come through it fine. We just can't take any chances with the infantas, can we?"

Amalia tried to speak, and found she had to swallow thickly for the words to come. "Leo—Leonela isn't telling the truth about me. The children did share the crib, for just a moment after the birds came into the nursery. But the rest isn't true, whatever she's told you. I—I promise that—"

Celia's face grew very still. "I'll have no theatrics in the nursery, Amalia. Whatever is going on between the two of you ends now." Amalia covered her mouth with her hands. Tomás started to cry again. "I cannot fault you entirely. Leonela is as pleasant as a crow at dawn," Celia said, and she smirked just a little. "Watch that he doesn't scratch his pretty face. A beautiful child like that shouldn't be marred, yes? I'll see you in two weeks," she said, bent over Tomás, and made the sign of the cross on his forehead. Then, she patted Amalia's cheek. Amalia imagined she would scrub her hands with lye before entering the palace again. Then, a stricken look came across Celia's face. "Ay Dios, what if Alfonso grows ill!" She ran up the palace steps without another word, as if she would beat the sarampión back with her bare hands.

As the driver pulled the carriage away, Amalia took one long look at the left wing of the palace, where the nursery and the aviary were situated. It was as if she could see right through the pale stone, right into the cream-colored room with the painted horses on the ceiling. There, she imagined Leonela holding Eulalia, whispering terrible things about Amalia to the girl. Her mind's eye traversed the length of the nursery, leapt into the Birdcage where the peacocks guarded the eggs in their nest—to her horror, Amalia had learned that there would be more peacocks in the Birdcage soon—and along the cobbled path of the aviary to a loose stone near the farthest wall. Underneath, she had hidden the jewel she had found in the confessional.

The breeze coming in through the open carriage windows carried a hint of rain, and Amalia took deep breaths of it. Let it pour, she thought, wanting a thunderous storm to envelop the carriage in darkness, shutting out the world, letting her sort through her noisome thoughts.

A thunderstorm erupted over Las Trinas, Burgos, just as the carriage pulled up to the house. Tomás had refused to eat on the way, and Amalia could feel him growing hotter, his cheeks red pomegranates, his diaper a damp mess. When he cried, he sounded hoarse, like a feral cat. The driver blinked wetly at Amalia through the carriage window. He removed his coat, and held it overhead, beckoning her to take cover. This way, she and Tomás were led up the short walk to the front door. Rubén opened the door.

"What happened?" Rubén asked, pulling Amalia inside. He motioned for the driver to come in, too, but the man deferred, returning to the carriage.

"The baby," Amalia said, and they both looked at him in the lamplight, now covered in angry red marks. Without speaking, Rubén fetched a wet cloth, and Amalia settled down with the baby in their bed, coaxing him to nurse. She shut her ears against the familiar sounds of the house—the drip of the water in the kitchen sink, the tinny ticking of the clock in the hall, the scrabbling of small, clawed feet in the walls and on the roof, rodents and birds that used the house as a stopping point. Soon, Tomás settled down, and Amalia took a deep breath.

Rubén had been pacing, back and forth from their room to the kitchen. "How is he?" he'd ask, and Amalia saw a recognizable look in his face, the same tense, furrowed brow and teeth clamped together she'd seen each time they'd lost one of the babies.

"It's sarampión," Amalia said. Rubén nodded, felt the baby's forehead, and seemed to settle down a little, though Amalia's own heart was fitful and full of fear.

After a while, Rubén sat beside her, twisting one of Tomás's curls around his thumb as the baby slept. "Did you notice?" he asked. "The windowsills? I replaced them."

Amalia, who did not see too well in the dimming light, squinted in the direction of the windows. "So much better," she said, though she couldn't see the difference.

"And look up," he said. "See? Patched the crack in the ceiling."

"You've been busy. That crack reminded me of a rabbit's silhouette," Amalia said.

"You won't miss it, I promise."

Amalia knew that her husband wanted her to be proud of him, of how he had kept himself busy while she was away. But Amalia's eyes, having seen new things, the caul of familiarity ripped away, saw her home for what it was—small, dull, suffocating.

She was silent in the wake of Rubén's chatter. She tended to Tomás, nursing him, pressing cool cloths against his body, bouncing him and snuggling his almond-scented neck.

In the morning, Rubén ate a quick breakfast, and left to do a quick repair job at the cobbler's, who had promised him a new pair of leather shoes. Amalia watched him go with relief. Tomás was asleep, his fever broken at last, his long arms spread out, his body forming a "t" on the blanket where he lay. She sat down for a bit, and noticed how her hands jerked every so often, like a dying snapper. It was a recognizable twitch, one that had last happened to her in the orphanage. "Nerves," Sister Damiana had said to her, holding Amalia's hands until the spasms faded. She was the only nun who was truly kind to Amalia.

Here they were again, her nerves, betraying Amalia, trying to tell her something. Perhaps she was only missing the palace, or worrying about what Leonela was saying in her absence. She thought of the jewel she'd taken from the confessional, which she'd hidden away back at the palace. She worried about Tomás all over again, and checked his skin for fever. Amalia sat on her hands to still them. Her eyes fell upon the sink, full of dishes, and a pillowcase that needed mending, and the steadily growing pile of dirty diapers. She recognized that old version of herself in those things that needed her attention, and so, reminded of who she used to be, Amalia got to work.

8

It was early in the evening when Amalia looked up from Tomás's face and realized that Rubén was still not home. Taking soft steps, she went around the house and lit the lamps in each room. She had grown accustomed to the pendant gaslights of the palace, which lit the rooms in a glow that was like the late afternoon. The candlelight and kerosene lamps in her house in Burgos were, by comparison, weak, sputtering things. She touched the peeling plaster walls and thought of the fine wallpaper of the nursery. She wiggled her toes on the rough tile floor and thought of marble cooling her heels. A bite of bread from the kitchen brought to mind the thin, airy pan de cristál the palace cooks served each night with dinner. She peered out the window every so often, hoping that Rubén would be coming up the walkway.

By the time Rubén returned, when the last of the day's brightness was gone, Amalia was determined to remake the peace she had once felt in that house. So she asked him, as gently as she could, where he had been so long.

"Wood rot," he said, as if that explained anything. When Amalia blinked at him, saying nothing, he added, "Everywhere."

"The cobbler's, you mean?"

"Yes, the cobbler's. An hour's job took all day. I'm sorry I am late. How is the baby?" Rubén asked.

"He's better. Come here," she said to her husband, and he sat beside her, taking Tomás into his arms. She leaned against him and played with the pleats in his pants.

Rubén leaned over and kissed Amalia, then yawned. She watched Rubén as he walked away. He favored his left leg. His hair had grown so that it brushed his collar. He was humming to himself, a tune Amalia did not recognize. *How can he know a song that I do not?* she thought. The song that he hummed was proof of a certain inexpressible sense that something had shifted, like a lock sliding into place.

Rubén yawned again, and scratched his chin. He smelled like iron things and sweat, and beneath that, a sweet something, as if he'd spent the day in a field of flowers. He bent over his son, and ran the back of his fingers along the baby's cheek. "The rash is better, I think," he whispered.

"I think so, too," Amalia said, and he looked up at her. Then, something changed in his eyes, and it was a look Amalia had not seen for months, and one she had forgotten she had missed. Suddenly, Rubén was kissing her hard, their teeth knocking together.

Amalia could feel a secret in that kiss. They both had secrets. She thought about the jewel hiding in the Birdcage. They made love that night while Tomás slept, but for the first time, Amalia felt as if they were each holding something very precious close and hidden away from the other.

By the fifth morning in Burgos, Tomás's skin was clear, his fever gone completely, and he'd even gained a bit more weight. Amalia groaned theatrically when she lifted him, and chattered away about how big he was becoming. As for Rubén, he had gone to work early, and Amalia had missed his going.

Because Tomás was better, Amalia went in search of Gisela. She put on the peacock dress Gisela had made. It was snug around her chest, and Amalia remembered something that Celia had said in her first week at the palace—that palace life can make one fat, and that palace cooks are at fault. Those in service grew plump on pastries divvied out after lunch each day, but the queen was plied with so much rich food that she seemed larger than life. Celia, who was small herself, always said that a woman built nearly like a man was hard to say no to and nearly impossible to look in the eye.

Gisela lived in a small cottage on Calle Milagros, which she rented for a surprisingly small sum. She'd been there when the landlord's wife was giving birth to twins, and had saved the woman when it seemed she was on the verge of death after the delivery. It was not far from Amalia's house in Las Trinas, and so she walked, pushing Tomás in his pram, dusty from misuse. There was a small hole in the bed of the pram, a mouse having made a nest inside

The curtains inside Gisela's windows were drawn that day. Normally, Amalia would see her within, standing at her kitchen, or in a corner chair, reading. Once, she caught Gisela dancing by herself, her mouth moving in tune to a song Amalia could not hear from outside. Amalia had teased her about it, and Gisela had said that Cubans cannot help but dance sometimes, and that it was a shame that the Spanish had no sense of rhythm.

At first, Amalia thought that Gisela must be attending a birth. But she remembered that she had never seen her curtains drawn. Not even at night. Curious, Amalia knocked on the door. "Gisela," she called. "It's me. Amalia." There was no answer. She walked the perimeter of the cottage, searching for slivers of light. She longed to embrace her friend, to tell her about the palace, and how she was always on her mind, how she was her little conscience, reminding her to love Tomás above everything else. She wanted, more than anything, to thank her.

At last, around the back where Gisela's bedroom was, Amalia saw a gap in the curtain. There was Gisela, asleep, one long, brown leg bare and tangled in the sheets. Her arms were thrown above her head, sleeping the sleep of infants. Her mouth was open. At first, Amalia mistook the bulge of her stomach for pillows, but Gisela turned, smacked her lips, and it was clear that she was pregnant, though not far along. Amalia searched the room for signs of a man, but she didn't see work boots, or men's trousers, or anything that suggested that Gisela had gotten married while Amalia was away.

No wonder the curtains are drawn, she thought. My friend is ruined.

Remembering the sleepiness of pregnancy, how it is the sweetest sleep one ever enjoys, Amalia decided not to wake her. Instead, she drew a pencil and piece of paper from her bag and left her a note.

> *Gisela, querida,*
> *Why didn't you tell me? How can I help? What man has done this? I will find him for you and beat him over the head until he comes to his senses, or else Rubén will. Come see me before I go back to Madrid.*
> *Tu amiga,*
>
> *Amalia*

Rubén arrived home late at night. "So much work," he grumbled, before kissing the top of Amalia's head and sitting in a chair. He waved his hand in the air at his wife, and she knew he was asking for his dinner. He hummed a bit to himself in that new habit of his, but she did not have the heart to sing.

"Why didn't you tell me about Gisela?" she asked him.

The humming ceased. Rubén stared at his shoes, which were muddy and loose fitting.

"I saw her today," she went on. "Through the window of her cottage. I saw what state she is in."

"What did she say?" Rubén asked. His cheeks were burning.

"Say? Nothing. She was asleep and I didn't wake her. What's wrong with you?" she asked.

"You didn't speak to her?" Rubén demanded now.

"No, I—" Amalia paused. Something thick was growing in the room between them, some wreckage taking shape. She wanted to beat back at it somehow. She put her hand on Rubén's wrist, and he began to weep.

"Oh God, oh God help me. The thing is done, Amalia." He was panting, and hid his face in his hands. "Forgive me," he kept saying again and again.

"What thing? What thing?" Amalia asked, trying to lift Rubén's face to hers, her hands in his curls, the scent of his hair filling her nose.

At last, he met her eyes. "Don't make me say it." His face twisted and the look of it robbed Amalia of breath. She remembered in that instant that when she was laboring to bring her third baby into the world, when things were still peaceful in the room and full of hope, Gisela had hummed to herself as she laid out towels at the foot of Amalia's bed. It was mindless humming, and soothing, too.

"You weren't here," Rubén was saying. "I was alone—"

"You made me go." Amalia cried.

"The house was so quiet all the time. Forgive me," Rubén wept into his hands.

Amalia backed away from Rubén, careful, delicate steps. "Oh, my life," she said, then ran out of the kitchen, into her bedroom, and locked the door. She cried in silence, afraid of waking Tomás. There is crying, and then there are the sobs that claw their way out like an animal.

Later, Amalia would pick at the embroidered peacock on her dress with her nails until it was a headless thing, colorful threads covering the bed and floor, like strange veins. She might have unraveled it all, unmaking what she could of Gisela's handiwork, but Tomás cried out for milk. It was a fool- ish thing to do, ruining the one beautiful dress she had. And the beds of her nails ached for days from the effort of it.

9

It was three weeks after Amalia had left the palace that the doctors from Madrid appeared at her door.

"We are here to examine the child, señora," they said. "You are missed at the palace." Amalia escorted them in, and Rubén shook their hands, grinning broadly. The days following the spilling of secrets had been fraught ones. Rubén spent each day trailing his wife, trying to possess her again. "You were gone, I was weak. You were gone, she gave me comfort. But I missed you, Amalia. Amalia, look at me." But Amalia would not look at him. Instead, she tended to Tomás, who grew stronger, his skin flushed and new, the sarampión gone now. Yet, when she cooked dinner, she cooked it for herself and Rubén, and when she washed her things, she washed his, too. How could it be otherwise?

The doctors from Madrid peered at Amalia's son through magnifying glasses, their eyes giant orbs. Amalia held Tomás, who by then was smiling and so fat that his arms and legs seemed like the segmented limbs of some strange creature.

"The light in here is not so good," one of the doctors said, squinting, and so they all stepped out the front door, where the afternoon sun bathed them.

The doctors held Tomás naked in the light, checking his skin. Amalia could feel herself leaning towards them, her arms twitching in anticipation of holding her son again, her breasts filling, all of her pulled in Tomás's direction. The doctors gave Amalia her orders, asked her to report to the palace.

The next morning, a carriage came to pick them up. She gave Rubén a perfunctory kiss before climbing into her seat, and he knew not to press for more. He stood a few feet from the carriage, and though Amalia tried hard not to look up at him, she relented at last, and felt a prickle in her skin at the sight of his pleading eyes. She had wanted to be like a stone in that moment, but she knew she was soft and yielding, even now. Nor had she meant to look back at her little house with the crumbling convent towering behind it as the carriage pulled away. But her head turned, as if of its own accord, and she was disappointed to see that Rubén had not watched them go, had not stood there with his arm raised in goodbye. She watched his back grow smaller as the horses led them toward Madrid.

10

The first thing she did upon returning to the palace was to snatch Eulalia up and kiss her head. "How I've missed you, princesa," she muttered into her blond curls while Celia looked on. The nursemaid seemed to have aged while she had been gone, her hands linked but fidgeting at her stomach.

She leaned forward and whispered into Amalia's ear, "I'm glad you're back. Leonela has made the nursery such a miserable place to be." Behind her, Leonela glared at the scene they made, like a strange, put-together family. "She has a hard time waking up in the night, and lately, I've caught her wandering about the Birdcage, talking to herself."

"Perhaps she is homesick," Amalia said.

Celia shrugged, and when she spoke, out came a torrent of gossip, as if Celia had not spoken to a soul the whole time Amalia had been away. "The entire palace feels out of sorts. Isabel keeps showing up in the nursery at all hours, and you know how Her Majesty is—she'd make the horses in the frescoes leap from fear with one look. That Sor Patrocinio wanders in from time to time, too, but I don't let her near the children. I half expect to see the knife she uses to cut her hands tumble out of her sleeve. Don't look at me that way, Amalia. It isn't blasphemy if it's true. But enough of that. How was your visit home? Your husband must have been glad to have you back."

Amalia wasn't accustomed to telling lies, had never had need of them. Even in the orphanage, she had been well-fed, and weekly confessions had a way of keeping a child honest. So, when she responded with, "He was. It was wonderful to see him again, like turning your face to the sun for the first time in a long time," she was surprised at how easily the lie came, like a song buried deep in her memory. Amalia worried about the stone, thinking that someone might have found it; she worried about Gisela, giving birth to her husband's child; she worried about Ruben, and she imagined him taking one look at the new baby and deciding to make a new life with Gisela, abandoning her and Tomás. She thought, too, with great bitterness, of the 24,000 escudos that would, by law, belong to Rubén. Heat would rise to her face when she thought of these things, and she would drop pacifiers and blankets as if they were lit coals, and Celia would reprimand her for her clumsiness.

That night, awake and fitful, Amalia wandered the nursery like a spirit, hovering over Eulalia, who had been moved into a room with her sisters. She listened to their breathing in trip-licate—three infantas with the world open to them, asleep on silk, and she felt, for the first time, envy.

Frustrated, she visited the Birdcage. There was the dusky female peacock, with six gray hatchlings nuzzled against her. The white male was perched on a limb above her, his long neck lying along the branch like a snake. They were all silent. Amalia found the place in the cobbled path where she had hidden the gem, felt with her toe for the lose tile, and lifted it. Underneath, a worm glistened and wiggled away, but aside from it, the space was filled with nothing but soil.

She flipped over a few more tiles, thinking that perhaps she had chosen the wrong one. She gave up soon after that. Curiously, it was relief that she felt. One of the gardeners must have found it. If asked, she would pretend ignorance, of course. She put the tiles back in place, and pressed them down into the dirt. A marvelous light that should have felt like a blessing poured into the aviary.

The male peacock wandered beside her, unfurling his brilliant white tail and shaking it about in that strange dance of his.

"Go away," she told him, but he persisted, waving his head like a cobra. Amalia turned to look at his mate and her sleeping chicks. "Don't you listen to him," she warned her. "Men are all the same." She had meant it as a joke to herself, but she had gone and made her eyes water and her throat tight, so she left the Birdcage in a hurry.

11

Four months had passed in relative peace, though Amalia had begun to count each full moon as it came, the waning moon bringing Gisela's baby another day closer to birth, and carrying Rubén further away. Amalia tried to put Gisela out of mind, but it was as if some poison had worked into her system, making her back ache all the time, giving her indigestion after even the most wholesome food; her heart fluttered every time she menstruated, like a bird caught in her chest, and an ear infection had sent her to bed for a few days. Celia worried her brow at Amalia constantly. How could Amalia explain? It was shameful and debilitating.

One time, Celia caught her reading Rubén's latest missive, in which he had written only two lines: "Not long now. If it is a boy, we will name him Martín."

"Love letter from your husband?" Celia had asked. Celia, who had never married, imagined that all of them—Amalia, Leonela, the queen—enjoyed a sacred, passionate romance with their respective husbands. She longed for what she thought they had, and no one had the heart to tell her the truth about marriage, and what goes on in the hearts of men and women who are bonded together by law, by life's momentum, and by convenience.

The letter sat in Amalia's pocket for days. She would read it so often that she called Tomás by his brother's name by mistake. Already she couldn't imagine a life in which this new baby wasn't present. He haunted her, so that she thought she heard him crying in the night, that bleating so particular to newborns, and her breasts would fill as if she had given birth all over again.

The only distraction that summer was the queen's masquerade. Elaborate Venetian costumes had been made for the children to wear, including a tiny one for Eulalia. The seamstress, who had been brought in from Venice, spoke in excited Italian at the children as they tried on their garments. Satin blouses and pantaloons in turquoise and red, small pointed shoes, their tips pointed upwards like vines seeking the sun, and glittery masks had been created for the three youngest infantas. There was even a tiny fabric mask for Eulalia, which made her cry and ball her hands into fists. That day, the queen came by for the fitting, and she groused about exposed seams and reds that were too bright, while the Italian seamstress, long pins pressed between her lips, flew about making changes. Meanwhile, the infantas were as well behaved as could be expected, though all three sent longing looks at the window, as if they could will themselves outside and beyond this tense flurrying. The scene was reminiscent of holidays everywhere, where the woman of the house makes herself mad cooking large quantities of food, making sure, as well, that the floor is swept, the children are clean and their clothes are pressed, worrying all the while about the coming guests. Such was the state Isabel was in, and her hands kept coming to her cheeks and pulling on her jowls in exasperation.

It was upon this scene that Tenorio entered, halting at the doorway when he saw Isabel there.

"Your Majesty," he said, and bowed.

She whirled to face him. "The red in Paz's outfit is all wrong. All wrong."

Tenorio seemed to take a deep breath before saying, "Yes, it is."

Isabel grew very still then. She faced Amalia, Celia, and Leonela. "It's too red, don't you think?"

They all curtsied. Pilár, who was the best behaved, curtsied, too, her pantaloons slipping off her waist.

"And what if I said that the turquoise was too bright? Or that we should give up on a Venetian theme and decorate the Salon de Columnas like a Moroccan bazaar?"

The pins fell from the Italian seamstress's mouth, but she deftly caught them in her hands.

Tenorio removed the hat from his head. "Your Majesty, if it is what you desire—"

"What I desire," she said, her voice sounding like it was caught on a hook, "is guidance for once. An opinion. For once." She reached out her hand to Tenorio, and he took it gently, his smallest finger floating away from Isabel's own, as if he were holding something quite fragile.

When he spoke again, it was as if the two of them were in a room on their own. "The red is just fine. The turquoise is beautiful. The masks, however, are ridiculous."

"Le maschere—" began the seamstress defensively, emboldened by what she'd just seen.

Isabel's eyes were hard, like pieces of jet, her hand no

longer in Tenorio's. "Sono ridicole," she said to the seamstress, who was silenced at once. "Get rid of them. We'll muddle through with the rest of the costumes as they are. Adios, tesoritos," she called to Paz and Pilár, who approached her and kissed her hands. Then she was gone. Tenorio hesitated at the door.

"Was there something you wanted?" Celia asked him.

He looked at Amalia. Paz shrieked. The seamstress had stuck a pin in her.

"You are busy. I'll take my leave," Tenorio said, and left them to deal with Paz's tears and the seamstress's apologies.

The morning of the masquerade, Celia surprised Amalia and Leonela with costumes of their own. "The servants have their own masquerade in the kitchens," she said. The costumes were worn, their colors drab. They had been through several incarnations, so that the dress Amalia was given looked like something that might have been at home at Versailles during the French Revolution, and Leonela's dress had a decidedly gypsy flair, with jangling tin coins threaded to the bodice. But the masks were new. "Gifts from Her Majesty," Celia said, her face in a smile so broad Amalia could see the empty places in her mouth where some of her molars had once been.

The infantas would appear at the masquerade with their mother, attended by her many ladies-in-waiting, who often visited the nursery and cooed over the princesses and brought them gifts. As for Tomás and Luz, Celia explained, they would go to the servants' party with their mothers. Amalia longed for a break from babies of all sorts, even her own. At breakfast that morning, she had listened to the scullery maids with envy as they described their costumes and whispered about the young men in service at the palace on whom they had set their eyes and hearts. As they spoke, Amalia counted the months with her fingers and thought that it was possible that Gisela was giving birth at that very moment, and she wondered if Rubén was there with her, holding her hand.

On the night of the masquerade, after feeding and dressing the infantas, Amalia and Leonela stepped out of their uniforms and traded their black dresses for costumes. When they emerged from their room, Pilár and Paz cheered and clapped their hands. Eulalia had begun to crawl just that week, and she came toward them, smiling.

"Look at her go," Leonela said, and got down on her knees before the littlest princess. Eulalia pulled herself up onto Leonela's thighs, and tugged at the coins on her bodice. "No, no," Leonela said, and placed Eulalia back onto the carpet.

"¡Dios mio!" cried out Celia, who was wearing a mask with pink and red feathers sprouting from the eyebrows. She pointed at Eulalia, who was on her side, turning blue.

Leonela screamed, and Paz and Pilár began to cry. Amalia rushed to the baby, knelt on the ground, and draped her over her legs. She pounded her small back once, twice, three times, her rib cage a hollow instrument. At that moment, the queen appeared, ready to retrieve her children. Though draped in silks and encrusted in gems, the queen ran, dodged the other children, and was at Amalia's side in the instant that Eulalia vomited a pale lump onto the rug.

The queen sat on the floor, her skirt a moat around her. Amalia passed Eulalia into her arms. "Thank you," she said in a barely audible voice.

They were all silent, happy to hear the baby crying, her face as red as the dress she wore. It was Celia who spoke first. "Look at this," she said, and held in her palm a dripping, blue gem.

The queen spoke in a whisper. "My lost aquamarine. It was a gift from my grandmother." Amalia began to shiver and a ringing started up in her ears. *I will spend the rest of my days in prison*, she thought. *Will it be like the convent? Or much worse? Much worse*, she imagined. So spellbound was Amalia in her fear that she did not hear when Pilár said, "It fell out of Ama Leonela's shirt. I saw it."

"I found it, Your Majesty. In the Birdcage. I was going to return it," Leonela was saying at once, her eyes brimming with tears.

The queen reddened. She lifted an arm in the air, and Celia ran to help her stand. She would not hand over Eulalia, who was still wailing.

"When did you find my aquamarine?"

Leonela opened her mouth, but no sound came out.

"I lost it months ago. How long have you had my aquamarine? Be truthful, and it will go easier on you." Isabel was now at her full height, and though out of breath, her voice did not quiver. Amalia's voice, however, was caught in her throat. *Speak up, speak up*, she told herself, and twice she did manage a weak "Excuse me" that no one heard over Eulalia's cries.

"Two weeks," Leonela said. "Two weeks. In the Birdcage, underneath a tile. I tripped over it and went to fix it. That's how I found the gem. Someone else hid it there, Your Majesty. I've only recovered it for you."

"You've only nearly killed an Infanta of Spain," the queen spat. Then she sighed, and her eyelids fluttered closed for a second. "Eulalia is eating cereal these days, and she does like her fruits, yes?" Isabel asked Celia.

"Yes, Your Majesty."

"Do we have need for two nodrizas?"

Celia looked at Leonela, who was holding herself by the waist, as if she might break in half, then returned the queen's gaze. "No, Your Majesty."

"We will say that your term has ended early. Pack your things and go. Tonight. A carriage will be made ready for you."

Leonela's expression resembled the one Amalia had first

encountered when they had begun together—hard and devoid of emotion. Without a curtsy, she turned on her heel and left the nursery to gather her things, and get her daughter ready for the return trip home.

Amalia began to cry then, her guts a twisted wreck.

"You tender thing. Don't cry. You have our thanks," the queen said.

Amalia found that she couldn't breathe. Instead, she bowed, and blinked back tears, nodding like a crazed person. The queen gathered Eulalia onto her hip, and said, "Come, my gemstone, my jewel, all three of you, come," and she motioned for Pilár and Paz to join her.

Then they left, and the only sounds in the nursery were of Leonela slamming closed her drawers and Luz whimpering.

"We had better go," Celia said, and Amalia picked up Tomás, who had watched everything from a corner of the nursery with eyes wide like an owl's, and they headed to the servants' party.

12

In the morning, Leonela was gone. She'd stripped her bed and folded the sheets carefully, better than she ever had. Before rising, Amalia contemplated her absence, noting that for the first time in her life, she had a room to herself. In that uncertain late summer, she had at least this—a place where she could think. What were those first thoughts in that quiet place like? Seething, restless, guilt-ridden things. One minute, she thought she would go mad if she didn't say something to the queen about the aquamarine, the next, she was calling to mind the time Leonela had tried to get her ousted, feeling like justice was finally on her side. The cool darkness of that room, the creaking bed, and Tomás's steady breathing acted like magnifiers of her hypocrisy, her longing, her boredom with the rituals of being a nodriza, her anger at Rubén and Gisela, all of it, so that she rose and dressed quickly, just to keep herself from thinking too much.

Aside from the grumbling of her conscience, the weeks after Leonela left were serene ones. Celia did not talk about the incident, except to say, "Peace at last," the morning after Leonela had left. Amalia only offered her a wan smile. The summer passed into autumn, and Amalia did not return to Burgos in all that time. She had nightmares about going home now, only to find Rubén with children clinging to his legs, in his lap, whispering in his ear, all of them resembling Gisela, humming discordant tunes. She would wake in a sweat.

Evenings, Celia and Amalia would tidy the nursery, then settle for a game of faro, using a set of playing cards Leonela left behind.

"Bad habits, that one had," Celia said when she found the cards.

"We are all of us a little bit bad," Amalia said.

Celia clicked her tongue and with a wink said, "Yes, everyone but me."

During a game, when it looked like Amalia was losing, they had a visitor. Tenorio knocked on the nursery door, though it was open, and the women rose and curtsied at the sight of him. He was dressed sharply, and had obviously been at a dinner party. At the corner of his mouth was a little smudge of jam, and he brought with him a strong scent of sugar, so that Amalia instantly envisioned a table full of pastries, profiteroles, puddings, and coconut cake.

"Do sit, do sit," Tenorio said, so they sat with their cards again. "I'm sorry to interrupt. Her Majesty wanted me to give something to Amalia."

Struck silent, Amalia stood again, the cards in her hand fluttering to the carpet. Celia groaned.

"She wanted you to have the aquamarine, as a reward for saving Eulalia. Her Majesty thanks you," he said, and in his palm was the gemstone, glittering and polished again. "I-I thank you," Tenorio said.

"I don't want it," were the first words out of her mouth.

"¡Niña!" Celia shouted. "You don't refuse a gift from Her Majesty. What are you thinking?" Then, to Tenorio she said, "She's in shock. She accepts the gift with gratitude, of course," and she pushed down on Amalia's shoulder so that she might curtsy, but found her stiff and unmoving. "Oh, this is ridiculous," Celia muttered, grabbed Amalia's hand, tugged loose her fingers, and presented her open palm to Tenorio.

Amalia watched as he placed the aquamarine in her hand. "Take it, with our gratitude, Amalia," he said, bowing deeply. "There is also this," he said, handing Amalia an envelope with a wax seal on it. This, too, Celia took on Amalia's behalf.

"You see? Isn't it nice to be appreciated?" Celia asked after Tenorio left, bending down and collecting the cards. "Thirty years of service, and I've never received any royal gifts, I promise you that."

Amalia's voice returned to her at last. "I did what any of us would have. Even Leonela would have saved the princess." She stared down at the gem and the envelope, not wanting to meet Celia's eyes.

Celia sighed. "You are right, of course," she said. "But she didn't save Eulalia. You did. Now, do something wonderful with that gift. Make a ring of it, or sell it, and take a trip when your service is over," she said. "As for the envelope—"

"I'll open it," Amalia said. Slowly, she peeled the wax seal off. It was soft and still warm. Inside were two letters. One was in the queen's hand, and the other was from the University of Valladolid.

"What is it?" Celia asked, touching the edge of the letter with the tip of her finger.

Amalia's could barely speak for the lump in her throat. "A scholarship. For Tomás," she said. He played quietly at her feet, underneath the table. Amalia bent down and peered at her son. His full cheeks puffed in and out as he played, and he babbled to himself, to his fingers, and to the small wooden horse he was holding, making it gallop in circles around the pen that his legs created for it.

"So this is my terrible deed's worth," she thought, as she watched her son play, and felt more confused than ever. There comes a moment when a person gets so used to guilt that the feeling of it becomes something like the warning signs of a headache. To dwell on it too long is to encourage the pain to grow stronger. So she wrapped up the aquamarine in one of Tomás's clean but worn diapers, and sent it off in a package to Rubén, with a letter that merely read: *This is a gift from the queen. Do with it as you will.*

As the days wore on, Amalia batted away her guilt over Leonela whenever it appeared, and thought of her son, books in the crook of his arm, glasses perched on his nose, handsome, brilliant, and far from Burgos. But still the guilt returned, in moments of quiet, when Amalia was all by herself, and it became her constant companion, a dim roar she heard at all times.

13

Amalia refused to take her days off. Celia worried, but Amalia would say that Rubén could not get away from work, or that she did not mind staying with the children, which was true. Pilár, Paz, Eulalia, and Tomás would sit on the carpet and push toy wagons around in circles, or else Amalia would read them stories about witches who stole naughty children, and they would squeal and cover their faces. When all of that was going on, Amalia could forget about her husband and her own mutable heart, which urged her to forgive him one moment, and curse him the next. As for leaving him, such a thought was out of the question. Where would she go? Even the church would turn her away for leaving her husband.

One day, while Amalia was alone with the children, Celia having taken one of Amalia's days off for herself, she heard shouts coming from downstairs. First one voice, then another, and suddenly, there was the sound of a single, echoing gunshot. Amalia could not help it—she screamed, and the children, all four of them, began to cry, startled out of a game Pilár had organized. Amalia gathered them all quickly, and ran toward the Birdcage, slamming the iron gate behind her. The shouting was dim there, and Isabel's two new macaws, both blue and gold, screeched at them as they ran to the farthest nook.

Pilár had buried her head in her lap, and was crying, "Ama, Ama, they have come to kill us!" The others, perhaps, were too young to understand anything, and Tomás and Eulalia both tried toddling away, chasing the little birds that hopped to and fro on the branches of the orange and lemon trees. Paz, true to her name, sat quietly beside Amalia, her small hands folded in her lap, her eyes closed.

Amalia had no way of knowing what was happening. Had the Carlists taken over the palace? Was Isabel, at this very moment, lying in a heap somewhere? What about the cooks and the maids? She imagined they were cowering in closets. Another set of shouts rose in volume, and the birds themselves went silent.

"I'm scared, Ama," Pilár said, and Amalia shushed her,

brushing back her dark curls. What do I do if men with weapons come for the infantas? Amalia's thoughts wouldn't organize themselves into coherence. The windows, the windows, she thought, then remembered they were thick and laced with lead, and that they were three stories up. Nothing in the Birdcage could be turned into a weapon—it was all moist dirt, budding oranges, and rainbow-hued feathers. She tried to distract herself, but her imaginings took her to the worst of places, to images of the little girls dead-eyed and bloodied, of her own Tomás ripped apart like the infant boys in the bible.

The turn of the lock and the creak of the gate tore her from her morbid thoughts. Panicked, she yanked Tomás into her arms, his legs flailing against Pilár's head. Eulalia was a few feet away and Amalia whispered to her, "Eulalia. Ven, niña. Eulalia," but she was pushing a twig into the dirt, swirling it this way and that, as if signing a piece of paper with her name. "Lala," she said, the name Amalia had privately called her since the beginning. The infanta looked up, repeated it, "Lala, Lala," and walked over, falling onto her bottom once, rising, and reaching Amalia at last.

By the time they could hear the crunching of hard soles over gravel, Amalia had a hand on all four children. "Ave María," she whispered, and Pilár, who understood, repeated the prayer after her.

The shadow preceded the man, and Amalia held her breath. She could make out the dark shape of the head, surveying the room, looking. Beyond him, the light in the aviary suddenly darkened, as if thunderclouds had appeared in the sky, and his shadow melted into the air. Amalia determined that they were about to die. She shut her eyes, then thought better of it, and opened them wide. When at last Tenorio's face appeared before them, etched with worry and half-covered by a palm frond, Amalia burst into tears.

"What has happened?" she cried.

He looked relieved to have found them. "A lunatic made his way into the palace. He's been caught."

"A Carlist?" Amalia asked, and Tenorio tilted his head, as if surprised that she had a sense of the world outside.

"As I said, a lunatic. Everyone is safe." Tenorio picked up Eulalia, then, took Paz by the hand. Amalia followed with Pilár and Tomás. "Next time," he said, as they passed the iron gate, "lock it from the inside."

"If there is a next time, I will quit my post, I promise you that," Amalia said. Her heart was still pounding hard, and it would be hours before she put Tomás down again.

Tenorio looked Amalia in the eyes, saying, "That would make me very sad, indeed."

He stayed with them all afternoon, saying he was not needed downstairs, and he played with the girls, who delighted in having someone new in the nursery. Tomás played at his feet, and every once in a while, Tenorio would glance down at him and say, "He's like a little man, this one," or "Look at him. Strong fellow." He sat with a notebook and drew each of the children, then composed a line of poetry below each picture. When it was time for their naps, he tucked Eulalia into her crib, then folded a page from his notebook into the shape of a bird, which Eulalia soon crushed in her grip before falling asleep.

Amalia drew closed the curtains and settled into a chair. Tenorio sat down too. There, in the dim glow of the nursery, he wrote in his notebook yet again. The sound of his pencil on paper reminded her of the sound of a rushing stream, of the woods in Burgos, and the peace of that city's afternoon hours, when everyone would feel drowsy, and sleep and dream.

Amalia did not ask what he was writing, and he did not show her. He only closed his notebook and tucked it and his pencil into his coat pocket. "Amalia," he said, rising. "Perhaps, on your next day off, we might—"

"Friday. Two weeks from now," she said.

Tenorio moved as if to take up his notebook again, then dropped his hands. It was a habit of his, and she suspected he kept drawings and poems there, yes, but also measurements and observations and dates. She would not need to write it down. Two weeks from that Friday. He studied her intently for a moment, his throat jolting the way men's throats do. They were tipping into something different, he and Amalia. She could feel it, how gravity was pulling her in a new direction. The peace of the palace had been intruded upon, and she, too, felt disrupted and thrilled.

Tenorio left soon after that, giving one last, long glance at the princesses, his daughters, snoring lightly.

When one is waiting, the days seem long, each minute feels like an eternity, and so it felt to Amalia as she waited for that Friday to come. Celia stayed with the children, even Tomás. "Is your husband meeting you in Madrid at last?" she asked, and Amalia told her yes. She felt as if she was a different Amalia in that moment, unfamiliar even to herself. What am I doing, meeting the queen's lover on my day off? she asked herself even as she bathed and perfumed her body before leaving the palace, even as she plucked wayward hairs from her thighs. She asked such questions as if the answers would be innocent ones, as if in the act of doubting herself, she could find absolution for what she was intending to do.

On the palace steps, she halted momentarily, and very nearly turned around. But Amalia thought of Rubén and Gisela together in her house, in her bed, and she trudged forward. The snow was falling lightly on Amalia's shoulders, and the cracks between the cobblestones were filling with white fluff. Madrid looked like a sugared dessert, and it made her feel brave. If a city could transform itself overnight, from its gray and bustling antiquities to a pearlescent, holiday scene, thanks to a little bit of cold weather, then she, too, could transform. God knew, her heart felt cold enough.

Tenorio had asked her to meet him at El Parque Buen Retiro. The grounds belonged to the queen, and she had spent considerable funds on planting trees and commissioning fountains and statues for the park. Once, a palace had stood there, but it had been long ruined when invading French troops used it as barracks years earlier. "Meet me at the old palace," Tenorio had said. The walk had taken Amalia half an hour, and by the time she reached the ruins, she was soaked through.

"In here," Tenorio said, when he saw her approaching, shivering as she walked. He carried a parasol, which he folded once they entered what was once the main hall.

"Are we allowed in here?" she asked.

"The queen gave me permission."

"She knows we are here?"

Tenorio paused, then he dusted some snow off her shoulder. "She knows *I* am here."

If there had once been tapestries on the walls, or rugs on the floor, there was no evidence of them now. The marble underneath their feet was chipped and stained, a long vine hung lazily from deep within the giant fireplace, as if someone had tried climbing into the palace on it from above. The plasterwork angels in the cornices were missing noses, or limbs. The whole place smelled damp and musty, and beneath that, there was the smell of gunpowder.

"She meant to restore it," Tenorio said. "But this place is a lost cause. I've run the numbers. It will be cheaper to build it up from scratch." Tenorio's gaze rested on the corners of the palace as if he were still assessing it, still adding and subtracting from Isabel's wealth. "I thought you'd like to see it, before it's gone forever," he added.

Amalia was chilled through, and peeled off her white gloves, wringing them out at her feet. Tenorio noticed, and pulled her over to the fireplace. He restacked the logs there, took out his notebook, and crumpled up a few blank pages from it. These he put in between the logs. Plucking kindling from a box beside the fireplace, he arranged things with precision. He produced a match from his pocket, and in short order, they had a small fire. They sat on the hearth to warm up.

"Have you enjoyed your time in Madrid?" Tenorio asked.

"I never could have imagined myself here," she said. "I grew up in a convent. An orphan." Tenorio blinked, as if his eyes stung. "Even a place like this, this ruin, is more than most of the nuns hoped for me or for any of us. I wonder where the other girls are now," she said aloud, realizing it was something she had never wondered before. Perhaps it was the feeling of the place, of time passing rapidly, indiscriminately eating away at everything. "What about you? Have you enjoyed yourself?"

Amalia regretted her phrasing at once. Of course he had enjoyed himself, in beds so tall one had to use a ladder to climb into them, among silks and satins. Her hands were folded in her lap, and she pinched herself, trying to stop her train of thought, which was threatening to derail.

"For all the busyness of the palace, I've had a lonely time of it. My wife—she died. I think she would have loved Madrid. Whenever we came to the city, which wasn't often, she would wander about with her pretty head tilted up at the tall buildings, and she would say to me, 'Can you imagine the people who live there? How smart they must be. How refined,' and what I think she meant to say to me was that the life we were living was not enough for her, that she had settled for me."

"How can you know what she was thinking? Did you ask her?" she asked.

He shook his head. "Perhaps I've let grief rewrite things in my head," he said. Then, "Has anyone ever asked you what you think, Amalia?"

"No, never," she said, realizing it was true.

He waited. The fire crackled lightly. Above them, the gilded ceiling had given way in the corner, and snow trickled in every so often and plopped onto the marble. Here, everything yielded to time.

"I think we are going to catch our deaths in this cold and damp," Amalia said, removing three long hatpins, then pulling off her hat. The pink ribbon affixed to it was drooping and sad.

"What else do you think?"

"I don't know what else to think," she said, which was true. At least, she didn't have the kinds of thoughts one can put easily into words. Tenorio, on the other hand, had much to say, and he regaled her with stories about Almonaster, and about his childhood (hadn't she wanted to know what that was like?), how his uncle was a dentist, and how he would go into people's homes and extract teeth, and how he would give these to Tenorio and his siblings to play with, and on and on he talked, as if the fire of his voice had been given more and more kindling. Why had she thought that this was a quiet man?

"Do you know what else I think?" he asked at last. Amalia took a deep breath, as if she had been the one talking. "I think you won't get warm unless you take off that coat." He leaned forward and touched the buttons of her coat. They were small, wooden buttons, rough to the touch. The coat had been Rubén's when he was a younger man, a fact she did not remember until Tenorio pulled it off her shoulders. Tenorio breathed hard, like a horse, right in her ear. "You aren't going to faint, are you?" he whispered, and she realized she had been staring at the dripping snow without blinking.

Amalia's voice had grown thin, but still she said, "No, I won't." Tenorio's dark eyes glittered in the firelight. He took up her forearm, twisted it gently, and kissed her wrist.

"Look at me," he said, when he caught her watching the snow falling again. But she could not look. With Rubén, such moments had felt as natural to Amalia as scratching at an itch, and just as insistent. This felt like picking at a wound. What she wanted most was to curl up and turn herself into a hard, impervious seashell.

"This place is—" she started to say, but Tenorio silenced her with a kiss. It seemed like ages since she and Rubén had lived in Burgos together, a lifetime since they had chosen their home behind the crumbling convent in Las Trinas, with hope alive in their hearts. That had been a ruin, too, but there had been something sacred in it.

In the end, Amalia could not do what she had set out to. She'd had a kind of vengeance in mind that stabbed at her heart, left her mute and introverted in the moment when she needed to be bold, when she needed the right words to come out of her mouth. None came. The wind coming through the fireplace whistled, and she heard Sister Damiana's voice, how she had told her once, when she had been very afraid in the orphanage, that though fear had called her, she need not answer it. There, with Tenorio, Amalia had come close to becoming too different from the person she had always been.

Amalia thanked Tenorio for showing the ruins to her, and he propped open his umbrella and held it over her head as they walked back to the Palacio Real. "I have some business to do in this direction," he said vaguely by way of goodbye, his lips thinned out and pressed together. Amalia tried to hand him the umbrella, but he said, "Keep it," and she did.

Amalia turned once to watch him as he went, cutting a path through the snow. It seemed like a path of what could have been, and she was glad when the wind whipped her skirts and blew snow over his footprints.

14

Shaken by her encounter with Tenorio, Amalia asked for permission to visit Burgos. Tomás had a runny nose that week, and, ever afraid of infections, Celia was glad to see them go.

By now, Amalia thought, Gisela would have had her baby, and she practiced what she would say to her the whole way to Burgos, thinking that it would be wise to prepare herself and ease into the hurt. She was still seething about Gisela and Rubén. Her failed attempt at the palace ruins with Tenorio only made her angrier and sadder. The only thing left was to wipe Tomás's nose every so often and to watch, as it scrolled by, the panorama of woods and hills, scampering deer, and, in the air, streaking cardinals like fresh cuts in the atmosphere.

Once home, Amalia opened the door with her key. She did not knock, nor had she warned Rubén of her coming. The sun was still out, and she expected to find the house empty. Instead, she found Rubén in a chair, sleeping with his hand over his face.

"Papá," Tomás said. Rubén opened his eyes slowly, blinking, the scales of sleep falling off one by one.

Rubén rose unsteadily, and she smelled the wine on his breath. He kissed Amalia with drunk lips. Then, Rubén said, "I've sent her away from Burgos."

Amalia put Tomás down and he toddled away. "What happened?" she asked, and Rubén cried fat tears. Beyond him, Tomás had gone straight to the damp fireplace to play with the logs. She watched as his hands turned black and sooty, watched as he left handprints on the carpet and the hearth and across his face whenever he wiped his upper lip.

"I did it for you," he said. There was the bottle of wine, empty and tipped on its side on the floor. A cat darted behind a chair. Since when had there been a cat in the house?

"Did what for me?" Amalia asked. Rubén sat again, straining to compose himself.

"The aquamarine. I gave it to Gisela before the baby, before the baby—She told me I was buying my freedom from her and the baby. I said, 'Take yourselves back home, to Cuba, or go somewhere else, anywhere but Burgos.' That's what I said."

"But the baby."

"Amalia, the baby did not live. A boy . . . It was a little boy." Tomás sat silent next to his father, tugging at his pants.

Even in her darkest hours, Amalia had not hoped for such a brutal resolution. What Amalia wanted at that moment, above all, was to fly to Gisela. She knew the pain in her heart. She knew it because she carried it with her at all times. Emilia, Francisca, Rubén, Alicia. Each night, she prayed for them. Emilia, Francisca, Rubén, Alicia, and now Martín. The list of innocents lost had grown by one. Amalia wanted to pull back Gisela's hair from her face, kiss her cheeks, and tell her that she had thought of her as a sister.

Forgiveness. It struck Amalia like a hammer and all at once. She began to pull her coat back on. "I'll go to her," she said. Rubén shook his head. "She is gone, I told you. She left."

"Oh," Amalia said, and her coat came off again.

There was a long silence as Tomás ran around the room, fishing buttons and needles from between seat cushions. Slowly, Rubén would take these from him and shake his head. Unfazed, Tomás would head toward fresh dangers.

"What will I do?" Rubén asked. Amalia could not answer him. Their lives had come unstitched, his in Burgos with all the shame and hope, fear and loathing blooming in Gisela's body, all of it being extinguished by Martín's death. Meanwhile Amalia's life had come to a standstill in the palace, inextricable from the routines of tiny royal people. She could not give him an answer because she didn't really understand the question anymore. What would he do? Live on, try not to think of all that his choices had wrought, and drink a bottle of wine on the days when the guilt would not go quietly.

Amalia picked up Tomás, who protested and kicked her stomach, and washed his face in the kitchen. As she did so, she sang his own name loudly to him—Tomás, Tomás, mi rey, Tomás—and he laughed. Beneath the sound of her own voice, she could hear Rubén crying out the name Martín like a ragged shout in the midst of the noise.

That night, Amalia dreamed of Gisela an ocean away, her arms cradling warm, salty air.

15

Amalia's time at the palace was drawing to a close and while the final months moved like molasses, when she was given her leave, it was all at once, catching her off guard.

Eulalia had been assigned eight maids at birth. They were voiceless, uniformed things, who came for her dirty clothes and diapers, stoked the fireplace in the nursery, and beat the rugs outside. Just before Eulalia's second birthday, eight more women arrived—the infanta's ladies-in-waiting. They were young, well-dressed, aristocratic Spanish women, who had come to the palace to serve the little princess, and also to learn the ways of the court. Who knows? Any one of them could be married off to a duke someday, and there was no better place to learn about protocol than in the Palacio Real.

Once Eulalia learned to say "Gracias" and walk steadily, she was made to attend all the feast day gatherings, cloaked in stiff brocades and taffeta. She and her sisters would stand in the hall while the gentlemen of the household stood in line to kiss their chubby hands, bedecked in bracelets and dazzling, tiny rings. Not that Amalia saw any of these proceedings with her own eyes. Now that the ladies-in-waiting were in place, Amalia was being etched out of the infanta's life, little by little, like a mistake in an engraving.

It was around this time, too, that Miguel Tenorio's visits to the nursery became practical, swift encounters. One day, he was taking inventory of the wool rugs, on another, he was merely passing through the nursery to get to the aviary, where a team had arrived from the London Zoo to gather the birds and take them away. The creatures had escaped too often for Isabel's taste, and, in a fit of temper, and because she hoped to get into Queen Victoria's good favor, she'd donated them. The little girls, remembering him from the day he had come to them in the aviary and played with them all afternoon, sought his attention. Paz would bring him her new doll, or Pilár would follow him about, singing him a song. Even Eulalia would light up in his presence. But Tenorio would ignore the children now, speak only to Celia, and leave without saying goodbye.

That he had been replaced in the queen's affections by another man was the gossip of all of Madrid. Carlos Marfori, the son of an Italian pastry chef, was made Chief of the Royal Household, and given the room directly beneath Isabel's that had once been Tenorio's. As for Tenorio, he seemed to be readying himself for a change in circumstances.

On one visit, he paused before leaving the nursery and asked, "Amalia, you wouldn't happen to speak any German, would you?"

Amalia started. They had not spoken since that day at the Parque Buen Retiro.

"I'll take that as a no," Tenorio said. He was leaning against the doorway, one hand in his pocket. "I'm going to Berlin, you see, as a minister of Spain."

"Oh," Amalia said, struggling to smile. "Congratulations."

Tenorio shook his head. "I'd prefer not to go," he said. At that moment, Eulalia toddled toward him, and he reached down to pet her head. He would cease seeing the infantas altogether soon, Amalia thought sadly.

She didn't know what else to say. So often, the people in the palace left her mute in this way. Any comment could be taken badly, and she had learned a few times that silence was often the best response.

"Here," Tenorio said, breaking the quiet between them. He handed her a folded piece of paper. "For you." Then, he left, dragging his heels a little, his long coat barely swinging behind him.

Amalia unfolded the thin sheet to find a poem, titled "Romance Escondido." The poem ended with a compromise: *If not your love, then your friendship.* At the very bottom of the page, Tenorio had signed his name. She took the poem and put it on the dresser in her room.

Eulalia had sixteen women attending her at this point. Paz also had sixteen, as did Pilár. This army of ladies lived in a wing of the palace all to themselves, though they flitted through the nursery constantly, plucking at the infantas' outfits in order to sharpen a crease here or there, and offering them advice that they were too young to receive: "Paz, querida, pinch your cheeks before you go out into the hall. You look pale as death," or "Pilár, such a somber, sickly thing you are! Here, have a sip of honey to tame that cough." They were allowed such critiques because they were noble ladies, and because Isabel had been assured that they were more Catholic than the Pope himself. Armed with rosaries, they practiced Te Deums with the infantas, yelling, "Louder. Louder! So that God may hear you!" They were gossipy, loud, well-dressed young women, and they were everywhere, skittering about the palace like an invasion of sugar ants.

The poem Amalia had left on the dresser was gone within an hour's time, dropped into some silken pocket or other, and delivered to Isabel before nightfall.

Amalia rose the next morning, bleary eyed. Tomás had been fussy overnight, sneezing and coughing, though not feverish. He had insisted on sleeping in his mother's bed, and she had let him, though his weight on her chest felt oppressive after a while, as if he were gaining weight by the minute. A knock on the door woke them both up.

"Come in," Amalia said, expecting Celia to bring in Eulalia for her morning milk.

It was Sor Patrocinio who darkened the open doorway. Her black habit pinched her forehead especially tightly, and her small, brown eyes peered into Amalia's. She tried not to stare at her hands, bandaged and immobile as they always were.

"Mi hija," she began, "it is time for you to go."

Amalia's first thought was of confession, and she counted backwards to her last trip to the confessional. She was about to argue that she had just been, when Sor Patrocinio spoke again.

"Pack your things. La reina has terminated your employment this morning."

"What?" Amalia sat up, nearly pushing poor Tomás off the bed. "Eulalia doesn't turn two until February," she said. It was early December, and it had snowed again overnight. Later, the carriage that took her back to Burgos would slip and slide over the icy roads, and Amalia would cry out from fear and sadness over her expulsion.

"It must be as she desires, hija," Sor Patrocinio said, then clasped her hands together lightly, the bandages making the gesture awkward.

"But why?" Amalia insisted.

Sor Patrocinio went on. "The infantas have their ladies and their ladies' maids now."

"Can I say goodbye to Eulalia?" she asked. Her voice broke over the infanta's name, so what came out was "Lala," the name she had kept for the infanta in secret. *Oh, my Lala, my sweet Lala, who I will never hold again,* she thought.

"Of course," Sor Patrocinio said, and for once, she seemed gentle and sweet. But that effect soon passed over her face like sunlight dampened by shadow. "Miguel Tenorio de Castilla has left already this morning, for Berlin," she said.

"What?" Amalia asked, confused, still drowsy. Why did she mention Tenorio just now? What did that have—she thought, then glanced at the dresser, the surface clean and dusted. While she could not determine what Tenorio had meant by giving her that poem, someone else had, impugning her in the process.

Amalia laughed. She couldn't help it. Isabel and her many lovers, Rubén and Gisela, and yet here she was, faithful and stupid, fired from her job at the palace. Tomás started to cry, and Amalia held him up to her shoulder and sang a song she made up on the spot, nonsense lyrics and an inharmonious tune. He calmed down, and she set about packing her things, thinking about Leonela, and how, perhaps, this was God's way of balancing the scales.

The hard part came later, when it was time to say goodbye to the nursery and Eulalia. It was as if the child had sensed that Amalia would not be coming back, and she insisted on several long embraces. "Mas," she said after Amalia had hugged her tight. "Mas, mas, mas," and Eulalia held on and on. "Ama, mas." It was Celia who pulled the little infanta off.

"Go," Celia said. "It will be better if you just go." Celia's eyes were tear-filled. She had promised to write, and maybe to visit Amalia in Burgos when she was ready to retire. Meanwhile, Eulalia howled, and tugged hard at her earrings, which she hated. She ripped at her ears and called Amalia's name until the little gems fell out, and her left earlobe was bleeding. Amalia backed away from the scene, choking on tears, clutching Tomás.

Later, she would say this to Rubén—that she had witnessed Eulalia's first act of rebellion the moment she tore out her earrings, and that she was certain it would not be her last.

EXILE AND BURGOS

Eulalia

At my baptism, they would give me ninety-three names. I could only ever manage to remember five of them— María Eulalia Francisca de Asís y Margarita de Bourbon. The world will remember just one—Eulalia. I am the first Eulalia in the Spanish royal line, a name, which means "well-spoken." I am not certain whether, in these twenty-nine years, I have really lived up to my name.

My mother was not in attendance at my baptism. But over a hundred Spanish nobles were there to watch as I received just as many names and was washed clean of original sin. If we indeed carry the sins of Eve on our bodies at birth, then I am certain that, in the case of my own conception, I was composed of sin entirely, every thread and fiber of my being one of secrecy. Officially speaking, my father is the prince consort, Francisco de Asís. I have seen him often enough in my life, and have glanced at a mirror often enough, to know that he bore no part in making me, or my sisters, Paz and Pilár, for that matter. My mother's first cousin, Francisco de Asís was not her choice for a husband. Married when they were still children, my mother was forced into her vows with a deliberate pinch on the arm from her own mother, my grandmother, in plain view of the priest and everyone in attendance. They both wept openly during the ceremony. Did Asís father my older sister, María Isabel, and my brother, King Alfonso, may he rest in peace? Nobody thinks so.

As for my real father, I am of a mind to believe it was my mother's secretary, Miguel Tenorio, who had the privilege. He kept his affections hidden from me, and for that I might hate him all my life, except that my older sister, Paz, has welcomed him into her life, and so I cannot fault either his taste or his heart, for she is an excellent woman. I saw Tenorio rarely, though he once sent me a fat envelope full of poems he had written about his dead wife, Belisa. Because I was thirteen or so, at an age when a girl swears nightly that she would sooner pitch herself off a balcony than succumb to the sentimentality on display among the adults around her, I tilted my nose at the poems. In retrospect, I believe them to be quite good, and I have a better understanding of my mother's choice in Tenorio. A woman is better off with a delicate man who writes poems than with a virile one who tosses and turns all night thanks to bloody memories of war. A kingless queen, as my mother was, holds more power than one who has to share the throne. And Tenorio, for all his worth, was no king.

What were they thinking, my mother and Tenorio, on the morning of my baptism? Neither of them was present, though Francisco de Asís was there, to hand me off to my many godparents. Perhaps they colluded together in her bedroom, whispering about the color of my eyes, whether or not I looked like him, my sleeping habits, or the quality of the newly hired nodrizas. I like to imagine them this way, having several long and unavoidable moments together, where they couldn't help but be drawn into one another. Whether my mother's many love affairs were tender in that way, I'll never know.

Passionate and gentle love of this kind is a concern for any woman brought up in a royal court, for it is forbidden to us. Neither my sisters nor my brother nor I have had a say in whom we have married, though I believe that my brother Alfonso, rest his soul, married for love. We have entire castles at our command, and armies, diadems, and thrones, respect, fine clothes. All of these things are like iron bars on a window to me—thick and cold and oppressive. I don't want any of them.

What do I want? I want to have read a poem and fallen in love.

Tomás

Back when my father was still alive, I told my parents that I wanted nothing to do with the farm that had been bought with the money my mother had earned as a nodriza. To my surprise, my father did not grow angry or morose. Rather, he asked, "What's the first thing you think about in the morning, hijo?"

"Books," I had said. What I might have said, instead and more accurately, was "Jules Verne." I was obsessed with him. At the time, I thought that my destiny was to beat Phileas Fogg's eighty-day record trip around the world. I imagined that underneath my feet were caverns, that Burgos might hold in its bowels a new world full of blind creatures and roaring waters. I read and reread Verne's novels until the bindings grew loose and the pages went soft like cloth, and in my pocket I kept with me at all times a little notebook with a dark red cover, embossed with the profile of an imperial eagle. It had been a gift my mother had given me before I left for the university, and I planned to fill it with stories.

"Books," I said, and my father, who could barely read, smiled and his eyes moistened. He looked at me that way often, with tear-filled eyes. Once, when I was around nine or so, I had woken in the middle of the night, thinking that I had heard someone crying. I found my father in the kitchen, his arms wrapped around a nearly empty bottle of red wine, weeping. I laid a hand on my father's shoulder and he jumped, looked at me with a sob in his throat, patted my head, and dissolved into tears. I had known then, even at that age, that to speak of the moment again would be a mistake. My father was the kind of man who cried easily. I did not understand it, could not remember the last time I had cried, and could not imagine the shame of doing so in public. But I loved my father very much, and his tears made my heart sputter and hiss in strange ways.

Instead of staying on at the farm, I attended the University of Valladolid, my tuition paid for long ago by a writ from the palace. I sometimes skipped classes to walk around Valladolid, which was a city where I thought great things happened. For example, in Casa de Cervantes, *Don Quixote* was finished, and one afternoon, I went there to see if I might sense something, some vibration of my spirit, writer to writer. Perhaps I felt something. Perhaps I believed it. In Valladolid, too, was the poet Zorilla's house, and Christopher Columbus's. One of my professors, Eustacio Flores, liked to say that there were towns and cities like Valladolid all over the world, modest places that, in spite of their humility, produced genius after genius.

I took it all to heart, and began to write stories set in the future, novels populated by beings from other worlds, homage after homage to Jules Verne. I dreamed about them even when I was awake, and would sit in cafés with friends and tell them what I was up to, talking too fast, exceeding their tolerance for optimism. No matter, I thought. They don't understand the spirit of Cervantes, of Zorilla, of Verne, and I felt superior to my classmates, whose hopes amounted to earning degrees in moral philosophy, Latin, or constitutional law.

I was nineteen years old then and, I suppose, people thought I was handsome. My mother had always told me that I was handsome, but who could believe a mother's praise? In classes, I would lean back in my seat, because my legs were too long. Professors would call on me often, sometimes with such an open look upon their faces that I thought that I could provide no answer that they would consider wrong. I knew they were not hearing me, only seeing me—my stature, my build. I might as well have been speaking in English. Inspired by the idea, I took an English class, and found it to be the one class where I excelled. The teacher was blind, and he walked around the classroom, tapping his cane before him, and leaning forward when the students responded, "Fine, thank you. And you?" to his "How are you today, good sir?" I gathered my good marks in English, and my devotion to writing stories, and thought that my future, if not entirely secured, would be an interesting and creative one.

I wrote every day, forcing myself to finish a story if it was begun, even if the ending was ludicrous and half-formed. Once, I presented my slim manuscripts to Profesor Flores, who had a reputation for scattered scholarship—he studied both the flight patterns of geese and the early diaries of Christopher Columbus. Profesor Flores took my pages and read them overnight. I barely slept in anticipation. In the morning, he called me to his office. He had shoved my work into a volume of Aristotle, told me that I had no foundation worth a damn, and suggested I study engineering. "The future is in machinery, Aragón," he said.

So when Profesor Flores had dismissed the one thing I thought I did well, the one thing that had little to do with my body and my face, I felt real despair. Whatever hope had resided in my heart was gone. After that meeting, I took my collection of Verne books and left them on the front steps of the building where I lived.

"May the wind take them," I said to no one, and slammed the door closed behind me. But soon, regret dragged me out again, and I gathered my books into my arms like feral kittens, and brought them home. I went to classes, but less enthusiastically than before. I attended mass, seeking empty pews where my long limbs would not disturb others, and would dodge the women who would push their daughters into my path, their lace veils covering their faces at mass, their hands trembling nervously just beneath their breasts.

Six months after Profesor Flores's assessment, my father died in a field in Burgos, and I returned home, my Jules Verne books in a rucksack, my classes at the university unattended.

"That good-for-nothing doctor!" my mother had moaned upon seeing me the day after he died. She pounded my back as I held her. "Just last week. Last week! The doctor had told your father that what he was feeling was the result of bad food. Bad food! Blaming my cooking, of all things. And it was his heart, Tomás, his heart." She sobbed onto my chest, then turned her face and cupped her ear against my heart. She listened for a long time, and then, satisfied that I, too, wasn't yet bound for the grave, let me go.

"Mamá, he died out in the sun, tall wheat all around him, his shoes three inches in mud," I told her. "It's what he would have wished for himself."

"Your father's heart was a mystery to me," she whispered, patting my cheek. It fell upon me at once—that I was my mother's caretaker now. My father, who was as big a man as I am, left behind an absence that was impossible to fill, so that the house I grew up in seemed to echo in a way it hadn't before. I imagined him everywhere, thought I could feel his hand on my head, caught the smell of his clothes from time to time, and hid from my mother to weep, because she had enough to bear. Ours was a typical grief, and yet I say it without believing it. When death becomes personal, then there is nothing typical about it.

After the funeral, I returned to the university to collect my things, and made the round trip back to Burgos. I thought I had left the university behind when, to my surprise, I saw Profesor Flores back in Burgos one Sunday after mass.

"So, you've left the university," the professor said.

"As have you," I said.

"I've just retired," the professor said, fiddling with his hat now. "I was born in Burgos," he said, though he had never mentioned it before.

"Well, at least you won't worry about my ill-formed imagination ever again," I said, sourness in my mouth like a lemon.

"Come now. I have just the thing in mind for you." I followed the professor through a tight alleyway bridged overhead by a medieval arch. The wooden figure of San Judas Tadeo loomed over us. I stole a glance at its bare toes and whispered a little prayer to the saint of impossible requests.

Soon we were on Calle Pozo Seco. There, a small store, the trim painted dark red, the window with a sign that read Libreria Flores, stood between a bakery and a hat shop. "It is my father's old bookshop, Aragón. I've managed it since he died—"

"My father died two weeks ago," I offered, then said, "I'm sorry for your loss."

"And yours. But mine was long ago. This seems more like fate by the minute. The store needs minding. We've had one bad manager after another. You seem the man with just the right interests to do it. Popular fiction of the sort you enjoy sells fairly well," he said, his mouth a smirk.

I knew it. What he said was true. My collection of Verne books had come from this store, which was always well stocked. I searched my memory for the countenances of the people who worked there and could not locate the professor among those faces.

"It was never a place I loved," the professor said. "An irony, I suppose. I prefer libraries to bookstores." He slid an iron key, a relic from some bygone era it seemed, out of his pocket. "Do with it what you will. Only send me a check of the profits, minus the bills and whatever salary you find appropriate, at the end of each month."

"Profesor, I don't know if—"

"Would you go back to the farm, Tomás?" he asked, and his mouth turned down a little. "There's an apartment upstairs. It's small, but functional."

I thought of my bedroom back at my mother's house. I saw myself surrounded by books, perhaps taking up my pen again on slow days.

Profesor Flores, his hand shaking a little, held out the key, and I took it.

Eulalia

Shortly after my second birthday, my mother, Su Majestad, La Reina Isabel II, was dethroned in a coup. A group of generals and politicians, opponents of my mother's regime calling themselves "Spain with Honor," sent us into exile. They were embarrassed by my mother's many lovers, by her superstitious ways, perhaps, even, by the look of her. She was not a great beauty. They selected a minor Italian prince to serve as king, while my brother Alfonso, the rightful heir, was sent to England, to learn about politics, Shakespeare, and how to cultivate roses in that wet, fertile climate. My mother, two sisters—María Isabel had just gotten married and was on her honeymoon when the news reached her—and I left Madrid by train. As the story was recounted to me later, I was covered in spots from a wretched case of measles, and my fever was high. Perhaps the heat in my body acted as a crucible for my first memories, which date from the start of our exile when I was only two.

We were on vacation in the north of Spain, at San Sebastian, when news of the revolt came. We didn't know we were leaving. Nobody had warned us that we would not return to the palace nursery again as children, or that when we next spent time in those quiet rooms, we'd be mothers ourselves.

My first memory is of my mother on that train. She sat like a mountain as Spain rushed by our windows. We had some nobles with us, and a few cousins who had remained loyal to the queen. Sor Patrocinio was with us, too, her hands freshly bleeding. None of the other servants were allowed to come. I remember my sisters crying about some of their larger toys that could not be sent for from the palace, like the dollhouse that was taller than Pilár, with working lights and running water inside. Pilár's tears soon became a tantrum and to shock her into silence, my mother told the story of the son of a Liberal and how he had been murdered by the Carlists in front of his father. The child, only four, had been placed before a firing squad. One of the Carlists threw an orange a few feet from him, and when he toddled towards it, the shots rang out and the tiny body crumpled. This was the story my mother chose to tell us as we began our exile into France.

In our exile, Spain was renamed a Republic. For my mother, it may have felt like a prison, being stuck in Paris as Madrid went through its seasons without her. But I would come to think of Madrid as a different kind of prison. A gilded one. A beautiful one. But a cage nevertheless.

In Paris, we lived in the Palais de Castille. Napoleon III reigned, and his son came over often for playdates. We took walks in the Bois de Boulogne, and in the Tuilleries, I skinned my knees and once I punched a little French girl for stealing a candy from me. My Spanish nannies scolded me, but I had no patience for them, or their tales meant to frighten me into submission.

"There are no such things as witches," I would say to them when they tried to convince me that a witch would come and take me away for being naughty. I didn't dare say such things to my mother, though. She not only believed in witches, but in even more frightening elements of the supernatural. Sor Patrocinio haunted the Palais, her bloody bandages needing changing, which she did not do often enough, so that all would see her "miracle" and be stunned into reverence.

My sisters and I were day-scholars at Sacré Cœur, and we wore dark blue uniforms every day. Gone were the taffeta gowns, the elaborate costumes my mother had seamstresses design for the many royal balls, gone were the high-heeled shoes, gone were the diadems.

We were not wholly free of the royal life, though. Sor Patrocinio, who did not like the French brand of Catholicism, insisted that our uniforms be equipped with multiple hidden pockets. Inside, she would hide medals, from which dangled small, golden lockets. Within the lockets were relics—the tooth of Santa Barbara rested in one, the thumbnail of Santa Marta was in another. San Damian's small toe bone was in Pilár's pocket, while Paz had the dubious distinction of carrying around a withered chunk of San Judas Tadeo's left earlobe. We clinked and jangled along with our unsuspecting Parisian playmates at school, and removed our uniforms in the evenings, careful not to touch the relics, which always felt cold, even in the summer.

At school, I gathered around me, year after year, an ever-larger group of girls who depended on me to lighten the mood. At age seven, I was horrified to realize that there wasn't a single mirror at Sacré Coeur. They were forbidden by the nuns, in an effort to curb our vanity.

What a shame, I thought. These French girls were so pretty,

with their tiny, upturned noses, and their wide-set eyes, their little waists and feline legs. My sisters and I stood out among them, stocky and Bourbon through and through.

So, I devised a plan. I took one of Sor Patrocinio's habits, which was black as night, and tore it in half. This, I brought to school. The classroom doors had small, clear windows in them, and when I put the black cloth behind them, the effect was that I created a mirror on the other side. Whenever one of the girls wished to check her hair, or just look at herself and admire what she saw, they would call out, "Lali, Lali," and I would come with Sor Patrocinio's torn habit and make a mirror at once.

"You are so beautiful," I would tell my friends, and they would embrace me and kiss my cheeks.

"Merci, Lali. Vous êtes très mignonne!" they would say, and I would float on air afterwards.

Those nine years in exile were the only time in my life in which anyone thought to shorten "Eulalia" to something else, something tender. I am still Lali in my heart, you see, though I haven't heard that name in many years, and to say it to myself would be beyond silly.

When my mother found out about Sor Patrocinio's habit, she yelled at me for an hour, and made me mend the cloth with needle and thread. I did a poor job of it, though not on purpose. My mother, examining the habit, sighed and said, "You are only fit for America," as if that was the worst insult she could muster.

Her dismissive utterance sparked in me an intense desire to visit that place. If only I could take a ship to America, I thought, then I should be really happy.

She also said this: "I have two sons. Alfonso and Eulalia," which was meant to insult me, but which I delighted in. If only I had been the second boy she had so wanted! What freedoms I would have had!

In short, my years in Paris were the happiest of my life. But it was in Normandy, on that cold, serrated shore, that I made my first real stand against the destiny set for me. As I think of it, I realize that perhaps the events at Normandy so affected me, so branded my way of thinking, that now, whenever I am near the sea, on a coast that looks alien in its jagged beauty, with my skin prickling into bumps, chilly toes going numb, I am happiest, and feel most free.

We were playing on the sand, my sisters and I, when a tall boy about my age came by with a pail. Inside the pail was a brown crab, clawing the smooth sides of the pail, trying to get out. My sisters squealed and ran from the sight of the boy and the crab, but I found that I could not move. The look of him— his scabby knees, his feet good and solid on the sand, held me steady. I hear him say, "Regardez ici, belle fille."

"Do not call me 'girl.'" I told him. "I am Su Alteza Real la Serenísima Infanta Eulalia," I said, giving him the full title I would later use. When he laughed, I laughed too, and he moved closer with his pail and his skittish crab. The magic of the moment was interrupted by one of the Spanish nannies, who came running toward us, her skirts fisted in her hands, struggling over the sand and rocks. I knew she was coming to shoo him away, and so I met her halfway and kicked her hard in the shin.

The nanny, whose name I no longer remember, cried out, and fell, clutching her leg. She told me that if I weren't an infanta, I would have been spanked long ago, and I told her that I wished someone would hit me, because I longed for a good fight.

"By my life, no one will ever harm a single, blond eyelash of yours," the nanny said as she lay on the ground. I ran away, following the boy into a stand of trees not too far away, while the nanny screamed and hobbled in our direction.

I was gone for several hours with the boy named Alain. He took me to his parents' orchard, and we ate apples that were not ripe, and gave ourselves a stomachache. There, in Normandy, a small fire grew in my belly, and Alain, gallant boy, kissed my knuckles with his sticky mouth.

Later, Alain's parents would drag me across the sands, apologizing to me the whole time, "Nous sommes désolés, princesse," again and again, before returning me to the Spanish nanny, who came toward us with outstretched hands, relief plain on her face.

The memory of Alain's little round face, of his mouth on my hand, served to perplex me for years. How is that I could not choose to stay in that orchard? My grandmother had abdicated the throne, leaving Madrid and settling in Normandy with her lover. She paid the price with exile, with the loss of her daughters and her crown. But she had chosen her own path. Why couldn't I?

This is what I learned: I may wear a crown, but I am powerless as an ant, as a fox dead on the side of the road, as a mote of dust, whipped by the wind. Crown or no, I have one life. Just the one. I wish I might have spent it munching on French apples near the shore, saying to anyone who passes by, "I have no plans for tomorrow, or the day after that. Come back if you desire. I may or may not be here."

Tomás

It was strange, at first, to have a set path, to have plans that unfolded. I took that uneasiness with me to the bookshop when I first went to see what it was I had signed on to do. Waiting outside, leaning against the door, was a young woman.

Her hair was hidden under a brown felt hat, and her dress, a burnt orange, had a high collar, with tarnished gold buttons trailing down her throat, between her breasts, and all the way past her waist to the hem of her skirt. She was staring at me as if I had done her some wrong. In her hands was a parasol that she was gripping tightly.

"Excuse me," I said. "I'd like to enter my shop."

"Your shop," the woman said. Her voice was quivering.

I dangled the key, and she leapt into motion, trying to snatch it away. I sprang backwards, then held up a hand. "Hang on a moment," I began to say.

"Your shop? Did the esteemed Profesor Flores simply hand you the keys because of your potential? Scholar maybe? Writer? The son he never had? Is that it?" The blood had rushed to her cheeks, and she squinted at me as if trying to peer into my heart.

"I don't know who you are, or what—"

"Juana Flores," she said. "The profesor's daughter. His only child." She was breathing hard, and her eyes were wet.

"Listen, you don't have to get upset. You don't have to cry."

"I'm not crying," she said through gritted teeth.

I noticed that, though her arms were crossed, she was pinching her elbows. I held up the key again, and gestured to the door. Juana moved aside, and watched as I inserted the key.

"Teeth up," she corrected, and I turned the key over and managed to get the door open.

Once inside, Juana walked purposefully through the store, and returned with a kerosene lamp. Then, she went behind the counter, opened a drawer, and drew a match, with which she lit the lamp, lighting the dark corners of the shop. I put the keys and my red notebook, still in my pocket and now soft and worn, onto the counter. The shelves were half-empty, and a rustling sound could be heard overhead.

"Bats," we both said at once, and she turned to me and smiled, reluctantly.

"You know the place well," I said.

Juana turned slowly in the center of the shop, her eyes casting about, taking it all in.

"I do," she breathed. Her deep breath filled her dress, her exhale loosened the fabric, and I watched it fill again, mesmerized by her. "Papá wouldn't let me manage the shop. No matter how I begged, even though I grew up here. Do you even know anything about the book business?"

I shook my head. "I like to read."

Juana laughed, but it was a bitter sort of laugh. "You like to read?"

"Verne, mostly."

She laughed again. "Wonderful. Just wonderful." She stalked over to the cash register, and popped open a secret door in the back. Inside was a folded piece of paper. This she gave me. "Here," she said. "It's the names and addresses of the people you need to know. The publishers and the accountant, the tax collector and the university librarian, and also . . . " On and on she went, retrieving other slips of paper with more and more names and addresses on them. Juana spent the rest of the afternoon in the shop, lecturing one moment, then setting up mouse traps the next, pausing to wipe her small face with a handkerchief, polishing the counter, then taking stock of the books still in boxes at the back of the shop. Every once in a while, she would take my hand and lead me down an aisle. Then, she would let go, and I would feel deflated, as if her very touch was a source of energy.

Opening up a new box, we found new editions of *Journey to the Centre of the Earth*. I ran my fingers over the covers and sighed deeply. "I've never read him," she admitted.

I picked up a copy and handed it to her. "Start tonight," I said.

"Look around. There is so much work to do. Top to bottom, the store needs—"

"I'll help. We will work until Libreria Flories is in good shape again. I'll go get some food, and in the meantime, Verne," I said, tapping the book in her hand.

I left her in the store in search of food to bring. A little box of olives, some jamón serrano, and a bottle of wine were easily procured at a shop around the corner. When I returned, she was flipping through my notebook.

"That's mine," I said.

"It's empty." Juana was right. I had never used the notebook my mother had given me. It seemed to me that I hadn't quite found the right story to put into it, and the small book had become precious to me in a way I couldn't explain.

"Even so," I said. Juana shrugged and left my notebook alone. Then, she picked up a pair of scissors to cut open more boxes, careful not to tear into the books themselves.

"More atlases," she sighed after attacking the first box, and gave the big books a slap, as if chastising them.

I motioned to the food. We ate with small plates on our laps. There were no napkins in the store, and it seemed we'd both forgotten our handkerchiefs that day, so we licked our fingers clean. I watched her cheeks turn red as she did so, which perhaps made me flush, too, I can't be sure.

"Well," Juana said, after finishing her last bite of food. "I should go."

"Wait," I said, but didn't know what else to say. For the first time since the debacle with my stories, followed immediately by my father's death, I felt light, happy even. I didn't think it was the bookstore itself that caused the change, but the creature before me, who seemed as if she were in her element among the stacks. "Why won't your father turn over the store to you?"

"A woman has no place in business," she said in a booming voice, impersonating her father. She shook her skirt a little and pointed her toe.

"Other women manage stores," I said, but Juana shrugged. I couldn't simply hand her the key. What would be the point? Professor Flores would only take it from her. "The truth is, I don't know what I'm doing," I said.

"I know."

"If you'd like, you can—"

Juana smiled and clasped her hands under her chin. "Yes. I would very much like to help. I have so many ideas," she went on. "Little signs designating local authors. There are three of which I know. No more atlases, of course. How many different kinds does a store need? A section on Shakespeare, don't you think? Children's books, too . . . " I followed her back to the store, listening long into the night to her flurry of words, watching her hands as they punctuated her speech. I didn't take a single note, but I learned the patterns her gestures made, like birds in flight.

Eulalia

I was eleven when my brother was proclaimed King of Spain. The revolution was over. Spain would once again belong to the House of Bourbon. My mother called my sisters and me to her room and told us, bouncing in her seat like a child. My sisters and I spoke French, and only a little Spanish at the time. My mother knew only Spanish. So, it is little wonder that we when she told us about returning to Spain, we were confused, understanding only a little why we had to depart Paris, which we loved, and where we knew some freedom.

At Santander, we were pelted with flowers, and red and gold bunting hung over every doorway. We rode a carriage through the countryside, and here and there, doves tied to leashes were released over our heads, then jolted away as soon as I reached out to touch them. My mother, who had become fearful of birds after Sor Patrocinio told her that they sometimes were inhabited by demons, would scream every time a dove was sent our way. Despite that, the people cheered and wept at our return, and my mother smiled at them, and looked young again in my eyes. It was as if there had never been a coup, as if my mother had always been loved this way instead of despised.

After the carriages, we boarded a train that stopped at each station through the night. At each stop, we were roused from sleep and made to greet the crowds that waited for us. By the time we reached the Escorial, the palace just outside of Madrid, we had to be carried in by the nannies, to sleep in that cold, dark castle. In the morning, we would greet our royal selves again in the Escorial's many mirrors. Standing there, seeing myself replicated so many times, I told myself that though my body was royal, my mind would not be. I even whispered it to the many Eulalias facing me. "We belong to ourselves," I said.

Sometimes, one thinks a particular thing, and the next moment, a thing happens to cut that thought to pieces. The following morning, my brother Alfonso appeared before us. Now he was king, and we embraced him, and said, "¡Viva el Rey!" He swung me around and kissed my sisters' cheeks. Then, a solemn look came over his slender face. "There is something I need to show you," he said, and took me by one hand and Pilár by the other. Paz trailed after us. We went from room to room, until finally, we arrived at our empty tombs.

"There you will lie, all of you," he said, pointing to four tombs, one for each of my mother's daughters. Alfonso, because he was king, would lie elsewhere. "And here," he said, taking us to the Pudridero, "is where they put you to rot for a while before you go in the tomb." His eyes glittered a little, and I thought at first that he was playing a trick on us, the way he used to prank the servants back in Madrid. Finally, he took us to another room, where the bones of centuries of infantas and infantes lay jumbled.

"I don't want to see any of this," Pilár whimpered. She was the delicate one, always. Paz quietly put an arm around her and shushed and shushed.

Meanwhile, I said, "I'll make sure to die in an explosion then. Or a fire. There will be none of me to entomb."

Alfonso took a deep breath. "Your Spanish is terrible, Eulalia. Try not to speak in public," he said. This was no prank, I realized.

"Alfonso," I said, my voice hurt. I reached out to tickle him, to make him laugh. I wanted to recognize the brother I had once known, the sibling I had loved best of all. He did break after a moment, and smiled, and called us all beautiful in perfect French. But something of my old brother was gone forever, I knew, and I was certain that ephemeral lightness, that playful, mischievous joy, evanesced the moment he was declared king.

"I was first shown the Escorial when I was your age. I was shown these tombs. I even walked into the Pudridero and held my nose against the stench. And what I learned from it was this—that we are all destined for this place, and that we have one chance to make the right choices. Our destinies weigh far more than those of the average man or woman, sisters." He spoke so solemnly that Pilár began to cry again. Alfonso ignored her. "We nearly lost Spain. We will not lose her again."

Oui, I thought at that moment, *mon frère n'est plus la.*

Our eldest sister, María Isabel, arrived the next morning. She looked so much like our mother that I was confused at first, and rapidly hid the novel I was reading. It was Verne's *The Mysterious Island*, and I had just reached the part where an orangutan named Jupiter falls into a volcanic crevice and dies. My eyes were full of tears, and I knew that if my mother saw my distress, she would confiscate the book. When I realized it was my sister, and not my mother, I sighed with relief.

"Oh, it's only you," I said, which made my eldest sister wrinkle her nose at me. She was a young widow, her husband having turned a hunting rifle onto himself, but grief had not softened her. Instead, she became more of an authoritarian, more devoted to the rules of court, and nuances of protocol.

It was no surprise that, after a light lunch served to us in our rooms, the first thing that María Isabel said to us was her rules for getting along in Spain. "You shall have no opinions and no friends," she said to the three of us, looking long at me. "This way, we will be sure that there will be no scandals, and no trouble whatsoever made for our brother, who is doing God's work in Spain." I was certain then that the trip to the tombs and the Pudridero had been her idea.

We answered her with silence, our forks halfway to our mouths. No friends! No opinions? I was bubbling over with anger, and I stuttered for the first time in my life, searching for the right words to say. The words did not come at that time. Instead, they came later, in the middle of the night. What I might have said to my sister was that I deeply wished for another revolution, another exile, one without end. But, like all good responses, the idea for it came too late. Would that I had been born in ancient Sparta, where people trained in the art of the timely bon mot!

María Isabel countered our silence with a quiet, "Viva Rey Alfonso," and we echoed the sentiment. In truth, we all four loved our brother very much. He was the best of us—the bravest and the kindest—and not many years later, we would pray at his bedside and wish to trade places with him, so that he would have that long life all of Spain wished him with every greeting.

*

María Isabel took charge of us shortly after we returned to Spain. It was my mother's own fault. My brother announced his marriage to Mercedes de Montpensier, our cousin, and the daughter of the man who many believed had had us ousted in the first place. Our mother fought the idea so vehemently that the courts decided it would be best if she returned to France, leaving us behind so that we might not be influenced by her.

It was not a tearful goodbye. In fact, one morning, we woke up and were told that our mother had left, that we would see her on holiday, and that was that. We were in María Isabel's dutiful hands from then on.

So we spent our adolescence in Madrid, back in the Palacio Real of our births. There were many visitors, many lessons in protocol, many strange trips across the country on horseback, where villagers would come out and call our names, and send birds in our direction. Once, marveling at the fact that we were so well known by these people, I turned to blow a kiss to a group of children, and realized that someone had pinned our names to the tails of our horses. At one of the stops, I switched the names, and laughed whenever anyone kissed my hand and called me Paz instead of Eulalia.

If we passed a priest on the way to give someone their last rites, it was customary for us to accompany him to the deathbed of the person. Many times this would happen, and María Isabel, who was as devout as our mother, would stop each time. My eldest sister was the only one of us who still kept relics on her person, the one who recited rosaries in order to fall asleep, and crossed herself whenever we passed a graveyard. Imagine the scene—a person, coughing, delirious, prone on a rough bed, his children weeping around him, and all of us, dressed in thick velvets, glossy taffetas, jewels glittering on our wrists and in our ears, sitting there like treasure chests in the corners, watching as the last rites were given. Then, when the person coughed his last, we would sometimes kiss their foreheads and say a prayer together. The family members would weep all the harder then. Sometimes, our appearance had the wrong effect. Relatives who should have been comforting their dying brother, cousin, mother-in-law, busied themselves about us, bringing us coffee or serving us sweets. Or they would go still from the shock of seeing us there. Once, the aunt of a dying child sat hard on a seat upon seeing us. She was a large woman, built like my sister and mother. She did not move at all during our visit, though she seemed uncomfortable, as if her back was hurting. When she rose at last, we learned the reason for her discomfort. She had sat upon the child's kitten, and had smothered it, unwilling to move while we were present.

That stop was an exceptionally hard one for me, not only because of the dying child, and the sad fate of the kitten, but because I realized the danger we posed simply for following protocol, which seemed to matter more than comfort, or love, or grief. My beloved sister-in-law, Mercedes, had died only months earlier, after complications following a miscarriage. Alfonso had laid in the Pudridero with her for three days, weeping so hard that there was talk of making María Isabel queen. In those days, we wore our mourning like a second skin, and it felt as if everyone was being taken from us.

Pilár was better in these situations, and she would sometimes hold the hands of the dying as they passed, or she would run her own hands over their heads and murmur a prayer. Paz and I hung back, often holding handkerchiefs to our mouths and noses. I did not trust Spanish doctors, who sometimes lurked during these death scenes, clutching their bags full of grisly tools and jars of who-knows-what.

During another stop, Pilár held a young woman, about my age, as she convulsed and died in her arms. I am not one for superstition, but the moment felt charged with darkness, as if something had passed overhead and marked us. Two weeks later, I fell ill with a bad cough. Weak lungs run in the family, and so when Alfonso, María Isabel, Paz, and Pilár left for the baths of Escoriaza, for a getaway, I stayed behind, and nursed my cough.

It was there, at Escoriaza, that Pilár fell ill. There, at Escoriaza, she fell into fits, dying while my siblings were out on horseback, enjoying the summer afternoon. Pilár, who had comforted so many others at their passing, died alone.

A legend sprung up around Pilár's death, a romantic one borne of the sadness that is the death of so young a princess, one untouched by any man. The newspapers devised a story in which my sister and young Napoleon Luis, the son of Napoleon III, once a playmate of ours, had fallen in love. He died in the Zulu wars, and in the stories, she died of meningitis in Spain. The story went like this—at the moment that Pilár first felt ill, a pressed violet, given to her by Napoleon III, fell out of the book she was reading, fluttering to the ground and turning to dust. At her death, Napoleon III's mother, the Empress Eugenia, grieving now her son and future daughter-in-law, sent a wreath of violets that hung outside her son's tomb, and ordered that it be fashioned into a floral circlet for my sister to wear in death.

In a way, I wish the story had been true. I wish Pilár had loved a man at least once. Such a ridiculous story. Why must everything about us be so fanciful? Why can't people understand that we are nothing, nothing. That we live and die, give birth, behave pettily, eat and suffer migraines, hate and love, just like everyone else does? We are sacks of flesh, and the gems at our hands are merely rocks dug out of the dirt.

We were never the same after Pilár died. She was all sweetness, all tenderness. She was, perhaps, the only tender Bourbon to have ever lived.

Tomás

It is impossible to pinpoint when I fell in love with Juana Flores. Though I do know that when she took my hand that first afternoon in the bookshop, barely knowing me, my soul felt suspended somewhere outside of me.

Most days, I felt like her student, and she presented her curriculum patiently. "No," she would say, "the orders come in on Tuesdays," or "Tomás, please don't forget the rent is paid the first of the month."

"Watch me," she would say as she took the parasols gently from the customers when they entered the shop, since so many had used the tips of their umbrellas to lower books too high to reach, sometimes damaging the merchandise.

"Tomás?" she would call, and I would reach up to retrieve the book in question. Sometimes, I wouldn't answer right away, just to hear her say my name again. She liked to wrap purchases in brown paper. "I read somewhere that they wrap all purchases in Japan just so," she would say. I would watch her run her fingernail along the paper to make a firm crease, and once, she cut her finger and I felt a tug in my stomach as if I had been the one injured.

Because I thought it would please her, I ordered the entire catalog of Routledge's Miniature Library, each book precisely the size of the palm of her hand. "For you," I said, when she opened the box.

"We must sell them! They are delightful," she said, but I plucked *Language of Flowers* from the top, and turned to the page featuring the peach blossom.

"It means, 'I am your captive,'" I said.

She turned to the pomegranate. "It means, 'foolishness.'"

Even so, I kissed her, and the tiny books that she had piled onto her lap tumbled to the floor. A customer interrupted us with a cough, and then she was all business again, though I noticed how she fidgeted with her hair the rest of the day, catching my gaze.

One midmorning, a rapid snowstorm blew through town, and we were barred from the street past closing, the doors half-covered in snow. We lit the stove in the back room, and talked about our families. I told her about my father, how he cried in the middle of the night, and about the stories I wrote. I found it easy to talk about in the dark.

"I had such hopes," I said.

"Tell me," she said.

"The stories?" I couldn't bear to, not at first. If she laughed, I knew I might not recover, not now, when we were so close to something I could not name.

"Tell me," she insisted. The crackling wood, the soft patter of snow on the window, like cat's paws tapping at a thigh, and her lips, parted, pink, all loosened something in me. I unraveled the stories for her, fixing them as I went.

"No, he wasn't a banker after all. He was a lighter of lamps," I would say, revising on the spot, and she would nod, whispering, "Go on, go on."

There are nights when all one does is talk to someone with an open heart, and at the end of the night, one's face hurts from smiling, the jaw aches from talking. That was the kind of night it was, and though I thought about taking her upstairs to my apartment, where there was a couch and a fireplace, I knew that asking such a thing of her might ruin everything.

In the morning, the snow had mostly melted, and what remained had stiffened into ice. Next door was a bakery, and we went inside for hot chocolate and bread. The baker and his wife had been trapped all night, too. Juana bought several pastries and a loaf of bread, which she put inside a canvas bag that was normally filled with books.

"For your father?" I said, and she nodded, concern settling in her face. She struck up a quiet conversation I couldn't make out with the baker's wife, who whispered in her ear. Juana looked relieved afterwards.

"What was that about?" I asked.

Juana said nothing.

"Come on. Tell me," I said. My eyes were heavy, but I wasn't ready to part with her yet.

Juana clutched the canvas bag, flattening the pastries inside, I was sure. "My father will wonder where I was all night," she said. "She promised, if he asked, that is, that she—"

"Oh, I see," I said. "You were trapped with the baker and his wife all night. At least it was warm."

She swatted my arm and grew happy again. I watched her go in the direction of her father's house, and I knew for sure that he had no idea where she went during the day. What would he say if he knew that she was helping in the bookstore, or that she spent nearly every waking hour with me? More likely than not, he was locked in his office, writing, studying, firing off one correspondence after another. Did he smell it on her, that particular scent of books when they congregate like birds? Or did he smell my cigarettes, which I smoked outside because Juana said they would damage the merchandise?

I soon realized I didn't care. I wanted the profesor to know. Then, I would tell him that of all the dreams I'd had—of writing stories like Verne, of perhaps seeing the world, of having Juana in my life forever.

Eulalia

On my eighteenth birthday, María Isabel decided that it was time for my debut, and I would be presented at the annual dance held by the Dukes of Bailén. I was ecstatic at first, but when I learned that María Isabel was to serve as my chaperone, the wind left my lungs, and my toes, which had floated above the ground at the announcement, touched cold earth again.

"But why?" I'd asked my brother, and he had looked at me softly, and tugged at a curl dangling down my forehead. "You need a chaperone, Eulalia," he said, offering no answer at all.

"Perhaps Prince Carlos Braganza can accompany me?" I said, and my brother arched an eyebrow.

"I thought you weren't interested in the Portuguese prince," he mused.

"Interested? He's certainly interesting," I said, and my brother kept wisely quiet. The truth was, Carlos Braganza was more than interesting. But he was to be king one day, and I did not wish to play the role of queen. Nevertheless, Carlos's letters were funny, and even his handwriting was all jagged, as if he were laughing as he wrote. His eyes were the sort one could look deeply into without growing nervous. I'd seen him dance at different festivals, and admired the way he took his partners by the waist—without hesitation! Yes, I was interested in Carlos Braganza in a way that would make the court gossips perk their ears in our direction.

"Our eldest sister is an appropriate partner for you, Eulalia," Alfonso said.

The dance was dreadful throughout, becoming more so by increments as the night wore on. First, I had to tolerate María Isabel by my side, telling me to "Slow down. You take strides like a giraffe," and I hissed at her that I had been raised in Paris, among city people who had places to go, and she pinched my elbow hard. It irked my sister that I was not raised as she had been—in the Palace, girded by golden arches and a million rules. Then I cursed at her in French, which was a language that gave her trouble, and the brief spat was over.

All of this happened before a crowd of nearly a hundred partygoers, who, if asked, would have said that María Isabel and I were as composed as an oil painting in the front of the room.

Later came the dances. How I longed to spin out onto the dance floor with a few of the young men in attendance, sons of dukes and marquesas, handsome in their evening finery. Instead, I was allowed dance after dance with ambassadors, ancient men who smelled of cigars and paper. If my eye caught the gaze of a young person like me, he would look away, turning as red as a pomegranate, for it was not permitted that anyone make eye contact with me aside from those stately politicians, men who deferred to the king and no one else.

By the end of the night, I was so bored I thought I might start gnawing my own hands. The final song played, and I danced with an ambassador from Constantinople, who asked me three times, because he was half-deaf, whether I drank coffee. When I said I did, he produced a tiny coffee bean from a gold-trimmed pocket. It was the oddest gesture, but I appreciated it. I tucked the bean into my glove and thought, "At least there was this one strange thing I can remember about tonight."

When María Isabel and I retired to my room, I threw myself onto my bed, fully dressed and prepared to spend the night in just such a state. I would deal with the crushed fabric and pins in my hair the next morning. But one of the maids, sighing and telling me to rest, removed my shoes, massaged my feet, and pulled me upright gently. She undid the buttons at my back, unlaced my whalebone corset, at which I sighed in happy release, and managed to get me out of my debut dress. I pulled on a white slip and fell back into my pillows, the sound of the maid rustling my dress reminding me of being on a ship at sea.

Suddenly, I heard a sharp cry, and then, my sister's name being called. I was nearly asleep, and thinking of the castles in

Portugal, when María Isabel came roaring into my room, holding up a tiny thing that glinted in her hand.

"What is the meaning of this?" she asked. Trapped between her fingers was a tiny golden arrow. The arrow was pierced through a sheet of cream-colored paper, tiny and translucent in the lamplight.

I held out my hand, removed the paper from the pin, for that is what the arrow was, and read it aloud: "I am an earthworm in love with a star, and that star is named Eulalia." There was no signature, but the hand of the would-be courter was steady and firm, with a flourish at the end of each word that I at once noticed and would adopt in my own handwriting.

"I've no idea," I said, returning the pin to my sister. I'd wanted to keep it, but knew it would be stupid to suggest such a thing. There was a strange fire burning in María Isabel's blue irises, making them seem both cold and hot at once.

"You must have felt it!" she yelled. "It was pinned to your skirt!"

"I've been half-asleep all night," I told her, though suddenly, it felt as if I would never sleep again.

María Isabel laughed, threw back her head, and launched the following at me: "If this is what happens when you are asleep, what will you allow when you are awake?" Her lip curled in disgust, as if I were a maid she had caught in flagrante delicto! I felt my cheeks burn, and I wanted nothing more than to be swallowed by the cushions on my bed, to be smothered like Desdemona, and die an innocent in order to prove my accusers wrong. Such dramatic thoughts, I know. But they were my sleepy and distraught ideas, and I must own them.

It was not Carlos Braganza who pinned the note to my skirts, since he was not in attendance at the dance. I wish it had been him. It would have made for a better story, and perhaps my sister would not have been so angry with me, since, at the time, Carlos was everyone's preferred choice for my husband.

I still have the letters that Carlos Braganza sent me. He was fair, like I am. His blond curls were like mine. His blue eyes were like mine. I am not so stupid as to think that wasn't part of it. I have always liked looking into mirrors. In his letters he called me his "dear friend," and the "joy of his heart," and his greatest wish was to marry me. I might have been the Queen of Portugal.

We met twice in Lisbon, Carlos and I. He would tell me, "Portuguese is the Rosetta Stone of languages. If you can speak Portuguese, then Spanish, French and Italian come easy."

"I speak all three," I told him, "and English too," and he laughed that loud, robust laugh of his, and cupped my cheek in his palms, and did other things, too.

Everyone expected I would marry Carlos Braganza of Portugal. But already, the diadem on my head was too heavy. I could not bear to imagine what a queen's crown would feel like.

The last time I saw Carlos, we met in Burgos. Whenever I passed through that city, I made sure to find my old Ama, and have a hot chocolate with her. Amalia sends cards at Christmas, and Easter, too. Inspired by those notes, which are so kind and effusive, I have made it a practice to visit her when I can. I have gone to see her in Burgos, and she weeps into my hair and praises me, telling me how smart I am. I bring her small gifts I know she will like—a lavender-scented candle, a new handkerchief, and once, a small painting of my namesake, Santa Eulalia, who looked so prim and innocent that she made me laugh. Amalia shows me her old uniforms, which she keeps in a cedar closet. My milk brother is never there, and I believe that Ama must send him away when I come to visit. I asked her about him once, and she said, "I want you all to myself," but I think there was something else troubling her mind, some notion about what her son might think of me, of his mother's past. I think he must be a very lucky man, to have had a mother like Ama. I wonder if that blind love so early in my life has wrecked my mind, so that I find it difficult to settle for anything less than pure devotion in my relations with others.

When I write letters to my mother, I sign off with the following, "I kiss your hand, respectfully," then scrawl my name beneath it. How much better would it be to say, "Te quiero, mamá, with all my heart, te quiero." I have never written those words before now, and I know that, should she read them, my mother would burn with shame. Not so with Amalia, who mothers me still, though I am grown now.

Sometimes during my visits, Amalia told me stories of her childhood in an orphanage, but mostly, she would regale me with stories of her son. Because she trusted me with her stories, I trusted her with mine, and one visit, I asked her if I should give in to my feelings regarding Carlos.

My Ama said nothing, only, "Yes, Eulalia. Yes, you may." But I am unsure whether she approved of me. I wish I could hear a word other than "yes" now and again, when the question is one I want a real answer to.

Days later, back in Madrid for the San Isidro festivities, I met Carlos Braganza. We were both young and afraid of scandal, of God, of our own bodies. That night, Carlos spoke to me of life in the palace at Lisbon. "You and I, side by side. Will Europe have ever seen such a pair?" He whispered into my ear as he spoke, seducing me with words. "Rainha, rainha, with the world at your feet," he said.

I was not yet engaged, and my argument against marriage was that I was still too young, a line of reasoning my brother, the king, respected because I was the baby of the family, and would always be too young in his eyes. Carlos Braganza could not know, nor could I explain to him, what it had been like for my mother, Queen of Spain, to be cast into exile. Perhaps his history tutors had told him about the many ways we Spaniards fought to keep a woman off the throne, the many intrigues, the many conspiracies, the blood that was shed. Sometimes, I would catch my mother looking at me and my sisters with such longing, as if she could will herself into our places. If a regular woman selling flowers on the street was freer than I, then I was infinitely freer, as an infanta, than my mother, a queen. Carlos would not have understood an argument like this, imagining that a king had more worries stitched across his brow than a queen. If we had tried to debate it, I would have listed my dead siblings, all of those attempts at creating a spare for Alfonso. I would have listed the many dead wives of Henry VIII, and then I would asked him who truly suffered the weight of the crown.

But this was not the kind of conversation one had in the dark, in hiding. As for Carlos and I, we parted ways in the morning, and that was that.

Tomás

On a book-buying trip to Madrid one day, I wandered into a jeweler's shop on Calle de Serrano. I had sketched a drawing on a napkin over lunch, the image as it appeared making me so nervous that I could not finish my soup. The jeweler took the drawing of a ring, the setting in the shape of an open book with delicate, fluttering pages. "The stone should be a garnet," I said, thinking of the color of the dress Juana had worn when I first saw her.

I described the ring to her later that night, showing her my sketch because I could not wait to have it in hand. We had been busy rearranging the books in the store by subject, rather than alphabetical order. It had been Juana's idea, and she planned on decorating the top of each shelf with an item that would indicate the books beneath it. A globe would sit on the travel shelf, and over the shelf with all of the Jules Verne books, Juana had picked out a brass telescope that gleamed when the sunlight struck it just right. She had just placed the last of the history books on the shelf when I stilled her hand, and slipped my sketch into it.

"It will be something beautiful to wear on our wedding day," I said. "I picked out a garnet, like your dress. But you'll probably want to wear white, as it's the fashion these days," I rambled, afraid of the silence that might follow my declaration.

Juana was, indeed, silent. She held the drawing lightly—a draft would have blown it out of her hands.

"Are you—"

"Marry me," I said. Juana circled her arms around my neck, kicking over a small stack of military books nearby.

"I'll have to ask your father," I muttered into her neck, but we pretended that that encounter was still far away.

Instead, I introduced Juana to my mother. She met her at the door like a schoolteacher, and watched with pursed lips as Juana stuttered through her introduction.

"Mamá," I said in warning, and my mother laughed, at last, said she was no good for such stern demonstrations, and embraced Juana.

"Listen, niña, you will give me the most beautiful grand-children in all of Burgos. How can I show you anything but love?" Just like that, she took Juana by the arm and led her into her home, where she showed her the room I'd slept in as a boy, her cuckoo clock, which was her prized possession, and her nodriza's uniform, as crisp and clean as the day she'd first worn it.

"Tomás never told me," Juana said. She looked at me quizzically.

"Never told you? That he was the milk brother to the Infanta Eulalia, Eulalia la serenísima, herself? We lived in the Palacio Real," my mother said, and her chin rose an inch, her eyebrows, too.

My mother brought out artifacts for Juana to see—her dark socks and polished shoes, which she'd been allowed to keep, the letter from Queen Isabel, with the details of my scholarship, a drawing that Paz had made for her, the "z" in her name written backwards, and a flower that Pilár had pressed into a book of saints for her, too. We crossed ourselves at the mention of Infanta Pilár, and the mood in the room turned somber for a moment.

In all, my mother had precious little to remind her of those days.

"Nothing from Eulalia?" Juana asked.

"Nothing," my mother said. "But she was my favorite, of course." My mother packed away her things into a fabric-lined box, and then she and the box disappeared into the house.

Juana turned toward me. "Why didn't you ever tell me? How interesting it all is!"

"I don't think much of it. I don't remember at all," I said. But Juana kept returning to the subject, and I learned that she had always longed to see the palace, that her father had met Isabel herself once, after her exile was over and Alfonso was king, and that Juana used to play infanta when she was little, fashioning crowns out of paper.

For me, the palace held no interest, and I told her so.

"If you could choose any place to live?" Juana asked.

It was America that I loved, with its expansiveness and its Wild West. I told Juana so, and that night, over dinner, I recounted a book I'd read about a man named Wild Bill, who'd been mauled by a bear and lived to tell the tale, and who went on to do a great many adventurous things before being murdered during a game of cards.

"Leave the palace to me, then. You can keep the saloons," Juana said, and my mother laughed.

That night, Juana slept in my old bed, and I in the front room. I heard her call my name, an insistent, worried whisper. I checked on my mother, snoring away, then slipped into a room that should have felt familiar, but just then, with Juana in it, felt as if I had fallen beneath the earth, into one of Verne's caverns, an otherworldly, beautiful place.

"I can't sleep," she said.

I sat on the edge of the bed.

"Perhaps these have something to do with it," I remarked playfully, pointing at various pictures on the wall of saints— Santa Teresa de Ávila was on one, her dark eyes and hair glinting in the moonlight, her delicate, white hand to her chin. There was the Virgin herself, full breasts, an obscured infant in her lap. On the other was an icon I didn't recognize, a little girl in a green dress, though her eyes, too, blazed darkly at us.

"Perhaps," Juana said, then, she took my hand. We discovered one another blindly in the dark. I thought, at the time, my hands on Juana's hips, that there were no rewards or punishments for love, not really, and that to think so was to believe in fairy tales.

Before dawn could wake my mother, I sat up in the narrow bed, Juana's leg heavy over my own. "That one is Teresa," she mused, pointing at the image. Then she laughed. "Oh, of course," she said, her voice lazy and full of sleep. "The little girl with the feather quill and the green brocade, now I know who she is."

"What?" I asked, delighted that Juana had been musing about the saints, too.

"Santa Eulalia, of course," Juana said. "Spain's favorite virgin saint," she whispered. I trailed my fingers around her belly button twice, then dropped a kiss there, which made her laugh.

Later, my mother would eye us with suspicion, but say nothing, and when I asked her where she got the picture of Santa Eulalia, she claimed to have no idea what I was talking about.

Eulalia

When my sister, María Isabel, became a married woman, she was seventeen. I was only four. My sister, who is more like my mother than my mother is sometimes, was the picture of mourning at her wedding. Under her blue eyes were dark circles that no amount of powder could cover. Her short, blond hair held gardenias that were going brown at the edges. And her hands shook underneath all of those flowers in her bouquet so that it looked as if a perpetual breeze was striking her. Paz, Pilár, and I wore matching dresses, with enough layers underneath our skirts to make us look like fat little macaroons.

All of us milled about María Isabel, laying our small hands on her, trying to calm our much older sister. Alfonso, so handsome in military clothes that were a touch too big on him, stood off to the side, unsure of himself in this world of women and girls. None of our susurrations or consolations worked. María Isabel's moist eyes gave themselves over to real tears, and they left bright streaks on her face.

This is how our mother found us, her five children, huddled around one another as if a great tragedy was about to descend upon us. It was a strange moment, made especially so by my older sister's acquiescence to our comforts. She was never a friend to us. She was our mother's shadow, in all ways mimicking her, practicing the same facial expressions and ignoring us the way our mother often did. She sniffed the air with her small upturned nose at the slightest of provocations. If Pilár flung a doll into the air, there went María Isabel's nose. When I tore my bullfighter costume, the one I was made to wear at the fair in Sevilla that year, María Isabel huffed like a bull herself.

But on that day, hours before she married that Prince Gaetan, who was as dim as twilight, we all felt tremendous love and pity for our sister. There we all were, the perfect picture of sibling affection, when our mother walked in, her heavy skirts announcing her presence the way the wind whips between certain buildings on certain streets in Madrid.

"Basta," she said quietly, but with tremendous force. "My own wedding to your father was arranged. He is my first cousin twice over, no less. And yet, I am content." She said this with downcast eyes. Not a one of us believed her. "Fondness will grow between you and Gaetan slowly, like moss at the base of a great oak," she said, and peeled us off our sister one by one, gripping our small shoulders and casting us aside as if we were barnacles attached to the hull of a boat. "You are the Princess of Asturias," our mother said, pinching María Isabel's cheeks so hard that they bloomed, making her look, for once, like the blushing bride of fairy tales. "Now act like it."

Hers was the most sorrowful wedding I've ever seen. Gaetan was an epileptic, a fact that had been kept from my sister. The man shot himself in the head only three years after their wedding, making my sister a very young widow, and giving her free rein to oversee my education like the dictator she was.

I thought of my sister in her bridal finery often, and darkly, days before my own wedding, which promised to be just as unhappy.

Like my mother and my sister, I was married to my own

cousin, Antonio de Orléans, to trade my Bourbon name for another man's. I did not have Pilár by my side, nor Alfonso. They were already cold in their crypts in El Escorial, while my empty tomb waits patiently for me. And God knows María Isabel had no pity, though my mother was against the marriage, since Antonio's father had sometimes helped the Carlists with their plotting. I had Paz, of course, who married a few years earlier herself, and in her eyes I found some of the comfort I needed.

I must explain what María Isabel did when Antonio was proposed for a husband. I refused hotly at once. His broom of a mustache, his implacable countenance, as if nothing ever pleased him—these I could not imagine seeing day after day. He was the only male infante in the royal family at the time, and he acted every bit the spoiled prince. His mother, the Infanta Luisa Fernanda, who also happened to be my aunt, spoke of him as if she were describing a misbehaving puppy. "What a poor student my Antonio was!" she would say at dinner as if this is the kind of thing anyone cared to listen to. "He was like a sloth. At first, he loved school, but then he became dissatisfied," she would say, chuckling and gazing at her son with a wet look. At this, Antonio would lift a well-manicured eyebrow at his mother, then sip his soup, as if deciding that, alas, she was right after all. I recall one dinner when the Duke of Veragua was supping with us. He is a descendant of Christopher Columbus, and has ridden that lineage the way one rides a horse on parade—with great pomp and style. The Duke was discussing the recent rebellions in the Caribbean, and the need for strong Spanish men (like himself, naturally) to lead the troops abroad and squash those "indios and negros" once and for all. I hid a mocking smile behind my napkin as he spoke. At once, all the men in attendance at dinner began to volunteer, as if the Duke of Veragua had summoned them to arms. One by one they vowed to fight in Cuba if the time came. Antonio, however, only tilted his bowl to catch the very last drops of soup onto his spoon, and was utterly silent.

One does not expect a puppy to go to war, I suppose.

When I told María Isabel that I would refuse my brother's arrangement, as I could not bear marrying Antonio de Orléans, she ushered me into my room by pretending that it would be a safe place for us to talk. I shouldn't have fallen for that trap. She had long been my teacher in all things related to protocol. Pilár and Paz would join me in making fun of her rigidity, curtsying dramatically behind her back. Yet, how many afternoons did I spend grinding my teeth in anger over some lesson my sister had tried to impart? In fact, the dentist told me I had the teeth of a sixty-year-old woman, and that soon, I would not be able to tear into a piece of steak if I did not stop grinding my teeth.

But I let María Isabel trick me that day. I was overwrought, trembling with anger at my brother, and full of sadness, too, that I had no choice but to defy him, he who was my king and sibling, and whom I loved very much. My brother had been sick of late, and at the moment, I did not know that our days with him were numbered. So, I allowed my sister to lead me to my room. At the threshold, she pushed me in, and closed the door behind me. I was so shocked by the shove I did not notice at first that she was screaming at me from the other side of the door. "The dynasty first!" she shouted. Her words sounded muffled through the thick wood. I told her I had a mind of my own, that I was my own woman, and she yelled, "You must learn to be an infanta before you can learn to be a woman!" Then, she threatened to keep me locked in the room without food or water until I consented. Of course, it was an empty threat. María Isabel is nothing if not punctual to meals, and she left off guarding my door by lunch.

While the court awaited my decision, and I bore my sister's cold looks, our brother died. The papers say it was tuberculosis.

Other reporters have claimed a bout of epilepsy. I don't know why the reports have been so varied, or what his second wife María Cristina (who was pregnant at the time, and pale and sickly herself with grief) was trying to hide. The truth of it was that he died of cholera, and the room my sweet brother died in smelled of death long before he died, and that his mouth had a blue ring around it I will never forget. Like Pilár, he had gone to visit the sick and the dying in the south of Spain, where a cholera epidemic had taken hold. He had been at the deathbed of the Mother Superior there. He returned a hero of the people, the Sword of Damocles already nicking the top of his head.

What could I do but acquiesce, and honor my brother's wish? I told the court I would go on a prayer retreat, to pray for my brother's soul and my marriage, and used the opportunity to go to Burgos, where I sought Amalia. I had only an hour with her, and she looked at me with her dark, roaming eyes, and told me that marriages can strain the heart, and how one must temper one's tears with an iron resolve. Thus counseled, I married Antonio de Orléans, while still in mourning. I demanded that the church sanctuary's statues, its candelabras, its stained glass windows, be draped in black cloth. María Cristina, whom we call Christa, said, "It will bring bad luck to you, Eulalia," and I told her that the bad luck had already come, that it had already had its way with me when it stole Alfonso from us. So I married that man of such delicate manners (offensive to me as they are), and thought of my duty to my brother even as I spoke my vows.

It should be noted, that Antonio and I are sometimes in love. Sometimes, he holds my hand when no one is watching, and rubs my palm slowly, so that a fire starts up within us both. He has given me two sons, whom I love with all of my being. But it isn't the kind of stable, lasting love a woman needs. There is an actress I know who has taken up residence in

Antonio's heart. He meets with her often, and the court knows it. They turn away, pretend to watch the sky for thunderclouds, to gaze down the street, to notice anything and everything except for the woman who takes my husband to her bed.

There are days when I want to answer the insult, as the English say, tit for tat. Once, on one of those trips through the countryside, I visited my Ama in Burgos, and told her about Antonio and his mistress. She cautioned me against retaliation, and told me the sad story of her own marriage. And yet, how kind my Ama still is, how full of love she is. If only I could preserve that part of me, too. I feel it going, though, slipping away like mist, and I am hardening, hardening, becoming like my mother and eldest sister with every turn and every betrayal, a not-so-slow poisoning of my heart.

Tomás

My engagement to Juana was a quiet, secret thing, because of her father. "He's an academic, in the end," she said. "And he will make a study of our relationship. It will feel like living under a magnifying glass, I promise you." Her description of her father's reaction seemed to coincide with what I had known of the man back in the university, so I agreed to keep silent.

In the evenings, Juana would return to her father's home and cook his dinner. She was certain he had not noticed the paper cuts on her fingers, or the occasional red splotches on her neck, leftovers from beautiful hours in the stockroom, the two of us lying upon empty boxes, our clothes in heaps at our feet, and the front door to the store locked tight.

Juana gave nothing away the night I visited the home she shared with her father with the intention of asking for her hand. She had steamed clams and a pot of rice, and had, that morning, bought good wine to have on hand for a toast.

When I arrived, the professor greeted me warmly, wiping his chin.

"Sit, hijo, sit. Juana has made too much tonight," he said.

I watched as Juana filled his plate. She would not meet my eyes, though I willed it, feeling one glance from her would supply the courage I needed. I ate very little, and answered the professor's questions, which came at me rapidly, as if I were in one of his lectures.

"How are sales? Did you talk with the publisher from Sevilla? It's an academic press. They don't sell many copies, but they did publish my latest treatise and so, of course, we give them shelf space. Juana, por favor, a bit more rice? I heard there was a robbery on Pozo Seco earlier this week. The watchmaker? Is that so? Maybe we can put another lock on the front door . . . " and on he went, his questions unanswered for the most part.

After a while, I sensed the professor slowing down, noticed that the man's belly was full, and that his plate was all empty clamshells. The professor absently stirred the shells together with his fork, and they sounded like castanets in the distance. I looked at Juana, and she, wide-eyed, nodded.

"Profesor," I began, my hands shaking slightly. "I have fallen in love—"

"Ah," the professor interrupted. "The store. I am glad you love it. I always felt it was a hindrance to me, to my own writing and my studies. You are well suited for—"

"With Juana, Profesor. I am in love with Juana. And I would marry her, if you would allow it." I said it all in a rush, as if it were one word.

In that moment, it seemed as if we had all turned into quite different people. Juana, so talkative most of the time, had covered her mouth with her hands, and was leaning forward on the table, as if watching a suspenseful play. The professor became red-faced, and his brow wrinkled, and I thought that if Juana had set the table with knives, the professor might have thrown one at me. As for myself, for the first time in my life it didn't feel as if I filled the room, but rather, it felt as if I had shrunk down to nothing.

The old man composed himself, and took a breath so deep that his nostrils flared. "Do not take offense, Tomás. Please do not. But Juana has other options in life. A colleague of mine, he is in Theology Studies, his son is a surgeon. Another colleague is the grandson of an Austrian duke, you understand? They are smart men. And both have indicated an interest in—"

"Papá, my preference is with Tomás. Mamá chose you of her own accord, didn't she?" Juana said in a very quiet voice. I wished she'd used stronger language. Her "preference?" *What about love*, I wondered.

So, I supplied the word. "I love her, Profesor."

"As do I," the professor said. "And I want every possibility for my daughter. You didn't even graduate, hijo. You didn't even do that."

I rose from my seat, and from where Juana and the professor sat, it must have seemed to them that a tree was growing before their eyes. Juana and I had not discussed the possibility that the professor would deny us. He had handed the keys to to me, hadn't he? He called me "hijo" all of the time, didn't he? Juana's face was drawn and her eyes were damp. Her hands were laced over her father's, imploring him, but the man had set his jaw, ground his teeth, and said no again and again.

"I was milk brother to the Infanta Eulalia," I blurted then. "Good enough to live in the Palacio Real."

"Hijo. My mother was in service once, too. You and I come from the same places. I look in the mirror and know what I am.

And what I am is not good enough for Juana. You are not good enough for Juana," he said, with the finality of a man at the end of a speech, awaiting the applause.

"Papá," Juana said, her hands flat on the table. "I can choose a husband for myself."

"Be quiet," the professor said.

"Papá, I will not. Tomás is a good man, hardworking, he has dreams, Papá, and they are beautiful dreams that include me, the bookstore, travel. You know very well what Mamá would say if she were here. She would appro—"

The mention of his wife, who had died when Juana was twelve, escalated everything. The professor rose abruptly, the chair he sat on tumbling backwards. "Leave," he said to me, but I felt heavy as a stone. My first thought was of Juana, whom I did not want to abandon in the house. Nor could I simply sweep her away, drag her by the arm out of her father's house, never to return.

"Am I as objectionable as all that?" I began to ask, when the professor clutched his chest suddenly, and made a wheezing sound, like a deflating rubber balloon.

Juana rushed to his side, righted the chair he had pushed over, and helped him into it. "You will kill me, the both of you," he said.

"Papá, Papá, please, take a breath, calm down," Juana said, pressing her hands, which were always cold, against his cheeks.

The professor looked at me and wheezed again, squeezing his eyes shut. "I'll go get help," Juana said. "Take care of my father." She brushed my hand as she passed me by in a rush.

What happened next would live on in my memory as precisely as the cut of a scalpel for as long as I lived. She was wearing her burnt orange dress, and it would appear in my remembrances as if the sun itself had streaked past me, warming me for a second and then leaving me cold the rest of my life. Through the parlor she ran, then out the door, into the cold winter air.

Then, we heard a scream, the whinnying of a horse, and a sick clatter.

The professor, who sat up suddenly as if he'd been doused with cold water, leapt from his chair, and I followed him outside. The old man ran nimbly, his earlier act utterly abandoned. There, upon the cobbled street, was Juana. The driver of the carriage was hovering over her, swaying from side to side. Her eyes were closed, and her chest did not rise and fall the way it should.

"Her skirts," the driver was saying. "Her skirts. I pulled them down. Her legs are twisted. Don't look, señores, don't look, por el amor de Dios." And then, "I didn't see her, I swear I didn't see her." The horse was nervous and pounding his back legs, making the carriage jolt every so often. The professor scooped Juana up onto his lap, and cried over her in silence. The lamplight near them threw the horse's scarlet shadow over the pair. I closed my eyes against the red of the open wounds on her left cheek, and the streak of mud over her right eye.

I kept silent, too, though it felt as if I were shattering within, piece by jagged piece. I choked and gagged in silence. I held myself about the waist in silence. And later, when the caretaker and the priest came, I found I had nothing to say. Though people had gathered around us, I felt perfectly still. What I wanted most to do was touch her hand, those hands that used to move about so elegantly. But the professor had taken her wrists, and he was kissing them. Each time his head bowed toward her, I took a small step backwards.

They lifted her body, the professor holding her by the shoulders, and started to take Juana inside. I went to follow, wanting to help, when Professor Flores looked up at me.

"Hijo," he said, and shook his head, his eyes as they grazed mine cold and taciturn. Then, he gripped his daughter harder and backed into his house. In this way, Juana and I were parted forever.

Eulalia

My third child, a girl, died shortly after she was born. The doctors placed her in her cradle just before she drew her last breath, and it seems to me I will never recover from that fact, more than any other: there was no one there to hold her little hand and kiss its warmth one more time.

We desire happiness. It is what marks us as different from the beasts that want only full bellies, and one another when the craving strikes them. But happiness is a dictator. It is a domineering god that one has to believe in without seeing. It requires faith, of which I have always had so little.

Happiness. Vaya. One cannot gaze upon the tiny, blessed face of a child one has birthed, then bury that same child in two days, and ever know happiness again.

I cannot say more. What more is there to say?

Tomás

In the end, I was not allowed to attend the funeral. The professor had placed one of his nephews, who was just as big and burly as I, at the entrance to the church. Understanding now that I had lost everything, I gave the key to the bookshop to the nephew, and told him to give it to the professor, please.

It was a week after Juana was buried that an envelope appeared in the mailbox at my mother's house, where I was staying. Inside was the key to the shop, and a letter from the professor.

It is yours now. I do not want it. She loved the store so much. Perhaps as much as she loved you.

That was all that the professor had written, as if he, a man who had made his living with words, could no longer conjure them. I, who had found such joy in word-conjuring myself, knew the feeling. The well of my imagination had gone dry, and whenever I picked up a pen, the name *Juana* was the only thing I could think to write.

CUBA

Q uerida Eulalia,
In regards to the unpleasant conflict in the Caribbean of which we spoke the other day, you should know that I think Cuba will always belong to Spain. How it could it be any other way?

We have come upon a plan to show the Cubans that we will not be moved. A symbolic gesture. I've heard that the people of the Caribbean grow weak before the idea of a party. All seriousness flees their bodies at the sound of music, and the notion of a holiday. And there is no greater holiday than a royal visit.

Additionally, it is the 400th anniversary of Christopher Columbus's discovery of America. In the American city of Chicago, there will be an exposition in honor of that anniversary. Americans being such as they are, things are a bit muddled, they will be celebrating the 401st anniversary, but c'est la vie. The exposition promises to be spectacular.

I think it would be wise if we sent you and Antonio on a trip abroad. You will visit the Columbian Exposition in Chicago, but on the way, stop in Cuba for a bit. For a party, you see. A party will lift spirits, show them that Spain wishes them well, that an Infanta of Spain deems them worthy of her presence.

Some say that Spain is destined to lose all her colonies, that her power is diminishing in the world, that America is a plant that has outgrown its pots, and that its roots are shooting across *the ocean floor in every direction. Spain has had its day, people say, and now the dusk is upon us. I say they are wrong. You, dear sister, are young, and beautiful. You are the face of Spain that the rest of the world needs to see.*

Affectionately yours,

María Cristina, Queen of Spain

1

When Tomás Aragón saw the Infanta Eulalia for the first time, he was in a room that was as dark and damp as a mouth. Of course, he had gazed on her before, during their infancy. He was certain that they played together, since his mother assured him of it. In fact, she assured everyone she met of it, as if the act of passing a silver rattle back and forth with a Spanish princess had left some kind of commendable mark on her son.

On the day Eulalia turned up in his life again, Tomás was curled up like a question mark in the back room of the small bookstore he owned in Burgos, on Calle Pozo Seco. The infanta was in Burgos that cold winter day in 1893 for reasons that remained a mystery, and she stopped at the bookstore at the precise moment Tomás had found a comfortable position at last on an under-stuffed and torn divan that had come with the shop. He had been thinking of Phileas Fogg, and imagining himself in the clouds, with the entire world beneath his basket. It wasn't hard to do. The shop was cold as a crypt, as he imagined being within a cloud might be. Tomás had just allowed himself to fall into that dense whiteness, and his limbs, at last, had settled after a good deal of turning when the little bell on the door of the shop rang. Tomás groaned loudly, hoping the intruder would leave. It was a Saturday afternoon, just before supper, and he had never sold a book at that hour.

Tomás sat up, ran a hand through his hair, tucked the red notebook back into his pocket, since it had fallen out in his sleep, and walked to the front of the shop. Eulalia was standing in the center of the room, her hands held at her waist. She wore a lavender-colored dress with a plain bodice, her sleeves small and lacy. Her blond curls were done up under a little cap, almost like a beret. She'd pulled off her gloves, silver ones, and these were draped over her bare forearm. The little bones of her wrists were exposed. Tomás's voice caught in his throat.

"Su alteza," he said, bowing deeply. With her was a lady-in-waiting—a sallow-skinned woman with dark hair and that distinctive Bourbon nose, which Eulalia had somehow escaped. Her skirt was covered in tiny fabric violets. A man stood near the door, in a waistcoat so black it sparkled. His chest was as wide as the doorway.

Eulalia appraised the shop with the wide blue eyes she was known for. Tomás hadn't quite yet looked her in the eye. The place, he thought, must have seemed shabby to her. Tomás was immediately aware of the balls of dust clinging to the corners, of the trail of mouse droppings near the shelf that held the Latin texts, and the bulging floor directly beneath his feet. Eulalia tapped her foot and her shoe made a clicking sound.

"I can't say I remember you," Eulalia said at last.

"I don't remember you, either," Tomás said, regretting it at once. "I mean to say, not like this—" He was still partly bent over, in an awkward half-bow. "What I mean is that we haven't, not since we were children, seen—"

"Yes, Señor Aragón. I understand perfectly." She smiled, and Tomás felt as if he were in the clouds again, dropping headfirst into that thick white world. "I've been to see your mother. She mentioned you owned a bookstore."

Tomás envisioned the scene at once—his mother, shocked to stillness at the sight of her old charge at the door to the modest farmhouse, grateful to the bone that she swept that morning, as she swept every morning, and glad, too, that the bacalao she'd cooked for dinner the night before had not left too fishy an odor. Amalia would not have been able to help herself—she would pat the infanta's cheeks, comment on how lovely and plump she was, and then tell her about her son's shop near the cathedral, all in one exultant breath.

"May I ask your highness how the visit went?" Tomás asked.

Eulalia paused, and it seemed to Tomás that she was considering her next words carefully. "She showed me her old uniforms, how proud she was of them, of my sister and me. We are passing through Burgos in preparation for a trip abroad," Eulalia offered, referring to her companions for the first time. The lady-in-waiting straightened her spine, as if the infanta's use of the plural pronoun was a sprinkle of holy water in mass—a sudden and surprising blessing. The man, a guard, simply stood near the door, his eyes firmly locked on Tomás's.

Eulalia pivoted to face the store window, cocking her hip to do so. Tomás noticed the gesture, as well as her delicate wrists, the roundness of her hip, pronounced even underneath the voluminous skirt.

"I see you carry the novels of Jules Verne," she said, still facing the window.

"Sí, your highness. All of them."

Eulalia nodded in appreciation. "There are quite a few. Your favorite, Tomás?"

"*Around the World in Eighty Days*, your highness."

"Impossible," she said, sniffing the dry, cold air.

"Excuse me?"

"It is impossible to travel around the world in that short a time," Eulalia said. "I've not yet been to every country, Tomás, but I can assure you the earth is bigger than eighty days' worth of travel."

"I disagree," Tomás said.

"Go on," Eulalia says.

"There's a genius about Verne that many people don't understand," he said, feeling bold. "Perhaps you've not read *Five Weeks in a Balloon?*" Bolder still. "Africa will be explored in such a way, your highness, you can bet on it."

"I don't bet, Tomás and I don't read Jules Verne for the plausibility." Her body started to turn away from Tomás in tiny degrees, towards the exit. He could sense it, the way one sometimes feels the lightest tremors from the earth—deep in his core.

"Nor do I," Tomás said. "I read him for the possibilities."

Eulalia stopped turning. "*Twenty Thousand Leagues Under the Sea*," she said. "My predilection. And as I am going on a sea voyage in a matter of days, I am hopeful that Verne's 'possibilities,' as you say, are actually impossibilities."

"You should be safe from le poulpe, your highness," Tomás said, risking a grin.

The payoff for his insolence and badly accented French was another smile from Eulalia, and a request. "I'd like to purchase a copy of *A Floating City*. Romances aboard ships are my favorite possibilities," she said.

Tomás packed the book in plain white paper, taking one last look at the embossed cover before tying the package with string. While he worked, Eulalia and her lady-in-waiting scanned the shelves, their long skirts brushing the floor and gathering dust at the hems. The guard watched Tomás closely, and as soon as he tied the string, the guard was at the counter, snatching the book from Tomás's hand, and putting money down on the counter for it.

"Su alteza," the guard said, surprising Tomás with the soft tenor of his voice. It was the kind of voice that carried through a room easily, the way a stringed instrument fills a space.

"Ah," Eulalia said, taking the book from her guard. "So, Tomás, how much of the world have you seen?" she asked.

"Not much. I have been to Paris once, for the World's Fair." He had been hoping to catch a glimpse of the future, but the place had been overrun by con artists selling pills promising to make women attractive and men muscular, and a recreated village of Africans, who had been brought over on ships and made to stand about in scant clothing. Tomás had seen nothing futuristic, nothing of Verne's imagination, in that place. If anything, it all felt as if progress had halted, leaving an open gill through which frauds could crawl through.

"So you saw the Eiffel Tower?" she asked.

"And climbed to the platform. That, I'll admit, was incredible," Tomás said, remembering how shocked he had been at the height of it, of the Seine like a glossy ribbon dropped by a girl, and the gray buildings so small, like petit-fours laid out at a banquet.

"I read that the Americans brought sharpshooters to the exposition," the lady-in-waiting said, speaking aloud for the first time. "There was a woman among them. How ridiculous! Perhaps we shall see her in Chicago," she added.

The intrusion cast a pall over Eulalia's face. It was a particular look cultivated by royalty around the world, perfected, Tomás thought, so that their dour images on coins and bills might seem all the more accurate.

"I should like to learn to shoot a rifle," Eulalia said after a moment, and smiled as her lady-in-waiting's mouth opened with a soft click of tongue against lips. "I would shoot a pomegranate off the top of your head, Rafael, what do you think?" she said to her guard, who nodded, as if accepting the dark fruit's weight already.

So the princess can be cruel, Tomás thought, intrigued.

The cathedral bells rang, marking the five o'clock hour.

"Closing time, then," Eulalia said loudly over the din. Tomás silently cursed the bells.

"Thank you for dropping by, your highness," he said, bowing once more.

Then, Eulalia turned to her lady-in-waiting and the guard. "Leave us," she commanded. Her guard protested, and whispered in Eulalia's ear. She shook her head, and then, reluctantly, her companions departed. The lady-in-waiting produced an umbrella from somewhere within her heavy skirt, and, popping it open, covered her head from the light rain that had begun to fall. The bells ceased their pealing as they left, but Tomás's ears rang with leftover noise.

"I shall be quick, Tomás," Eulalia began, searching her voluminous skirt and producing from a hidden pocket in the folds of raw silk sheaves of paper bound with a thin blue ribbon. "Your mother tells me that Pedro Medina is a university friend of yours."

"He is."

"Would you please deliver these pages to him? It would be my greatest wish to see them in print."

She gripped the pages tightly, as if there was a great wind roaring past, when in reality, the stillness of the bookshop sealed them in as if they were both sitting in a pot with the lid on.

"I will see him soon," Tomás said, and without thinking, reached for her hand and held it, as if to reassure her. Eulalia took a deep breath, then slid her hand away from his.

"Thank you," she said. "We are greatly pleased. Tell Señor Medina that he can send whatever money he deems it worth to your mother. I am glad to know that she hasn't remarried, so the money will be truly hers. She may do with it whatever she pleases. And I'd ask you not to mention it to anyone." Then, she unlocked the door, and stepped out.

2

He carried Eulalia's manuscript under his arm, and walked over to a café he knew would still be open. There, he ordered a soup and a coffee. He ate the food, and only when he was done, did he begin to read at last.

The manuscript was in English, which surprised him for a moment. At first, he thought it was merely a diary, the musings of a princess, interesting only because of their authorship. But soon, it steered toward something else, a sense of an audience, hungry for her revelations. Tomás plunged in, and soon was with Eulalia through her childhood in Paris, felt himself growing angry at her mother and eldest sister, both so stern and unyielding. There, every once in a while, was a mention of his mother, Amalia. Tomás would thrill a little at seeing her name, anticipation running through him each time, each time thinking that perhaps he would be among her memories, too. But that made no sense and he knew it. Eulalia did not remember Tomás, in the same way that he could never remember her.

It was a brazen book. On several occasions, Tomás would read a sentence, then read it again, disbelievingly. He would raise his head, look from side to side, the way one does when about to engage in gossip in public, and make sure no one could read over his shoulder. When a waiter approached to refresh his cup, Tomás laid his hands over the manuscript. Beneath the boldness of the book, some other sentiment rumbled. It was as if Eulalia no longer wanted to think in terms of duties, of promises kept. He wondered whether if, in every room she entered, she first sought the location of the door, longing for the space beyond it. Indignation, righteousness, and an independent streak that Tomás had never encountered in a woman pulsed along the sentences. It seemed to him that Eulalia had been kept in beautiful rooms for too long.

He read as much as he could before the the café began to empty out. The voices of the remaining customers sounded hollow, the way voices often sound in dreams. Eulalia's voice, however, felt resonant in Tomás's ear, as if he could hear her whispering her life's story to him.

Soon, the café owner came out with his broom to sweep the floor, eyed Tomás as he got closer and closer, and finally, swept over his feet. Taking his cue, Tomás put the pages together, and left money on the table. He tried not to think of an old superstition Amalia always repeated, about not allowing anyone to pass a broom over your feet, or else you'll never marry. If she believed in such things, Tomás thought, he could imagine Eulalia passing a broom over her own feet. There had been a sentence in the book about his mother's "sad" marriage, and it had struck Tomás as curious and, ultimately, wrong. Perhaps Eulalia had misremembered. His mother was sad, yes, but that was because she was a widow now. To tell the truth, Tomás also felt sad most of the time, a secret sadness that crept up on him like a shadow, and when he cast a light on it, he would find memories of both Juana and his father, Rubén, the source of the darkness.

Tomás kept a brisk pace, the infanta's manuscript under his coat, careful when stepping over cobbled parts of the road, and seeing absolutely no one. He took a left turn down Calle Paloma, and shortly thereafter, climbed the steps of a bright, white house with black gates and a bicycle leaning against the wall. Pink roses, fragrant and sturdy, brushed his cheek as he went past them. Tomás rang the bell.

"Mr. Aragón, we weren't expecting you," said the woman at the door in English.

"Good evening, Mrs. Medina."

The woman, dressed in burgundy, her hair loosened from its usual bun, seemed halfway toward undress, as if Tomás had interrupted her bedtime routine. He glanced at his pocket watch. Seven fifteen.

"Pedro, my darling," she called into the house, then gestured for Tomás to enter.

Pedro Medina and Tomás had met at the university. They were both scholarship students and shared a passion for Jules Verne. They ferreted out other common interests during a long night of drinking after midterm exams one term and became fast friends. When Juana died, it was Pedro who slept over in Tomás's apartment, who filled his wineglass and who covered his face when Tomás would begin to weep, so that both men might keep their dignity. Like Tomás, Pedro had left the university early. He had gone to work with a publisher in Madrid—Ediciones Garza. His father had been a tailor, and Pedro had learned some of that trade. "What's the difference between sewing a sleeve to a suit and sewing pages together?" he'd asked Tomás once.

"I've no idea," Tomás said. His socks had holes in them so often his toes had blisters where his feet rubbed against his shoes.

"Neither do I," Pedro said, laughing. "But I intend to find out!" He proved to be a keen reader with a good eye for the editorial side of things. The work took him to America, to New York City, specifically, to seek out American novels that might be translated into Spanish. This was where he'd met Eliza Jane Hartwell, the daughter of a publisher, Sylvester Hartwell. Pedro had married Eliza Jane and brought her to Madrid, where she refused to learn Spanish and spent her father's money on parties and new gowns each month. When Pedro returned to Burgos years later, he showed up at the bookshop in a tailored suit. The first thing he'd done was hand Tomás an Ediciones Medina card with his name on it and the words Editor in Chief underneath. Being married to the daughter of a New York City publisher brought with it some privileges.

Pedro descended the stairs in pajamas, a cigar in his hand. "Mi hermano," he asked, "what brings you here?"

"The Infanta Eulalia came by the bookstore today," Tomás said without preamble.

"What was that?" Eliza Jane asked. She supported the royal families in spirit, thinking herself like them in some way. "Something about one of the princesses?"

"Her Spanish is improving," Tomás said to Pedro.

Pedro clapped Tomás on the back and laughed, sending a plume of smoke in the air. "No, she merely knows when the talk turns to money." Eliza Jane stared at them with pretty, wide eyes, her hands laced together just under her breasts, resting on her belly.

"You're making fun, I can tell," she said, patting her stomach as if warning, *You have your confidant, I shall have mine.* Eliza Jane excused herself with a terse "goodnight," or so it seemed to Tomás. English sounded terse in his ears no matter how well he had learned it. Even so, Tomás did not know how Pedro could withstand it, sleeping with a woman who always seemed as if she was annoyed every time she opened her mouth to say something. But she reappeared a few short minutes later, after Pedro and Tomás had settled down in the living room with cigars in hand. Her hair was up again, and an ivory mantilla rested across her shoulders.

Tomás had never known a woman like Eliza Jane, so eager to join the conversations of men, unwilling to leave them to their discussions. Pedro did nothing to dissuade her, blaming her strange manners on her American upbringing. "In New York City, the women smoke cigars," he said, puffing two perfect O's into the air. "They argue with their husbands in the street, in plain daylight, for everyone to see."

"So you said something about Eulalia Bourbon de Orléans," Eliza Jane said. Her belly bounced a few times. She patted herself and readjusted her body in the chair. "She's quite the independent woman, the infanta," Eliza Jane went on. "You know," she said, leaning forward as far as her body would allow, "she only married that cousin of hers out of guilt. Eulalia, as everyone who knows anything at all can attest, does not love him," Eliza Jane said. "But her two little boys . . . at least she has them."

Eliza Jane hiccoughed into her hand and glanced down with furrowed brow at her belly once more, as if chastising the little being within for reducing her to so many small crude confirmations of her humanity. There was no room for such things—belching and stretching, the cracking of knuckles and the grumbling of stomachs—at certain levels of society, as if people of a particular class had evolved beyond their bodies.

When she spoke again, it was in a voice strained and interrupted by the gases and perturbations within, which cut off her words and made her blush. "She was once in love with King Carlos of Portugal. Everyone knows that. What a match they would have made! Instead, she's stuck with that first cousin of hers for a husband."

"Eliza Jane," Pedro said, but she continued.

"I've a friend in Lisbon, her name is Anamary, isn't that lovely? I like that name very much, Pedro, if we have a girl. Anamary, bless her, married a Portuguese shipbuilder, and has come to know, quite well I might add, the lady-in-waiting to Queen Amélie—"

"Por Dios, Eliza Jane!" Pedro said at last, crushing his half-smoked cigar in a dessert plate at hand.

Eliza Jane smiled at her husband, revealing very white teeth that were not crooked at all. It was a smile that said "I don't like you very much," and it stripped the heat out of Pedro's voice, so that when he spoke again, it was to say, "Our friend here has had a long day, and a story of his own to tell, you understand, amor?"

"Of course," Eliza Jane said. "Perhaps I should cut to the

chase. Eulalia is false to every man she meets, be he king, duke, cousin, or husband." Eliza Jane looked at Tomás and smiled that indelicate smile again. Then, excusing herself, she rose with a groan and left the men to their cigars gone cold.

"My friend—" Tomás started to say.

"Say nothing. She'll grow accustomed to our ways. And soon our little Pedrito will be here and Eliza Jane will soften, I know it."

"What if it's a tiny female tyrant, my friend?" Tomás asked.

"All women are tyrants." Pedro did not seem to be joking. A long line of sweat collected at his hairline. "So, what impulse brought Eulalia to Calle Pozo Seco tonight?" Pedro asked, turning the conversation in the direction Tomás had hoped.

"I think my mother sent her."

Pedro laughed out loud, as if this was the funniest thing he had heard all day.

Tomás pulled the manuscript out of his pocket. "She brought this and asked me to pass it on to you. I think my mother tipped her off about our friendship."

Pedro placed a pair of thin spectacles on his nose. His eyes narrowed over the script, which was beautiful and swirling. Tomás imagined Eulalia bent over the pages in moments of privacy.

Tomás waited as Pedro thumbed through the pages. Above them, gaudy cherubs flitted around the cut-crystal chandelier. There were clouds and bursts of sunlight, and bluebirds done in imperfect strokes.

"It's atrocious," Pedro said.

"Her writing?"

"No, the mural," Pedro said, noticing where Tomás's gaze had rested. "It came with the house. Eliza Jane likes it."

"I like it," Tomás said truthfully, thinking of his own home and shop, how empty and gutted they seemed, like bones without flesh.

"You think Eulalia sleeps under a ceiling like that?" Pedro asked, chuckling. He stood and poured some port into two glasses.

"God knows." Tomás sipped his drink.

Serious again, Pedro held the manuscript with both hands, testing its weight. Tomás could almost see the ciphers running in his mind.

"It's an autobiography?" Pedro asked, "My English is not so good."

"Something like it," Tomás said. "It reads like a confession."

"Confessions are sacred."

Tomás shrugged. He went to mass out of habit, not because it moved him in any particular way. "I think it's very interesting. The things she writes about her mother, how cold and distant she was, about her sister, that brute. It seems very modern to me." Tomás did not mention Eulalia's relationship to Carlos Braganza, now the king of Portugal, nor say a word about her tryst in his mother's house. When he'd read about it, his arms and legs had grown cold, the way one feels when suddenly afraid, the way he remembered feeling the night Juana died. He wondered if Eulalia and Carlos had come together in his bed, and he realized, counting backwards, that he must have been away on a school trip at the time. Let Pedro read all of that for himself, he thought.

"This could spell trouble," Pedro murmured to himself. "Does anyone else know you have it?" Pedro's hands crinkled the pages a little.

"Not that I've told."

"Let's keep it that way, then. The palace has eyes and ears everywhere. Only the one copy?"

"As far as I know," Tomás said. "If it's published, the logical conclusion for the infanta is—"

"Unclear? Would Alfonso send her away? Strip her of her titles? I am not sure. Royal intrigues are Eliza Jane's area of interest, and Eulalia is so far down the line of succession . . . I'll need more time with it, you understand?"

"Of course." Both men took long sips from their glasses. "I've been thinking," Tomás said after a while, "about closing the bookshop." He leaned his elbows on his knees as he spoke.

Pedro looked alarmed, like an animal caught in a trap. "I don't have a position for you at the publishing—"

"No, that's not what I meant," he said, waving him off.

Tomás glanced up again at the painting, then down at the gilded flowers that decorated the handrails on the staircase, and finally rested his gaze upon Pedro's slippers of dark green velvet. There were American dollars behind all of it, the gifts of Eliza Jane's publisher father plentiful. *America, America*, he thought, remembering that nearly a third of Verne's novels were set there. The man had been fascinated with America, a world between worlds, neither old nor new anymore. The mysteries of the sea, the bottomless, cavernous depths of the earth below, all of these things echoed America for Verne.

"I must go to a place were there are possibilities, Pedro. Where a person can hope for more than a second turn at his mother's breast as a baby, and more than a ratty shop on a shabby street," Tomás said. "I want to go where the women shout at their husbands in the street. I want a woman like *that*, Pedro. And a new language to fill my mouth, and something . . . something other than this."

Pedro had been blinking rapidly the whole time, then surprised Tomás by clasping his left knee hard and giving it a shake.

"Absolutely, Tomás. I've always thought that a man has to travel to know himself. Visit America. I can recommend it with all my heart," he said, putting his hand over his heart as if it beat too strongly.

"Will there be money in it? The manuscript, I mean?" Tomás asked. He remembered what Eulalia had said, that his mother could keep the proceeds for herself. Perhaps there would be enough, he thought, for a trip abroad for himself.

Before Pedro could answer, Eliza Jane returned as if the mere mention of her home country had drawn her in like an overheard whisper. "What did I miss?" she asked, and Pedro told her that she'd missed nothing of import, tucking the manuscript between his thigh and the seat cushion.

"In truth," Tomás said, "I was telling Pedro that I'd like to visit America." Eliza Jane's eyes lit up, the way some people's eyes do when a thing they love a great deal enters the conversation. It is almost as if a full theater appears before them, a podium rises from nothing at their feet, and they are off, declaiming their passions. One can't help but sit in thrall of such people, and Eliza Jane was one of them.

Tomás left Pedro's home later that evening, after being regaled for over an hour by Eliza Jane's descriptions of America. She told him of winters so bitter that the locks of doors froze; of buildings in New York City that seemed to tear into the very firmament, they were so tall; of the library in that same city, with shelves so tightly packed that not even bookworms could sneak in between the pages; of the mountains in the Hudson Valley, gray and jagged; and of the clog of smoke and clouds that encircled cities like Pittsburgh, so dark that when Eliza Jane stayed there in the summers as a child, she would awaken with soot in her blond hair, "and so I knew what I would look like as a brunette. Hideous, is the answer if you're wondering"; she spoke at length of her uncle who had died in the Civil War, how her mother always told her about the way his body had come home wrapped in muslin, his left hand missing, which the doctors in Alabama had removed, "like butchers, Mr. Aragón"; she described her nursemaid, who was "black as sin," but golden-hearted, and the maid's little boy named Raleigh for the city in which he'd been born, and how he had been Eliza Jane's companion and how he, too, died in the war, fighting on the side of the North, "so brave-looking in his blue uniform." In the end, Eliza Jane had painted a portrait of an America so vast and complex that Tomás's resolve faltered for a moment.

At the door, Pedro had said in a whisper, "Come back next week and we'll talk about the Infanta's book. But don't tell anyone about it." Then he closed the door with a heavy click, and Tomás went home.

3

It being a Sunday, Tomás decided to spend the day with his mother. In the stillness of the morning, without a single man in the fields, the view of the house surrounded by the growing wheat appeared like a postcard. Amalia had left her broom outside, the handle painted bright red, leaning against the yellow stone of the house. The look of it all prepared him for a particular scene inside—perhaps his mother would be rolling dough for bread, or, still in her slippers and robe, she might be sitting at the kitchen table and saying a rosary, her eyes closed and her lips parting and closing, parting and closing like a fish.

Instead, Tomás found a quiet house, the curtains still drawn, and the kitchen sink dry. "Mamá," he called out, worry coursing through him like alcohol, making him stumble as he turned the tight corners of the house.

It is a particular trait to the Spanish that their minds turn instantly to tragedy. Tomás had already killed his mother in his imagination. In an instant, he had pictured her dead of the same miserable heart failure that took his father. In the next, he imagined her drowned, pale and waterlogged, in the bathtub. He did not consider that she was, perhaps, soundly asleep.

"¡Mamá!" Tomás called out again, reaching her door and pushing it forward with all his strength.

There he saw it, a pale arm hanging over the side of the bed, the fingers curled so that the hand resembled an open shell, soft and pink and alive inside. The breath that filled the room in sound and scent was like a young animal's, milky and moist. The blankets were wrapped around legs still in their gray stockings, and the toes, hidden, twitched when Tomás took a step forward. The figure on the bed, who Tomás was now sure was not his mother, roused a little. Her head turned toward the light of the door, eyes still closed. There, sleeping like a baby, was Eulalia Bourbon.

"¡Por Dios!" a voice behind Tomás whispered.

He turned at once, and saw his mother standing behind him, dressed as if she had been up for hours. "How? I mean . . . how is it possible . . . "

"Come away from the room and close the door. She needs her rest, la pobrecita," Amalia said, dragging him away from the entrance to her room by the elbow, pinching his skin and bringing him back to the moment. She pushed him toward a chair in the kitchen and immediately began to make hot cocoa.

Tomás said nothing as his mother grated a chunk of chocolate into a pot. The flesh on her arms wriggled with the effort, and his mind drifted to the slender limb he had seen peeking out from under the blankets on his mother's bed.

Tomás did not say a word until he had half of the warm drink in his stomach. "Why is she here?"

"Speak up," Amalia said, her hand on her hip. She was testy with him, as if his intrusion had been premeditated. It reminded Tomás of his seventh year of life, when he found he suddenly could not sleep in a room without his parents. He would wail upright in bed, and his mother would stand in the center of his room, darkness all around, and point a finger at him. "I swear, Tomás, if you don't lie down this instant—" and he would cry, "But I can't, Mamá! I need you!" He used to imagine a little pale boy hiding under his bed, calling his name in the dark. Amalia would not hear of it. She would seem like a terrible monster in those moments, cloaked in shadow. She was a genie, a dragon, death itself, and yet his mother whom he loved more than anything else in the whole world. In the morning, her eyes would blink over dark circles, and it always seemed to Tomás that she held her tiredness against him.

"Why is Eulalia Bourbon de Orléans sleeping in your bed?" Tomás asked, his thoughts turning to Eulalia's descriptions of Carlos Braganza again.

"You ask as if I've committed some sin allowing the poor girl to stay here on occasion," Amalia said, sitting down. "Bah!" She stood, then sat again, then stood, like a windup toy.

"What are you doing?"

"You've made me nervous," she said, clutching her apron.

"Sit, Mamá. I apologize." Tomás thought of his hopes to leave for America soon. How many more chances would he have to sit with his mother in her kitchen again? He felt his whole body soften, and he touched his mother's thick wrist. "Sit, please."

She did, folding her hands in her lap.

"She came to the shop yesterday," Tomás said.

A smile rose like a sunrise on Amalia's face, illuminating her countenance at once. "I wasn't sure she would visit you."

"She did . . . And she came with a woman and a man. I'm wondering where they are? Did they sleep in the barn?" Was the giant man nestled in the hay, next to the quarterhorse named Fulano?

"No, she was able to convince them to stay in town," Amalia said, and the comical image of horse and man vanished from Tomás's mind at once. "Pobrecita," she said, sighing again.

Tomás bit his tongue. Quite literally, he bit down on his

tongue to stop himself from saying what he wanted to say. No matter how many times his mother pronounced Eulalia "la pobrecita," there was no arguing that there was nothing "poor" at all about the woman. Pobrecita, pobrecita, and all along, the hem on his mother's dress was undone, and Tomás counted two mouseholes in the kitchen alone.

"Why is she here?"

"Her husband, that Antonio de Orléans."

"What about him?"

Amalia glanced behind her,then leaned forward a bit. "Not just him. Lots of little things. She's spent."

"Pobrecita, is that right?"

"Don't be so hard-hearted," Amalia said. Tomás wondered if, when his mother looked at the infanta, if she saw the adult woman Eulalia, and not the chubby, squalling baby. *How does my mother see me?* he thought. *Does she see a man?* A mother's heart, Tomás decided, was a complex and formidable thing, able to shape the story of a person's life in such ways that made them more than what they really were.

"He embarrassed her during dinner the other day by questioning the cut of her dress. They were hosting the Duke of Austria in the Palacio, so everyone that mattered was there. Antonio kept asking her to hand him bread, as if she were a footman. Finally, he told everyone within earshot over dessert that she read too many books and would soon have to hide her beauty behind bifocals. She comes here sometimes, to get away from all of that," his mother said.

Tomás had been raised with similar stories—of the palace nursery built next to an aviary, of the spare nodriza, who made an enemy of Amalia, blaming her for every little thing, of Eulalia's blue eyes, the queen's infrequent visits, the fear that the Carlists were taking over casting a pall over their days. Instead of fairy tales, Tomás was told tales of palace life, so vivid in his mother's memories that sometimes, it felt to him as if the walls of their small house were disappearing, replacing themselves with gilded plasterwork and worn tapestries.

They heard a cough coming from the bedroom. Two, three in succession, and then a light sneeze. Amalia stopped talking and leapt from her chair to attend to the infanta.

He waited in the kitchen a long time, listening to his mother chatting effusively with Eulalia, but never hearing Eulalia's voice in response. To pass the time, Tomás made a list for himself. Back at the university, one of his teachers had insisted that the students make lists at the start of each seminar session. "Write down what you hope to learn, you young men. Write it down, so that you might know the tessellation of your own minds!" he would say, and hop up and down a little as he spoke. He was a favorite among the students, and they made up their lists diligently.

It was a habit Tomás had grown fond of, and in the bookshop there was evidence of the routine. He had lists of books he hoped to acquire, and of ads he hoped to place, of stories he hoped to write when he found the courage again, and bills he hoped to pay if enough customers came to the shop. Hope. He had so much of it sometimes it spilled over in large messes that were hard to clean up later when reality set in.

The list he made now was meant to guide him during his travels. He searched the drawers in the kitchen for some paper in order to make his list, and found none at all. How strange it was to live in a world without much paper in it, he thought, when his had so much. Tomás drew out his red notebook from his pocket. It was a bent thing now, and the pages inside were thick with ink. Shortly after Juana had died, he had written down everything he felt was true about her in that notebook. It was the only story that belonged in the notebook, he told himself. Writing it down had helped, and after he did so, he did not think of her quite so often. When he did, the memories were gauzy and lit from behind somehow, and he never reread the pages, though he carried them with him at all times.

But now, the making of a list seemed very important, as if it might contain the hopes to end all hopes, and he turned to the last page of the notebook quickly, not wanting to see any of what he had written before.

At the top of the page Tomás wrote, "Onward," and beneath that, his first objective:

1) Go to America.

He overheard his mother saying, "You've gotten so thin. I have some condensed milk I bought for emergencies. It's fattening and will fill you back up again nicely." He laughed softly at his mother's insistence, and wrote:

2) Eat well.

He would like to drink champagne out of a flute and tinkle it lightly against another's. He imagined who that other might be, and he saw her at once—a woman whose laughter pealed like a bell, the kind who throws her head back and reveals white teeth and a quivering pink tongue, who pretends shock when Tomás tries to be scandalous, who might lean her head on his chest, or take his hand in a dark theater.

3) Fall in love again.

He felt a lump in his throat. He crossed it out, then wrote it again. Tomás leaned back against his chair. A slash of sunlight grew stronger by the moment, warming his hands as they held pen and paper. It felt like a blessing. At least, Juana would have thought so, and he paused to cross himself. Sometimes, he would catch a particular shade of orange out of the corner of his eye, and he would want to fall upon the ground, wherever he was, and weep. His mother's voice bubbled up again, "Your books, dear. Where should I pack these?" and at last he heard Eulalia speak.

"Thank you. At the top of my bag. I want to be able to reach them." Her voice was huskier than it had sounded at the shop.

"These books," Amalia said. "How my son loved reading these books."

Tomás thought of the many hours he had spent reading in the small house. At the kitchen table, he would read passages to his parents. His father would listen and laugh at the right places, but his mother, tired from the housework, from Tomás's chatter all day, would say, "Ay, mi hijo, read to yourself for a while," and he would feel as if she had clapped a hand over his mouth. But Rubén's eyes would drift to the ceiling, as if he, too, were being transported. Once, Tomás read to him a story about Christopher Columbus discovering Cuba, and Rubén had put his hands over his face and wept, as if he could feel the melting warmth of the tropics, see the sheer gold of the sunsets there. The memory of that night was one Tomás thought of often, and it drove him to write one last mandate for himself.

4) Do the impossible.

Soon, Amalia appeared in the doorway to the kitchen, with Eulalia right behind her. The infanta was in a cream-colored dress of simple cotton, though the shawl around her shoulders was embroidered with silver dandelions, their tufts floating away in pearls. It was the kind of thing one might hang on a wall like a tapestry, and yet it graced Eulalia's shoulders like a queen's robe. The silver made her blue eyes sparkle.

Tomás couldn't help it. His breath caught in his throat again.

"Buenos días, Tomás," she said.

Tomás rose. "Su alteza," he said, offering a small bow.

"Writing so early in the morning?" she asked. "Your mother has told me you were a bit of a scribbler."

"A scribbler, yes," he said, swallowing thickly. His mouth suddenly tasted as if he had been hoarding coins in his cheeks. *What of your own scribbling?* he wanted to ask.

"Sit, sit," Amalia urged Eulalia, and she took a seat beside Tomás, who closed the notebook, shoving the thing into his pocket.

"Not a viable story, then?" she asked.

"It's nothing."

The three of them ate breakfast in silence. Between swallows, they all spoke at once:

"So, tell me about—"

"Your mother says—"

"How are the eggs?"

Then they were quiet again.

"Tell you about what?" Eulalia asked.

"America. You said yesterday you would be going there. I'd like to go myself," Tomás said. "Someday."

Eulalia put down her fork. "I'll be going there for the Columbian Exposition in Chicago. And to some other places in the Caribbean. Cuba. Puerto Rico. I'll be leaving in two weeks."

"Is it safe?" Amalia asked.

"America? Safe as houses, as they say in England," Eulalia said.

Tomás thought of the house they were in, how old it was, how the stones in the walls were as big as skulls, and how the lead windows, bubbling and warped, were thick as bone. He thought, too, of what he knew of the Caribbean. Revolution, war, chaos. He could not picture Eulalia there, in the midst of it.

"You'll be going by yourself?" Tomás asked.

Something darkened Eulalia's expression, but it flitted away like a shadow. "Of course not," she said. A tight smile. "Antonio will come with me. And other members of the court. We will be a small party, to be sure. This was delicious, Ama," she said, changing the subject. She dabbed her lips with a napkin. "I must be going, however."

Amalia put her hands on Eulalia's cheeks, her eyes welling up with tears. Eulalia relaxed, her spine curving a bit, so that she shed some of that regal posture and looked for a moment like any woman on earth.

"Thank you for breakfast," she said, rising, and they all stood with her. She kissed Amalia's cheeks and then turned to Tomás. "Tomás," she said, her lips parted, her eyes wide. He wondered why she didn't just ask about her book, whether he had delivered it. The question died on her tongue, but still she looked at him.

There was a knock at the door and Amalia rushed to answer it. Eulalia and Tomás were left alone in the warm kitchen.

"Might I ask you a question?" Tomás ventured, and Eulalia nodded. "The book. Why did you write it?"

She was very still at first, deciding, it seemed to Tomás, whether she wanted to answer the question, or whether she trusted him with her response. "It wasn't a book, not a first. Just a thing I did to pass the time, to try to rid my mind of memories that seemed too heavy, holding me down when what I wanted to do most was float."

Tomás nodded, and went on, "I don't mean to suggest anything by this, but sharing such memories, su alteza, is—" he struggled with what to say next. "It is courageous." Tomás wasn't sure if that was exactly what he wanted to say. He'd wanted to warn her, though he suspected that whatever consequence came from publishing the book, Eulalia would face it, perhaps even delight in it, if it gave her more freedom.

Eulalia folded her hands on the table. "I accept your concern, Tomás, because you are something like a brother to me. You must know that what I may have lacked in regal grace, as my eldest sister María Isabel often reminded me, I have made up for in moral courage, as you say. I do not mean this as any kind of excuse, intellectualization, or defense. What it strives to be is a statement of fact, that this book is a testimony of my own experience as a member of the Spanish royal family, of my own sense of what constitutes love, and my own untrammeled view of the history of my life, which others have been so quick to write for me from the moment I was served on a platter for Spain's nobility to feast on." Eulalia took a deep breath. "So, have you approached your friend, the publisher?"

"It's done, your highness. We should know more about it in a week," Tomás said.

Eulalia sighed and mouthed the words *thank you.*

She turned to leave, but he reached out and held her wrist lightly. She stared at him, her mouth open.

"My apologies," he said, withdrawing his hand. "I was just, just wondering something about—"

"Go on," she said, holding her wrist in her hand as if he had injured her.

"Why is the book in English?"

Eulalia pursed her lips, and then smiled. "Not many in Spain can read it."

"I can," he said.

Her eyes widened for a fraction of a moment. He had wanted her to know that he had read the book without having to say it.

"Can you?" she asked. She seemed to consider how that changed things, that Tomás had read the book. "Well," she said, "you may write me here, in English if you'd like, should you have news." She drew out a card with an address in Madrid from her purse and handed it to him. She left him there, twirling it in his fingers.

Watching her go, Tomás could feel the pulse in his wrist, in his fingertips, and at his throat.

Amalia escorted Eulalia out the front door, where her guard

was waiting. Tomás watched as his mother cleaned up the kitchen, sighing every so often as she went.

Hanging in the Museo del Arte in Madrid, there is a portrait of his mother and the Infantas Paz and Eulalia on her lap. In it, Amalia's face is bent towards Eulalia, her mouth soft and open. The painting is called *La Nodriza*, and her name isn't anywhere on it, or on the description on the little white card beside it. His parents had taken him to see the portrait when he was young, and they had held one another before it, and Amalia had wept. Then, they were asked to leave by one of the guards, who must have seen their worn clothes, their dirt-caked shoes, and wondered what they were up to.

Tomás often thought of that portrait. He thought of her in her youth answering an advertisement that would lead her to Madrid, to live in a kind of wealth she could not have imagined. That one choice—to apply or not to apply—had sent their lives on a course that led to this moment.

Tomás wondered what the decisive choice in his life would be. Was it when he first let Juana into the shop? Or was it when he delayed her that Monday morning with a kiss that lingered too long? What if he hadn't? Perhaps the carriage would have rolled down the street in her wake instead, her hair unmussed. Or perhaps he was now on the cusp of such a decision. The important choice. The one that changed everything. Tomás took the notebook out from his pocket and opened it over his thigh.

Amalia had been watching him, deep in his thoughts. "Mi hijo, you're getting too emotional. Eulalia's visits always do that to me, too. Sit, sit. I'll make you some broth." Then, Amalia, who treated every calamity with food, got to work.

4

Tomás spent the next few days scouring the newspaper for mentions of America. An ad by the Pinkerton National Detective Agency caught his attention. They sought big men, men like Tomás, to join their forces. "Built like a Bear?" the ad read. "Then Join the Pinkerton Men!" An eye looked out from the center of the advertisement, and beneath it were the words, "We never sleep." The address was in Pittsburgh, and Tomás remembered that Eliza Jane had mentioned the place. He tore out the advertisement and plotted his letter of interest.

He was interrupted by a soft, fluttering sound. A handwritten note from Pedro slipped into the mail slot at the shop. Tomás opened the door and saw a boy in shorts running down the street, the message now delivered and his job done. *Come as soon as you can. Quiet about the book, yes?* Tomás refolded the note and put it in his pocket.

It was a busy day at the shop, as Tomás had expected it to be. Verne's *The Carpathian Castle* has just been published in France, and customers had been coming in all day to buy their copies, a full stock of which he had ordered in advance. He had not had a chance to read much of it himself, but Tomás had skipped forward to the end, a habit he had had since childhood, and slowly, ponderously because his French was not that good, thrilled at Verne's technological imaginings again—a projected image of a ghost, paired with an eerie phonograph recording! More than once he thought—*how wonderful it is to be alive in 1893, where such ideas can live.*

By the end of the day, Tomás had only two copies left, and one of those he kept for himself. He locked up the shop, and made his way to Pedro's house.

Pedro himself opened the door. "Hello, friend," he said. His face was flushed, there was a nearly empty glass of port wine in his hand, while Eulalia's manuscript was tucked under his arm, the pages folded here and there, his notes on the margins in black ink.

Tomás followed him in, asking after Eliza Jane's health. "She's fine. Asleep. The damn woman found the manuscript in my locked desk. My locked desk, Tomás, which she unlocked without permission!" he said, waving a finger in the air as if he could slice the atmosphere with it. "She read it and I've had to fight her all week about keeping quiet."

"I can hear you," Eliza Jane called out from another room, and she waddled in, her own cheeks flushed, too. "Hello, Tomás. Your mother is about to become a very rich woman," she said.

"Or a very imprisoned one," Pedro replied. "Sit, sit," he urged.

"What's going on?" Tomás asked.

"This thing is a national embarrassment," Pedro said, waving the manuscript around. "Why didn't you tell me what this was?"

"You're exaggerating," Tomás said.

"It's very good. A revelatory look at a royal upbringing," Eliza Jane added. "We'll need to translate it into Spanish, of course. Maybe Portuguese, too. Certainly, Germany might—"

"She accuses her mother of infidelities, her sister of emotional abuse. Need I remind you her mother was the queen? That it implies that King Alfonso himself was a bastard? That she was unmarried when she slept with Carlos Braganza? That she seems to think religion is merely a superstition? That the Carlists are just slavering arthropods?" Pedro trembled as he spoke. "I can't publish this in Europe, Tomás! Nobody could."

"It only confirms the rumors everyone has already heard," Eliza Jane said, drumming her fingers on her belly.

"Not in print, for Christ's sake. I could go to prison for slander. More likely, Eulalia will be kicked out of the country," Pedro said.

Eliza Jane sighed. "This is why we shrugged off kings and queens one hundred years ago."

"She proclaims that Spain is destined to lose all of its colonies," Pedro said. "That's treasonous. What kind of princess is this?"

"She's Eulalia. She has always been this way. At least my mother says—" Tomás began to say.

"She sounds like an American," Eliza Jane put in, ignoring Tomás, her mouth tight around a grin she was trying to control.

"It's the gossip that you love," Pedro said viciously, then pulled the manuscript out, bent over, and spread the pages one by one on the carpet. The pair ignored Tomás, as if the manuscript had come to them of its own accord. Pedro walked around and around the pages on the floor, running his hands through his hair.

"We should publish!" Eliza Jane said, stamping her foot on the floor.

"It's too risky," Pedro said, though doubt seemed to creep into his voice at his wife's insistence.

Eliza Jane, sensing the opening, pushed on. "You Spaniards are such prudes. Meanwhile, your queen and your princesses are busy lifting their skirts for any man who—"

Tomás watched it all with anxiety building in his chest. His dreams of travel were evaporating as the couple before him argued. There would be no profits from a book that could not be sold.

"Listen friend," he said. "It's almost the twentieth century. In America, a man named Edison is lighting houses without kerosene, without oil. They are running electric trains underground in London. I just read it the other day, the universe, all of it, is growing. Expanding, Pedro. And we should expand with it," Tomás said. What was it Eulalia had said, he thought, that she was served on a platter for the nobility to consume?

The memory of it spurred him on. "Everything is changing, and the books we publish should change with it. Look at Verne! He gives us a fantastical future in his books. This is your chance to provide a glimpse into a realistic one, with Eulalia leading the charge." Eliza Jane sidled up beside him, laid a hand on his forearm as he spoke, as if to give him strength, and nodded and nodded.

"Enough!" Pedro said, firm again, gathering the pages. "Those novels you read are about the future, Tomás, those aren't real life. The crown heads of Europe care little for expanding universes and electric trains." Pedro slumped into a chair nearby. "Eliza Jane, the letter," he said.

"Pedro, listen to reason," she began.

"I've had quite enough of women and their reasons. The letter."

Eliza Jane set her mouth grimly, walked slowly over to a writing desk in the corner, opened the small drawer beneath it with the turn of a key, and retrieved an envelope from within. This she handed to Tomás.

"Return the pages to the infanta," Pedro said to Tomás, "and give her this letter, with my regrets. This manuscript of hers will not see the light of day in Spain. Ediciones Medina will have nothing to do with it. And if anyone here asks if I've seen it, please tell them that I have not. I'd rather not be on the bad side of the people at the Palacio Real."

It was raining, and Tomás clutched Eulalia's manuscript under his coat. As he walked, he composed his own letter, which he would send to Eulalia, telling her that he could not do what she had asked of him. He imagined her mouth turning down as she read. Inside, Tomás placed the manuscript on a shelf beneath the shop's cash register, Pedro's letter on top, and retreated to the back room. There, he picked up his old copy of *Twenty Thousand Leagues Under the Sea*, let the book fall open, and allowed his eyes to settle on the first words he saw, ones he had nearly memorized: *The sea is everything.*

It was an old soothsayer's game, to choose a page in the Old Testament at random, and allow the first phrase to rise from the print to predict one's fate. It was a fun trick, and one Tomás and his friends had played on each other in grammar school. If a boy had the misfortune of turning to Lamentations, his classmates would suck in their breaths, and determine that he would fail the next exam, or worse, fall down a manhole. But if a boy turned to the Song of Solomon, they would predict that the girl he had been pining for was waiting for a kiss. Tomás thought of Verne and his sea, of the Atlantic, which he still hoped to cross, and of America, which he still hoped to see.

The sea is everything, Verne wrote. *It is the Living Infinite.* Tomás had always loved the phrase. There was so much possibility in it. The Living Infinite. As old as the sea was, he mused, it killed and reproduced with the stamina of youth. As for Tomás, he felt his own finiteness keenly. How Juana had come to love Verne. She would read to him at night, and they would wonder whether their children would see the future Verne had imagined. Children. Their living infinite.

Tomás closed his book and made his way back into the shop, determined to be useful, dust a shelf, or tally an account, anything to keep memories of Juana and disappointment about what had happened at Pedro's at bay. But he froze when he saw Eliza Jane standing there, Eulalia's manuscript in her hands.

"Señora, what are you—"

Eliza Jane was suddenly before him, whispering as if she had been followed. "My husband is right. We can't publish the book here, but I may have a solution," she said. "My father, Sylvester Hartwell," Eliza Jane continued, "he's a publisher, you know this. He lives in Chicago now, and I would like him to read the manuscript. As you can imagine, we cannot trust the Spanish post with this delicate material. I would be glad to sponsor you so that you may deliver it to him."

"Chicago?" Tomás repeated, and Eliza Jane corrected his pronunciation.

"No. Shh. It starts with a whisper. Shh-cah-go." She tucked a strand of hair behind his ear. "Yes, he's moved Hartwell & Company to Chicago. Abandoned New York for a new city, I can hardly believe it. I sent him a telegram the moment I finished the infanta's book. He's very interested in it. It could mean some money for your mother. Eulalia will have to agree to the terms. Daddy will draw up the contracts. The Columbian Exposition and Eulalia's visit will be good for publicity."

"What about Pedro?"

"That old Royalist?" she asked, her eyebrow arching. "I'll smooth things over."

Tomás looked hard at Eliza Jane. Am I dealing with a woman after all, he thought. She rubbed her expansive belly in slow circles.

"You know, Eulalia will be there. In Chicago," Eliza Jane said, "for the Exposition."

"Yes, I kn—"

"You can be sure the city will put on airs for her. What perfect timing for a book of letters written by the infanta herself! Do nothing so drastic as letting my husband convince you to do away with, this . . . important historical record. Take the book to my father. Let him publish it. Eulalia wanted the proceeds to go to your mother. You and your mother will be rich, and you, handsome as you are, will find America to be a place of many possibilities. Leave Burgos, chase your destiny. The Exposition will be the place for you," Eliza Jane spoke in hurried tones, casting about for reasons that Tomás did not need. He had made up his mind the moment she appeared at his doorway.

Tomás took the pages from Eliza Jane, and messy as they were, started to tidy them up. He smoothed his hand over the top page. They were silent for a moment.

"So, you'll take the manuscript to Chicago?" Eliza Jane asked.

Tomás thought of his crumpled-up list. He thought of his dusty shop and of Jules Verne, traveling the world in search of story ideas, of the infinite sea, and of himself, Tomás, a finite man. He thought of Eulalia, who seemed capable of burning the world with her pen. He thought of his father, crying in the middle of the night and clutching a bottle of wine. He remembered Juana, and his eyes stung.

"It would be my pleasure," he said at last.

Eliza Jane shook his hand like a man, her face grim. She plucked a small white card from a pocket in her skirt, then wrote on it. "Here is my father's address in Chicago," she said, handing him the card. Then she pulled a long ticket from that same pocket. "I knew you'd say yes," she said. "The ticket is for passage on a ship to the United States, with a stop in the Caribbean first. I've always wanted to see Cuba. The Pearl of the Antilles, they call it. And here," she said, producing another envelope from a fold in her skirt, "a little something for your efforts." When he took the ticket and the envelope, from which peeked out several bills, Eliza Jane clapped with stiff hands, tiny claps, as if she was flattening dough between her palms.

She left a few minutes later with the words, "Let's not tell Pedro just yet, shall we? Perhaps after the little one comes. He'll be all soft butter then, you'll see. And you? You will be rich!" She scurried out into the rain without an umbrella. Tomás called after her, shaking his own umbrella in her direction, and she stopped and returned, her hair dripping wet.

Tomás put the umbrella in her hand, and offered her his handkerchief, which she used to pat down her face. She handed it back and grew serious for a moment. "I think you are an interesting man, Tomás. A different kind of man. Perhaps you might understand why Eulalia's book, which I found both stimulating and important, means so much to me, and as the son of a woman who was in service during his infancy, you will understand what I am about to say better still. Women are victims of duty. We learn at our mothers' feet how to clean a house, how to feed a man, how to arrange a party, how to apply rouge to our cheeks in order to dissimulate health and happiness. We learn how to give birth to new life, and how to keep it alive." Eliza Jane took a long, tremulous breath. A raindrop trembled on her chin, but did not fall. "For this, we receive no recompense. And when we grow old, we are forgotten, silence becomes a new womb for us. And since you men die off young, we are alone, prisoners to widowhood, to a duty that does not end. So I think that Eulalia, in writing this book, has shaken off duty. I think that because of it, she, at least, won't be forgotten. By extension, perhaps some of that remembrance will rub off on all of us, don't you think, Tomás?"

"Remembrance. The Living Infinite," Tomás said.

"What was that?" Eliza Jane asked, but Tomás shook his head.

"Nothing. Thank you." Before he could say another word, Eliza Jane was gone again, once more forgetting the umbrella. He called to her, but she waved him off and went down the road with quick steps, seemingly dodging the rain as she walked.

Tomás glanced at the ticket again. The first stop was in Havana. War was still brewing there, the Cuban rebels fighting the Spanish in pockets of violence. The ship was set to leave from Santander on the 19th of April. He had a week to gather his things and secure the shop.

5

The next morning, Tomás began his preparations. He packed a small bag with his clothes and Eulalia's book. He nestled a pistol that had belonged to his father between a pair of pants. He did not know if he would be welcome in Cuba, though so many Cubans were once Spaniards. Later, he made arrangements with a regular at the store, a college student named Daniel, who studied literature and leapt at the chance to keep the bookshop in order while Tomás was gone.

He wrote a letter to Eulalia, and hoped that she would receive it in time. He was careful not to say too much, lest the book be revealed too soon. He wrote:

> *Su Alteza, Eulalia,*
> *The project of which we spoke will be delivered, by me personally, to Chicago, where it will progress as you desire. Am eager to see more of the world, beginning with Havana, where my ship will dock first.*
> *Your servant,*
>
> *Tomás Aragón*

As for the letter that Pedro Medina had written, Tomás kept it wedged between the pages of the manuscript, unsure of when to show it to the infanta. It can wait, he thought.

The manuscript now in his possession was packed carefully and wrapped in paper. Tomás had read it twice now, and itched to make edits, especially regarding his mother's "sad" marriage, which he was sure was an error on the part of the infanta, and would hurt Amalia's feelings were she to read it.

His plans were made so easily, and fell together so neatly, that Tomás could not help but hum as he made his way to his mother's. This would be the hardest part, he thought. She would not want him to go, she would chastise him for his hard heart. He would give her Eulalia's book to read, and perhaps she would be moved by it the way Eliza Jane had been. Tomás prepared his arguments as he walked and hummed, certain that, in the end, Amalia would understand. Hadn't she gone on an adventure of her own long ago, living in the palace for two years, far from her husband? Surely she wouldn't deny him an adventure of his own.

It was a warm day, and the door to his mother's house was open. A slight breeze pushed it back and forth. Tomás stepped in, went to call out to her, and stopped short. Amalia was sitting in a cane chair by the fireplace, an envelope on her lap, her hands over her face as she wept.

"Mamá!" Tomás cried out, running to his mother. "What happened? Are you hurt? Is it bad news?"

She looked up at him, surprise all over her face. She wiped her cheeks and shook her head. "It's nothing, nothing," she said, rising and pushing Tomás away. "What are you doing here on such a nice day?"

"What's this, Mamá?" Tomás asked. The envelope on her lap had fallen to the floor.

"It's nothing," she said, and tried to take it away.

"It clearly isn't nothing," Tomás said. He was speaking softly, as if there were a sleeping baby in the room. It was addressed to Amalia, though there was no return address, and Tomás could tell that the envelope was very old. He wondered whether this was an old letter from his father, and he checked his memory to make sure he hadn't forgotten an important date—his father's birthday, or his saint's day, or the day of his death. No, he hadn't forgotten, and he sighed in relief.

"May I?" he asked gently. Amalia's eyes widened, and then, to his surprise, she relented with a nod.

The paper was brittle, and some of it flaked off. Tomás began to read.

Querida Amalia,

I'm sorry, my friend. I love you. I do not know how else to say it, or how many more times. I know you remember the gem, the one from la reina. I hope you do not miss it too much. Know that I took it gladly. In its clear blue facets I saw an ocean, the blue crystal ocean of my island. I am not sorry about that, because now I am home, and when I take a deep breath, I smell the tropics. I can visit my mother's grave.

You should also know that I have stopped attending births. I feel as if I can no longer do it. The first three babies I helped bring into the world here in Havana died within the hour. Maybe I bring a curse with me into every birthing room. I can no longer bear it. Instead, I have found work in a photographer's shop. He photographs the dead, who are brought in by their relatives through a widened back door, propped into chairs and posed as if they were living. The dead always consent. The pay is good. Tell all of this to Rubén, please, though he may not want to know of it. You may not want to know of it, either. But you must. We are bound, you and I.

I miss you very much. Write me. Forgive me. I have more to tell you, but I'll await your response.

Your sister, in Cuba,

Gisela

Confused, Tomás read the last page to himself. "Gisela?" he asked. The name was familiar, as if he'd heard it spoken before, long ago.

Amalia sat back down in her favorite chair, weeping openly, her mouth wide and full of spit. Every once in a while she muttered, "Oh, my friend."

"Speak to me, Mamá," Tomás urged, confusion making him dizzy. "Who is Gisela?"

"She was my dearest friend," Amalia said, looking away.

"She used to speak of her island so much. We would be sitting right here, right where we are now, and the topic of home would bubble up in our conversation, like an unexpected burst of scent from an open window. She said that in the summer, every place smelled like the sea, and that the spring, which came in February, made the breeze crisp and the air cool, but that the summers felt like living inside of an oven, with a wet rag over your mouth and nose. This is the only letter she ever sent me after she left. I've read it so many times, I could recite it."

Tomás recognized a secret unspoken in the room. He thought again of Eulalia's book, of his mother's "sad" marriage. Something was missing. "Why haven't you mentioned her before?" he asked.

Amalia, reading the letter on her own now, said nothing, and Tomás was struck with the same feeling he always had when he first opened a novel he had wanted to read. There was so much possibility, and such a vast world in his hands, that he often stumbled, closed the book, and took a few encouraging breaths before plunging in again. Gisela's letter was such a thing.

Amalia's cries grew quiet. A tick-tock accompanied them, and though Tomás didn't notice it at first, the eventual realization of what it was he was hearing got his attention. Shortly after Rubén died, Amalia had bought a cuckoo clock from a Bavarian merchant coming through town. The merchant was at the end of his journey, and he practically gave away the clock. Tomás was there when Amalia unpacked it, carefully removing the paper from around the weights, which were molded to look like long pinecones. She hung it outside her bedroom, gently pulling the chains, each click soft and precise. At the half hour and the hour, the red-beaked cuckoo would peek out from behind tiny wooden doors and call out loudly. Amalia, her voice weak from grief, would mimic it, saying,

"Cuckoo, cuckoo, did you hear that, Tomás?" When he asked her why she had bought a cuckoo clock of all things, she said that she thought it would comfort her at night to know that something, even if it was just a little wooden bird, was awake too. She didn't keep up with it for long, and in the years since Rubén died, the chains were slack and dusty, and the iron pinecones rested on their sides on the floor. But as Amalia sat there crying for the friend she once loved, Tomás heard the cuckoo call out eight times, and he knew that his mother feared loneliness again.

Tomás reached into his pocket and felt the ticket that Eliza Jane had given him. Images of jungle canopies and men with machetes crowded his imagination. The ticking clock urged him on. "Come with me to Cuba," he blurted out before he could think too hard on it.

"What are you talking about?" Amalia said, sniffing loudly.

Tomás pulled the ticket from his pocket, and he told his mother the story of the last few days, of Eulalia's manuscript, and Eliza Jane's father. "The infanta mentions you, Mamá. A few times, in fact. She's fond of you. So fond. And she said the book's profits would be yours."

"Why would she do such a thing?"

"I imagine the earnings will be paltry compared to what Eulalia has socked away. Consider it a gift, Mamá. You should come with me. We can sell one of the horses in the barn, can't we? No one rides them anymore since Papá . . . well, it's feasible. First Cuba, then to Chicago. We will see America together." This was not really what Tomás wanted. A man could not shape his destiny with his mother at his side. But she looked at him with wide, wet eyes, and a slow smile emerged from some deep place within her.

Even so, she said, "Tomás, I am too old for such a trip."

"The warm air will be good for you. The sea and all of that. We can find your old friend. Say hello."

Amalia shook her head. "I am too old, Tomás."

Tomás was a bit relieved to hear it. It was love that possessed him to invite her in the first place. Perhaps it was Eliza Jane's ideas about old women being forgotten. That, too, stuck in his head like a refrain. Still, what man wants to travel with his mother? It was absurd, really.

Patting the seat next to hers, Amalia urged Tomás to sit closer. He wished now that he had brought Eulalia's manuscript with him to share with his mother. "Sometimes," he said, "it feels as if you and Papá kept a great many things to yourselves." He was thinking of his mother's friendship with Gisela, and the life they had had together before he was born, and he thought of his siblings, and their little graves in town.

Then, as if he had unplugged a dam, Amalia told him all of it in fits and bursts, interrupting herself with talk of the neighbors, or rising every so often to wipe down a side table or shelf, as if she could not bear to just sit down and let the story pour out. It took her the rest of the afternoon to tell it all, while Tomás listened.

He had known of men with secret families. In fact, just the other day, Daniel, the student now taking care of the bookshop, told him about an aunt he'd only just learned of, the product of a decades-long affair his grandfather had had with a woman from Barcelona. "I can't seem to call her 'Tia,'" Daniel had said, and Tomás had commiserated with him over a cup of coffee. But the scenario was different in this case. Gisela was not so much a secret to anyone except to Tomás. And the baby Rubén had fathered had died at birth. Martín had been his name. The list of innocents his mother had recited all her life, the babies she had lost before Tomás came roaring into the world the size of a three-month-old, must have included Martín, too, in the breaths between names.

Tomás had always imagined his shadow brothers and sisters. But this Martín would have been his little brother, and that made it different. He would have liked to know him, to have had someone looking up to him. He would have liked his brothers and sisters with him on the day they buried Rubén, to lean against them, to bring red carnations for Amalia on the day of his death each year, to ask them what they thought about Eulalia and her book.

"Don't be angry with your father," Amalia said, and Tomás searched for some evidence of anger, but could not find it. Rather, he felt alone. The cuckoo called again, as if in answer to Amalia's question. It was uncanny how often that had happened, the ridiculous tiny bellows inside the clock going off at just the right moment during Amalia's story, and there it went again, answering on Tomás's behalf. Of course I'm not angry, he thought. Dios mio, I am tired, though.

"I will always love Papá, and honor his memory. What's past is past," Tomás said, and his mother burst into fresh tears, and she cleaned her cheeks with the inside of her housedress.

Now Tomás feared leaving his mother behind. How lonely her life had been. How solitary in its grief. He was moved again to ask her to join him on the trip to Cuba and Chicago. Amalia went to bed without answering him, and Tomás stayed up late in the night thinking it over. He would sell the horses for her passage. Take some money he had been saving to replace the bookshop's back door, which had warped and splintered last winter.

In the morning, Amalia woke her son with an answer in the form of a question. "But what will I say to Gisela if we find her?" she asked.

Tomás had no answer, and Amalia thought for a moment. "I don't know," she said, in response to herself. "I have so much to say. You don't understand what women can mean to one another. I haven't spoken to another woman since Gisela left."

"You talk to women all the time," Tomás said, rubbing sleep from his eyes, thinking of the neighbor, who had come over during Amalia's story to apologize because her dog had trampled the geraniums again.

"No conversations of the heart, I mean. I haven't had a soul to talk to in twenty years," Amalia said. Tomás found he had no ready response. What can she possibly have to say to Gisela that she cannot say to me? he wondered.

Later that night, back at his apartment, his mind returned to his mother's assertion that women talked to one another in a way that men did not understand. He considered Eulalia, baring her soul, page by page. Who was her story for exactly? Perhaps there was something in the book that had spoken to Eliza Jane in a way that was not possible for Pedro, or for Tomás. Perhaps Eulalia's book was, after all, a conversation of the heart.

It bothered Tomás to think so, to imagine that Eulalia had not meant to speak to him through her book, that he was merely the vessel through which the book would enter the world.

6

Tomás and Amalia left Burgos on a cool, damp morning. It was a three-hour train ride from Burgos to Santander, where their ship, the *Triunfo,* was docked.

On the train, they shared their compartment with a quiet family. It was tight, and Tomás's knees were up near his chest. The family introduced themselves to Tomás, then gestured at his mother, who had fallen asleep soundly.

"Your mother?" the wife asked. "Que Dios la bendiga," she said, and Tomás wondered if there was something about his mother's sleep that suggested she needed a blessing, or if it was just something the woman liked to say. The husband wore a long beard, quite unfashionably, and he was silent as death after their initial introduction, latching his gaze onto the floorboards and keeping it there. But the daughter, who was not much older than thirteen, gave Tomás a tight smile, sat down with so much force that her skirt ballooned a bit around her, and produced a notebook out of her skirt pocket. This she opened to reveal clean, white pages. Tomás could smell the newness of the pages and thought with a pang of his bookshop.

After rattling her pencils about, the girl proceeded to sketch a portrait of Tomás, without his permission. He felt unsettled as he watched his face slowly appearing on her paper—his hair parted far to the right, curls appearing at his temples. She captured his eyes, which were set deep in his face, satisfactorily. She managed to see that his irises did not quite fit the wells of his eyes, and that a sliver of white was always visible beneath them. It was a feature that Juana had loved. She had called them her "hypnotist eyes," and he would playfully cross his eyes at her whenever she said it. The girl set his ears just right, his strong, angular jaw, and even dotted in his stubble. She looked up once or twice to study him, and Tomás winked at her, which made her blush.

When she was done, she flipped her notebook over to show Tomás.

"Your daughter is very talented, sir," Tomás said to the husband before really looking at him. Like Amalia, he had dozed off, his jumble of a beard serving as a kind of cushion for his chin to rest on. Tomás looked to the wife, but she said nothing. Instead, she reached over and slowly closed her daughter's notebook, then patted her knee. But the girl had slipped her thumb between the pages, stopping her mother. Carefully, as if she were handling a delicate thing, she tore the page out of her book and handed it to Tomás. The paper quivered in the air between them for a moment.

"Sign it, please," Tomás said, and the girl quickly took the page back and put her initials in the right-hand corner. Then the girl tucked her pencil into a pocket in her coat and stared out the window for the remainder of the trip. Later, Tomás placed the page inside Eulalia's manuscript, so as not to crease it.

They arrived at the docks in Santander on a gloomy April afternoon. The *Triunfo* seemed to hover over the water, as long and white as a cloud. Behind it, the *María Cristina*, another ship, was being loaded for an upcoming voyage. Onboard of the latter, Tomás knew, was the infanta. Her trip to the Caribbean and the United States had been in all the newspapers, and now, crowds had surged upon the docks in the hopes of seeing her go. The ships' tall masts and their dangling ropes resembled giant knitting needles from afar, tangled up in yarn. Horse-drawn carriages toted passengers and their luggage. The horses snorted and pounded their hooves, and one nearly trampled Tomás, who was not paying attention. Off in the distance, the hills of Santander rose in gray mist. The lamps within the ship were already lit, and they glowed brightly enough to be seen through a few portholes.

Amalia struck up a conversation with an elderly man, who was helping her with her bag.

"We'll be stopping in Cuba, which is where I plan to stay. My family is there. Are you both going on to America?" he asked.

Tomás nodded.

"Well, Cuba should be interesting," he said to Amalia. As their tickets were punched, he added, "Perhaps we'll get to witness a war."

"I should hope not," Amalia said.

Onboard, they watched Santander disappear on the horizon

as the ship pulled away. As darkness fell, lanterns brightened the windows of the homes set on the hills, and the light trembled on the water. "Que lindo," Amalia said again and again, and Tomás wondered what it was she saw in those delicate lights that struck her so. Hadn't she lived in a palace? Hadn't her eyes rested upon strings of diamonds lacing a queen's chest? Tomás thought that if he had seen such things, there would be no light impressive enough to make him sigh in such a way.

Later, the sea roiled as if it has been unchained from some giant anchor, and Tomás and his mother spent an unpleasant night inside their cabin, wide-awake, and talking in whispers about the state of their nausea.

Most days, Tomás and Amalia rose before dawn to sit on the deck and watch the sun come up. In those quiet moments, she told him about life in the Palacio, the details she had left out before. She traced the patterns of Sor Patrocinio's injuries on the palms of his hands. She described Isabel's lovers, and, specifically, a man named Tenorio, who climbed the spiral staircase into the queen's quarters at night.

"They all seem so sad," Tomás said.

"The Bourbons? Yes. Some say they are cursed," Amalia added.

"Eulalia once mentioned that you were unhappy, too. With Papá, I mean." Tomás spoke quietly, softly. The dark of their cabin and the rocking of the ship put him in mind of his childhood, when his mother held him at night. Boyish secrets would tumble out of his mouth, and she would listen, commenting only so often.

"Some days were very hard. Very sad. This is true," Amalia said. She reached out to hold her son's hand. "We sacrificed so much to secure your future. Even our happiness. I know you understand, hijo," she said.

Tomás did understand. Some days, he would think of Juana

and find he could not breathe or think, and he knew in those moments that he would spare every ounce of happiness in his life to see her again.

They began to see lines on the horizon after the sixth day at sea. Amalia befriended the old man who first spoke with them as they boarded. His name was Grimaldo, and his family awaited him in Cuba. It was Grimaldo who pointed out the islands as they passed them by. "The Virgin Islands, and there, that bright spot is San Juan, Puerto Rico. Soon we will see my Cuba," Grimaldo said, a hand over his heart.

Amalia looked up at her new friend and blinked slowly in his direction.

In another life, Tomás could imagine them together, how this Grimaldo might have been his father instead. So many "might haves." Tomás felt unchained, like the sea, and spoke without thinking, "Your Cuba? You are a Spaniard, señor. These days, it's best not to forget that."

"My daughters are in Cuba," Grimaldo said. "They are all I have left. Where they are, my home is. My Cuba then. You can keep your Spain." Grimaldo left them by the railing without saying goodbye, and Amalia scowled at her son. "Look what you've done," she said. But she wasn't really angry. The open air had been good for her. She had grown used to the rocking waves, and now she couldn't stop talking about Cuba, about the warm air, how it felt in her lungs, and the dolphins she kept spying off the side of the boat.

When Cuba finally appeared on the horizon, it stretched lazily on and on. It felt like summer, though it was still April. In fact, it felt as if someone had bottled the summer up, allowed it to grow and expand in a confined space, and had just released it. Before they even set foot on the island, Tomás had already had four glasses of water that turned warm before he could take a proper drink.

*

They tried to find lodging at several inns close to the harbor. Each time, they were turned away, and walked deeper into the city. Tomás carried his mother's bag and his own, and they seemed to get heavier with each block. The city reminded Tomás of Sevilla, which he had visited once. The buildings were stacked close together, as if a child had imagined the entire place and created it with toy blocks. On balconies and roofs, people lounged about, fanning themselves with pieces of paper, or painted silk fans. Every once in a while they turned down a cobbled street and caught a glimpse of a long, low fortress, the walls of which seemed to circle the city and keep the sea out. Waves crashed against the sea wall every so often, sending glittering sprays down on the people walking along the path beside it. "Que lindo," was all Amalia would say, even as she stepped over a cat that had seemingly been dead for a few days, never missing a step, her eyes gazing up at the balconies and around buildings.

When they finally found an inn with a vacancy, Tomás booked two rooms for them. "So expensive," Amalia said, but he waved her off. The money he'd taken out of the bookshop's bank account, paired with Eliza Jane's sponsorship, was sufficient, and there would be money enough when Eulalia's book sold.

"We've had a horrible time finding a room," Tomás told the innkeeper.

He shrugged. His Spanish was different than Tomás's. His vowels more open, the endings of his words trimmed off like so much fat. He stuttered a little, too. "The city is f-full. A Spanish infanta is coming to Havana. I f-forget her name," he said.

Amalia began to say something, "Yes, we know. In fact—" But Tomás cut her off. It was best, he thought, not to let on to a stranger that they knew the princess. What if he assumed too much, that, perhaps, their pockets were deeper than they actually were because of the association?

"Do you know when she will arrive?" Tomás asked. He didn't know. They had lost sight of the *María Cristina* right away, and according to the newspapers, Eulalia's itinerary had her stopping in Puerto Rico first.

"Tomorrow," the innkeeper said. "The whole city has been cleaned up for her visit. To be honest, it used to smell so bad down this street. And now? F-fresh as roses. I wish more of these princesses would come to Cuba." He handed Tomás the keys to their rooms.

"Mamá," Tomás called, and found her standing before a picture on the wall.

"Tomás," she said, breathless. "Look."

The painting was of three little girls, each with a diadem on her head. They were dark-eyed things, standing in size order. The smallest, on the left, held the end of a diamond leash, and at the end of the leash was a blazing white peacock, a circlet of gems around its neck.

"It's them, my girls," Amalia said.

"Mamá, the infantas are not brunettes. They are blond and blue-eyed," Tomás said, and started to pull her away.

"No, no, it is them. I've missed seeing them this way, when they were little, so—" Amalia's hands fluttered towards the painting.

"Don't touch it!" a shrill young woman shouted from behind the tall desk. She was a squat girl with a piggish, upturned nose.

Surprised, Amalia gripped her son's wrist. "Ay," she cried.

"Let's go to our rooms," Tomás urged, and she let him lead the way. "This is a strange country," he muttered as they climbed the stairs, but Amalia only said, "Que lindo," again, like a guitar with only one string.

7

Tomás could not sleep from the heat. He drank glass after glass of water, which sent him to the bathroom downstairs again and again. Sometimes, there was a line for its use, and he waited for nearly twenty minutes at one point for a woman and her daughter to emerge from the toilet. Her eyes were red from crying, and the girl held her mother's hand tightly. He slapped mosquitos away from his arms and tried not to itch. Such were the disturbances at a Cuban inn in the middle of the night.

In the morning, Tomás and his mother met for breakfast, and it looked as though she hadn't slept either. Even her hair, usually wound into a small bun at the nape of her neck, was beyond her control, and ringlets had sprung up around her face, giving her a girlish look.

"It's too hot," she said, fanning herself. Overnight, streamers had been placed inside the hotel, hung from roof beam to roof beam in happy loops.

The shrill girl from behind the desk the night before was rigging up the last of them, and as she did, she hummed the "Marcha Real," missing some notes here and there.

"How is that for a welcome?" Tomás asked his mother, who didn't seem to recognize the Spanish anthem in the girl's off-tune trilling.

Feeling better with some toast in his belly, Tomás teased the girl, "Te agradezco la música," exaggerating the "z" for effect.

"It's not for you," she said at once. "Neither are these," she said, gesturing to the decorations. "But should the infanta find her way here, she will know we support her in Havana. It's the Orientales, out there in Santiago and those backwoods, who are fighting our king." The girl shoved the last tack into the wall, stood back, admired her work, and disappeared into another room. The streamers were not red and gold, however. Nor were they red, blue, or white. Neither Spain nor Cuba was represented in them. Rather, the streamers were green and orange, and the ends were frayed from multiple uses.

"Eulalia arrives today," Tomás said to his mother, who was still spreading butter on her toast. It occured to Tomás that she seemed smaller than before somehow. Older, too. Suddenly, he regretted bringing her with him.

He spoke cautiously. "Mamá, we don't have to look for Gisela. We can go see the princess arrive. Enjoy the sights some. Go on as we have been." Even as he said these things, he knew the ways she would refute him. He considered how he might escape one night and try to find Gisela on his own, though he didn't know what he would say to her.

"We should see the infanta arrive, of course," Amalia said, then sipped her coffee. Sweat pooled under her eyes and on her temples.

"Mamá," Tomás began, unsure. "You . . . you shouldn't get your hopes up about finding Gisela. Even if we do, she may not want to see you again. I don't know what you intend to say to her, but she might call the police if—"

"I'm not going to attack her, if that's what you think," Amalia said. Irritation seemed to rise in her, gaslike. She was a hot air balloon. "Besides. How many photography studios could there be here?"

"In all of Cuba?" Tomás asked. "It's a big island, Mamá," he said gently.

"I mean only to talk. To see my old friend again." Amalia laced her fingers tightly. "I miss your father so much, Tomás. You can't understand how much. And I haven't had anyone to talk to for so long about him."

"You have me," he said.

"A son does not remember his father the way a wife recalls her husband."

Tomás crossed one leg over the other and looked away. Behind the front desk, the innkeeper was talking to a guest dressed in a military uniform. The little sabers on his epaulets clinked as he spoke.

"Gisela and I remember Rubén in a way you cannot, I'm sure of it." Amalia opened her mouth to say more, but stopped herself. "Forget this. I have business with Gisela, that is all. You understand that? Business? It's a man's word. Business. That's what she and I have to talk about now."

Up until that moment, Amalia's face had been pale, but now it was florid and her cheeks quivered.

"Fine," Tomás said offended. "Leave it. Today is for greeting Eulalia, fresh from the sea. We will wave our handkerchiefs at her and she will recognize you in the crowd, her blessed nodriza, and she will greet me like a brother.

Amalia looked at her son hard for a second, then softened. "Don't get your hopes up, hijo," she said before rising from the table and returning to her room.

At the docks later that day, Tomás and Amalia joined a mass of sweaty, excitable people awaiting the arrival of Spanish royalty. The *María Cristina* appeared on the horizon and they watched it approach rapidly. It was a faster ship than the *Triunfo*. It had likely passed that vessel somewhere in the Atlantic, resembling a whale or a bird in the distance. Tomás and Amalia waited in the blazing sun for another two hours before the ship was allowed to dock. It was a torturous, stinking wait.

"What is that smell?" Tomás said. His mother had covered her nose and mouth with the sleeve of her dress. Before them stood a man and his son. Their pockets bulged, and Tomás noticed a pool of blood at their feet. He pulled his mother away from them. "Sickness," he whispered, imagining some tropical disease.

But Amalia pointed at the boy's pockets, from which poked out what appeared to be pig intestines, dangling against his thigh like snakes.

"They mean to throw them at the princess," Tomás whispered, the meaning clear at once. He began to notice other potential weapons. Beside him, a little girl bobbled a tomato in her hands. Ominously, a man to his left clicked two stones together. Ahead of them, the little boy's socks soaked up pig's blood.

"I thought they were supposed to be in support of the crown here in Havana," Tomás whispered in his mother's ear. She took a deep breath, but kept her silence.

A woman in the crowd stood on a box and called out, "¡Compatriotas! ¡Cubanos!" She held a fringed parasol, and wore a white mutton-sleeve top and a gray skirt. She didn't seem likely to be throwing anything, but her voice cut through the din. "The infanta is one of our oppressors. She reeks like rotten pork. She doesn't even speak Spanish! How dare she govern us?" the woman cried, and several people cheered. Others hissed at her, and a man tried to pull her down from her box, but she hit him on the head with the handle of her parasol. On and on the litany went until, finally, she was consumed by the crowd.

"We should leave," Tomás said to his mother, but she disentangled her arm from his.

"Eulalia needs us," she said. "I am like a mother to her. I cannot abandon her to this mob. She will sense that I am here. It will give her strength." Amalia's eyes were fixed on the ship's empty deck.

Some authorities will come soon, Tomás thought. Authorities sympathetic to Spain, rule makers of some sort, and the people will be subdued before the first egg is thrown. But he didn't want to risk it.

"Fine. But let's move to higher ground," he said, scanning the area for some kind of elevation. They found it toward the back of the crowds, in the shade of a shop selling flowers. From that distance, it was clear that the dissenters were in the minority. Most of the people clutched small Spanish flags, and even where they stood, there was a happy buzz in the air, like bees in summer.

When Eulalia finally appeared on deck accompanied by her husband, the crowd gasped, and then went eerily quiet as Eulalia waved.

"The colors of the rebellion," the shop owner behind them said in awe. "¡Viva la Infanta!" he cheered, quietly at first. Eulalia wore red, blue, and white. Antonio, dressed in a military uniform, stood a little off to the side, as if Eulalia's presence was coincidental to his own.

Tomás knew a little about Edison's electricity, how it is supposedly meant to light a room with a single switch being pulled. This moment was like that. The crowd had gone from pain, despair, shadows, and threats to cheerful cries of support. A switch had been thrown over Havana, and Eulalia was the filament that had lit up the place.

Atop her head, Eulalia wore a crown made up of three rows of diamonds. The rest of her was all Cuba—her blue dress; the white lace atop her shoulders, at her collar, at her waist; and around her neck, a thick ribbon of bright red velvet. Tomás thought that, should a star come down from the heavens and perch itself atop her head, nobody in the crowd would be surprised at all.

Rotten fruit and rocks and animal entrails dropped from many hands, which, wiped on pants and skirts, were soon raised in support of an infanta of the House of Bourbon. Eulalia smiled at them, and they cheered ever more loudly.

Amalia had closed up her fan and crossed her arms over her breasts. "Eulalia! Eulalia! Viva Eulalia!" the people around them shouted.

Tomás watched as Eulalia waved, pivoting slowly like a figure in a music box. Beside her, the Infante Antonio and the ship's captain waved too, tightly, their faces in grimaces. Though no shadow fell upon them, the light did not seem to reach them, either. It was all on her. Tomás felt a stirring in his gut, one he had not felt in a long time, since back when Juana was alive. Juana would have liked this moment, he thought.

On the way back to the hotel, Amalia was very quiet. Tomás, on the other hand, was all energy. "Did you see her? So beautiful. She's never been more beautiful. It's the light here, this Caribbean light," he went on.

"You're smitten," Amalia said with a smile, and Tomás gently bumped his mother's shoulder.

In his heart, he knew it was true. And he did think Eulalia was beautiful, the way a shard of glass catching the sun was beautiful. She was the talk of the city. They heard her name everywhere, and to Tomás's ears, it felt strange in this tropical place, the way an irregular pulse feels, causing a vague sense of alarm. They passed a newspaper stand, and Tomás stopped. There were many different kinds of newspapers to choose from, and the many tiny columns of print seemed like crawling insects. There, in the center, was a front page with a drawing of Eulalia on it. The artist had captured her poorly—giving her too heavy a fringe and too prominent a chin. He paid for the newspaper, an edition of *La República*. The stand owner took his money, then opened a box at his feet surreptitiously, as if he'd dropped a coin. "Psst," he said, and pointed at another paper, one printed in yellow. It was called *El Yara*, and on the front page were drawings of mustachioed men in straw hats. And there, in the center, was a caricature of a Spaniard, with a long nose and fangs for teeth.

The snarling sketch on the paper was a small insolence, and yet it sent Tomás's Spanish heart racing in a way that surprised him. He did not consider himself a patriotic man, and was usually deeply uninterested in talk of politics. Sometimes, his mother would tell him stories of her youth, of the Carlist days that had been so bloody for Spain, but Tomás's attention would drift away, and she would leave off the telling. Still, the sketch had bothered him, a small thorn had lodged in his heart and ruined the afternoon.

Tomás unfolded the newspaper. The writer of the article fawned over the infanta, calling her "the most beautiful Bourbon," which wasn't wrong in Tomás's estimation, and a "blessing from Spain." It said that Eulalia would be meeting with supplicants and admirers the following day, and this he pointed out to his mother, who suggested they go. The rest of her itinerary was listed, too. She was set to meet with dukes and duchesses, attend a bullfight, meet with nuns, visit a university, and on and on.

Tomás wondered for the first time what was being accomplished by sending Eulalia to Cuba, especially when she arrived dressed like a rebel flag. How wonderful it was to see her, though, radiant and luminous in the afternoon light. She seemed, in that moment, beyond the rules of protocol, of her own womanhood. Tomás thought of Juana when she didn't think he was watching her, how she tapped her foot to some unknown song, scratched her ear, smiled openly at a thought that had crossed her mind, and how different she was when she was conscious of him, how still, how controlled.

Eulalia, he thought, here in these warm climates, seemed more herself, free of the social order that forbid her to stand in the sunlight, dressed in all her own choices, daring those around her to challenge those choices. Tomás searched for that freedom in himself, tested himself to see if Cuba had inspired such a sense of liberty, but he could find no difference within.

8

Amalia had not mentioned Gisela again, though Tomás knew she was present with them anyway, the shadows of her trailing them as they walked around the city the previous day. Tomás saw how his mother looked at the shop names up and down each block. He knew she was hoping to see Gisela's photography studio among them. The next morning, dark shadows encircled Amalia's puffy eyes.

"You look beautiful today, Mamá," Tomás said, hoping to make her feel better. She patted his hand but said nothing.

After breakfast, the two made their way to where Eulalia was meeting supplicants and admirers. The building was painted a creamy color, and it was flanked by two rows of palm trees, their thick, smooth trunks gleaming in the sunlight. The line of people waiting to meet Eulalia was not as long as Tomás had feared, and many people merely passed by, lost in their day-to-day routines. They waved at one another, dashed across streets, removed their hats, or adjusted their skirts, they peered up at the buildings and pointed at the balconies, threw rocks at cats, or else peeled an orange, dropping the skin of it on the ground and moving on. The busy nature of the living struck Tomás, and he realized that he, too, was a blur, tapping his fingers on his thigh as they waited to move up in the line.

A policeman moved down the line, questioning everyone present. He held a piece of paper and a pencil, and every once in a while he jotted something down. Sometimes, he stopped, removed his cap, and dried the sweat off the top of his bald head. When he reached Tomás and Amalia, he asked for their names and places of birth.

"Burgos," Amalia said, and Tomás added, "This is my mother. She was her highness's nodriza."

The man smiled, said, "Bienvenidos a Cuba. ¡Viva el Rey!"

They responded, "¡Viva el Rey!" and several others around them said so, too.

"My mother was born in Barcelona," the man said, eager to talk. "Is Barcelona close to Burgos?"

"No, very far apart," Amalia said.

"Ah, well. Ven," the man said, and they followed him out of the line. Around them, the others in line murmured their disapproval as Tomás and Amalia were escorted in. They waited in a breezy courtyard, with a fountain tinkling away in the center. The tiles beneath their feet were small and colorful, each small square different from its neighbor. Arches led off in different directions around them. Above them was the sky. On a table, a silver dish held translucent candies peppered with sesame seeds. A bouquet of pink roses sat on a different table. Suddenly, four men in firefighter hats walked through one of the arches, patting each other's shoulders and smiling broadly. One of them carried a large flag draped over his arm. Eulalia's audiences were varied in that way. Moments later, a group of schoolchildren exited from another arch, and each one carried with them a pink rose, just like the ones that made up the bouquet in the courtyard. Then it was quiet again, and now and again, a green parrot swooped in and squawked at them from the floor.

"Shoo!" a voice exclaimed as the bird startled, and flew away. Tomás looked up to see Eulalia. "Parrots, of all things," she said. Her arms were pale and bare, but her face was flushed. Her green dress swept the floor as she walked toward them.

"Su alteza," Tomás said, bowing. Amalia forgot courtesy, and sped toward Eulalia, her arms aloft.

"Mi divina, que bella te ves," she said to the princess warmly, familiarly, and they embraced tightly.

"Come, come," Eulalia said, and led them through one of the arches. Inside, there were chairs and sofas surrounding a glass-topped table, upon which a pitcher of water sweated, puddling on the glass.

"You were both on my mind this morning," Eulalia said. "I received your letter, Tomás. I'd hoped to see you here, but Amalia. Oh Ama, what a surprise."

Amalia beamed at her. "You look flushed, mi vida," she said, laying a hand on Eulalia's cheek.

"I asked them to put ice in my bath this morning, and the maid here nearly fainted from shock. 'You'll catch your death,' she said to me, but I insisted. I've always had ice baths. This heat will be what kills me," Eulalia prattled on to Amalia. Tomás thought of her in a porcelain tub, ice cubes floating against her breasts and shoulders.

"It is very warm, your highness," he said.

"Tomás," the princess said, arching an eyebrow. Then she fell silent, waiting for him to speak again.

"Eulalia," he said.

The infanta laughed. "It feels good to hear my name out of the mouths of people I'm not related to." Eulalia relaxed against the cushions of the couch, and wiped sweat off her upper lip. "Did you see the firefighters? Brave souls. They asked me to be the godmother of their flag when it is blessed in a few days. What a thing to do! I agreed, of course. But enough of that."

Eulalia looks so different here in Cuba, thought Tomás, as if she is another person entirely. Meeting her now, one would not immediately think that she was a princess at all. She reminded him of Eliza Jane, so brash always, like one of those little green Cuban parrots.

"Have you read the papers? I caused a stir yesterday, didn't I?" Eulalia said.

"You did. It was an accident, of course," Amalia said, and patted Eulalia's knee.

Eulalia squinted for a moment, as if she was trying to make something out in the distance. "Well, what I told Antonio was this—that it is a women's prerogative to wear what she likes. And besides, I'd already gotten dressed, and it takes so long to get in and out of the corset. It wouldn't have done to keep the people waiting."

The excuse seemed practiced, as if she had already told this story a dozen times. An emerald dangled from her neck on a golden chain. A circlet of diamonds and more emeralds sat half-buried among her blond curls.

Amalia's smile faded a little, and her face took on a look of worry that Tomás recognized from his more reckless days, back when he thought climbing roofs in Burgos and teasing wild dogs until they chased him down cobbled streets were good ideas.

"Princesa," Amalia began. "Tomás told me about your book. I am worried about what people will think."

Eulalia straightened in her seat slowly. "They will think what they are prone to thinking always—of the ways in which royalty should be untouched by real life, how we are supposed to be an unseen hand in the lives of the Spanish and the people in the colonies, and how my book bares that hand to the world—disfigured knuckles, hangnails, and all."

"It is unwise of you, all of it," Amalia said. Tomás realized he was holding his breath.

"You, too, Ama?" Eulalia said, and her blue eyes waterd. "Everyone tells me what to do."

"Think of your sons."

"I do. All of the time. I think how, already, they keep quiet when they should be shouting. They keep secrets from me, Ama. I never know what they think. They do not know how to think."

"Sometimes silence is a blessing," Amalia said. It sounded like something one hears from a nun, and Tomás wondered if she was digging into her own past for this advice, down, down to her childhood days in a convent, where silence must have been the unspoken eleventh commandment, where her little girl giggles and her little girl squeals were hushed down to nothing.

"And the injustice I feel in that silence? Is that blessed,

too?" The tears dried in Eulalia's eyes. She was unblinking, and even though Amalia was still talking—about wisdom, and protecting her family, and how she wished she had had a mother, how she would have loved her mother given the chance, how Isabel deserved that love—Eulalia had gone still. She did not nod. She did not even appear to be listening anymore.

"We should go, Mamá," Tomás said.

"You are implicated in this, too," Amalia said.

"I am only delivering a manuscript, one I did not write, to an American edito—"

"Tomás," Eulalia spoke at last, but her voice was different now. Smaller.

"Eulalia," he said, but the humor was gone from the moment.

"What do you think?" she asked.

Tomás looked down at his feet. How thrilling it had been to read her book, to see in neat handwriting what one always thought—that behind the politics and the pomp were real people who fell in love, felt sadness, knew the patterns and permutations of a broken heart. It had made him think of Juana, who would have loved to have read such a thing.

"Does it matter what I think?" Tomás asked, cautious now.

Eulalia nodded. Her lips were parted. Her hands were clasped at her throat, as if she were waiting for a great shock, or some terrible news. He imagined Juana again, curled up in the back of the bookshop, Eulalia's printed book in her hands and a small crease between her eyes.

"Your highness," he began again, and looked into her eyes. "I think you're very brave, and your book very good." Later, he would hear his own voice playing in his head again and again, and he would revise what he'd said, adding flourishes, or taking her hand in his imagination, ridiculous flights of fancy that kept him up all night.

But in that moment, Eulalia responded simply. She drew two cards from a small basket at her feet. Each had been printed with her official name: *SU ALTEZA, EULALIA BOURBON DE ORLÉANS, INFANTA DE ESPAÑA*. She signed the back of each card, and handed one to each of them.

"A memento," she said.

Amalia took the card and tucked it into her purse. She sighed so quietly that Tomás thought Eulalia might not have heard it. Then, she said, "The truth is, I did not come here, to this island, for you. I came to forgive a friend for a terrible decision she made a long time ago." Amalia took several deep breaths before speaking again. "Mi querida niña. Eulalia. When Tomás first told me about your book, I thought as he did. That you were brave. But you did not see the men holding rocks and entrails for you yesterday. You do not know the danger you face. I only want your safety, mi niña." Amalia's hands were before her, imploring. "May Spain forgive you. May they always love you, the way I love you," she said at last.

Eulalia nodded, and the diadem atop her head quivered. She reached out and grabbed Amalia's hand, squeezing it for a second before letting go.

Then it was over. They left Eulalia to her next visitors—a couple in fine, heavy clothes despite the heat, whose smiles as they passed them by were so fixed to their faces that they seemed elusive even to themselves.

"Mamá, how are you?" Tomás asked his mother as they walked back to the hotel.

She looped her arms in one of his, and he felt her weight as she leaned into him. "Eulalia has always been like an untamed horse. I worry about her. The same way I worry about you," she said. "The card is very nice," she said after a while, looking at hers as they walked. Tomás took his from his pocket, and flipped it around to Eulalia's signature. But instead of a signature, she had written, *Mañana, Quinta de los Molinos, ten sharp, EBO.*

9

Oro y sangre, Tomás thought, as he approached the Quinta de los Molinos, a farm on the outskirts of the city, where Eulalia was visiting. The gates had been wrapped in gold and red cloth, of a type of material that glimmered in the sunlight. Beyond the gates was a meticulously kept tropical garden, and off in the distance were fields of tobacco, the broad leaves waving in the breeze. A man in a straw hat, wearing a crisp white shirt, greeted Tomás at the gate.

"I am here to see Her Highness, the Infanta Eulalia," Tomás said formally.

The man smiled, revealing protruding gums that were dark and glossy. "You would do better here to speak of the beautiful 'woman' visiting our island, rather than any 'infanta.' Perhaps you don't know it yet, but you've just met a man who believes in liberty." He extended a hand but Tomás did not take it. The man let him in anyway, and pointed down a path, where Eulalia was said to be having her photograph taken after laying a cornerstone on the farm.

Tomás was confused by the red and gold bunting and the man he had just met, one contradicting the other. Back in Spain, the revolution on the island no longer made front page news. It was diminished, made small and insignificant. But Tomás had seen the people awaiting Eulalia with his own eyes, and understood the man at the gate clearly. As in all things, Tomás understood, there was more than one story. More than that, the man's sudden declaration had given Tomás pause, and a bubble of fear grew within him, that Eulalia was not safe in this place, among these people of many faces.

When Tomás saw Eulalia at last, she was sitting sidesaddle on a large black horse. She was dressed in a dark blue dress, buttons high up her throat, and a tall top hat on her head, jauntily cocked to the left. Near her, were three other women, also on horses, also sidesaddle. A photographer stood nearby, his head deep within the well of his camera, a black cloth covering his neck and torso. The flash popped, then smoked, and Eulalia relaxed on the horse, fanning herself with her hand.

"Your highness," Tomás said loud enough to be heard.

Eulalia nodded in his direction, then called forth another man in a straw hat, leading a speckled mare. The animal was heavily pregnant, and it ambled as it walked.

"Señor, para usted," the man said, and motioned at the mare.

Eulalia began to laugh, covering her mouth with the back of her hand. Tomás scowled at her, which made her laugh harder until an indelicate little snort escaped her. The women on their horses looked away, pretending to fuss with their skirts, or the reins, or the horses' manes. With a laugh of his own, Tomás conceded, and climbed up on the mare.

"Let's assess the tobacco fields," Eulalia said, and she trotted away, the women riding behind her. Tomás's slow horse plodded, and though he didn't want to do it, he gave it a swift kick in the ribs, and the animal picked up speed until he was beside Eulalia again.

"You look ridiculous on that creature, Tomás," she said when he appeared at her side. "How is Ama? Is she angry with me?"

"No. She could never be."

"Good. I hardly slept last night thinking of her. This way," she said, and pulled her horse into a sandy stretch of land, dotted here and there with fruit trees. She slowed her horse down, then, pivoted in her saddle. "Señoritas, damas, perhaps you would like to see the north end of the fields? I was told they are very lush."

"Sí, su alteza," they murmured, turned their horses, and trotted off in a different direction. Then Eulalia faced Tomás, hiked her skirt, and straddled her horse, slipping her heeled boots into the stirrups.

"Better," she said.

Worry gripped Tomás all of a sudden. He was unarmed, and ahead, the stands of trees grew denser. He envisioned men with pistols behind every trunk. "Eulalia," he said. "You aren't safe in this country. The man at the gate told me—"

"The only thing I fear is this heat. It's liquefying my brain, I can feel it," she said, smiling at him.

"I wish you would be careful," he said.

"I am careful. So very careful. Perhaps too careful. Though, sometimes, I find a way to slip out from under the gaze of my watchers." She motioned to her ladies-in-waiting, whom they could hear in the distance, laughing among themselves. "Early in the morning, when the streets are still sleepy, I wander about, prop open a parasol to hide my face, and take in the city. It's a wonderful old city. Then, as soon as it gets too hot, I go back to my room. The ladies wake up and tell me I look flushed, and they pat my cheeks and check me for a fever."

"And you laugh and laugh at them?" Tomás put in.

"No, never. I'm as serious as a funeral. Havana is wonderful, isn't it? Where are you staying?"

He told her about the inn, where it was located. She listened intently, as if mapping out the city in her mind. Afterwards, she was off again, and the pregnant mare could not keep up. Tomás lost sight of her at a bend in the path, and so he sat there, sweating, unsure of which way to go. The sun was high and blinding. If a rebel were to appear suddenly, gun in hand, machete in the waistband of his pants, what would he do? Die on this horse, most likely, he thought. As for Eulalia, she was capable of anything. Perhaps she, too, had a gun strapped to her thigh, like one of those western women in America that he'd read about.

She returned after a few minutes, flushed, her hat no longer on her head, but lost somewhere in a tobacco field.

"I'm glad you didn't chase me," she said, out of breath. "That poor horse might drop dead, or decide to give birth right here."

"Are you feeling well?" Tomás asked. Eulalia's face was very red. She swayed, and her hands gripped the horse's mane.

She breathed out of her mouth. "This heat," she said, unbuttoning the top buttons at her neck. She veered to the side again.

Tomás climbed out of the saddle, and reached up to Eulalia, helping her down, her voluminous skirts brushing against his face. When she came down at last, she landed hard on his feet, the heel of her boot crushing his toe, making him yelp. "Perdon, perdon," she said weakly, and leaned against his shoulder.

They walked toward a large mango tree and sat in its shade. Its tiny orange flowers flutterd down into Eulalia's hair every so often as she rested.

Tomás fanned her with both hands. She recovered a bit, and her cheeks no longer seemed to burn. "Oh, this heat," she said again.

Tomás did not dare tell her that the dark dress with the high collar and long sleeves was a mistake. Or that she should not have run off into the fields with an unknown horse in an unfamiliar place. There were things one did not say to an infanta.

Instead, he asked about her book. "My mother was right, you know. What do you aim to do about the chaos that will ensue, Eulalia?"

She leaned into him, as if she were going to drop her head

on his shoulder, but, at the last moment, thought better of it. "Get thrown out of the country?" she posed.

Tomás did not answer her, or offer other conclusions about her future. He was about to change the subject again, say something about the scar on his wrist, when the horses bolted and ran off back in the direction of their stables.

"A snake, maybe? I thought I saw one earlier," Eulalia said.

Tomás stood and scanned the horizon. The man who let him into the finca appeared from behind a bushel of hay. His hat was in his hand, and he walked slowly toward them. "We have been looking for you," he said. He did not add "su alteza," or anything of the sort.

"I am not a lost object, señor," Eulalia said.

The man smiled, his teeth peeking out a little. "Of course not. Your husband is finished shooting his pistols on the other side of the finca. He is ready to go."

"I'm sure Antonio had a delightful time," Eulalia murmured, but there was something distant in her voice and in her manner. She followed the man out, and Tomás went after her.

"I don't trust him," he said.

"He only works here," she said. "The farm belongs to the Captain General of Havana."

"Even so," Tomás began, but she ignored him.

All the time, his heart was pounding and he felt breathless. At any moment, this man might round on them, gun in hand. At any moment, they might hear the shout, "Viva Cuba libre." It is coming, it is coming. Look at the muscles in the man's neck, extended and pulsing. Look at his fingers as they flex open and closed. His pockets are bulging with something, no? Rocks? A weapon? He removed his hat and Tomás jumped. But Eulalia was still and composed as ever.

"Doesn't anything frighten you?" Tomás asked her as they approached the main house again. There, he got his first close look at Antonio de Orléans. The infante was wearing a straw hat, too, though it looked awkward on him, as if he was only wearing it because it was a gift. His thin mustache looked damp. Everything about him looked damp and wilting. Tomás instantly imagined his face on paper money, wrinkled and moist. He had rolled up the sleeves of his white shirt, and his pants were dusty and clinging to his knees.

Eulalia had seen her husband too. She acknowledged him with a nod and said without looking at Tomás, "Yes, many things frighten me." Antonio walked toward them and Eulalia said, hurriedly, "I have more pages for you, Tomás."

He blinked at her several times. "More?" was all he managed to say.

"Does that frighten you?" she teased, and then she left him there, her small feet creating puffs of dust as she walked away.

He watched her slip her arm through Antonio's, and he leaned his head forward to talk to her. The photographer, who had been fanning himself under a tree, came to life again, ready to set up another portrait of the couple.

"This way, señor," the man from the field said to Tomás, pointing to the front gate. Once at the entrance to the finca, he said, "Cuba será libre. There is no infanta beautiful enough to stop it." Then, after a moment, he added, "But she is beautiful."

10

That night, Eulalia sent a boy to the inn. He was a black boy, and Tomás wondered if he had once been enslaved. He thought about it often while in Cuba, such a tropical, beautiful, terrible place. But he did not dare ask the child. The practice seemed like such a relic to Tomás, even as he smoked

cigars, poured sugar in his coffee, and marveled at the soft-
ness of American cotton. Tomás's own hypocrisy had struck
him in Cuba. Perhaps it was the heat, oiling the cogs in his
brain. There was something about the feeling of languor in
the air, the soft shuffle in everyone's walk, the loose ankles
and wrists. There was a certain sense of how the world should
work, one with fewer rules, less protocol, but these were
thoughts Tomás could not follow long before getting interrupted, or feeling a line of sweat running down his back, dis-
tracting him, or waking him up in the middle of the night
from a dream about Eulalia, one that kept him from closing
his eyes again.

The boy carried with him a book, and when Tomás turned
it over, he saw that it was a copy of *A Floating City*, the very
same novel he had sold to Eulalia back in Burgos. At first, he
thought that she was angry with him, that she was returning
the book like an unsatisfied customer. But when he flipped it
open to test the binding, wondering if she had actually read the
thing, two pieces of paper fell out.

One read:

> *There will be a dance tonight in my honor at the Casino
> Español de la Habana. You might enjoy yourself, and spend
> the night dancing with a lovely Cuban woman. I will be con-
> demned by etiquette to stay put and watch the festivities, but
> if you come, I will be able to watch you dance and laugh,
> which should be enough.*
>
> *EBO*

The other paper was an invitation, inked in gold, with such
a flourishing script that Tomás had difficulty reading it. He
showed it to Amalia, who was flushed and tired after spending
a day wandering up and down the Malecón. Her hair was stiff
with sea spray, and she had brought back a seashell, upon

which someone had painted the Spanish flag and sold it to her for a few centavos.

Amalia's countenance darkened a bit. "It's notes like this one that Queen Isabel used to install the men she favored in the palace. I love Eulalia, but she is the queen's daughter at the end of the day."

"I'm going, Mamá."

"You should, of course. But be careful. Eulalia is a married woman."

"It's not like that."

Amalia looked away for a moment, then said, "Of course, hijo. I—I asked the innkeeper if he had heard of Gisela's photography studio, and he hadn't. I'm not meant to find her," Amalia said.

"Perhaps not," Tomás replied, glad in his heart. It wasn't that he hoped his mother would fail, but it felt to him that she was reopening a wound.

"By day, I look for Gisela, and at night, I dream of her strange eyes," Amalia said. "I had hoped that coming here I would feel things out within myself, decide what I might say to my old friend. When I was young, I could not think of Gisela without anger brewing in my belly like a sickness. I could not think of her in any way other than this—that she was calculating and heartless—and the thought made my queasiness fade because I had the moral high ground."

"And now?" Tomás asked.

"Things are more complicated than that. There are so many layers, hijo. If only, if only, then, then," she said, marking turns with her hand in the air.

Tomás chest tightened. *If only, then, if only, then.* His mind had settled into that pattern without his permission. Regrets were strange, corrosive things, he thought. And yet, he could not imagine an existence where he didn't think of Juana often, where he didn't mourn her, or mourn his father.

"Are you still angry at him? Papá, I mean," Tomás asked. The question left his lips before he could consider whether it was a good thing to ask.

Amalia shook her head. "I don't think I'm angry at anyone anymore," she said. "It takes so much effort."

Later, the two of them sat on a balcony and watched the sun set over Havana. The buildings seemed to soak up that golden light, and the sea breezes whipped Amalia's hair across her eyes. Groups of pelicans in the distance skimmed the water, and below them, a fat iguana marched down the sidewalk, slow and confident like a politician.

Tomás told his mother about his morning at the finca, about the heat and Eulalia's near-fainting spell, and about the strange man at the gate, who seemed primed to stir up trouble. "It's a strange country," he said. "But I like it. I feel like I can come and go here, like the waves. Can you imagine spending a day with Eulalia in Spain? I'd have to be her husband's valet. Or a tutor to one of her boys."

"And even then, you wouldn't see her," Amalia said. She was holding the invitation to the dance in her hands, and she spun it around and around. "Perhaps, before the dance, we can go see the Cathedral, you and I?"

"Of course, Mamá. We should see the sights while we can. Soon enough, we'll be in the United States. And before we know it, we'll be back in Burgos, and all of this will feel like a dream," Tomás said. In his hand was a tumbler of rum, the ice long melted. But his face was sleepy, and the smiles came lazily to his face.

"I like to see you smile, hijo," she said. "You should drink more often."

"Mamá!" Tomás protested, laughing, then he took another sip. They watched the sea for a while as it darkened. Spanish naval ships dotted the horizon, and Tomás could just make out the holes on the sides of the ship made for cannons. He pointed them out to his mother.

"No more talk of war. Tomorrow, we'll light a candle or two in a beautiful cathedral far from Burgos, hijo. And at night, you will attend a dance, maybe meet a nice girl, yes?"

Tomás took another swig of rum, nodding at his mother. *A nice girl*, he thought, and his mind filled itself with memories of Eulalia that afternoon, her skin glistening in the heat, smooth as paper, and he, thinking how he might write a story upon it.

11

In the morning, Tomás dressed, put a blue handkerchief in his shirt pocket, and knocked on his mother's door, ready for their excursion in Havana. But Amalia emerged from her room with groggy, swollen eyes, and complaining about her back.

"I couldn't walk all that way," she said.

"Perhaps just down the street a bit, to get some air?"

Amalia shook her head. "You don't understand what it means to get old. You will someday, God willing." Behind her, open on her bed, was the old letter from Gisela. Tomás opened his mouth to say something about it, but she closed the door. Tomás had only recently started to notice these spells of hers, when her aching body matched an aching mood. Sometimes, he would force her out, and for short moments, she would be herself again. But the little windows would shut again, and she would complain about her legs, or her shoulders, and it would be a hard night for them both. Better to let her rest, he thought, then stepped out into the morning.

The sun was just up, and the streets were still wet from the night. Vendors were setting up outside their shops, rows and rows of papaya and guanabana, and a few early mangoes. Some were split down the middle, and the colorful flesh of the fruit attracted flies and made the air sweet.

Tomás palmed a small mango, wondering what it might taste like and searching his pockets for some coins, when a woman in a parasol brushed against him as she passed. "Me perdonas," he began to say, looking up to find Eulalia, her face shaded and fresh, smiling at him.

"Walk with me?" she said, and he left a few coins, he didn't pay attention to how much, and put the mango in his pocket.

"Let's go," he said, and she took his arm. Her touch no longer shocked him. With each encounter, Eulalia became more real to him, more tangible, warmer and varied.

"You're up early," she said.

"With the dawn. Mamá wanted to go sightseeing, but she wasn't feeling well this morning. She's fine, fine," he added, when he heard Eulalia suck in a small breath. They walked in silence, pausing every so often to admire the sky, which was blushing in pink and orange. As often as he could Tomás stole a look at the infanta. He hoped she could not feel his pulse in his arm. What was it about these Bourbon women that entranced men so? he wondered. Was it only in the depth of their power, or was there something else in their faces that sang out to others? Suddenly, Tomás stopped in the middle of a dusty road.

Before them was a small shop, with an extraordinarily wide door. Above the door, a sign read "Fotografía Cesár."

Tomás had stopped in another photography studio the day before, only to find that the man inside was French, and did not know anyone named Gisela. Curious, he began to open the door.

"Tomás, wait," Eulalia said, but he released her arm and pressed forward. The windows were draped within with heavy, black curtains. The awning over the door was striped black and gold. Two bronze angel wings flanked the doorknob. The place seemed rich somehow, like a miniature palace of the supernatural.

Tomás turned the doorknob, and disappeared into the dark interior. Eulalia followed him, her parasol still open.

"Gisela?" he called out, his eyes adjusting to the dark.

A tall man emerged from the shadows. "We aren't open yet," he said.

Tomás gasped. "Dios mio," he said. "Ay, Dios santo."

"What is it? Who is this?" Eulalia whispered.

The tall man nodded, as if in understanding. "These things are hard. I am so sorry for your loss. With a photograph, you can remember your loved one always. Death is inevitable, isn't it?" he chattered on as Eulalia slowly approached and leaned against Tomás.

Outside, the sun dipped behind a cloud, and behind this man, the shadows darkened in response. "Look at him," Tomás said. "He is my father all over again," he said, his knees beginning to buckle.

This tall, formidable man looked so much like Rubén. Answers to questions he had not known to ask were making themselves known, like pebbles washing away in a stream, revealing the mud beneath. A name from the past, a name he once heard his father crying out in the middle of the night came to mind at once.

"Martín?" he asked tremulously, and the man's brow furrowed.

"Yes, I am Martín."

"How is it possible? Your mother? Where is Gisela?" Tomás asked.

Martín said nothing, only led Eulalia to a cushioned seat in the corner. It was over-stuffed, and covered in a deep purple velvet. "The lady should sit," he said. Tomás wondered how many corpses had been posed on it.

"Señora," Martín said, gently, folding Eulalia's parasol for her. Her eyes were wide, and she tried in vain to catch Tomás's gaze. "Gisela, my mother, died ten years ago. Did you know her? Back in Spain? I can hear your accent," he said to Tomás.

Tomás felt his mouth drop open, but no sound came out.

"Now, now," Martín was saying. "She was quite ill, and now she is with our Lord."

How practiced he was. How smooth. How comfortable with death, even that of his mother. His patience bothered Tomás.

"I am sorry to hear about your mother," he said. "And I'm sorry that you are an orphan now. We thought you yourself died nearly thirty years ago, so pardon me. It's a bit of a shock. Your father died ten years ago as well."

"Tomás, what's going on?" Eulalia began to say, rising from her seat.

Martín's gently worried face froze and it was as if Tomás could hear his poise shattering seconds before it actually did. He rose to his full height, which was considerable.

"You look like him. Just like our father, Rubén. Did your mother tell you that?" Tomás said.

Martín stared and Tomás could tell what he was thinking— that in some ways it was like looking in a mirror. "The shop is closed," Martín said at last. He walked over to the door, his long legs taking slow strides, then held the door open. A blast of heat came in. His hand shook on the door handle.

"Let's go," Tomás said to Eulalia. Halfway there, he paused, thinking of his mother, the shock and anger wearing off. "We are staying at the Reyes Inn. Come see an old friend of your mother's. She'll have many things to tell you."

Martín stared as if Tomás and Eulalia were not there at all, as if he were seeing right through them. Then he wiggled the door, shooing them away like a pair of mangy dogs who had wandered in. They went through the door, and it felt to Tomás as if he were closing the coffin on Rubén's face again, seeing it for the last time.

The lock turned with a click. From deep within, they heard a loud sound, and Tomás imagined that Martín had kicked that velvet chair with all his strength. He would know—it's exactly what Rubén would have done, too.

He stared at the door, lost in thought, when Eulalia hit him with her parasol. "When in the presence of an infanta, one does not drag her through unknown doors and subject her to unknown dramas. If you wish to maintain our company, then you will do well to follow protocol," she said, her face flushed, her hands trembling.

But Tomás was still staring at the closed door, as if he could see through it. Eulalia struck him with her parasol again, breaking the spell.

"Protocol," Tomás said acidly. "I thought you didn't care for it? I read your book. Soon the whole world will. So what is it, su alteza, do we follow protocol or don't we?" Tomás said, his voice rising, sure that Martín could hear him.

"Hush," Eulalia said, glancing at the door to be sure it did not open again. "If I'm found here—"

But Tomás was walking away from her, down the narrow street and back toward the inn.

"Where are you going? You can't leave me here," Eulalia said. She struggled with her parasol, the opening mechanism stuck.

Tomás stopped. He took a deep breath, his thoughts racing. Had his father known that Martín lived? Was he not there when Gisela gave birth? Tomás couldn't imagine he stayed away long enough for her to go through it alone. He could almost see the scene—Gisela, her son just an infant, and Rubén, guilt-stricken and miserable. In his hand is a valuable gem, and he proffers it to Gisela and tells her to take it and disappear. He kisses the top of his son's head, he holds him in the light, and he realizes that light can sometimes burn, and so he walks back into the darkness and the shadow. Later, he tells Amalia that the child is dead, and she believes it because she has intimate knowledge of those kinds of losses.

"Of course, su alteza. I will walk you back." He unjammed the parasol, and handed it to her silently. She held it tight against her head, her face obscured. They passed newspaper stands with her face upon them, and Tomás could see Eulalia turning away from them.

After a while, she spoke. "I don't mean to pry—"

"Then don't," Tomás said.

Eulalia stopped walking. "I don't have many friends. I have not had any, really, since I was a child in Paris. You were my first friend, weren't you? And I've not been kind," she said.

They walked on, clouds darkening the sky rapidly. "I thought it only rained in the afternoons," Eulalia said, but Tomás only hurried on.

Soon, a tropical storm broke and great big flashes erupted overhead. Eulalia began to cry without shame, the thunderbolts masking the sounds she was making. The rain hurled itself against them, and she huddled against Tomás, trudging on. When they reached the home where she was staying they were soaked through, and surprised to find that the foyer was empty. They made such a sloshing noise with their shoes that they tiptoed up the stairs to the wing of the house Eulalia was using. It was still early in the morning, and the ladies in waiting were still sleeping. Antonio was staying on the other side of the house. "He hasn't even been to see my rooms yet," Eulalia whispered, and Tomás could not tell if there was regret in her voice about that or not.

She opened a wide wooden door, and together they stepped inside. Above the door was a half-circle, set with colorful glass panes. Red, green, and blue splashes of light were cast upon the tiled floor. They left wet footprints behind them, and Eulalia skirted the large oriental rug in the center of the room. She gestured to a pair of chairs by a bookcase. "Not that one," she said, when Tomás chose the upholstered chair. "You're all wet." So he picked a cane chair instead. "Perhaps you don't want to tell me—" she began to say.

"No. It's fine." He told her what he knew quickly, his eyes on his shoes. Eulalia said nothing, only held herself by the waist. When Tomás was done, he looked up, and noticed she was shivering.

"You should get dry," he said.

"I'll be right back."

She disappeared behind another door set in the back of the room. Tomás went to the window that overlooked an enclosed garden. A small lawn was dotted with blooming gardenia trees. Tomás cranked open the window and the scent wafted up at once, filling the room.

"Such a scent," Eulalia said behind him. She had changed into a taffeta dress of vertical stripes in brown and white. The cuffs of her sleeves were trimmed in white lace, and stopped just shy of her wrists, exposing those small bones Tomás always found himself contemplating. Her hair was loose about her shoulders, much longer than Tomás had imagined. The curls were still wet, though no longer soaked. "What do you think?" she asked, and spun slowly. "Good enough for the bullfight later this morning?"

"Is that on the itinerary, too?" Tomás asked. He'd never been to a bullfight, but as a child in Burgos, he had climbed trees outside the ring and watched from a distance. They were only thrilling for a moment or two, when the bull charged. But the animals exhausted themselves so quickly, and the sword tips were so deadly, that Tomás lost interest after a while.

Eulalia nodded. "And the dance at the Casino Español tonight, do remember. You're going, yes? Would you like to come to the bullfight as well?" she asked, adjusting a lace cuff.

Tomás almost said yes. But he hadn't forgotten about Martín. Being there, in Eulalia's room, almost made him forget. He had to go back to Amalia at once, tell her what he had learned. "I can't," he said.

"Your mother, of course. It's been a trying morning, hasn't it? So many secrets," she said, almost to herself. Tomás thought about her book, the queen's indiscretions with men like Tenorio. At the very least, Tomás knew that Rubén was his father. That couldn't be denied, they resembled each other so much. But Eulalia, he supposed, would never know for sure whom she took after.

"It has," he said. "I should go, before anyone knows I'm here."

Eulalia frowned a little. "Wait," she said, walked over, and plucked the blue handkerchief from Tomás's pocket. "You've left your handkerchief behind and will have to return for it later."

Tomás laughed, and reached for the handkerchief, tugging it harder than he'd planned. Or else, Eulalia had held onto it too fiercely, because he'd pulled all of her toward him, so that now she was closer than she had ever been. They stayed that way for a second, long enough for him to catch the mint on her breath. Then, they broke apart swiftly, and the handkerchief fell to the tiled floor.

"I'll see myself out," he said, leaving her standing there in the center of the room, her hand still working the lace at her wrist.

Back at the inn, the innkeeper was busy sweeping and humming to himself, barely acknowledging Tomás as he passed him by, even though he had been caught in another rainstorm and was leaving a trail behind him.

Tomás stayed in his room a long time, going over everything that had happened with Martín, with Eulalia. He heard his mother in the room next door, snoring still. The thought of going to her now, and telling her all of it, exhausted him. No, he thought. For Amalia, time was a chasm that could not be bridged, and this would only make a hard day even harder. He would wait until tomorrow, until after whatever was to happen at the Casino Español that night happened.

12

Tomás arrived very late in the evening. The building resembled some in Spain, with its many small balconies tucked into dark arches. There were no statues of haunted saints, but instead, sculptures of overgrown vegetation and fruit decorated the building here and there. Outside the Casino Español, women milled about in small groups, wearing long lace dresses and glittering shawls about their shoulders. Some wore lacquered peinetas in their hair, in a style that was more Spanish than Cuban. Men in fine suits, and others in military dress uniforms, smoked cigars, crushing the stubs out with their boot heels. Tomás overheard them talking about *Il venditore d'uccelli*, which they'd just seen over at the Teatro Tacon earlier in the evening, and Eulalia's name was on everyone's lips. Every once in a while, a man and woman broke off from their chattering groups and linked arms, then headed into the theater. Tomás followed a happy pair—he was large and ambling, his suit stretched to fit his wide girth, and she was thin and angular, with a sharp nose and large knuckles. If my mother were here, Tomás thought, she would say they were un diez—she the one and he the zero.

Inside, the ceiling was painted blue, and all around, there were cane chairs draped in gold fabric, and small, lace-topped tables. Lace was the predominant fabric on the women and on their fans, which they beat rapidly, the mother-of-pearl handles clicking in time with the movement of their wrists. Suddenly, the Marcha Real began to play, and the crowd inside the Casino Español hushed, people rose from their golden seats, and only the click-click of the fans could be heard. A light was thrown onto a balcony above the main stage, where an orchestra was now standing at their instruments. Eulalia and her husband appeared, their arms raised in salutation. Enthusiastic "¡Viva!"s erupted all around, and Tomás watched as Eulalia became happier when they reached her ears, how her smile grew and grew until she pulled it back a bit, in control again. She, too, wore lace—an intricate design in silver lying over blue fabric. The diamonds in her hair sparkled. Antonio was waving, too, and giving the crowd his indolent smile. Her right arm was linked to his left, and when she waved, she shook him, as if his spine was made of something soft, like bread.

The orchestra announced the Mignon Overture, and they took up their instruments and began to play. It was not the kind of music that was good for dancing, but the Cubans around Tomás swayed anyway, so fluidly, so like the water that surrounds the island, that he believed the blood in their veins must thrum in time to secret rhythms. Tomás watched as Eulalia and Antonio sat farther back in the balcony, and how, one at a time, they greeted visitors—mainly ladies who held the hems of their long gowns by the tips of their fingers as they talked.

As Tomás watched Eulalia, the music became livelier, the

members of the orchestra grew sweatier, and pairs started to form on the dance floor, each making elegant rounds, fans dangling from the hands of the women and striking their partners' backs, whipping them lightly as they spun. Up in the balcony, Eulalia was nodding in time to the music, even as someone spoke to her. Her cheeks were full of roses. Her hair had taken on a reddish glow. Tomás breathed fast, and before he knew it, he was standing on the stairs to the balcony, waiting for his turn to greet the royal couple.

He waited in line without making conversation with the others. They chattered about Eulalia's dress, the Casino's decorations, the food, the weather, the state of the sea lately, their shoes; they chatted about everything under the bright, Caribbean sun, but not one of them mentioned the war. It was as if a revolution was not happening at all. From what Tomás understood, the battles were happening in the east, in the province they called Oriente, in cities like Santiago de Cuba. But there in Havana, among people of a certain kind of wealth, the revolution was only a little bother, like a mosquito that had landed in one's milk.

Eulalia noticed Tomás while she was speaking to an elderly couple—he in a top hat and she in lace, of course. The infanta's eyes widened and her nostrils flared a little, and Tomás could see that she was hurrying the couple by offering her hand for them to take. They kissed it instead, once, twice, taking turns as if she were a dessert they were sharing. It was Antonio who stopped them by alerting a guard.

Tomás stepped forward, bowing deeply. "Su altezas," he said.

"Antonio, this is the son of my nodriza, Tomás Aragón," she said. He bowed again before the prince.

The infante seemed to appraise Tomás from head to toe, looking up at him, his mouth pursed, his hands laced behind his back.

Then, Antonio sat in his seat and stretched his legs. "How interesting. I don't even remember my nodriza. I'm sure I had many."

"You must not have had any good ones, because I remember mine," Eulalia said.

Laughing, Antonio leaned forward, as if he was about to tell Tomás a secret. "How would she know? She claims to remember her own birth. Don't believe a word of it," he said.

Eulalia's own smile faded a little, but she rallied, and asked Tomás how he was enjoying the dance.

"It is a beautiful building. The orchestra is good," he, stumbling about for conversation. The formality of it felt so strange after what had happened between them that morning. He could still feel her hand on his cheek, her cool, phantom touch. "I haven't tried the food. Crab, I think, and, and some wine," he rambled on. Thank God, a danzón, Tomás thought as the music started up. Both Eulalia and Tomás smiled at once at the sound of the clave knocking together in a one-one-two rhythm. Below them, the Cuban women opened their fans, and they gestured with them to the men, who sauntered forward. A cheer was heard from the back of the room, and the couples started to dance, moving their feet together in sequences of four small steps, with sharp turns every once in a while, their heads still, their eyes locked on one another.

"Antonio, the music," Eulalia said, reaching out her hand to her husband, but he shook his head.

"Is it proper? Sounds a little vulgar to me," he answered, nervous now at the sound of the song that was growing louder and louder. "What would your mother say?"

"I don't expect she can see us here all the way from Spain," Eulalia said.

"You write her every night."

Eulalia leaned forward a little, a laugh in her voice. "I won't tell her that we enjoyed a danzón," she said, but Antonio frowned, and Tomás could see the laugh dying in her, like a light diminishing in the early morning.

Eulalia stood at the balcony. Tomás stood behind her and followed her gaze. Her feet moved a little, mimicking the dancers, her fingers drumming on the handrail. Antonio had risen, too, and struck up a conversation with another visitor to their box, a man in military dress who was showing off his silver-plated pistol.

Tomás was standing between them—Antonio, now holding the gun up and peering down the sight, and Eulalia, her back to Tomás, her hips moving left and right. He took a few steps forward. "If I could, I would dance with you," he whispered. She stilled. Tomás could hear his mother's voice in his head. *Tomás, no, no, no.*

"We called this the contredanse back in France," she said to Tomás, to the air. "But this is better. Faster."

"I've never danced once in my life," he said. It wasn't exactly true. Once, Juana had tried to make him dance at a festival. She had grabbed him by the waist and he had let himself be pulled into the crowd. But while she danced, really danced, he only swayed, unsure of himself and delighted into stillness by her beauty.

"I know I have," Eulalia said. "But on my life I can't remember when or how. So you see why I wrote my story?" she asked.

"The new pages you mentioned, I'd like to see—"

"Later. You may see them later," she said. Another danzón had started, this one even faster than the last. Her voice was soft, different sounding. Tomás fought the impulse to reach for Eulalia's hand and walk out of the Casino Español with her, to take her to the east, to Oriente, to show her some small, dusty barn and say to her, "Here you are free," to bang out a rhythm with a pair of sticks and watch her dance and dance . . .

"I need a secretary," she said out of nowhere. Behind them, Antonio was back in his chair, and the man with the pistol was now in Eulalia's seat, the two of them chuckling over a joke. Tomás caught the punchline and, against his wishes, found himself thinking that the infante was a genial sort of fellow, more at home with men than with his wife.

Tomás said nothing in response to Eulalia's statement of need. He felt strange and out of place. Had Eulalia suggested that she, like Verne, would visit the center of the earth, Tomás would not have been surprised.

"I need a secretary," she said again, this time to Antonio, who stood, and asked her to repeat herself over the loud music. Below, people were clapping and shouting to the sounds of a song familiar to them, but new to everyone in the balcony.

A waiter came in with three sweating flutes of champagne, one for each of the infantes and one for the military man. Tomás was left empty-handed. The military man raised his glass and said, "Viva el Rey," to which they responded their vivas, Tomás with his hands behind his back for lack of a better thing to do with them. Antonio downed his drink in one, the heat, even at night and indoors, oppressive.

Eulalia sipped, and said, "Tomás is a scribbler." That word again. "He is going to Chicago anyway. Perhaps he can accompany us on our steamship, serve as my secretary."

Antonio thought about it for a moment. Tomás wondered whether he knew about Isabel's many secretaries, that Tenorio had been one of them for many years. Antonio walked over to Eulalia, and kissed her lips firmly. Her arms dropped to her sides at once, as if his kiss was a blow to the head and he had stunned her like a fish. The orchestra trumpets blared, and the crowd was singing along and clapping. Antonio and Eulalia parted, his lips wet. "Of course, Eulalia. Whatever you desire," he said, then returned to his military man for more conversation.

"It's settled," she said to Tomás after a moment. "Tell Ama, she will be so happy. We depart in four days."

"I'll think it over," he said, and she widened her eyes.

"We would be most pleased if—" she began.

"I am grateful, I am." Tomás pictured the road ahead, what it might be like to be with Eulalia night and day. He remembered his mother, in service for so long, how she kept her old uniforms pressed and clean, as if she might be called back at any moment. Would he be tethered to her, like a shadow, for a lifetime?

Eulalia interrupted his train of thought by putting a gloved hand on his own. "I have another page for you," she whispered. She went over to where a small, pearl-encrusted clutch had been set on a table. She opened it up, and pulled out a folded sheet of paper. She took one furtive glance at Antonio, saw that he was still chatting with the man in uniform, and brought the page to Tomás. "Here. Things change moment to moment, and I intend to capture them as they do," she said. "Perhaps, after you've read this, you will be firmer of mind."

The music changed again to a slow waltz, and suddenly Antonio was at her side. "If you'd like, we can dance now," he said, his tone bored, his smile seductive.

Tomás left them to it, and as he went, he heard Eulalia's unrestrained laughter, which beat in his ears all along the quiet walk back to the inn.

Eulalia

Soon, I will be leaving Cuba and heading to New York, to Washington, D.C., and then on to Chicago, for the Columbian Exposition. I've heard stories about the many wonders I will see there, including a contraption called a Ferris Wheel, which takes one up into the sky to view the city and brings one down again. It is no Eiffel Tower, I'm sure.

I am eager to see it all, but sad to leave this island. They say that it is easy to win over Cuban hearts, and I believe it is true. How else can one explain the kindnesses these people have shown me, even as they war against my country and my family?

I have been fed well here, adored here, seen impossible things here. But even so, it feels as if the crown of Spain, in my person, is saluting Cuba for the last time. This visit that Antonio and I are in the midst of making is a farewell, of this I am sure.

Other things are ending, too.

Recently, I discovered a letter among Antonio's papers, directed at him, and full of errors and misspellings. "Sielito lindo," it begins, that wayward "s" at the start of the word an affront to anyone who has ever read a book. The letter ends with the name "Carmela," in a signature that is torpid and brutish.

This Carmela, this actress, I've discovered, has a round face and a head of dark curls. In her portraits (of which there are a few), she wears dresses with low necklines and bare arms, and she is all cream-colored skin. In rumors I've heard her called "la Infantona." I've heard that Antonio is taking money to build her a home, a miniature palace where he can keep her like a pet. Each time, I find that I cannot breathe when I hear it.

If I ever meet this Carmela from Cordoba, this actress, I will say to her, "Take my place, if you want it. Be courageous and show your face to the world the way I have always had to do. Behold this platter. Undress and lay upon it."

I would do it. I swear I would.

Thus Spain releases her hold on Cuba, thus Antonio shakes me off, and I him. Carmela writes him letters? So will

I write letters. Many of them. And they will come together and shake the foundations of Spain so that women in my country will feel the tremors of it and grow bold.

13

That night, Tomás read Eulalia's addition to the manuscript. It was written so recently that tiny pockets of ink were still fresh on the page. These he patted, and left his fingerprint on the edges of the page. Eulalia, he knew, would shatter his heart. He was somehow entertaining to her, a respite from her husband's hard words and the hungry glares of the adoring public. Tomás knew that he, with his country manners and his bookishness, was no Portuguese prince, no Carlos Braganza. Was he capable of making her wilt like a daisy in the heat, or would his knees be the ones to buckle?

Then, a thought came to him, and the pity of it made him hold his breath—*she will make a Tenorio out of me.*

In the morning, the child that had delivered the book with Eulalia's note within was back. He waited calmly in the lobby, and in his hand was another note. When he saw Tomás appear, he ran to him, whispered, "Señor, para ti," then waited with his hand outstretched. This time, Tomás gave him a few centavos and watched him go into the bright sunlight, running as fast as he could go.

Once again, the note was in Eulalia's hand, on creamy paper, and it read: "Another bullfight. Two o'clock. This one presented by the mayor. Do come this time."

Tomás tucked the note in his pocket. He did not want to see her again so soon, not when he hadn't made up his mind yet. Besides, there was still the business with Martín to take care of.

He decided he would tell his mother what he had learned over breakfast.

"I have something to tell you. I found Gisela's shop."

Amalia stopped eating. She put her hand over her mouth, and with the other clutched at Tomás for support. Her shaking hands fumbled at his wrist.

"Mamá, she's gone."

"Ay," Amalia said, and crossed herself.

"Martín, Mamá. Martín lives," he told her then.

Amalia shook her head. "He wouldn't have lied to me, not about that, not after all he put me through," she said, and Tomás knew she meant the other babies, the ones she had lost before. "She must have had another son."

"He looks like me, Mamá. We are the same height. It was like seeing Papá all over again," he said. "He must not have known."

Amalia listened quietly. Tears clung to her eyelashes. The innkeeper's niece, wearing a crisp white apron, brushed past, and cleared the table next to theirs, her presence reducing Amalia's speech to whispers. Sorrow and fear troubled her voice. "Take me to him, mi rey. I want to see for myself."

Their walk was long and laborious. Halfway there, they skirted a scene in which a donkey had died while still attached to its cart. The owner struggled to get the harness off, and passersby remarked that the poor animal's hooves were over-grown, and that its ribs were showing. As the owner sweated and cursed, people chastened him, and petted the dead crea-ture, giving it succor it no longer needed. They passed a church with three graceful arches, and a priest standing out-side, offering to bless people as they walked. Amalia stopped and the priest put his rough palm on the crown of her head.

Tomás couldn't tell if the blessing had lent her any strength, but she walked a little taller than before as they made their way to Martín with renewed purpose, and they did not stop again until they were at the front door of the studio.

They let themselves in. In the dim twilight of the room, they could make out Martín positioning the body of a small child on a bed. The boy's long, dark ringlets he took in his fingers, twirling them just so, and laid them on his shoulders. The bed was merely a box, upon which Martín had draped a lacy coverlet. In the corner, the boy's mother wept quietly, nodding every so often. Martín stood back to assess his work. Tomás felt his own eyes pricking at the scene. How was this a comfort? he thought. Emilia, Francisca, Rubén, Alicia. The names his mother had recited her whole life came to mind, his long-dead siblings. Had she prayed for Martín's soul, too?

But there he was—alive, and tall, and gentle. He caught sight of Tomás, but said nothing as he went back to work. He whispered to the grieving mother, then stood behind the camera, which he had rolled out and put in place. He adjusted the plates in the camera, then, lifting the black sheet, he ducked his head within. Holding his hand aloft, he squeezed a bulb and the camera snapped. This Martín did a few more times, then he walked the mother over to her child, placed her trembling arms around the small shoulders, and took another photograph. He whispered something else to her, before rolling the camera away to a back room.

The woman began to wrap the child, carefully, in a muslin sheet.

Martín appeared again, nodded at them, and led them outside. He held the door open for a man, one Tomás took for the father of the child, who was just then walking in. He and Martín exchanged a charged look and before the door closed, Tomás heard the woman inside let out a plaintive wail at the sight of her husband.

"My mother always said that the dead were amenable," Martín explained there in the shade outside his shop. "There was never the danger that they might blink or move and blur the picture. But, unlike a bowl of oranges one might photograph, the dead were colorless, ossified, and cold. When my mother married my stepfather, I was quite young, and had not yet spoken my first words, though the time for that had passed. I do not know how they fell in love, or even if they were ever in love. But I do know that my mother had been a midwife once, that she had ushered many Spaniards into life, and that now she was memorializing the deaths of many more, an ocean away from Spain. Is that the woman you knew? Is that your Gisela?"

Amalia nodded.

"The photographer was your stepfather, then?" Tomás asked.

"Yes. The only father I knew."

"I was told you had died. I prayed for your soul every night, but here you are," Amalia said at last.

Martín was silent, his face cast in doubt.

"Gisela chose this work?" Tomás asked, hoping to keep the conversation going. He didn't want Martín to throw them out like he did last time.

"She always says the work chose her, but never told me why. The death portraits were endless, she would say. The appointments never stopped. This small studio became known for them, and so old ladies on their way to church crossed themselves when they passed her studio, as if they were walking past a cemetery. The back door was enlarged to accommodate stretchers. My first words, in fact, came at last when I was almost six years old. My mother and stepfather were posing a man in a Spanish soldier's uniform. They had seated him in a chair, and had asked his grieving wife to lay her hand on his shoulder. Just as the weeping woman touched him, the corpse fell forward, his hat tumbling over my feet. Three teeth bounced out of the man's mouth, scattering like marbles. From what I'm told, I screamed, and yelled, 'Mamá, no!'"

Martín was silent then, perhaps realizing that he had said too much, too soon.

"You would think the war would make for good business," Martín said, shaking his head. "I'd rather take portraits of living people," he said, "but I'd need a new sign, a new shop even." Then, he rubbed his fingers together in that universal gesture for money. "Times are hard." Inside the studio, someone coughed and coughed, and the sound filtered outside to them.

"How did Gisela die?" Amalia asked.

Martín cleared his throat. "She was ill for a long time. Seizures, fainting spells. They would happen without notice. They got worse when my stepfather died." This time, Martín did not elaborate.

Then it seemed as if none of them knew what else to say. He was a stranger to them, and while they shared a father, Tomás felt no kinship with the man, aside from the fact that they both had a strong, angular jaw, and hair of the same rough texture. Tomás had always wanted a sibling, and the litany of names her mother spoke at least once a day did nothing to ease that desire for him. But the emptiness he felt in the moment surprised him. Finally, uncomfortable with the silence and his own distant feelings, Tomás asked, "Do you have a family?"

It was a strange choice of words. He has one, Tomás thought, and he is standing before you awkwardly.

But Martín alleviated the tension, saying, "You can meet them. Give me a minute to close the shop." The mourners within had gone out a back door and the place was quiet again, the box with the lace coverlet on it bare and sad. They watched Martín go about the end of his day. He counted his money, he straightened furniture, he gave the counter that held a stack of photographic plates one quick dusting, he pulled his keys from his pocket and locked the back door. All the while, he hummed and hummed.

"I had a shop of my own," Tomás said. "A bookshop."

"I'm not one for reading," Martín said.

"Most people aren't."

"But everyone dies. The profits go to me," he said. The joke settled flatly between them. They followed him out of the shop, around the corner of the building. Amalia began to say something about Burgos as they walked, but they were cut short when Martín started to climb a flight a stairs that seemed to appear out of nowhere.

"You live above the shop?" Tomás asked, and Martín nodded.

He opened a small white door, and what lay beyond made Tomás catch his breath. Arched windows covered an entire wall. The floor was composed of thousands of colorful tiles, gleaming in the sunlight. Bright white walls begged for art, but they were blank, save for a cross dangling over every doorway. A woman emerged from the kitchen, and with her came a wave of scents—garlic and onion and cumin. Then children came running toward Martín, pushing into wicker rocking chairs and banging into low glass tables.

"¡Papá!" they cried, and he gathered them to him and kissed their cheeks. In his indulgences, this was the life Tomás had imagined for himself, back when Juana was still alive—to be a man surrounded by children who loved him, to have a beautiful wife, to live in a place that was so full of sun that he would have to squint in order to see. The scene made his heart ache.

"My wife," Martín said, and she was beside Tomás in an instant, offering her cheek for a kiss, then doing the same with Amalia. The woman gestured a good deal. Her dark hair, nearly black, was so thick that it had escaped the pins that held it back in places. She was very tall, taller than Martín. Her voice cut and carried, and Tomás imagined she was likely a good singer. This woman, named Teresa, was all superlatives, and she was enthralling.

"Martín told me about your surprise visit," Teresa said. Tomás couldn't tell from her expression if he'd told her more than that old friends of Gisela's had arrived from Spain. She pointed to a rooftop courtyard. "Would you like to see it? We have the best views in Havana."

They followed her out, and the children trailed behind them. A pair of blue jays hopped from one branch to another. Buildings rolled out like hills in the distance, brightly painted like jewelers' boxes. Beyond that, the sea glimmered like a mirage in the heat.

But Teresa was pulling their gaze away from beauty in the distance, directing them to the garden she had grown. "Mango," Teresa said, pointing to a potted tree. "In flower, too. You see them? This one here is avocado. She won't flower until later this summer. Guava over there. Let's see, that's fruta bomba. Guanabana in the corner. Limes you recognize, yes? I have to give the trees away when they get too big. I wish we had a plot of land of our own," Teresa said.

Tomás took in deep breaths of the sweet air. Teresa, sensing perhaps her own distant future, picked up the baby, who was fat and happy and dimpled all over. His hair was curly and his skin browner than that of his siblings, so that he looked as if he'd spent all of his short life in the blazing sun. Teresa placed him in Amalia's arms and said, "Manolito, this is Señora Aragón."

"Can you say 'Ama,'" Amalia said to the baby, and touched his nose with her own. "He looks like Gisela, this one. Beautiful boy," she cooed, bouncing and humming a tune Tomás did not know.

Martín, who had been watching in silence, grew serious at

the mention of his mother, and turned back to the apartment. Tomás followed, and they left the women in the garden.

"It's been hard here, my whole life. Very hard," Martín said when they were inside.

What Tomás thought he meant was the arrangement of his life, thrust out of Spain by his own father.

"Our father was a good man," Tomás began to say in Rubén's defense, though why he was defending him was unclear to him. If Rubén had known that Martín lived, would he have sent him away like this? It seemed unbelievable that he would. Rubén, who had always loved Tomás with an affection that was nearly maternal in its tenderness, would choose one child over another? Tomás couldn't make sense of it.

"Does it matter? Both my parents are dead, and death, being so final, is not concerned with a person's goodness. Am I a good man? That's more important to me. Besides, my life was not hard or easy because of my father. It was hard because this colony has been at war my entire life, and war is tiresome and sad, and because my mother was quiet and let her sorrow eat her up."

What might they have been like together? Tomás wondered. Perhaps Martín would have been the philosopher, Tomás the dreamer, making lists, creating universes built on his brother's philosophy. Together, they might have remade the world.

"We've interrupted your peace," Tomás said. "I am sorry."

"So you thought I was dead," Martín said.

"I did. So did my mother."

Martín's eyes were reddening and growing wet. "And who spread that lie?"

"I don't know," he said. Tomás said nothing else, and only watched, horrified, as Martín sat hard on a wooden chair and moaned, his face hidden in his hands. It was a brief thunderstorm, and he quieted almost at once, and soon stared hard at the floor, his toe following the swirl of one of the tiles. "Do not pity me, cast away into the Caribbean, like some Caliban."

"I thought you said you didn't read," Tomás said.

"I went to school. They have schools here."

"I didn't mean to—"

"I don't know what you want from me," he said.

Who am I to bring him the dusk? thought Tomás.

"I came here for a job. I have a delivery to make, you see," Tomás began, trying to explain himself. "And my mother always remembered Gisela, always loved her, and she hoped to see her again. Instead, we found you. And you have found a brother in me. I want you to know that. I'm a good man, Martín, and I think you are too, and we had nothing to do with this mess our parents made together."

Outside, Martín's children squealed and laughed, and Tomás could see them embedding themselves in Amalia's heart like a spoor. He already guessed what his mother was thinking, that Martín was the vine that bore fruit, and such vines needed tending.

Amalia and Teresa came in from outside, red-cheeked and sweaty. Teresa went off to the kitchen and returned with cold water for everyone. She set a pitcher on the table, and four crystal glasses, and the four of them drank in silence.

"Mi hijo," Amalia began after a gulp.

"Would you like to see where she is buried?" Martín asked, his voice gravelly.

Amalia nodded, and with a trembling hand, set down her glass.

They weren't far from the cemetery, and Martín led Amalia and Tomás without speaking much. Teresa had stayed behind with the children, but first had clipped some orange blossoms. She wrapped the stems in a wet towel, and handed the bundle to Amalia. "Gisela was a kind mother-in-law. Do you know, she refused to be my midwife? Even though I begged. Wouldn't see the babies until they were a week old. Such a mystery," she said.

By the time they reached the cemetery, the orange blossoms were already wilting and draping over Amalia's hands like tiny snakes. Once among the graves, they walked slowly past the rows of white tombs, each of them pensive and solemn. The statues of angels and weeping Marías seemed to reflect the sun like a photographer's flashbulb. Here and there, children played among the graves, alighting atop the big ones and jumping off, their arms wide as if they might slip onto a stream of air and fly away.

At first, Martín missed Gisela's grave and had to backtrack. It was modest compared to the others. There was no statue, no marble urn, only a simple headstone.

Gisela Castillo de Rusál, the headstone read.

Martín patted the headstone once, twice, then wiped his eyes with the back of his hand. As for Amalia, she put the blossoms on the grave itself, and then, as if Martín and Tomás weren't there, listening to every word, she began to speak:

"I miss you, dear friend. Thank you for bringing my children into the world. Thank you for grieving with me. Your tears made me feel as if my own were worth shedding. Thank you for the peacock dress, the one I destroyed. I wear it still, in my dreams, where I am still young and full of hope. Thank you for the humming that filled Ruben's days, for the humming I hear in Tomás's throat when he is busy and doesn't think I am listening. Thank you for leaving Spain, for taking that gem that I had stolen and that was later given to me, and making a life for yourself far away from us, so that Rubén might come to me at night and tell me he loved me without distraction."

Halfway through, Martín began to walk away. Tomás watched him from a distance, saw as he stood among unknown dead, his hands in his pockets, swaying a little. He watched as one of the urchins running about slammed into the back of his legs, and how Martín turned slowly, said a few words, then resumed his position.

"Mamá," Tomás said, and touched his mother on the shoulder. She wrapped her arm around his waist.

When they returned to Martín, they found him near a large hedge. "Look at these," he said, "Miniature peppers. They look like small pumpkins. Aji cachucha. Teresa will love these."

"You sound like your father," Amalia said to him, and his face grew serious as he handed her a few of the peppers. "I used to watch Rubén planting the wheat. He wasn't always a farmer, but a carpenter, and so we had good, sturdy furniture in the house. Outside, the plants sometimes died and the crops failed because Rubén was only just learning to be the man he wanted to be. I helped him on occasion, and he would say to me, 'One only has to believe that these seeds will become plants. There is as much faith in this as there is in anything.'"

Martín nodded, as if sealing his father's words somewhere deep inside. Then they left the cemetery and headed back to Martín's shop and his home, where they parted ways.

"Do you think we will see him again?" Tomás mused. They had only three days left in Cuba.

Amalia popped a small pepper into her mouth and chewed slowly, the sweetly sour taste making her scrunch up her face.

14

The next morning, Tomás read about Eulalia and the bullfight. "Any news?" his mother asked over breakfast.

"The bull lost. They always lose. Eulalia gave her ring to the torero, and everyone cheered. She's very generous," he said.

"Did the torero accept right away? Or did he protest?" she asked.

"Let's see," Tomás said, reading further. "It doesn't say, but we can imagine it, can't we. The torero did not deliberate for a moment. Then he slipped the ring onto his pinky finger and held it aloft for everyone to see. Antonio's face was priceless, of course. It looked like someone had slapped him. The torero was very handsome." Tomás's own laughter died then, and he seemed pensive. Despite his reservations, the possibility that he might not return to Burgos, that he might accept Eulalia's offer and see the world at her side, thrilled him.

"Mamá, I have a decision to make."

"What decision?" she asked, confused at the sudden shift.

Instead of telling her, however, Tomás asked her another question. "What do you think of visiting the old nursery? I could buy you a lace gown, like the ones the women at the Casino Español were wearing."

"Don't be ridiculous," she said. "I am not going to be invited to the palace. And you cannot afford a dress like that on a bookseller's salary."

"Mamá, Eulalia wants us to come with her. On her steamship. I will be her secretary and you will be—"

"What?" Amalia asked. Her face had hardened, and looking at her, Tomás felt as if the floor between them had opened up, exposing the lobby below.

"She's offered me a job. Secretario de Su Alteza." He went on, trying to convince his mother and himself. "I failed as a writer. The bookshop is in debt, did you know? I'm not the farmer Papá wanted me to be. My fiancee died and I wasn't allowed at her funeral. Yet, here I am, about to be handed the seal of the house of Orléans."

"Is that what you want? A wax seal in your pocket?" she asked.

Tomás did not know how to say what was in his heart. That

Eulalia thrilled him, and that, at the same time, he feared what she would do to him. That she presented an impossible future made possible. That all his life, he had merely been the milk brother, even after Amalia's service had ended, and how sometimes in her presence, he felt like more. That when she touched his cheek he had felt the boundaries of his life crumble.

But they both grew quiet, collecting their thoughts, building their silent arguments. "Tenorio wrote poems for me for a long time," Amalia said at last. "He would send them to our home, bold as he was, and I would read them, then burn them in the fireplace, did you know that?" Tomás shook his head. "I believe he loved me, I'll have you know. But I was true to your father, even when he wasn't true to me. Because the queen was jealous, I was dismissed." Amalia let the words settle between them before going on. "Your father couldn't read well, you know. But he suspected what the letters were. I never saw Tenorio again, and he seemed to me like a used-up rag. Grieving his wife, used up by the queen, by the government, and left to dry, stiff and awkward and lonely. Keep him in your thoughts, Tomás. Where Tenorio went, you now follow. The life of a secretary is not the life I dreamed of for you, even if it does take you to Chicago and places beyond that."

Tomás hated hearing his own thoughts and fears echoed this way. He might have resembled Rubén physically, but inside he was all Amalia.

"Don't you think that the queen listened to him? That he helped her in some way? I could help Eulalia. I could teach her to be more like you," Tomás said, his voice raw as if he had swallowed too much water. He knew, even as he said it, that it seemed like the worst kind of foolishness, to think that people could change those in charge of them, those who planned the courses of their little lives in lavish rooms and never asked them what the people thought.

"If I couldn't even change Rubén—" Amalia began.

But Tomás spoke over her. "After we return to Spain, I'll probably move to Madrid," he said.

"You're slipping away from me, not by measures, but in long leaps," Amalia whispered. "You'll follow Eulalia around like a lapdog, and when she is done with you, you will come back to Burgos without your bookshop, without anything, not even your dignity. This is not what Rubén and I wanted for you."

Amalia left before Tomás could say another word. He knew it would be hard, telling her, but he could not have guessed this. He thought darkly of Tenorio, that mysterious man from her past, the man Eulalia thought of as her real father. What a mess these men and women had made, even before Tomás and Eulalia could utter their first words, their first "No," in rebuke of all of it.

He put his hand in his pocket to retrieve his wallet in order to pay for breakfast, and felt a small piece of paper flutter down to the floor, like a dying butterfly. He took it up and saw his list again. This he carried outside to sit for a bit, right on the step in front of the inn.

Couples walked by hand in hand, fresh from the Malecón, that long, low seawall girding Havana. Their hair was stiff from the salt spray. Some of the couples seemed sure of one thing—that they loved one another, and that this was a jewel in their pockets, one they could not lose. It wasn't true of all the pairs that walked past him. Just a few. But Tomás could tell. He had had such a precious thing with Juana, hadn't he? It was in the ease of their walk, the way their hands folded together, or the way they laughed—without fear that they were too loud, showing too many teeth, or embarrassed by their guffawing. He looked at his list again, on paper so soft it felt like a handkerchief.

3) Fall in love.

Tomás tried to imagine walking casually like this with Eulalia, the way he had so often with Juana, saying something so funny that she snorted with laughter. He could not picture it. He tried again, but he was tired, his brain was fuzzy.

Where is my happiness? he wondered. Where is my place? Eulalia and I have this in common. Our miseries can be braided together, can't they? Together, can't they make two broken, meandering lives whole?

A church bell tolled the hour somewhere in the distance, and it joined the other noises of the morning, of dogs yapping, and a trumpet blaring, of the sea's rushing and a woman singing in some bright place.

15

Tomás spent his last days in Cuba at the inn. Eulalia sent another note, which he ignored, the request folded up and stuffed in his pocket. The newspapers detailed the rest of Eulalia's trip—her visit to the Sagrado Corazón, to greet the Mother Superior there, and the detailed description of the white feathered fan the nuns gave her, mounted on a small conch shell; of the delegations of freed slaves who, also armed with painted fans as gifts, met with Eulalia and told her tales of their enslavement and emancipation; and of the small fracas that occurred when she slipped out into the Plaza without chaperones, how the people held her by the shoulders and shook her, and begged her never to leave Cuba.

The effect of reading the newspaper, with doting stories about Eulalia on the front page and tales of the grisly revolution in the war against Spain in the pages that followed, was much like sleeping after a long boat ride—the disorienting waves of royalistas and independistas persisted in making

Tomás feel off balance—and he wavered back and forth on his decision to go with Eulalia.

As for Amalia, she was sullen in the mornings around Tomás, and each day she left early and returned late in the afternoon, with more stories about Martín and his children. Only then was she animated. "The little one is so rough," she laughed. "Look at this," she said, pointing at a little cut on her forehead. "He threw a seashell at me. He needs a firmer hand." Or else she would recount one of Teresa's meals, the amount of garlic they used on the island, and how the onions made her eyes water, but she loved it. She would talk about Martín, how he resembled Gisela and Rubén, how he was a perfect mixture of the two of them. She told Tomás about what she had learned about Gisela, how her mother was from Barbados, and her father a Spaniard from the Canaries, how they raised her in a place called Pinar del Rio, in the shadow of a huge green mogote, like something out of a fairy tale. "Her parents died in a fire, Tomás. Que horror. Poor Gisela, unmothered and unfathered, just like me," Amalia would say, and go on and on until Tomás thought that he knew more about Gisela and Martín now than he knew of his own past.

So, he was not surprised when his mother interrupted his packing to say, "I am staying in Cuba. With Martín. Teresa is pregnant again. She will have her hands full."

"They seem full enough," Tomás said.

"Yes. And, la pobre, she has no family." Amalia wrung her hands, spinning her wedding band around her finger.

Tomás struggled with the trunk, finding it difficult to close. "This stupid thing," he said out loud.

"Did you hear me, Tomás?" Amalia asked.

"What was that again?" He had heard her perfectly well. He had very nearly expected it. If Juana had lived, he thought in that moment, if she and I had had children of our own, we wouldn't be having this conversation.

"Teresa, you see, has difficult pregnancies, and I was telling her that I knew a thing or two about that, and about raising babies, as a nodriza, you see. She is all alone. Martín is all alone. No uncles, no aunts, nobody but me."

"You are nothing to them," Tomás said.

Amalia pursed her lips. Her hands ceased fidgeting. "It isn't only about them. I like it here. I like the weather. I like the way the people hug you after meeting you only once. I like the drums one hears at night, when the air is wet and thick and the sound feels like you are inside your own body and what you are hearing is your heart."

"Mamá, Eulalia wants us to come with her. On her steamship. I will be her secretary and you will be—"

"A servant again? Ay, hijo," she says, shaking her head. "Do you know why I became a nodriza? Because I wanted to take those 24,000 escudos and have you see the world. I used to have dreams of you living in a huge city of white columned buildings and wide, paved roads. I wanted you to see mountains and plains and islands. But your father insisted that you would be a farmer. Perhaps I was wrong to dream for you. Perhaps I was merely dreaming for myself. And here I am, in this beautiful country, adventuring for once. Let me have it, Tomás. Por favor. Let me have it."

"Chicago is a big city," he said, and a sad little laugh escaped him. He still did not know if he wanted to take the job that Eulalia had offered. He thought of his bookshop with a pang of longing, and thought he could smell old books in the air.

"So is Havana, hijo," Amalia said. "And Burgos is full of ghosts." Because she was decided then, they sat in silence, and enjoyed the last quiet moments they would have together. Tomás was aware that the moments he spent with his mother could be counted now, that they were small, diminishing units of time.

"Mamá," he said carefully, "you don't owe Martín anything."

Amalia could not speak. She had convinced herself of her own guilt, Tomás now understood. There would be no other way to mitigate that beyond doing what she had always done—caring for those who needed her as if they were her own, her heart beating forgiveness with every thump.

Then, with great care, and sniffling as she went, Amalia removed her things from the trunk she and Tomás had shared.

16

Tomás had ignored two of Eulalia's notes. When the boy arrived a third time, his small head sweaty and dark circles under his eyes, Tomás almost hid from view. But the boy was quick and standing before Tomás in an instant, with a new note and his hand, once again, upturned.

Tomás had two centavos left in his pocket, and these he gave to the boy. He opened the note, and was surprised to see that the hand was not Eulalia's. It read:

> Join me in the Sala de Armas on la calle del Prado at three this afternoon. —Antonio

It was not a request, Tomás thought, but a summons. This note he would not ignore, though he considered it. He dressed carefully, picking lint off of his only jacket until it was clean.

It was hot as ever, and Tomás soon regretted the suit. The Sala de Armas sat on a square, and was surrounded by cobbled streets on three sides, and, on the west side, a parquet of wood. When carriages passed over it, their hooves went silent. Along the wooden road was the governor's home, and Tomás noted the closed curtains, imagined the sleepy politicians inside, and knew at once why the streets were laid with sound-deadening ironwood.

The Sala de Armas was across from the governor's home. Even from outside, Tomás could hear the commotion within. Grunts and shouts were punctuated by clashes of metal. Outside, the sign "Club de Esgrima" hung on a golden cord, and a pair of foils had been crossed and secured to the wall above it.

Tomás stepped inside and leaned against a wall to watch two men fencing, clumsily, it seemed to Tomás. The words "Honor y Caballería" were painted on the opposite wall. The men lunged and parried, and every once in a while, the tip of a foil connected, and the movement stopped for a moment. The men were of the same build and height. With the masks on, they might have been reflections of one another, except that one of the men was lighter on his feet. The director of the bout halted the action after a while. Tomás watched as Antonio, who was the lithe fencer, pulled off his mask, and watched as the men in the room surrounded him, one coming out from the shadows with a bottle of champagne and flutes in his arms.

"A toast!" the man called. Tomás noted how some of the men drew back. A few refused the glass, but Antonio did not seem to notice. Of course, thought Tomás, they understood protocol well enough. In the presence of royalty, there was only one toast that could be made, and that was to the king, a king half the island was currently rebelling against.

Antonio spotted Tomás there, against the wall, just in time. "Come here, Tomás. I have just the toast for you. To my wife," he said, as his glass was filled.

This they could do, the others joined in at once, and soon they were all toasting to Eulalia. Antonio locked his eyes on Tomás as he drank.

"Gentlemen," Antonio said, pulling Tomás close by the shoulders. "This is Tomás Aragón. He and my wife have known each other since they were children. And now, he will be her secretary."

The men congratulated Tomás, and then another round of fencing began. Tomás sat down on an ornate sofa with turned feet, and Antonio sat down next to him.

"She's up to something," Antonio said, his voice low. "More and more, she makes me wish I had been a Carlist. The whole trouble with them had to do with women on the throne, you know. For my part, I'm glad she's nowhere near the line of succession."

Tomás knew now, though he had guessed before, that Antonio had no idea about Eulalia's manuscript. Otherwise, he would have known how she felt about the very idea of sitting on the throne. She would sooner die, Tomás thought.

"You'll take the job, I know you will," Antonio said. "Do keep an eye on her. I know she wanders early in the morning. Sometimes at night." Antonio was staring at Tomás, who found it hard to hold the gaze.

"She's like a sister to me," Tomás said.

"One shouldn't take those kinds of liberties with our persons," Antonio reprimanded. But the sternness wore off immediately, and soon he was pounding Tomas's back. "Gentlemen, get this man a mask and a foil!" he called out, and before Tomás knew it, he was dressed in white, and facing a masked stranger.

He knew nothing of fencing, and he waved his weapon wildly, ducking successfully once then taking touch after touch to his chest. It was all over before Tomás had gotten truly out of breath. Over on the couch, Antonio was laughing, and Tomás felt as if he were twelve, fourteen, sixteen years old again, back when an older boy would decide on mockery as a form of entertainment.

"Well done," Antonio called, and slapped Tomás on the shoulder again.

Tomás shed the fencing gear and watched as the men fawned over Antonio. Yet they hadn't wanted to toast to the little king back in Spain. Their binary feelings betrayed them, and Tomás, who was only just learning what it meant to rub shoulders with the rich and powerful, made a mental note to remember this moment.

Antonio did not speak to Tomás again, and it was as if Tomás had somehow disappeared from his vision. At the last minute, as Tomás headed out the door, Antonio looked up. His expression was blank as if he had grown so accustomed to Tomás that he was now more fixture than person. He did not nod, only held Tomás's gaze.

Tomás made his way to the home where Eulalia was staying. One of the guards greeted him as Señor Secretario, though Tomás had not said a word about accepting the job yet. He found Eulalia downstairs, meeting with members of the Santiago Society of Women, who had traveled all the way from the eastern province to greet the princess. The mood was tense, Tomás could tell. It was in the east where the fiercest battles were being fought, and as they spoke with the infanta, the women leaned forward, their hands clasped, their brows furrowed. They were war-touched, and he saw evidence of it in the faded colors of their dresses, and in their hats, which were a few seasons behind the fashion.

Tomás sat in the empty kitchen. He peeled a banana and ate it in three bites, listening to the conversation in the other room. Eulalia was comforting in her speech, she even laughed once at a joke that was not very funny, and when the women left, Tomás peered into the room and watched how Eulalia kissed their cheeks. He could never imagine such a thing in Spain. It would cause a minor scandal. Yet here, Eulalia leaned forward as if these women were cousins, and she allowed them to squeeze her arms, and when they separated, the infanta's face was lit up in a genuine smile.

Then, she was alone, and Tomás stepped out before her. "You are incredible," he said, took her hand, and kissed it.

Eulalia snatched her hand from his. "Two invitations ignored," she said.

"Is that why you sent Antonio after me?"

Confusion flickered in her eyes. "We need an answer, or else we will assume that you are an opportunist of the worst sort, and having abused our childhood link in a manner most—"

"We went to Gisela's grave. Mamá and I," Tomás said. "And she's decided to stay here in Cuba. For good. The last few days have been—"

"Difficult," Eulalia supplied. She had softened at once. Perhaps, thought Tomás, she is thinking of her own mother, or of Tenorio, and the stories she will never know, the secrets that have been kept from her, too. They were quiet for a moment before Eulalia asked how the meeting with Antonio had gone.

Tomás rubbed his chest where the foil tip had touched him particularly violently. "We fought with swords, I'll have you know. And I bled to death before his eyes. It was incredibly gruesome."

"So you didn't win?" Eulalia said, picking up the joke. "Then I have no use for you."

Tomás grew serious again. "You sent him after all," he said, and she nodded. "He encouraged me to take the job."

"And you will?"

Tomás nodded, and Eulalia flung her arms around the barrel of his chest. "Perfect!" she said. Tomás flailed a little, then, slowly, as if embracing a hollow, delicate structure, he put his arms around the infanta.

Overhead, green parrots flew in widening circles, led by a

bright blue macaw, and the noise they made broke up their embrace. The two of them watched the birds until they looped off, one by one, into the distance.

"We grew up beside an aviary, did you know? I think I remember it," Eulalia said.

Tomás nodded. "I'm not sure that I do. My mother told me about it, and I think her stories have become memories that aren't real. I'd like to see it again sometime."

"The birds are gone," Eulalia said, meaning the aviary. "My mother sent them away."

"Shame," Tomás said, still gazing at the sky.

"Oh no," Eulalia said. "I prefer to see them fly."

17

Tomás and Amalia did not speak of their parting, only going about their remaining days together as if every day would be slow and routine in the same way. When he embraced her and kissed her cheeks for the last time there on the docks, she called him "Mi rey," and then she could no longer speak. As for Tomás, he said that she should visit soon, as if she were young and wealthy and such a thing were possible. But what else could he say? Goodbye seemed too permanent. Amalia had nodded, and held him, and called him her king once more, before letting go. Martín held her firmly, his arm around her shoulder, and the oldest child gripped her arm. "Adios, Tio," they told Tomás, as if they had known him their whole lives. Tomás promised to send them gifts from Chicago, these new nieces and nephews of his.

And so Tomás left Cuba, and his mother. They did not stay

to watch the ship weigh anchor and drift away, because the baby had a cough, and it was best to get him home. Tomás knew that the baby had nothing to do with it, of course. It was that Amalia could not bear it, and Tomás, for his part, was glad to see that Martín understood that. It was the loneliest sort of departure, and for the first time in Tomás's life, he felt as if he could easily disappear, plunge into the sea or be taken by the wind, and not a soul would know or care.

When Eulalia and Antonio boarded the ship, the Marcha Real played, though Tomás did not see them come up the gangplank. Instead, his eyes were fixed on the sea, that "living infinite."

Later, Eulalia would knock gently on the door to Tomás's stateroom, which was larger than his old apartment above the bookshop. She would stand awkwardly there, her fingers tapping one another, as if she were fussing with a hangnail.

"You cannot imagine, Tomás, how much I loved Havana. It was as if we formed a single thought, that country and I. Ama will be happy there, I think," she said.

"I can't imagine it, no. My mother's happiness in a place so foreign." Tomás was in a dark state of mind, questioning everything. He wanted his mother's firmness of purpose, or else Eulalia's strict protocol, which told her what to do at every turn.

"We will not be able to keep her," Eulalia said, as if talking to herself.

"My mother? She has made up her mind, I know tha—"

Eulalia shook her head. "I meant Cuba. Spain cannot keep her."

"They won't forget you," Tomás said to her.

Eulalia laughed. "Yes, I will be remembered the way people remember comets. Once, every four hundred years, a Spanish princess visits Cuba and leaves in her wake a mantle of stars."

"A poet and a princess," Tomás teased, forgetting about

Tenorio for a moment. Perhaps she had inherited his lyricism after all.

They were quiet again. Eulalia turned to leave, and he bowed for her.

"I am glad you are here," she said, then she was gone. He considered reading her manuscript again, but that would have been his third time through it, and perhaps there was such a thing as knowing a person too thoroughly.

Tomás hardly slept that night, thinking of the people on board the ship and who they might be missing here out at sea, and if they were missed.

THE UNITED STATES OF AMERICA

1

T omás's stateroom onboard the *María Cristina* adjoined
Eulalia's and Antonio's, who each had their own rooms.
A massive desk was placed by a porthole, and upon it
sat a gleaming new typewriter. A cane chair with a green velvet
cushion was tucked into the desk, too. "I tried to imagine your
taste in these kinds of things," Eulalia said to him when she
first showed him the room.

"It's—it's just fine. This will do, of course," Tomás stammered. *My taste?* he thought. His apartment's kitchen table
was a sturdy box, upon which he had draped an oilcloth.
This he did not reveal to Eulalia. Instead, he gently pulled
out the chair and sat upon it, then laid his fingers on the
typewriter keys. The ribbon inside was black and moist, and
he could smell the ink and the oil that greased the delicate
typebars.

"We'll arrive in New York in four days," Eulalia said. "I'm
to meet with President Cleveland and his wife. Then we'll
make our way to Chicago."

At that moment, the ship lurched, and began rocking
slowly. Tomás adjusted quickly, but Eulalia soon turned pale,
and went up to the private deck above their rooms. She would
spend most of her time there, fanning herself, having little to
say to Tomás, who sometimes asked if she had a job for him to
do, out of utter boredom. Eulalia seemed melancholy, and
when she spoke, it was of their days in Cuba.

"The wide avenues lined with palms, the ones on Avenida

Isabel? How lovely they were. Tomás, if I had my canvases and paint, I would try to capture them before I forget."

Or else she would lament, "I know it in my heart, Spain and Cuba will separate. It will be a divorce from which we will not recover. Like a man who loses a beautiful woman because he was a brute. The spike of shame would live in his heart forever, don't you think?" she said. Her brow wrinkled then, and she became lost in thought, the fan in her hand slowing almost to a stop.

They passed the lighthouse at the tip of Florida, past mangrove hammocks and gnarly woods, all the way up the coast of the United States. Little by the little, the heat of the tropics dissipated, so that by the time they reached New York Harbor, and that vertical, heaving city, Eulalia had wrapped herself in a shawl on deck, a cocoon trembling on a leaf.

There was a parade when they arrived in New York, but Tomás had missed it. He could hear, in the distance, the sound of trumpets, and the faint cheers of onlookers. The sounds of rifles discharging ceremoniously rocketed through the streets. Later, Eulalia and Antonio, and a small retinue of ladies, were transferred to another ship newly christened the *Infanta Eulalia* in honor of her visit, and embarked for Washington, D.C.

Eulalia had described her itinerary to Tomás before they docked. "It would be my greatest wish to have you come with us, Tomás, and see the White House, plain as I've heard it is, but—"

"I understand," Tomás said. In truth, he was glad he was not going, that he would have the private deck and the stateroom to himself, and time besides to walk about in New York. Eulalia had been so melancholy upon leaving Cuba, as if she had left a country she had always known, as if she were a Cuban woman in exile.

"They are fighting for their freedom, Tomás," she had

sighed one night above deck. "Why shouldn't they have it?" She didn't even bother to look around, to see if they were alone when she said it.

In New York, Tomás wandered up and down Fifth Avenue, passing the Savoy Hotel, where Eulalia and Antonio would stay when they returned. Down Madison Avenue he went, stopping in a café for a sandwich, his ears full of a language he understood a little more with each passing moment. Everywhere he looked were women that reminded him of Eliza Jane, bustling up and down the streets, in such a hurry. Does time move more quickly here? he wondered. It seemed so, as if every passing person was trying to make the most of their waking hours. He stopped to look into a little souvenir shop when he heard the Marcha Real playing. Across the street, in the Garden Theater, an orchestra was practicing the song, and they would start and stop every so often, then begin again. How strange to hear that tune playing, and watch as the people went past, little noting the music. The exception was a small boy in shorts and a cap, a rucksack on his back, who stopped before the theater, lifted his arms, and pretended to conduct the music for a while. Then he was on his way again, walking as swiftly as the adults around him.

Did he stand out, there on Madison Avenue, as a man from Burgos and not a man from New York City? Tomás imagined that he did. In Cuba, the men leaned against carriage wheels, smoked cigars that dangled from between their fingers, the glowing ash flitting away like spirits in the sea breeze. Here in New York, men shoved their hats low upon their heads, nearly covering their eyes. Tomás had bumped into one, and before he could utter his "Perdón," the man had walked on, his heels loud on the pavement. Tomás knew that Burgos had shaped him. The frigid winters of Burgos had made him sturdy in the face of grief—he knew cold inside and out. The hilly landscape had made him dogged—Amalia often said that Tomás was like a crab, incapable of going backwards. Even so, even though his very bones were Burgos and Spain, Tomás could see the way a person could shift into a new man in a place like New York. He could see how his spine might grow more fearless, here among these bold, tall buildings. He could imagine himself in new shoes, his own heels making purposeful sounds across a gleaming floor. And no one in New York would know, or care, that his mother had been in service, or that he had once been a milk brother.

Tomás could only read about Eulalia's visit to Washington, D.C., in the newspapers, but these, being in English, were ponderous to read and in the end, revealed little of import besides what Eulalia was wearing and what the weather had been like. Bored, Tomás decided to make himself useful, and began to type up Eulalia's writings. It seemed like a sensible thing to do, since, as far as he knew, Eulalia had only written out one copy. He found he understood them better that way. It was as if he were studying Eulalia now, like a scholar, and within her elegantly scripted lines he would discover her more fully. Sometimes, there would be a perfectly quiet moment, wherein Tomás would cease typing, the gulls outside would quit their shrieking, and the ship and all of its histrionic noises would settle. In that space, Tomás could almost feel Eulalia standing behind him, her hand on his shoulder, urging him on. *See me, see me*, she seemed to say to him, then, he would type on.

Eulalia and Antonio returned to New York a few days later. Tomás packed a small suitcase, placing the typed manuscript and the original at the bottom, and left the rest of his things in the room on board the ship. He carried his suitcase all the way to the Savoy, where a room had been set aside for him. By the time he reached the hotel, his hand had blistered from carrying the bag, but his eyes were so full with the Savoy that he forgot all about his hand.

The iron door was pulled back for him by a young man in a uniform, a little boxy hat on his head. The lobby was immense—pale pink marble columns flanked the walls, beautiful soldiers. Leather chairs lined up before the columns, which led to a tinkling fountain. The ceiling was painted with images of angels on a blue sky, and in the corners, silver baskets hung from silver chains, and these were filled with fresh flowers. Opalescent jewels were encrusted within filigree. A sign pointed left to the Ladies' Restaurant, and another to the right towards the Gentlemen's Restaurant. Men and women spoke quietly in small groups here and there, whispering, their eyes casting about. Tomás was sure that Eulalia and Antonio had either just passed through, or were about to.

Tomás approached the front desk, suitcase in hand, and waited for his key. From where he stood, Tomás could see into the Gentlemen's Restaurant, and he had a clear view of a sculpture within, of two figures in marble. In it, the man stood behind the woman, their right arms entwined by her hip, their left arms lifted, fingers laced, high above their heads. His chin rested on her shoulder, his nose nearly in her ear, and his gaze fell upon her bare breasts. It was a large sculpture, and the men dining there would note it, and, perhaps, rush through their meals in order to return to their rooms, their wives, or their mistresses.

Eulalia and her cortege were lodged on the second floor, in the Louis XV suite of apartments, and there Tomás found her, sitting on a chaise lounge in the Marie Antoinette room, a scowl on her face.

"I am told this is an exact replica of Marie Antoinette's residence," Eulalia said. "Perhaps they mean to lop off my head, too."

"You're in a terrible mood, su alteza," Tomás said, and he

sat down. Sometimes, he wondered if he went too far, and he expected her to send him back to Burgos at once. But he had decided upon taking the job of secretary, that he would be himself, or he would simply not be a part of the adventure. Hadn't his mother warned him about Tenorio, about the sad man he had become? Tomás had no intention of following in those particular footsteps. Sometimes, Eulalia would sour at him, and she would speak in the third person, and Tomás would know he had crossed a line of protocol that meant something to her. But often, she merely looked at him the way one looks at a child learning to tell jokes for the first time, and then, won over at last, she would smile.

"Washington, D.C., was a fine city," she said, though he hadn't asked. "The president and I spoke in English, and the First Lady spoke with Antonio in French the whole time. Thank goodness for that, or else he would have been sour-faced and confused for days. I had my photograph taken more times than I can count. Why do they love photography so much here?" she asked, running her hand down the bodice of her dress. "The corsets alone," she sighed. "And the light hurts my eyes." She leaned back and pinched the top of her nose.

That was when Tomás noticed there was a Spanish newspaper on her lap, opened to a review of a play in Andalusia starring Carmela Flores. The name clicked into place in his mind at once—Antonio's mistress, la Infantona. Slowly, Tomás lifted the newspaper off of her. Her hand came down at once to snatch it back, but he pulled it away in time, folded it, and set it down on a table. When he turned around, Eulalia was seated upright, her head in her hands.

"Eulalia," Tomás began to say, but she sniffed loudly and lifted her face, which was dry, though her cheeks were blooming.

"We are tired, that is all. Did you know that Spain sent three caravels to New York in honor of our visit?" she asked, changing the subject. "Exact replicas of la Santa María, la Niña y la Pinta. They sailed all this way. We are to see them later today."

"Oh," Tomás said. He had hoped to spend more time with her. She had been in Washington for six days, and with each passing day, Tomás had begun to feel slightly broken in a way he couldn't name but it felt like seeing a favorite building torn down for something new, or passing a potted plant that needs water.

"Would you like to see them? The caravels?" Eulalia asked.

His face very nearly broke into a smile. But he restrained himself, and only nodded. Eulalia seemed pleased, leaned back again, and closed her eyes. Tomás took the opportunity to slip the newspaper he had taken from her under his shirt.

The caravels had come all the way from Spain in the old way, dependent on good winds and sturdy sailors. So it was that they looked as if they had gone through a war. The sail on la Pinta was torn, and the cannons, which were antiques themselves, were crusted over in salt, looking as if they had been at the bottom of the sea for years.

"They mean to fire them," Tomás pointed them out to Eulalia, and they watched the bedraggled sailors struggling with the weapons.

"In our honor, yes," Antonio put in. He and Eulalia had changed clothes again, and Tomás wondered how big the trunk that held their wardrobe was.

Eulalia gripped Tomás's arm. "They shouldn't, Tomás. They shouldn't," she said. They were close to the ships. Close enough that in ten strides, they could touch them. The cannons were aimed down the Hudson, and the royal salute would make the windows in New York tremble.

Eulalia broke from Tomás, and walked slowly toward the mayor of New York City, a man named Thomas Gilroy. There was a strong breeze coming off the water, and his iron-gray hair rustled about, like miniature storm clouds over his head. Tomás watched as she spoke to the mayor, pointed at the caravels and the cannons, and expressed her dismay. But the mayor frowned at her, laced his fingers over his belly, and shook his head.

Beside Tomás, Antonio sighed deeply. "She can be so difficult," he whispered. But the cannons were unprotected, bare upon the decks of the caravels. The boats were rocking to and fro, and three men held each cannon, which rolled about, in place.

"Perhaps we should move away a bit," Tomás offered, and Antonio shrugged. He had seen enough cannon salutes for a lifetime, he said, and walked away as if going off on a stroll. Eulalia and Tomás followed him, until all three were safely away from the ship.

Exasperated, Eulalia rejoined them. "Is no one reasonable here?" she asked, and in that moment, the first cannon fired. The sound was horrifying, and everyone watching the ship jumped backwards. Tomás was swept by a feeling of protectiveness, and he slipped his arm around Eulalia's waist and pulled her back against him. She did not upbraid him, or even look up to meet his eyes. She was very still, though not entirely calm. Tomás could feel her rapid breathing. The smoke cleared, and there, upon the deck of la Niña, lay three men. One covered his eye and screamed for help, while another clutched his leg. A third was unconscious altogether. The cannon was on its side, still smoking.

Eulalia now stood between Tomás and Antonio, and the three of them packed tightly together. Tomás's hand still lingered on her back, the force of feeling that the misfired cannon caused still lingered in him, thrumming in his veins. On board the ship, furious agitation reigned. For his part, Mayor Gilroy, had backed away even further, and was shouting orders at the sailors, who could not hear him.

Eulalia had her hand on her throat and was saying, "Dios mio, Dios mio." Antonio reached out to her and his hand brushed Tomás's. The latter took a step away, instinct taking over, prompting him to approach the ship and ask if he could be of assistance. He did not turn to see whether Antonio was watching him, and his voice, as he spoke to one of the sailors, trembled with a violent tension. He felt exposed, as if in one small gesture his feelings for Eulalia had been confessed.

Because he loved her. This he now understood deeply. Somehow, rereading her book, commiserating with the injustice she had felt her whole life, had released in him a sense of possibility. How different were they, really, wondered Tomás. They both had been born with someone else's vision of what their destiny would be. Rubén had wanted Tomás to be a farmer, Isabel had hoped her youngest daughter might be the model princess Spain had always lacked. But the plow and the diadem do not suit us, he thought. At night, he could not rest thinking about Eulalia. When she was in Washington, D.C., he felt like he was starving. He ate at fine restaurants, thinking of the list in his pocket that was as worn thin as an onionskin now, and he marveled that the food did not satisfy him. But when she returned from the capital, and Tomás saw her again, how sated he felt. He gorged upon her then, taking in every detail of her being—how her eyes appeared fathomless in bright light, the sturdy column of her back when she sat in a chair, the flickering movement of her throat when she spoke, and the roll of her eyes when she thought no one was looking. He caught himself protracting every meeting with her, commenting on the weather, or the cut of her dress, or the city, the plans they had heard from the mayor about the underground train, "like an earthworm beneath the city," he had told her, and she had scrunched up her face briefly, then laughed, saying "I've seen the Underground in London, Tomás, and I'm not easily impressed." Later, he would chastise himself for sounding so desperate. I am merely a secretary. Merely her milk brother, he would remind himself, and then he would unfold the notes she had sent him while they were in Cuba, one by one, and think that perhaps there was something more. In the dark, as he lay awake, he sometimes thought, I am merely another Tenorio. Then he would force himself to think of other things, and so would find sleep at last.

In the end, the injuries on board the ship were not grave ones, but the event had shaken Eulalia. She had held onto Antonio's arm all the way to the carriage, while Tomás walked far behind them, chatting with one of her ladies-in-waiting who described the events at the ship as if they had happened long ago and she had been the only one there.

Antonio and Eulalia had plans to attend the theater later that evening. But it was raining hard, and she decided instead to stay in at the Savoy. "I would like to sit quietly for a while with my own mind. I want to cast my thoughts out across the Atlantic, and think of my sons, and try to get this ringing in my ears to stop," she had said, entering her suite and closing the door. Antonio went to the theater anyway.

Tomás ate alone at the desk in his room. He chose a dessert instead of dinner, a pêche Melba bigger than his fist. He pulled out Eulalia's manuscript again, turning the pages slowly, studying the curvature of her letters, the beating heart of each sentence. He was frustrated as he read, his leg bouncing up and down under the desk. He had hoped for an occasion when Eulalia was in a good humor to talk to her. But the accident on the Hudson had drawn her away and into herself. Instead, he read and fantasized what he would say to her. It seemed to him that no one came to Eulalia with their feelings exposed, as if sitting upon a plate. Rather, if they spoke to her it was a request, or a decision that had been made regarding an issue of protocol. Speaking to Eulalia felt a little like uttering a prayer. Reverence, respect, and then, a plea for the self. One never asked God how He felt, and Tomás supposed not many others asked Eulalia the same question. As he read, he noted how often she had plated up her own feelings for others, and how those had been rebuffed—by her mother, her oldest sister, her brother, her husband.

"How many times have you read that?"

Tomás stood at once, his heart pounding. Several pages fell to the floor. Eulalia was in his doorway, still in her dress from that afternoon. Her hair was undone. The rings that had been on her fingers were gone and her ears were bereft of their jewels. She looked like a girl who had tried on a dress at a fancy shop.

"Once or twice. How are you?" he asked, his earlier train of thought still running.

Eulalia smiled. "Better. Thank you. It was frightening today, wasn't it?"

Tomás nodded. He bent down to pick up the pages, reordering them swiftly. He recognized the pattern of the book so intimately now that he barely needed to note the words on the page in order to know where it went. Merely the swing of her "M" or the off-center dot of a particular "i" told him all he needed.

"What is this?" she asked, bending down to pick up an envelope with her name written on it.

The letter from Pedro Medina had tumbled out of the manuscript. Tomás had been using it as a bookmark, so accustomed to moving it back and forth that he had forgotten what was inside.

"Keeping things from me, are we?" she asked playfully, and began to tear open the envelope.

"Eulalia, don't," he said, and watched as she read, her smile turning down, lines creasing her forehead.

"It is only one man's opinion," Tomás said.

"A forceful one," she whispered.

"Sylvester Hartwell will think differently. This is America."

Eulalia took a long, shuddering breath. "You keep this, Tomás. Let's pretend it doesn't exist. There is hope yet," she said. Her eyes were wet, but she blinked them rapidly. When she put the letter down, she wiped her hands on her skirt. When she glanced at Tomás, she smiled, and he could tell that it took great effort.

Tomás took the letter and placed it on the corner of his desk, away from Eulalia's book.

When he looked up, he caught her in a curious moment— she was leaning against the doorjamb, her head touching the gleaming wood, her eyes closed.

"Eulalia?" he asked. He dared not approach her as he spoke. "Are you all right? Truly?" The distance between them was not so big that he couldn't bridge it in two strides. And yet, he was keenly aware of her in his room, his own bed not so far away, and Antonio at the theater for at least another hour.

"Pedro is a friend of yours. Let us not speak of it again." She removed a glove and folded and refolded it in her hands. "Sometimes," she said, "it feels as if I am not here, but rather, an ocean away, and only dreaming of this place. Look at it, Tomás." She gestured to the window and the view, overlooking Central Park, which was in full bloom. Below, carriages trundled by under a bright moon. "I have never felt less like myself. I think about my sons, their tender faces, and wonder who their mother might be. Perhaps she is in those pages you've read. I think about their future, and wonder if they will feel this way too."

"What way?" Tomás asked. He wanted to know. He wanted to hear her express herself to him as she had done with no other. He could not claim her as a wife, but perhaps he could claim her mind, be the man with whom she could be honest.

"Like this," she said, curled her hand into a fist and rested it on the wall beside her. "A stranger to their own instinct, so determined by their titles of 'infante' that even their hearts beat only with permission."

Tomás took one cautious step forward. Eulalia reached up and touched her left temple, as if adjusting a phantom diadem. "I see the future, Tomás. In it, I am an old lady, sitting in a tufted chair, staring out of a window. In Paris, perhaps. Would that I could imagine the scene in Havana or here in New York. I am old, and alone. The light is fading. And yet, someone comes in with a paper for me to sign, more duties, Tomás, more duties. And a photographer will take one last posed photograph of me, one that will run in the newspapers after I'm buried in the crypt with all of the other Bourbons—"

"Eulalia—"

"And I will think to myself that all I had wanted in life was to be able to dance when a song played, laugh myself to tears in public, or steal an apple from a cart when no one was looking." She was talking to the floor, her face expressive and her eyes teary, watching her own foot make circles on the carpet, pushing the pile to and fro.

Eulalia was just about to say something else when Tomás, who had taken just one more step, kissed her on the mouth. For a moment, she returned the kiss, and Tomás could feel her adjusting to his height. Then she moved her head away and found his palm, which had been upon her cheek. There she dropped a light kiss, and then pushed against him so that she was outside the doorway.

They stood in silence for a moment. Tomás was shaking, and he could not still his knees. Eulalia looked past him, out the window. "The rain has stopped," she said hoarsely.

Tomás turned to look. When he turned back, Eulalia was gone.

2

Tomás and Eulalia did not speak of what happened. The following day saw their departure from New York, a two-day trip by train that kept them separated from one another. Tomás rode in a car for gentlemen, and among these quiet, smoking men, he found a measure of peace. The kiss had rattled him, made him feel certain that Eulalia would dismiss him, or that Antonio would somehow know, and that he would wake in the morning staring down the barrel of a pistol. He reminded himself that such turns of event happened in novels, and not at the Hotel Savoy in the Louis XV suite. The line of reasoning helped only a little.

On the train, he spoke to a Chicagoan, who delighted to hear that Tomás was part of the Spanish assembly. "Wait until you see Lake Michigan," said the man. He was ruddy-cheeked, and his lashes were long, looking to Tomás like a strange, grown doll. His hair was trim, and he wore it combed forward, covering a bald spot, the curls of the ends tickling his forehead. "I've just been to a funeral," the man said, thumbing the threadbare edge of his coat. "They say one shouldn't wear anything new to a funeral."

"My condolences," Tomás said. He caught most of what the man was saying, and felt as if his English had improved since his arrival in America, as if somewhere in his brain, ties that bound him linguistically were being snipped and set free.

"Jim Hawkins," the man said, and extended a hand. "I work for Mr. Burnham. The architect for the Exposition." He wiped at a line of sweat on his upper lip, then removed the shabby coat. "I'll tell you what, your visit seems a kind of miracle. A prince and princess among us, imagine that. Makes us all proud, the hog butchers, the schoolchildren, the carriage drivers, and the architects. The best part is that Chicago won out as the location for the Exposition, beating almighty New

York and trouncing St. Louis. You and your people being here is the stamp of approval we needed. Chicago delivers on its promises, I tell you that."

The man was only the beginning of Tomás' encounter with a kind of pride of city he had never witnessed. Perhaps it was the Exposition. Perhaps it was the sense of a city finally maturing. Perhaps it was the country, having gotten so large, proclaiming not one great city but two, and a future that promised, three, four, five great cities, just as populous and gleaming.

Once in the city, they were greeted at the Palmer House by Mrs. Bertha Palmer, the wife of Potter Palmer, who had built the hotel for Bertha as a wedding gift. Bertha Palmer waited in the center of the hotel's main floor in a white gown. A circlet of diamonds rested in her hair, a diamond lavaliere hung from her neck, and a diamond pin shaped like an eagle sat on her shoulder.

"Demasiado," Eulalia whispered to Tomás, and he agreed. Under the chandelier, Bertha Palmer absolutely glittered, but the effect was garish rather than refined.

"Su alteza," Bertha Palmer said, and curtsied stiffly. Then, without a word from Eulalia, she told them about the Exposition, and her role in it. "I am the president of the Board of Lady Managers, and as such, I have had the honor, a true honor, su alteza, of organizing the Women's Building. Such art! Such murals. And look," she said, snapping her fingers. A maid scampered forward at once, and held in her open palm a glossy coin. "I petitioned congress for it. A quarter, in honor of your ancestor, Isabella the First." This, Bertha Palmer plucked from the maid's hand and presented to Eulalia, like a communion wafer.

Eulalia took the coin, thanking her hostess, who beamed and put her hands over her heart and was silent, at last.

The Spanish assemblage was shown to their suite of rooms,

which were decorated with white lilies atop every surface. From the windows they could see, in the distance, the buildings of the Exposition, which had been nicknamed the White City. In the sunlight, they were blinding to look at, such an intense whiteness, that Tomás thought of Jules Verne's air balloon among the clouds at once. In such a place, thought Tomás, the impossible might just be possible.

The infanta was scheduled to see the Spanish Building, the Women's Building, the Electricity Building, and the Palace of Fine Arts the following day. But that afternoon and evening were, for once, hers. Maids came in and out of the parlor that connected all of the rooms. They watered the lilies and set up plates of cookies and a steaming pot of tea. Antonio, meanwhile, excused himself. He had suffered from a sore throat all day, and a doctor had been sent for. The physician, a burly Chicago man and Bertha Palmer's personal doctor, diagnosed him with an allergy to the dust in the city, and gave him a drink of honey and laudanum, then ordered him to have bacon for dinner. "The grease will be soothing," he said, before leaving without a bow or "good day."

Antonio retired to sleep off the medicine, and, once the maids were done, Tomás and Eulalia found themselves alone again.

"I want to see it all," she said. "But not as Eulalia. Do you understand?" Tomás understood at once, and he set off to explore the hotel, discovering two back entrances near the kitchens, and a stairwell used by the maids. Together, the two of them left the Palmer House without saying a word to anyone. They would need a carriage to get to the exposition, so instead, they wandered up State Street, her arm in his, and were soon lost among the bustling Chicagoans. In one direction, dozens of carriages of all kinds rumbled by, and in the other, streetcars, stuffed with people, rang their bells.

Tomás walked with his gaze to the sky. The buildings were so tall here, and once or twice he stumbled.

"They block the view," Eulalia said, meaning the buildings. "The lake is right there, and yet we can't see it."

"They can," Tomás said, pointing at the windows of the buildings, and at one or two very tall homes.

"Yes, but down here, I cannot. Nor can you. It seems selfish to me," she said. "In Spain, we let the common people have the best views. Think of Santander. A palace would suit there, what with the spectacular cliffs and the sea, and yet the palace is in Madrid."

Tomás thought for a moment before speaking. "I think you overstate things sometimes," he said. Eulalia stopped cold, and Tomás thought, I have ruined it.

But she was not concerned with him. Instead, she was suddenly stopped by a newspaper boy, thrusting the evening edition in her face, yelling over the ruckus of the traffic.

"A princess on Lake Michigan's shore," he yelled. "Won't you have her? Won't you have the Spanish Infanta?"

Amused, Eulalia said, "I suppose I'd like to see what she is like, yes," and she paid the boy with the Isabella coin she had received that morning, plucking it out of her glove.

"I d-don't have change," the boy stammered, but Eulalia waved him off, her nose already in the paper. The boy ran as fast as he could down State Street. She wandered into the shade of a building and Tomás followed her.

She smiled as she read, and Tomás knew the stories must be flattering ones. "If they could see me now," she said, "all rumpled from two days on a train, they wouldn't say such nice things."

Tomás held his tongue. What he wanted to say was, "Dios, who cares what they think?" and other things that were too full of feeling. What he said was, "My mother would have liked to have seen this place, blocked views and all."

Eulalia sighed, folding the newspaper as she did so. "If

Ama had come with us, I don't believe we would be taking this stroll." Tomás laughed. "Probably not." How he missed her, he realized. Knowing that he could not longer go to her, or feel her soft touch upon his cheek, brought him to the edge of tears.

"Tomorrow, we will see all of it, and we will toast to Amalia somewhere in the White—"

A streetcar clanged past, obscuring Eulalia's words. Tomás heard none of it, but he smiled at her anyway and said yes.

The White City was a young woman in a wedding gown. It was an undiscovered country. A calliope being played for the first time, crisp and raucous. The feeling of falling from a great height. It was all of these things to Tomás, and upon seeing it the next day as part of Eulalia's cortege, he felt as if he was no longer the same man. He stood transfixed at the Court of Honor. White buildings surrounding a basin of water, silvery statues all around, posed athletically. In the lake floated Columbus's caravels, having been brought to Chicago from New York City. Tomás could no longer see the cannons, and now the decks teemed with fairgoers, and the ships teetered in the water.

Eulalia was led from one building to the next. In the Manufactures and Liberal Arts Building, she tried on a glass dress. It swayed like real fabric, and under the electric lights, it glimmered. She ordered one on the spot, and the dressmaker, who wore magnifying lenses over both eyes, took the order with tremendous seriousness. They saw Bach's clavichord, and rode an elevator up and down three times. Each time, Eulalia clutched her stomach and said, "Do you feel it, Tomás?" and he would nod and say, "Of course, su alteza, of course I do." The Remington Company exhibited forty different typewriters, and Tomás lingered here longest, laying his fingers along the keys. There were Arabic typewriters, and Chinese ones, too. The

Spanish typewriters, with their "ñ's" were, not surprisingly, his favorites. He smoothed the ribbon of one of the machines, and a salesman was beside him at once.

"What's your profession, sir?"

Tomás began to say he was a bookseller, then a secretary, stammering so that when he finally said, "I am a writer," the salesman merely patted his back and moved on to another potential customer.

In the Tiffany exhibit, the salesman drew a heavy black case out for Eulalia. Within were ten different diadems, composed of every gem imaginable. "That one," Tomás whispered, pointing to a circlet made of aquamarines over Eulalia's shoulder.

"Aquamarines?" she wondered. "Why those?"

"Like your eyes, princess," the salesman said, answering before Tomás could. The moment had felt charged with history for Tomás, but how to explain that to Eulalia, who had not heard Amalia's stories? So he dropped it, agreeing with the salesman. This seemed to disappoint her, the compliment so lacking in imagination.

It was an exhausting day, and when they returned by carriage to the Palmer House, they found Antonio dressed and ready for dinner. He was feeling better, and had even spent some time at the fair.

"It's spectacular," Antonio said to Eulalia upon seeing her. "I've bought souvenirs. It seemed the thing to do," he said, a sheepish grin on his face. He had laid them out on the table. There was a brass spittoon, with the words Chicago Columbian World's Fair on one side. He'd bought a pitcher, etched in gold paint, with an image of the Court of Honor on it. There were cuff links and a hairbrush for Eulalia, three model caravels for their sons, and a miniature Siberian mammoth, too. He'd also bought a stereograph and some pictures to go with it. Eulalia brought these to her eyes and saw a half-naked woman, her arms aloft, and strips of lace frozen above her head. "Danse du ventre," Antonio said. "From Cairo, that one." Eulalia put down the stereograph slowly.

"It seems we had very different experiences," she said. Later, she would learn that Antonio had visited the Midway Plaisance, which was made up of private exhibits with a decidedly Bohemian sensibility. Antonio's souvenirs stayed on the table in the parlor, untouched by the maids, though the stereograph was often moved and passed from hand to hand, the ladies in particular gasping at the vision within.

While Eulalia and Antonio had dinner and later attended a concert at the exposition, Tomás sought out Sylvester Hartwell. His offices were near the Exposition, and from the street, Tomás could see the Midway that Antonio had visited. A circular contraption spun like a windmill in the distance. It was an enormous revolving wheel with passengers in small cars dangling from each spoke. He was still staring at it in the distance when he reached Hartwell & Company. Tomás held the typed manuscript in his arms. A strong wind whipped off the lake, and at one point, he had to chase the first page down a street, watching in terror as it flipped and soared, and, finally, wrapped itself around the trunk of a maple tree. The page was crumbled, but the manuscript was whole, and this he presented to Sylvester Hartwell in his lush office, with a view of the fair. The original copy, the one in Eulalia's hand, was safe in Tomás's room.

"A man named Ferris came up with it," Mr. Hartwell said, when he caught Tomás looking at the wheel outside the window. "Death trap, is what it is," the man grumbled. He had a full head of white hair, and a white beard, too. Like his daughter, Eliza Jane, Sylvester Hartwell had the kind of voice that rose above the rest. Here was a man who made himself heard, a man, Tomás thought, who could not be ruled.

"Let's see it then. Eliza Jane seemed rather enthused," he held out his hand and took the whole manuscript upon it, weighing it like a piece of meat. He put reading glasses on, and sat in a green leather chair to begin reading.

"Shall I—" Tomás began to say, pointing back toward the door from which he'd entered.

"Wait," Mr. Hartwell said, a fat finger in the air. It was a crooked finger, bent a bit from arthritis, and yet Tomás thought that such a hand would have once upon a time delivered a tremendous, crippling punch. He looked at his own hands, large and knuckly. How easily had his hands lain upon the keys of the typewriter once. How they had covered the keys almost entirely.

Mr. Hartwell read for nearly an hour, turning pages slowly, like peeling back wrapping paper one intends to save. Every so often, he would make a clearing sound in his throat, or else he would pause and make a note on the margin. A secretary came in after a while with a pot of coffee. This she set down on Mr. Hartwell's desk, and the man gestured to Tomás, who filled two cups, then drank the bitter stuff without sugar, which was not his habit.

When Mr. Hartwell was done, he leaned back and let the final page float onto his desk, where it slipped off the pile and sat askew. Tomás tamped down the desire to right it. He had been the guardian of the book for so long that he felt an animal desire to protect it, and by extension, her.

"Arrange a meeting with the infanta, son. I would like to speak with her," Mr. Hartwell said. "There may be risks."

"She understands the risks," Tomás said, though he wasn't sure that was true. Eulalia had joked about leaving the country, abandoning Spain if she had to, but did she mean it?

"I'm sure she does," Mr. Hartwell said. "Don't presume to know what's in my mind, now. Or hers. Don't ever presume that."

3

On one side it read 1492 and on the other, 1893. An F and an I, joined by a cross, represented Ferdinand and Isabella. Eulalia turned the silver ring in her hand. Etched inside, and on the back, was the name Carmela. The unassuming ring had sat upon the parlor table among Antonio's souvenirs for days, but now Eulalia had found it, and she sat with it for a long while in her room, slipping the ring on and off. It was big on her, a size eight when she was a size six, and she wondered if Carmela was much larger than she was, or if Antonio had simply guessed. Earlier that month, when Eulalia had been packing for the trip, she had discovered that one of her diadems had gone missing. It was a colorful piece, made up of diamonds, sapphires, rubies, and emeralds, and had belonged to Pilár. They turned their home over looking for it, and Antonio himself interrogated the servants, one by one, and threatened to fire them all. But the diadem had not appeared. A gossip column later described the "rainbow gems" atop the head of a little-known actress from Andalusia, and Eulalia had guessed what had happened.

That morning, just before she had found the ring inscribed to Carmela, she had had tea with one of her ladies, the Marquesa de Arco, who had brought with her a Spanish newspaper, which had, in small print toward one of the back pages, described the viscounty of Temerens as now belonging to one Carmela Jiménez-Floréz, a noble title being recently arranged for the woman. "He will bankrupt me," Eulalia had said to the marquesa, who, hedging her bets, could only pat Eulalia's hand.

Tomás, who had taken the morning for himself to walk about the White City, returned to the parlor flushed and sweaty. He had seen a hot air balloon crash on the Midway that morning. The balloon was tethered to a post, and a wind had carried the balloon and smashed it to the concrete below. Two women and a man tumbled out of the basket, dazed but unhurt. Around the scene, people screamed, and the Midway emptied out, as if balloons were going to continue falling from the sky. Tomás had stayed to help the balloon's owner unleash the basket from the balloon, and take out the post.

"You won't believe what—" Tomás began to say, when he found Eulalia in the parlor, her left hand over her face, and the silver ring in her right, resting there. "Su alteza, are you—"

"I am not. I am not well, Tomás."

"I'll fetch the doctor," Tomás said.

She waved him off, her movements languid, as if she truly had fallen ill. "Look," she said, and held up the ring. "The inscription."

Tomás turned the light ring over in his fingers and read the name, inscribed not once but twice, inside and out.

"If only it were just this ring," she said. The rumors had been about for months. Antonio's gifts were lavish ones, and now Eulalia began to list them for Tomás. "Grecos and Goyas, a farm in Maestra, a mausoleum in Cabra, chains of pearls. Diadems that once had rested on my sister Pilár's head, Pilár's innocent head, now sit atop that woman," she cried, and flung the ring across the room, where it tinkled against a glass lampshade and bounced to the floor.

Is this what Amalia had been like, when she learned about Gisela, Tomás wondered at once. He had not considered his mother's feelings when she told him the story, only his father's, only Rubén, torn between two women, between two sons. But now, seeing it for the first time, seeing the way her face shaped itself into contortions, Tomás felt a different sort of anger, except it had doubled in his heart—anger on behalf of his mother, and absolute rage on behalf of Eulalia.

What could he do? Were Antonio not a prince, he would find him and he would throttle him. His size alone was good for that. In school, he had never had to fight anyone. The mere thought of coming to blows with Tomás Aragón scared the other boys away. Now, too, he thought of something else for the first time. Eulalia, small as she was, had only her mouth and her money as her weapons. If Antonio had control of her wealth, then all she had was words.

"Sylvester Hartwell wants to meet you. He wants to help you change the world," Tomás said. Mr. Hartwell had said nothing like that, of course, but it seemed to be a helpful thing to say in the moment.

Eulalia brightened a little. She rose, went to the ring, and bent down to pick it up. Then, she placed it among the other souvenirs, as if it had never been touched.

"Where is Antonio?"

"Touring the Military Building," she said.

"Come with me then. To the Midway."

Eulalia's lips parted, she leaned forward, but she stopped. "I can't. Tonight, Bertha Palmer is hosting a party in our honor."

Tomás knelt before her and took her hands. Eulalia's eyes were wet, her face drawn. He said, "Su alteza would let an innkeeper's wife keep her from enjoying herself?"

Eulalia laughed a little, and settled her hands in his. "It is the Columbian Exposition after all. What would the occasion be if not for Columbus, and who would Columbus have been if not for Spain?"

"For Spain, then," Tomás said, and kissed the backs of her hands.

Later, the newspapers would turn on Eulalia, prompted by Mrs. Bertha Palmer, who told the press that the haughty infanta had stayed at the festivities she had organized in her Highness's honor for less than an hour, and then, complaining of a headache, had left. "We had mountains of food prepared, an orchestra, the very best people of Chicago, including artists and singers, and yet Eulalia is too good for us here in Chicago. Thank heavens," she told all who would listen, "that we threw off monarchism when we could."

Later, Eulalia would see those newspapers and her heart would pound with regret. But that night, she had no such feelings. She and Tomás climbed aboard the steamship that took fairgoers into the exposition and went wholly unrecognized among the crowds. At night the White City twinkled like the firmament. The electric lights were better than candles, she had remarked. Searchlights atop the buildings swept the sky, as if giants were running about, lanterns in hand, looking for their kin. But it was the Midway that drew them both.

They wandered through a Turkish bazaar, and Eulalia stood still as a woman fit a little red cap over her head and handed her a mirror with which to see herself. They saw a chamber of horrors, where, for a dollar, they witnessed Marie Antoinette being executed. The woman who played her screamed even when her head was supposed to be off her shoulders. Eulalia had not liked it, though Tomás had laughed and clutched his throat. Then, as the night cooled, they climbed aboard the wheel, just the two of them in a single car. As the wheel spun, it reached its greatest height, and all of Chicago was laid before them, the White City like a jewel on one side, the lumpy shapes of buildings in the darkness on another, and almost at their feet, the waters of Lake Michigan.

Up there, they were girded by silence all around. The sounds of the Midway did not reach their ears. Up there, Tomás and Eulalia had nothing to do but take stock of the moment.

"All my life," Tomás said, "your name has been in my ear. 'Eulalia,' my mother would say whenever she saw a little blond girl. Or she would reprimand me when I was being a boy, just a boy, and say that I was raised in a palace, where boys had to be men from the start. Always Eulalia in my ear."

"I am sorry," Eulalia said, laughing a little. She was leaning against him, the air cold and biting. "I can't say the same about you. I gave no heed to you in my memories, because I had no one to keep a memory of you alive for me."

The car rocked violently then, jolting them both. Eulalia yelped and Tomás gripped the handrail. He had forgotten the crashed hot air balloon from that morning until that very moment, and now his heart was pounding.

"We wouldn't survive this fall," he said, looking down to the ground.

"No, we wouldn't," Eulalia said softly. He knew she had meant something else altogether. There were facts running through his mind now—the fact that she had acceded to this little escape, the fact that she had returned his kiss, the fact that she did not love Antonio. Yet it was silence that held them in place, static as strangers to one another as they slowly dropped all the way down to the ground again.

The Midway was closing for the night, and so Tomás and Eulalia headed back toward the lights of the White City. Edison's incandescent bulbs would burn the whole night, and only a few dark spots remained along the Court of Honor. They walked without talking, Eulalia taking deep breaths of the night air every so often, shivering a little. They walked toward the Palace of Fine Arts, which was closed for the night, glowing along the banks of the basin. Inside, figures in bronze and marble embraced, draped themselves lazily upon rocks, and peered into far-off distances. Outside, Eulalia and Tomás formed a different pair of figures, as Tomás helped Eulalia board a small boat. He sat, too, and released the rope that had tied it down. He wasn't an experienced rower, and so they meandered a bit before he got the rhythm of the oars in the water. Still, they kept to their silence. Tomás had wondered if she would follow as he led her to the boat, and she had asked no questions. In the distance, the small island was lit by lanterns. There, a Japanese palace had been erected, replete with gardens and blue-tiled buildings. They tied the boat to a post on the shore and disembarked, their shoes sinking in the mud a few inches.

"It's a favorite of the Exposition, I've heard tell," Tomás said, meaning the Japanese island. It was the only permanent exhibit by any country, a gift from the Japanese to the Americans. How odd the architecture seemed to Tomás, with its gently curved roofs held up by dark posts, its paper walls, and the large gables, covered in gold leaf.

In one of the buildings, they could see the silhouettes of people settling in for the night—Japanese men and women who were spending their summer in Chicago to work at the exposition. Faintly, they heard laughter, and the tinkling of plates from within. The other buildings were dark, as were the gardens.

"It's closed for the evening," Eulalia said, and wondered about the time.

Tomás fumbled for his pocket watch, but he couldn't read it in the dark. "Should we go back?" he asked.

"Not yet," she said.

Tomás and Eulalia stumbled along the wooded paths without making a sound. Without light to guide them, Tomás let the fingers of his free hand trail above the short hedges that lined the walk. He closed his eyes as he led her, feeling better in a darkness of his own making. A light rain started up. Lightning forked in the sky directly over the Palace of Fine Arts, then again a little farther away, but the rain did not thicken.

"Over there," Eulalia suddenly whispered, her chin brushing against his arm. A smaller building emerged from a stand of pines. They slid open the door and went inside. They listened as the light patter on the roof slowed, then stopped altogether. Thunder rumbled in the distance, but it seemed far away now. It was just a room, and inside, flat blue cushions lay on the floor, with a low table in the center. Small teacups and teapots sat on shelves along the wall. The air was fresh and green-smelling inside. "It feels so proper in here," Eulalia said.

"I feel like a giant in here," Tomás said, nudging the table that was only as high as his shins.

"You *are* a giant," Eulalia said.

"Grande por gusto," Tomás said.

"I wouldn't say that." She sat on the cushion and pulled her knees up to her chest. She rolled her head a little, stretching her neck, then sighed.

Tomás sat down beside her. Yes, he thought, the place felt very proper. All proper, and more importantly, true. He felt that they had been meant to come to this place, their lives' decisions leading them, meandering, to this moment.

Eulalia looked up at him, her lips parted, and she asked, "What do you think of Bertha Palmer?"

"Oh, I—" Tomás began. He hadn't given the woman much thought. "She's lovely, But not as lovely as y—"

"I envy her," Eulalia said, only half-listening to him. "The Women's Building is magnificent, and she managed it. The hotel, too. These American women do so much. All of this progress, Tomás, and women have had a hand in it. Is such a thing possible in Spain?"

Tomás thought of Juana and her love for the bookshop that she could never run, and of Amalia, who sometimes had referred to her past self as una vaquita de oro, then laughed darkly. He thought of the innkeeper's niece back in Cuba, and her perpetual scowl, and then, of the women he'd seen everywhere in Chicago, pushing children in prams, helping their old mothers onto the deck of the Santa María, crashing in a hot air balloon. Just that morning, he had read in a Chicago newspaper about three missing women in the city, and a woman who had once been a slave in Alabama, found dead in Lake

Michigan, bruises around her neck. The freedom Eulalia spoke of eluded Tomás's imagination.

"Is this freedom?" he asked, gesturing to the room around them.

"No," she said.

"Just an indulgence then?"

Eulalia said nothing, only lay, face down, across Tomás's lap. He ran his fingers up and down her back, wondering if she could feel it through the whalebone corset. She turned to face him. "Tell me it isn't vengeance, Eulalia," Tomás said, his voice not quite steady.

She sat up, shook her head. Slowly, she undid the black ribbon that laced up her dress in the back, expertly tugging on the ends, as if she had always dressed and undressed herself. Then she stood, and stepped out of the dress, out of the hard corset. It was dark, and so the shape she took was all shadow, all confusion. Down she sat again upon the blue cushion, and then, all at once, Tomás's mouth was on hers. His lips parted and hers followed. He undressed with one hand, warming his other hand on her skin, upon her arms, her hip, and lower still.

Eulalia, gasping in his ear. Eulalia's breath warm in his mouth. Eulalia's thighs alongside his own, her own shattering happening in silence, her teeth upon his shoulder, pressing only just so. *Lala, Lala,* Tomás thought, and then he said it aloud, into her hair, the heat of her rising, volcanic, his face feeling as if it were on fire.

4

They dressed slowly, talking in quiet tones about the room they were in, the exhibits they had seen, the food they had eaten. Tomás knew it was strange, but he had no words for what had just happened between them. The scent of it was everywhere, the proof in Eulalia's reddened lips, and Tomás's wrinkled clothes. They made their way back to the boat, passing a gray-haired Japanese woman carrying a red lantern. She eyed them with suspicion, and said something to them in Japanese. It sounded like a scolding, and Tomás and Eulalia hurried away from her. Tomás rowed hard, until the woman's red lantern could no longer be seen.

The White City did not go dark at night. The searchlights swept the sky without ceasing. Even so, the Exposition was asleep, and there were no carriages to be found anywhere. The steamship that brought passengers to the fair via the lake was docked and shadowy. Dawn was not so far off, and soon there would be carriages again, and streetcars. But in that moment, sleepy and spent, Eulalia and Tomás could do nothing but wait there on the steps of the Palace of Fine Arts.

They stared out at the little wooded island together, watched as soft butter-yellow lights flickered in the buildings. Time and again, the red lantern would appear like a dying star, and they wondered whether the old woman was looking for them, whether she knew what they had done.

"The light is like a message, isn't it? Like Morse code," Tomás said.

"I don't know what that is," Eulalia said. Tomás resisted the urge to explain it. "Do you mean it's like a sign? It might be a sign," she said. Eulalia leaned her head against his shoulder. He felt her sigh, her whole body moving up and down. He felt himself a peculiar shock running up his spine, a trembling that came and went so fast he could attribute it only to the astonishing fact that Eulalia was there, beside him.

"A sign then," Tomás said. "But of what?"

Eulalia leaned forward, rested her elbows on her knees, and gazed intently at the woods, as if she could derive meaning from the lapping of the water, the chirping of the cicadas, the curling smoke that rose above the tree line like a spirit.

"If I leave him," she began to say, then stopped. The noises of the night filled in the pause.

Tomás held his breath. He felt as if anything was possible. His stomach constricted in a tight knot of hope, and then the feeling was gone. Of course she couldn't leave Antonio, not permanently at least.

"My grandmother left my grandfather for a soldier. And Heaven knows my parents never shared a bed. But they pretended for everyone else's sake, that they were still together," she said.

"Would you live separately then? The church would frown—"

"The church is not God," Eulalia said fiercely. "The church may judge me, but God will not."

Tomás looked down to see her face, her open, gorgeous face, which was set hard now, her eyes narrowed, tears collecting near her lashes. He knew those were angry tears, not sad ones. Otherwise, she was very still, almost as if she were ready to sit for a photograph. Juana's was a warm, heated anger. When incensed, Juana would stomp around the store, slamming drawers and stacking books as if they were heavy bricks. Eulalia, however, ran cold.

Tomás took her hand in his, felt her resist briefly then relent. "You don't have to get a divorce," he said. "I won't go anywhere. I'm your secretary, remember?" Even as he said it, he felt unease, heard his mother whispering Tenorio's name in his ear.

Then Eulalia looked at him slowly, sleepily, the anger he had seen in her eyes now fled deep within, seeded inside and turning into something new. Tomás understood it at once— Eulalia wanted a divorce for reasons that had nothing to do with him. She patted his hand and commented on the coming dawn, which was coloring the sky a bright coral.

"The carriages will be back soon," she said, and they rose from the steps and made their way to the edge of the exposition grounds, where they could hear the clop-clop of horses bringing the first guests of the day.

Tomás and Eulalia went through the kitchens of the Palmer Hotel, via doors that Tomás had discovered earlier. They climbed a set of spiral staircases, then reached the suite of rooms. The sky was still blushing in the dawn, and the snores of the ladies-in-waiting could be heard coming from the adjoining rooms. The parlor itself was dark, the curtains drawn. A fire was set in the fireplace. So it was they did not notice Antonio, sitting nearby, Eulalia's manuscript in his lap.

He said nothing to them, only lifted a page he finished reading, crumpled it up, and tossed it into the fire. His movements were liquid, gentle, as if he had merely decided to destroy old school notes.

Eulalia gasped and rushed forward, stumbling over her own skirts on the way and righting herself without falling. Antonio snatched up the manuscript before she could reach it.

"Leave the room, please, Aragón, I need to speak with my wife," Antonio said.

Tomás hesitated. Eulalia turned to look at him, her eyes round and wild.

"Thank you, Aragón," Antonio spoke again. "We will not be needing you again this morning."

Tomás found his voice. "We were only taking in the Midway when the carriages stopped running for the evening. The Ferris Wheel, isn't that right, su alteza?"

Antonio crumpled another page and fed the fire again.

"It's her life's story. She has a right to tell it," Tomás said, taking a step forward.

"Go!" Antonio said, standing. The remaining pages, of which there were now only a few, fell to the carpet. Eulalia dropped to her knees to gather them up. She turned to Tomás and mouthed the words "Just go," before picking up the pages.

For as long as he lived, Tomás would remember the feeling of backing out of that room. He would dream of it often, and in his dream, his feet would feel moored to the floor, incapable of movement. In his dream, Antonio would ask him to leave, ask again, beg and beg, but Tomás's legs would not move. They were oaks rooted in the ground.

But in real life, he left, walking backwards, finding the doorknob without looking at it, and falling into his room, where he could still hear everything that was going on in the parlor.

He listened as Antonio called Eulalia "cousin," as he brought up Isabel's infidelities, and those of Isabel's mother, and all the way down the line of Spanish queens and princesses who knew nothing but betrayal.

And then, Eulalia's voice, shrill as a hurt bird, the name "Carmela" on her lips, again and again.

Finally, after a long while, they were quiet. Tomás opened the door to the parlor and found it empty. Around the room, other doors opened, the ladies-in-waiting peering out like frightened cats. In the fire, the rest of Eulalia's book crackled, her words turning to ash, the bright embers floating for a second before falling.

Tomás slept through most of the day. He would pack his things later. Hartwell had a copy of the book, and this, at least, gave Tomás comfort. A knock woke him from a dreamless sleep. An envelope was slipped underneath the door, containing a letter from Martín. It read:

Querido Hermano,
Yesterday we received your letter, and were happy to learn that you are well and that you enjoyed New York City and your time with the infanta. Amalia had just complained that

morning that you never write us, and you can imagine how she felt when your letter was in her hands at last. But our happiness was short-lived. In the evening, your mother fell. It had rained, one of those tropical thunderstorms so common here, and the steps were wet. Her hip is broken. So is her wrist. In addition, she is running a fever. The doctor's countenance upon examining her was quite serious. We are frightened for her, hermano. If you can get away, please come.

   Tu hermano,

Martín

Tomás reread the letter several times. Then, his heart in his throat, he went downstairs to the lobby to inquire about train tickets. He saw Eulalia in passing, Antonio at her side. Her face was pallid, and she gripped a parasol tightly with two hands, the handle at her chest, as if she were holding a sword. He thought of her manuscript, how the fire had flared when it touched the pages, and the light piles of black ash that had been left behind, and Tomás wondered how it was that bright, blinding things could be reduced to almost nothing so quickly.

Later, they would watch a different kind of fire from rooftop of the hotel. The Cold Storage Building at the Exposition, which housed an ice skating rink, had gone up in flames overnight. They could just make out the towers, their flags ablaze, and tiny figures jumping from the top, trading one kind of death for another. Antonio held Eulalia about the waist as they watched in horror, while Tomás hung back with the ladies-in-waiting, and a few other servants, unsure of everything now. The fire almost distracted him from the ache that had settled in his chest. Around them, the air shuddered, as if the violence only a few miles off had reached them too.

5

"Come with me," Eulalia pleaded with Tomás as he packed his trunk.

Tomás did not look up to see her. It would hurt too much to see her round face, her precise little curls. He did not want to think of her tomorrow, or the next day, or twenty years from now, beautiful beyond the wreckage of time, existing without him.

But that was folly, of course, and he knew it.

"My train leaves tomorrow, early. Mamá needs—" he stopped himself, raised his head to look at Eulalia, pale and trembling in the doorway. "I shouldn't have left her there, alone."

She held up a piece of paper. "It's from the editor. He wants to see me today. About the book." The paper, which was a telegram, Tomás could now see, shook in her hand. "I can't tell him that Antonio destroyed it, of course. I'll have to make up another—"

"Mr. Hartwell has a copy, Eulalia. I typed up a spare."

Her mouth dropped open, the corners of it twitched a little, almost a smile. "Why didn't you mention it? How I wept for those pages," she said.

"I did. I told you about it days ago. You were in the glass dress, remember?" Tomás felt frustration grow in him like a weed, tangling up his feelings.

"Oh," she said. "I must have been distracted. Your train leaves today?"

"Tomorrow," Tomás repeated, and folded a sock carefully.

"Oh. Well, then, you are free to come with me to Mr. Hartwell's today, aren't you?" She placed her hands, one folded over the other, upon her stomach. She was holding her breath.

He thought of his mother, frail, hurting, in a strange bed, in a strange country. What a mess Tomás had put them in. And all for what? Because that American woman, that Eliza Jane, had dangled something like hope and progress before Tomás's eyes, and he, like a hungry fish, had swallowed the shiny thing that concealed a hook.

Eulalia took a step into his room, stopped, then took another. "I don't know what you are thinking, why your brow is so furrowed. Perhaps your mind is on Ama. I can feel it in my heart," she said, her hands coming up to rest between her breasts. "Ama will be well again. I'm not saying that to convince you, I just feel it. I knew when my brother would die, and I knew about Pilár, too. I just knew. Ama will be well again. All I am asking for is one day. One more day. With you."

Tomás nodded. The truth was, he had dreamed all night of the moment he would say goodbye to Eulalia, and in his dream he reached for her face and she said, "I belong to no one," and then he was hurled away from her, as if by a mighty wind. When he woke, he searched for who he had been before Eulalia came into his bookshop, and could not find that man anymore. It seemed to him now, with Eulalia before him, that he would do best to see the adventure through, to put an end to the story he and she were writing, a *fin* that would propel him back to Cuba, back to Ama.

Eulalia approached him slowly, like a person coming toward a feral cat. She put her hand on his shoulder and applied pressure there. He bent to her will, lowering toward her, until she was able to plant a soft kiss on his stubby cheek. "Thank you. This afternoon, at two, the carriage will take us to Sylvester Hartwell's office."

"Antonio?" Tomás asked.

Eulalia hardened before his eyes, and it was clear that she had been thinking perilous thoughts about Antonio since he had destroyed her book. She spoke in a vicious whisper. "Our marriage is only a memory of what once was. Or, better yet, what never was. Antonio knows it, as do I. If a woman like Bertha Palmer can curate masterpieces, name a building after female artists, and run a hotel, then I can separate from half a man who is draining my wealth and embarrassing himself with a little-known actress."

Hope flared and died in Tomás, all at once. A liberated Eulalia would be free to—do what? Live with Tomás? She would still be a married woman, the law permitted nothing else. A mirthless laugh nearly escaped him. Besides, his mother needed him.

"Two o'clock, then," he said.

Eulalia opened her mouth to say something, perhaps to ask his opinion about what she had just said, but she thought better of it, nodded, and left his room without another word.

Sylvester Hartwell did not keep the Infanta of Spain waiting. Rather, he stood outside his building, hat in hand, and helped her out of her carriage himself. He led her and Tomás to his office, which was spacious and carpeted in jewel tones. His desk was large, and glass-topped, with many small drawers in it. On the front of his desk gleamed a copper shield with an engraving of the New York City skyline.

Four chairs sat in a half-circle before his desk, and Eulalia and Tomás took their seats. Eulalia wore a yellow dress with a lower neckline than usual. She had folded her gloves on her lap and sat comfortably, her ankles crossed, her fingers tapping on the arm of the chair. Tomás was astonished by how much she had changed while in Chicago, how her body seemed to have grown languid, more at ease in the world. Or, perhaps, not in all of the world, only here, in this place.

Sylvester Hartwell rounded his desk and sat down, his chair set so high on its legs that he appeared to tower over them. Eulalia sat straighter in her seat, pretending not to notice that her gloves had tumbled off her lap.

The typed manuscript was at Hartwell's fingertips, and he fiddled with the edges of the pages. "We would be very honored to publish your memoir," he said, without further preamble.

Eulalia looked at Tomás and reached out, grabbing his forearm and squeezing.

"You should be prepared for, ah, repercussions, however, back home, in Spain, I mean," Hartwell continued.

Eulalia cleared her throat. "Spain has never felt like home to me," she said. "I've lost nothing there that I can't find somewhere else."

Tomás took a deep, tremulous breath. One of the things he had worried about when he left Spain was that he would spend the rest of his life missing it.

"You are everything the newspapers say about you and more, your highness," Sylvester Hartwell said, leaning back in his chair.

"What do they say?" Eulalia asked. She was flushed with excitement. Her chin lifted, all of her agitated.

Sylvester Hartwell opened his mouth to answer her when he was interrupted by someone opening his office door. A woman came in, dressed in dark brown, her face tight, chewing her bottom lip.

"Birdie, come in. Your highness, this is my wife, Birdie."

Birdie curtsied, and Eulalia rose and shook the woman's hand. Tomás stood, too, and offered his own hand. "Tomás Aragón, at your service," he said.

"You are Eliza Jane's friend, yes?"

Tomás nodded, and suddenly, Birdie had sprung all of her attention on him. "Here," she said, and pulled a small bible out of a pocket in her skirt. The cover was embroidered with Eliza Jane's maiden initials—EJH—in tiny pearls. "Her childhood bible, you see. I thought she might want it at a time like this."

"A time like this?" Tomás asked.

"The baby. The baby died," Birdie said, choking back a sob. "And our Eliza Jane isn't herself anymore. And now, now she'll never come home, will she, Lester," Birdie said, turning to her husband. "Not now that her baby is buried in Spain. How could she leave it? It was a girl," Birdie said, dissolving into tears.

Eulalia's hand was on Tomás's forearm again, and she was gripping him hard. *Emilia, Francisca, Rubén, Alicia*. The names came like whispers to Tomás, and he knew Eulalia was thinking of her own baby, and, perhaps, her own siblings, the ones Isabel could not keep alive.

"Forgive me, your highness," Hartwell said, though he did not rise to comfort his wife.

Then it was as if Eulalia remembered herself again, and Tomás wondered how she did it, how she rose and embraced Birdie. Tomás recalled the stories of Eulalia and her sisters attending the deathbeds of others, how that must have hardened them, made them strong in the places where everyone else was weakest.

"Thank you, your highness," Birdie said, and curtsied again, even though she was gripping Eulalia's arms still. "As a woman, you understand. You have children, yes?" Eulalia nodded. "Then you know that we do what we can to protect them. It's our lot, and it's a consecration upon us, isn't it?"

Eulalia nodded, and Birdie excused herself. The infanta sank slowly into her seat. Her hands reached out to the manuscript, and little by little, she pulled the book back onto her lap. "We are afraid that we cannot proceed," she said, her voice small.

Tomás felt as if his bones were suddenly shifting within him. He looked into Eulalia's face, which had gone blank, and felt as if he understood her thoughts. He mouthed the word no, and then he spoke it out loud. Eulalia turned to look at him, held his gaze for only a moment. Her blue eyes were glossy, and she gripped the pages of her manuscript forcefully, as if strangling the life out of them. Tomás tried to focus on what had just befallen them in Sylvester Hartwell's office. There would be no separation for Eulalia and Antonio, no scandalous book to provoke it; as far as the eyes of Spain were concerned, the Infanta Eulalia would return from her trip abroad with a trunk full of souvenirs and cheeks lightly sunburned. She would be a pretty bird with clipped wings. Her sons would be infantes, own property, marry young duchesses and marquesas, and he could see in her tenacity her hope for them, for their future. Eulalia, Amalia, Gisela, Birdie, Eliza Jane, Juana, he thought woefully of them all, imagining them bent down, laying cobblestones on the ground, creating pathways for the futures of men.

Hartwell shifted in his chair. He picked up a pen and set it down again. "Perhaps," he said carefully, "there is something still in Spain that you cannot find elsewhere."

Eulalia did not nod, or say anything other than a curt thank you. Tomás followed her out, feeling in her wake as if the courage were leaving her moment by moment, as if he were wading in its residues.

"Eulalia. Eulalia!" he called to her, but she would not turn. She walked past the carriage, her manuscript tight against her body. "Eulalia!" he cried again, taking long strides to match her pace.

"Which way is the lake?" she asked him then, frantic, and he pointed toward it, peeking out blue and knifelike between buildings. Eulalia marched toward the watery horizon in silence.

"Your sons, is it?" he asked, and got no answer. Hadn't Amalia done the same for him? Changed her life so that his would be easier? "You're putting them first, aren't you?"

Eulalia stopped. "Do you know that Luis Fernando writes

me letters from school? In the letters he tells me, 'Papa is more like a bear than a man, more like a beast, a brute. I have never loved Papa, never, never.' This is from a child. Yet I hide these letters so that Antonio does not see them." She was breathing hard, and two parallel lines of sweat ran down her temples, like the ties to a bonnet. "I will leave him, Tomás. I will light my love in a new lamp. But this, this?" she said, gesturing to her book, "I realize now, it can ruin everything for my children."

They walked on until they reached the lakeshore. A path had been made between a stand of brush and the water, and they went along it. Tomás held back branches so that Eulalia might duck under them, and soon their feet were in the muck of the lake's edge. The sun was low in the sky, and the wind pushed at them a little, as if it might toss them into the lake. Droplets of water fell onto the manuscript, and Eulalia wiped them off then, but there was no point to that.

Hartwell had bound the pages with a gray ribbon. Eulalia peeled the ribbon off first, and let it go.

It whipped into the sky, fluttering like an insect, before landing in the water, where it floated for a bit.

Tomás knew that Eulalia would not listen to reason. He remembered how his mother had always said that it was impossible to argue with an unreasonable person, that the only counter to their irrational thinking was a startling act. Eulalia peeled the first page off the manuscript and let it go. She took the second page in her hand, held it aloft, then stopped.

"One of the servants in Cuba told me how people there sometimes throw bunches of flowers into the ocean, sometimes tied with ribbons of different colors. They are offerings to the African gods. I liked the idea of it."

Tomás noticed then that there were tears in her eyes. He reached over and gently took the book from her. Then, with a suddenness that made Eulalia yell out, he threw the bundle into the sea.

"All at once, is how you do it," he said. Some of the pages flew off, wrapping themselves along the slimy legs of a nearby pier. Another page sailed deep into the city and disappeared among the buildings. But the bulk of the book scattered across the surface of the lake. They watched as page after page was pulled down, some very quickly, so that Tomás imagined a school of fish feeding on Eulalia's words.

They sat in silence until the last of the pages were gone, Eulalia's written life sucked into Lake Michigan, parts of it strewn deep in Chicago. The water glittered in the afternoon light, the very color of an aquamarine, and Eulalia said so to Tomás.

"Never been rich enough to have one," he said.

6

Tomás woke early the next morning, before the sun was up. He heard movement in the parlor outside his room, and cracked his door open to see who it might be. He had hoped it might be Eulalia, and she did not disappoint. She paced the parlor, back and forth, still in her creamy silk dressing gown. Her hair was loose and curled against her back.

She started when she felt his hand on her arm, pulling her back gently into his room. With a quick glance backwards, she followed him in. Tomás palmed the back of her neck, a perfect fit, and she tilted her face up at him. He kissed her gently, and felt her warm lips responding for a moment, but pulling away too soon.

"Sometimes, I think too much," she said, averting her

eyes. "I deprive myself of joy from overthinking. But I cannot help it."

"Then don't think. Come with me, back to Cuba. We can send for your boys, change our paths." Overcome with the intensity of his feelings, he stopped short. The words he had uttered, so full of hopefulness, felt empty hearing them out loud.

"That would be for me. For us. Not for them," Eulalia said. She rested her forehead on his chest, and Tomás could smell her perfume, not cloying, but clean, delicate.

"My train leaves this morning," he said.

"We leave tomorrow for Niagara Falls," she said. "I should like to throw myself into the cataracts," she whispered.

"No, you wouldn't," Tomás said, his lips touching her hair.

"No," she said. "I wouldn't."

"You can write your book again. Someday. Later."

Outside, Chicago came to life again, and yet inside the room, Tomás and Eulalia were very still, the stillness and the quiet making them shiver. Something else, too, affected their nerves. Perhaps it was the feeling that they would not see each other again, not in this way. Tomás would see Eulalia's face in the newspaper, and a sigh would escape his lips, an exhausted sad sound, and he would wonder at how the feeling of it would haunt him for the rest of the day, as if he had once been a very rich man who had lost it all. As for Eulalia, she would think of Tomás whenever she thought of her trip to the New World. He was bound to it in her imagination, as rugged and large as America itself. He was mountainous, protective; he was rushing rivers, and large, oceanlike lakes, buildings of steel. All of these things reminded her of Tomás.

They said their goodbyes, her lips on his throat, his cheeks, his mouth, and his hands at the nape of her neck, her back, her thigh. In that moment, Eulalia and Tomás were only lovers parting, their love a guttering candle, as so many others had parted before them, with a slim understanding of what the memory of the moment would become for each of them.

Later, Eulalia would ride with Tomás to the train station, accompanied by two ladies-in-waiting, who held handkerchiefs over their mouths the whole time. There was a strong smell in the air, and the driver had said that the wind had shifted, and the stench from the slaughterhouse had descended on that part of the city. Tomás and Eulalia merely covered their noses with handkerchiefs and looked upon one another as if in shock. They stopped to let a trolley pass, and watched as a newspaper boy called out the news of the day. "Bon Voyage, Bad-Tempered Princess," the boy called out. Tomás whistled at the boy from the carriage window, and purchased a paper on the spot. He and Eulalia read in silence as the editorial described Eulalia as rude and frivolous. "Does the enfant terrible know the difference between informality and frivolity? The editors of the *Tribune* think not."

Eulalia pushed the paper away, ignoring the ladies, who asked, "What did it say?" and, surmising the truth, advised, "Ignore them, Eulalia. These Americans are far too breezy, far too daring in their opinions."

But Tomás understood. She had loved Chicago, and Chicago, desperate to see a princess acting like one, had rebuked her.

The carriage pulled up to the train station, which was busy with tourists arriving for the fair. Those leaving carried overstuffed bags full of souvenirs they would take home to Missouri, to Oklahoma, to Los Angeles and Raleigh.

Tomás and Eulalia watched them all for a moment, and then the carriage driver thrust out his hand and banged the side of the door, making them all jump.

"Tomás," she began to say. "I'm sorry I wasted your time." She meant the book, he knew. Then, a thought occurred to him. "Your sons," he said. "I've never asked. Where do they go to school?"

"Merry old England," she said without any mirth at all. "They are good English chaps, as they say."

They were quiet, and to his credit, the driver waited patiently, though other carriages jostled to get by, and a few drivers yelled at him to get out of the way. Tomás knew then why her book had been written in English, knew who it had been for, why destroying it had meant so much.

"Su alteza," Tomás said, his voice breaking. He took Eulalia's hand and kissed it. She closed her eyes, but kept her lips pressed together. Then Tomás left the carriage with tremendous effort, the ladies watching him, their faces obscured by handkerchiefs still.

Everyone on the platform seemed frozen in time. In the distance, Chicago smoked and churned with industry. Farther beyond was the exposition, out of sight now, and above were fat, roiling clouds. Tomás blinked a few times. He peered down the tracks, which went eastward forever. For the first time, he did not quite know where life was taking him. He took a deep breath and smelled nothing at all. He caught his reflection on the side of the train, which was glossy as a mirror. Tomás reached into his pocket and drew out his notebook, the one with memories of Juana in it. He regretted that there were no more pages in which to write down a story about Eulalia. In the back of the notebook, he found his old list where he had tucked it away, the page petal soft. He looked at it a moment, then dropped it by the side of the train, for the wind to take where it would.

EPILOGUE

February 12, 1915

M*i querido Tomás,*

I have not received a letter from you in such a long time, but I hope that this finds you happy and well. Just this morning, I found the prayer card you sent me after Ama died. I keep it in a box with other treasures, small things that break my heart when I look at them.

It is my fifty-first birthday today, which seems like such a large number I cannot believe it applies to me. It is morning here in Paris, and by evening, I will have received a great many gifts from friends and family, and they will distract me from memories of you for a little while, at least. But here is a small gift for you—I've enclosed this picture of me, taken a few years after our trip to Chicago, just before Antonio and I parted ways for good. I am seated on the steps of the palace in Lisbon, and standing beside me is the Queen of Portugal, Amélie, who has that title that might have been mine, you remember. I think of Amélie often, a bouquet of flowers in her hands, her only weapon against the men who killed Carlos Braganza and their young son in the coup of Portugal. You must have heard of it. It stopped my heart to learn the news. Amélie still wears her mourning like a shadow. Sometimes, when I wear bright-colored gowns, I think of Carlos, of my brother, of Ama, and I seek a midnight-colored mantilla to throw upon my shoulders.

Anyway, the photographer in the picture caught me in a pensive moment, and I've sent it because I suspect it will be a familiar look to you, who were subjected to my most brooding days.

I don't brood as much these days. This is not to say I am wholly satisfied. I have wanted many things all these years. To have seen stability in Spain and peace in Europe, to have raised my boys outside of court intrigues, to have arranged for a different tomb for myself, away from el Escorial, to have seen you again in Cuba, and imagine you there in your tropical world, fanning your handsome face, taking shade under fruit trees. Europe is not who she used to be, and I long for the peace of the New World.

Mainly, I would have liked to have seen you again. You were a good friend to me, always, more than a friend, more than a milk brother, more than a secretary. I cannot say what you were. To put it into words would be too indecorous. It would be too much. But if I could, oh, Tomás, if I could, I would write a constellation of words for you. I became bolder in your wake, braver for having known you.

Enclosed is a copy of my first book. It was published in 1912, but with the war here in Europe, I have just now sent it to you. I have named it Au fil de la vie, *and it is nothing like the book you remember. You may be happy to know that you are not in it. It wouldn't be right, to cast a spotlight upon you or Amalia, que en paz descanse. What would your daughters think? They must be so grown now. I have set aside some rings for them, which I will send you soon. There is one, too, for your wife, lucky woman that she is.*

As for my book, in it I have defended divorce and feminism, and for that, my nephew, Alfonso XIII, has banished me from Spain. Paris is nothing like Madrid, nothing like New York or Havana or Chicago, but it is the home of my best childhood days, and I am free here. I have already begun another book, and this time, we won't need to go off on an adventure to get it in print. Exile is a small price to pay for speaking my mind. The penalty for fear is silence, and, at last, I lived up to my name, and learned to speak.

With all the affection that time and space allow, I remain, ever yours,

Eulalia

The popularity of the Infanta Eulalia at the end of the 19th century was akin to that of Princess Diana at the end of the 20th. Both were intelligent, independent, and beautiful. Eulalia was a writer, too, and went on to compose several books about her experiences at court. I included many of Eulalia's well-known sentiments regarding her position in the world as a woman, her destiny as an infanta, and her desires for freedom here in *The Living Infinite*. For example, she did, indeed, say that a queen's crown was too much of a burden, weighing far more than a princesses' diadem, and she expressed admiration of and envy towards women like Chicago's Bertha Palmer, who had such freedoms and ambitions that were unattainable to Eulalia. There are other examples that the astute Eulalia-phile will discover throughout the book, put down in an attempt to preserve her wit and intellect in these pages as much as possible.

Was there a wet nurse and a spare? Yes. It is important to name them. They were Andrea Aragón and Lorenza García. Andrea's husband, Juan Ontañon was a carpenter. They lived together in Las Trinas, and he was given 24,000 escudos for her two years of service as a nodriza. For a glimpse of what a nodriza of the Palacio Real might have looked like, the portrait of Alfonso XII's wet nurse, entitled *María de los Dolores Marina* by Bernardo López Piquer (1858), is a good start.

Are Andrea and Juan my Amalia and Rubén? They are not. The characters here are inventions, though I've borrowed the factual details of the real nodriza's job and village. Was there a milk brother? Assuredly. But I do not know his name, or what his destiny might have been. This question was the first I had before putting pen to paper. Who might a milk brother become?

As for the story of Eulalia making her debut in Havana wearing the colors of the rebel flag, that particular tale is up for debate, with some seeing it as merely legend. In her letters to her mother, Eulalia takes care to describe her dress in that moment, and it was, indeed, blue and white. Perhaps those present imagined the touches of red that would complete the tricolor of Cuba's rebel flag. Or perhaps she let that detail out of her letter. In any case, this was the first story I ever heard about the princess, and, true or not, it is how I see her in my mind's eye, with a sea breeze running through her hair, and a look of defiance on her face.

A novel is, ultimately, a fictional dream, and while I am a fan of history, I am not a historian. My admiration for the work of scholars runs deep and I am grateful for their efforts. For those interested in learning more about the Infanta Eulalia, as well as the Columbian Exposition of 1893, the following excellent sources may be helpful:

Norman Bolotin and Christine Laing's *The World's Columbian Exposition*

Eulalia de Borbón's *Cartas a Isabel II*, a collection of the infanta's letters to her mother, Isabel II, during her trip to the Caribbean and the U.S. in 1893

Eulalia de Borbón's *Court Life from Within*, a memoir of her experiences in several European courts

Eulalia de Borbón's *The Thread of Life*, the infanta's first book, a collection of essays about feminism, divorce, the role of the family, etc. and the book that triggered her exile from Spain

Erik Larson's *Devil in the White City: Murder, Magic, and Madness at the Fair That Changed America*

Dulce María Loynaz's *Yo fui (feliz) en Cuba*, a reimagining of Eulalia's visit to Cuba

Theo Aronson's *Royal Vendetta: The Crown of Spain 1829-1965*

Robert E. Wilson's "The Infanta at the Fair" *Journal of the Illinois State Historical Society (1908-1984)* Vol. 59, No. 3 (Autumn, 1966)

José María Zavala's *La infanta republicana: Eulalia de Borbón, la oveja negra de la dinastía*

ACKNOWLEDGMENTS

Many thanks to Jana Gutierrez, friend, scholar, and Eulalia-devotee. You told a story about a rebellious princess in Cuba to a rapt dinner audience, and I was forever changed. Thank you for introducing me to la infanta, and to Dulce María Loynaz's important work.

To Hallie Johnston, for being my first reader, and a friend of Eulalia and Tomás from the very beginning. To Ash Parsons, for plot-busting help whenever it is called for. You're a wonder, dear one.

To my colleagues and students at the University of Miami, for their support, invaluable kindness and inspiring talent. Thank you for bringing me home.

To my wonderful agent, Stéphanie Abou—thank you for believing, and for shining your light in dark places.

To my editor, Michael Reynolds, who understands the power of stories from around the world and acts as their champion in so many ways, and to everyone at Europa Editions for bringing these stories to a wider readership, thank you.

Finally, and always, to my family—my mother, Marta, husband, Orlando, and daughters, Penelope and Mary-Blair. You give me strength, and I love you all.

ABOUT THE AUTHOR

Chantel Acevedo was born in Miami to Cuban parents. She is the author of *A Falling Star*, *Love and Ghost Letters*, winner of the Latino International Book Award, *Song of the Red Cloak*, and *The Distant Marvels*, a finalist for the 2016 Andrew Carnegie Medal for Excellence in Fiction. Acevedo is an Associate Professor of English in the MFA Program at the University of Miami.